I0452082

FANTASY WORLD

Book One
of the
Fantasy World
Trilogy

C. R. STURGILL

Second Revision Copyright © 2022 C. R. Sturgill

Copyright © 2016 C. R. Sturgill
All rights reserved.

ISBN: 0988565358

ISBN 13: 978-0988565357
Library of Congress Control Number: 2016914943
DreamHeart Books
Marion, Virginia

Other Books by C. R. Sturgill

Sea of Hearts

Blood Tides

Dreams from the Heart: Tales of Hope & Love

For More Information & Updates:

Follow on Facebook
https://www.facebook.com/crsturgillauthor/

Visit Website
http://www.crsturgill.com/

This book is dedicated to the best and most supportive parents and grandparents I could have asked for: James & Janet Sturgill, Clifford & Dean Wilcox, and June Sturgill. I stand on the shoulders of giants.

Table of Contents

CHAPTER 1

The man scrambled to his feet and peered into the inky forest behind them. The ground trembled beneath his feet, and thunder rolled in the distance. Only he knew it wasn't a storm coming for them. "Run!" he shouted over the rumbling.

The woman slowly stood beside him, favoring her bandaged left knee, and stared into the darkness over her left shoulder. The man seized her hand and jerked her into a staggering run behind him, ignoring her cries of pain. The ground now shook violently beneath them as the thunderous din behind intensified. The sounds of splintering trees and snapping limbs joined the thunder. They more stumbled than ran out of the trees and into a rock-strewn clearing.

"What is it?" the woman screamed, making her voice heard over the booms and crashes.

"I don't know! But I'm sure it's another nightmare creation of the gods," the man yelled.

They paused for a moment, and both turned to identify the source of the calamity. Soon they saw the trees parting—the larger ones twisted and bent, the smaller ones snapped and scattered like twigs. The couple stood frozen, no longer even panting from the run. The last line of trees ripped apart, and a monstrous beast appeared. The creature stopped at the edge of the clearing and sniffed the air, its nightmarish head rotating side-to-side. Its head resembled a gray wolf's, except ten times larger. The eyes glowed red, and its huge, bared teeth glistened in the fading daylight. Its body resembled a giant lizard or dinosaur, with large, scaly plates covering it like armor. Long, curved claws tipped each toe, and a massive tail extended behind it, ending in a spiked ball. The creature stood twelve feet high at its shoulders and was at least thirty feet long.

***

"Your new creation?" Enki asked.

"Indeed, brother. You said it was time to end this quest. It will be over very soon," Odin replied.

"What is that beast?" Enki asked.

"I call it my wolfosaur," Odin said.

"Mixing a modern animal with a long-extinct one…impressive," Artemis added.

"Intriguing, but hardly sporting," Ra interjected.

"We are running out of time for sport. The pair have camped on that mountain for days, and he was not leaving the injured female. They have also proven they are not the ones," Odin replied.

***

The red eyes landed on the human statues. The head lifted, and the nostrils flared. The couple could discern the saliva oozing between the teeth, over the lips, and splashing onto the ground even in the dim light. The beast emitted an earsplitting sound—beginning as a high-pitched roar and ending in a blood-curdling howl. It lowered its head and then charged. Its claws scattered rocks to both sides, and its mace-like tail whipped in the air behind it.

The man finally sprang to life, turned, and sprinted away from the charging monster. This time, he didn't try to drag along his companion. She screamed in terror and attempted to follow. Even if she were not injured, she couldn't have escaped the creature in the open. The beast's hot, moist, reeking breath enveloped her just before the mouth did. Her screams abruptly ended as the jaws clamped over her, severing her in two at the waist. Her legs continued running for several steps and then toppled forward just as the beast chomped her torso twice and swallowed.

The man knew his partner was gone from the grotesque sounds behind him. He raced toward another patch of forest at the far end of the clearing. The trees offered his only hope of eluding the beast. Suddenly, a rock rolled underneath his right foot, nearly sending him tumbling to the ground. He regained his balance but knew instantly he had lost too much time. He glanced over his shoulder to determine how close death was. The glowing red eyes smoldered like coal embers. Dark streaks, which he knew were blood, smeared the bared white teeth. Something flashed to the left side of the monster. The man turned just in time to see the spiked ball swinging toward him. His heroic leap couldn't lift him above the spike that proceeded to impale his body. He screamed until the blood turned it into a gurgle.

The monster swung its tail with the skewered prey up to its mouth. Two quick bites picked the spike clean.

***

"One day, you will create something you cannot control," Enki said.

"Nonsense. We are gods, after all," Odin replied.

"That thinking is what led to our current…situation. And we cannot even locate a missing human."

"You worry too much, brother. We will locate and deal with him. Remember, we have all the power—to create and destroy."

"Unfortunately, we seem more adept at destroying," Enki said. He turned to Artemis, "Now, who are the next questers?"

"Ah, I think the next group has great potential. I have watched them for some time. They are young, with very diverse personalities, and possess unique skills. They also dislike each other, so they will not have the loyalty of the last pair. We will have to do some work on one of them, but it should not pose an issue."

"I hope they are good. We are running out of time to find our champion and complete phase one," Enki replied.

"We will know more after the arena," Ra said.

"Give them the amulets just in case. And let the quest begin," Enki said.

CHAPTER 2

"Crap!" Spence shouted, slamming his fists onto the table on both sides of his laptop. "No!"

"You weren't supposed to attack yet, newb!" Cody exclaimed from across the table. He stared intently at his laptop screen, his fingers gliding in a blur across the keyboard and the buttons on his mouse. "You just pulled all the ads."

"And here comes the boss. Yet another wipe, sponsored by Spence the Great," Kyle said, shaking his head as he furiously clicked his keyboard.

"I didn't mean to cast the spell! I was trying to select a target, but my stupid sat-card is lagging," Spence said. He stared in horror as the pool of acid dissolved his character. He watched helplessly as the boss and his ads slaughtered the raid party. *No!* In addition to the anger of his friends at the table, the online raid characters were giving him a nasty beating through instant messaging. Thirty seconds later, the twenty characters' bodies lay strewn across the cavern floor. The instant messages continued.

"And the vote to kick," Kyle said.

"It wasn't my fault! Give me another chance," Spence pleaded, his voice quivering. The vote was unanimous, and Spence's character suddenly appeared by itself back in the city. "Even you guys?"

"Spence, how many times do we have to wipe because Twitchy the Mage can't keep his finger off the cast button?" Cody asked.

"Uh oh," Kyle said.

"What?" Spence demanded, logging out of the game.

"You've been kicked out of the guild too."

Spence slammed his laptop shut, shoved it into his backpack, and placed the pack on his lap. He then pushed hard on the wheels of his chair and backed away from the end of the picnic table. "You all suck! And so does the stupid guild. I'll join another one, and they'll appreciate me and Anniswind—the greatest mage in the realm. You'll all be sorry."

Spence heard Kyle and Cody laughing behind him as he quickly wheeled down the concrete pathway leading away from the shelter and toward the nature trails. He struggled fiercely to fight back the tears. Before his car wreck, he was used to getting teased and bullied. After being confined to a wheelchair, he had immersed himself in online role-playing games and somewhat escaped reality. He was able to become an anonymous, powerful mage. He was reasonably good at it but still usually found a way to screw things up when it counted the most.

"Spencer," Ms. Stephenson's voice called from up ahead. "You're just in time to join our group."

Spence looked up to see a group of students and his history teacher gathered on the trail. He had brought his laptop on the trip in hopes of playing *World of Warcraft* for the entire time. For most of the week, the other students had climbed trails and explored parts of Sedona that were much too difficult to do in a wheelchair. Besides visiting the Chapel of the Holy Cross, he had avoided the rest of the excursions by staying on the bus or finding shady places outside to play on his laptop. Occasionally, his pseudo-friends, Kyle and Cody, gamed with him.

He inhaled deeply and tried to regain his composure. He knew his cheeks still glowed, probably redder than his hair. "Uh, Ms. Stephenson, I'm not sure if I can do any of these trails."

"I think this one is paved most of the way and should be pretty easy, at least to Red Rock Crossing. There you'll be able to see Cathedral Rock and hopefully feel some vortex energy," Ms. Stephenson replied.

"I can help out my bud too," a student volunteered.

Spence swallowed hard as the cold chill raced down his spine. The student was none other than Trey Morrison. Trey was a star football player and all-around jock but also one of the worst bullies in school. Even though Spence and Trey were in the same grade, Trey had helped the upperclassmen introduce him to a swirly in the bathroom on his first day of freshman year. Since Spence's accident, Trey had stopped most of the physical bullying, but the verbal and mental abuse was about as bad. As much as Spence tried to avoid him, Trey was impossible to escape totally. Yet somehow, Trey never seemed to get into trouble. He could always talk or smile his way out of anything.

Spence watched the large blond-haired student stride over to him. His khaki shorts and red football team T-shirt displayed his muscular physique. His face was full but not fat, and his eyes were bright blue. Trey patted him on the shoulders roughly and then walked behind his chair and grasped the handles. "Don't worry, Spence, I'll get you there," Trey chirped.

Ms. Stephenson smiled, nodded, and then led the group down the trail. Spence tried to enjoy the scenery but was tense and distracted by the thought of his fate literally being in Trey's hands. This part of Sedona little resembled a desert. There were green trees and grass on both sides of the trail, and Oak Creek rolled and splashed to his left.

The concrete walkway soon transitioned to a red-dirt path, although the new trail was still wide and relatively flat and smooth. A comfortable breeze blew, and before long, Spence unclenched his hands slightly from his chair handles and began relaxing his upper body. It was a beautiful, peaceful place, and Spence was actually feeling a little bit fortunate at having stumbled into the tour. Maybe he could even experience some healing vortex energy.

They rounded a bend in the trail and suddenly spotted the majestic red spires of Cathedral Rock in the distance, stretching high above the green treetops. The rocks seemed to radiate their own red glow against the azure background. Spence had seen pictures of the formation but seeing it in person was breathtaking even from this distance. He knew some of the other students were going to hike up to it and climb it if Ms. Stephenson allowed or if they could do it without her seeing. He would have to be content just studying it from afar.

He was too enthralled with the view to notice the big rock on the path. He just felt the jolt, the chair stopping and tipping forward, and his body sprawling onto the dirt and rocks of the trail. He fell hard onto his backpack, forcing the breath from his lungs. He lay there desperately struggling to breathe again as the cloud of red dust rose around him.

"Fail," a voice said from somewhere in the line of students.

"Stupid gravity," another added.

Spence listened in silent rage to a mixture of snickers and outright laughter. It had been bad enough being physically bullied before his accident. Now, he was utterly helpless, like a turtle lying on its back. He didn't know whether it was more upsetting that most of the others laughed at him or the fact that he wasn't surprised by it.

Finally, Ms. Stephenson's voice rose above the harsh comments and laughter. "Trey, do you want to be suspended?"

"Suspended? It was an accident, Ms. Stephenson! I was staring at those cool rocks in the distance and didn't even notice the one on the trail."

Spence was finally breathing again by the time Trey arrived with his chair. Trey reached down and, despite Spence's girth, snatched him to his feet and dropped him back into the wheelchair. He roughly patted Spence's arms and shoulders, sending more clouds of red dust into the air.

"Sorry about that, Spence. Still bros?" Trey leaned around the chair, grinning.

Spence was too mad even to reply. His body shook, and his stomach churned. He wanted so badly to punch Trey in his smug face. He didn't hate many people, but Trey Morrison was at the top of the list.

"Are you OK, Spencer?" Ms. Stephenson asked, having walked over to check on him.

Spence nodded silently. His bottom lip quivered slightly.

They proceeded without incident a little further until the trail intersected the creek. "OK. This is Red Rock Crossing. We'll take a break here for pictures. Everyone pay attention to the stone cairns and the twisted limbs and trunks of the juniper trees. They say the cairns mark where the vortex energy is the strongest and that the vortexes actually bend and shape the trees. We'll stay here for half an hour. You may get into the water, but no horseplay," Ms. Stephenson said, her gaze lingering on Trey.

The group of students quickly dispersed. Some headed for the water, some took pictures of Cathedral Rock, and others took photos of the cairns and juniper trees. There was plenty of posing and selfies too. Thankfully, Trey abandoned his position behind Spence and went to talk to some of the other football players.

Spence wheeled himself a little further up the trail. When he reached a side trail to the right that led into a thick patch of trees, away from the creek, he thought he heard, or more felt, some type of humming or buzzing. He thought it must be his imagination, with all the vortex talk, but he didn't want to spend any more time with his classmates, who would tease and laugh at a crippled kid being dumped out of his wheelchair. He wheeled his chair through the loose dirt and disappeared into the trees.

The trail was wide enough for his chair and reasonably smooth. It was tough to push the wheels in several places, but he managed to power through and make decent speed. The trail twisted back and forth through the juniper grove, slowly leaving the voices of the other students faint in the distance. The humming gradually grew louder, almost like the sound of powerlines. But he wasn't sure if it was in his head or if he actually heard it. After a couple of minutes, the trail ended at a clearing surrounded by twisted and contorted juniper trees. The ground was smooth and covered with red desert dirt. In the center was a ring of the stone cairns—little stacks of smooth stones—around twenty feet in diameter. Above the trees to his left, he could still see the top half of Cathedral Rock.

Spence's gaze was immediately drawn to the figure standing in the middle of the cairn ring. Her black Goth garb appeared supernatural in the bright red and green setting. He knew without seeing her face that it was Morgan Turner. She must have headed here right after Trey dumped him from his wheelchair.

"Can you feel the energy?" she asked, not looking at him. "It's amazing!"

Spence glanced behind him and realized he was the only other student in the clearing. He was stunned she actually spoke to him. He didn't think she was mean, but the Goths were weird. They usually brooded together in small groups and complained about this or that injustice in the world. "Uh, yeah, I think so. It's like some kind of humming or buzzing. I thought maybe I was imagining it." He cautiously wheeled his chair to the edge of the circle of stones.

She turned to face him. Her tightly curled, long, mahogany brown hair framed her light brown face. She wore black eye shadow and liner as well as black lipstick. She had piercings in her bottom lip, left nostril, right eyebrow, and numerous ones up and down both ears. "Yes! It's like a tingling feeling…electricity…energy. This area is supposed to have a powerful vortex."

Spence realized Morgan was an attractive girl, despite being weird and a little freaky looking. She always reminded him of Zendaya, only a little rougher around the edges. Even in her unrevealing baggy black jeans and black Marilyn Manson T-shirt, her body was very shapely. He wheeled into the ring of stones until he was beside her, hoping to experience the energy.

"Wow. What kind of geek fest is this?"

Dang it. Spence didn't have to turn around to know who had found them. His heart instantly raced, and his body went numb.

CHAPTER 3

Trey walked up to stand close behind Spence and Morgan. "Are you two like having a séance or something and making weird sounds?"

"Sure, genius. That's exactly what we're doing. And instead of summoning a Native American spirit, we summoned a living Neanderthal," Morgan replied.

Spence turned his head, grinning.

"What are you smiling at, dork? And we need to chat about you almost getting me into trouble earlier," Trey said, stepping closer to Spence.

"You freakin' dumped him out of his wheelchair, thug! That's a new low even for you," Morgan said.

"Shut up, Twilight. Now, Spence. What can we do to teach you a lesson?" Trey grabbed the back of Spence's shirt.

A shuffling of feet at the edge of the clearing caused Trey to release Spence and turn around. Spence pulled his shirt down in the front and looked past Trey's side to see a tall, lean boy standing at the trail's end. He wore camouflage pants and a tight green T-shirt. His face was gaunt and chiseled, with thin lips and deep brown eyes, and his brown hair was cropped close to his head. He held a pocketknife in one hand with the blade extended, using it to dig dirt from underneath the fingernails on the other hand.

"Wow. This place attracts freaks!" Trey said.

"And apparently big piles of shit," the boy replied, not looking up. "Guess the buzzing I heard were the flies on you."

Morgan cackled, and Spence, despite his fear, couldn't suppress a smile.

"Don't think I'm scared of you just because of what you did to Austin. You just got in a lucky sucker punch anyway. What are you going to do, stab me with your pocketknife?"

Spence froze. Caleb Stone was a loner. Despite being athletic, he wasn't a jock, and he wasn't a nerd or Goth or part of any other clique. Caleb didn't bother anyone, and nobody messed with him. Some thought both he and his father were crazy. They were rumored to be preppers—preparing to survive some kind of global disaster. Caleb usually wore some camouflage articles and was frequently seen with knives, despite the school strictly banning weapons. Most suspected he had guns in his locker and car too.

A few weeks prior, Caleb had walked past Trey and Austin Parker and some other football players in the Wal-Mart parking lot. The story was that Austin had insulted him and his crazy father. When Caleb stopped and walked over to him, Austin continued insulting, followed by a shove. Caleb wordlessly erupted with a fury of blows on Austin's face and head. He added some kicks, even after Austin lay unconscious on the pavement. Austin was rushed to the hospital with a broken jaw, a fractured eye socket, a punctured lung, and several broken ribs. Some thought the jocks might retaliate, but they must have deemed Caleb too much of a loose cannon. Spence was surprised Trey confronted him now, alone.

"I can field dress a deer with this knife in ninety seconds. I'm thinking I could do you in seventy-five."

The two stared at each other like old-west gunfighters facing off. Trey was much larger and probably stronger, but Caleb's dark eyes stared calm and cold. His body language didn't reveal whether he was scared or nervous. Spence glanced at Morgan. She met his gaze and then turned back to the showdown.

"Whoa, do you feel that?" Morgan suddenly asked.

Trey warily turned away from Caleb, and the three stared at Morgan. She spun around in the middle of the cairn circle with her arms spread wide. The air shimmered in front of her like heat rippling off the desert.

The humming sound intensified, and Spence felt it throughout his entire body. The hair on his arms and the back of his neck stood. His body tingled as if a weak electric shock coursed through him. The air shimmered close to him now too. He felt warmth, but comforting warmth, unlike the miserable desert heat. "Is this a vortex?"

"I think so!" Morgan exclaimed.

The shimmering began to tint with color, taking on a blue hue. Then the shimmering began swirling, with flashes of light and streaks of blue, forming a mini-tornado, except with no wind. The air hummed, along with occasional crackles and pops. The funnel was just a couple of feet from Spence and Morgan. It slowly expanded in size until it was several feet wide and taller than Trey.

"What the heck is that?" Trey asked. He walked over next to Morgan.

"It's called a vortex. Some people claim there are centers of energy in Sedona that give off positive energy. This area is one of the four main sites. I've never heard of them being visible, though," Morgan explained.

"Sounds like a bunch of new-age hippy babble," Trey replied.

Caleb had joined the three, standing on the other side of Spence. His knife had disappeared into a pocket. Spence assumed they all felt the same energy now. He glanced behind them to see if any other students or Ms. Stephenson happened to be witnessing the event. There was no one else. He turned around just as Morgan stretched her hand into the vortex. He considered shouting a warning, but he didn't speak, too curious to see what would happen.

Morgan let out a little squeal of delight as her arm slowly disappeared into the swirling chaos. She ceased smiling when her arm had vanished up to her bicep. After a brief struggle and scream, her entire body was sucked into the funnel. A few flashes of her black clothing swirled amid the blue and white, and then she was gone.

"Holy shit!" Trey exclaimed. He began to retreat when the vortex suddenly expanded as if eating Morgan caused it to swell.

Spence tried to roll his chair backward too, but the vortex tugged at him. Out of the corners of his vision, he saw Caleb and Trey fighting similar losing battles. The vortex moved closer, and the pull intensified until Spence's grip on his chair finally gave way. He flailed his arms wildly, striking Trey once or twice, and then was jerked headlong out of his wheelchair and into the energy tornado.

CHAPTER 4

Spence's body was like a ragdoll as he twisted and spun within the vortex. He didn't know whether his eyes were open or closed, though he saw flashes of blue and white. An intense roar drowned out his screams. He lost all concept of direction and couldn't determine if he was swirling in a circle, falling, or flying up. His stomach churned as if he was riding the Mind Eraser roller coaster, only worse because he was in the dark. Electricity charged the air, ranging from gentle tingling to lightning bolts.

He had no concept of time, but the blue and white faded away to total darkness at some point. He now seemed to be speeding in one direction, although he didn't know which direction. But he was traveling extremely fast. White points of light appeared and streaked past as if he were traveling at light speed in a *Star Wars* movie. The roar was still mighty, and he was unable to move. Then suddenly, there was only blackness and the sensation of slowly floating down, like a falling feather on a windless day. He drifted for what could have been minutes, hours, days, or years.

Finally, Spence's body came to rest, and he slowly opened his eyes. He stared at an overcast, gray sky. Instead of the warmth of the vortex or heat of the desert, there was cold—both in the air and on the surface he lay upon. His head pounded, and his body was weak and achy.

My legs. Spence instantly realized he had sensation in his feet and legs. He moved his toes and feet experimentally, and then he moved each leg. *I'm not paralyzed!* It had to be a dream. He had dreamed a lot over the past few months. Half of the dreams relived the accident. In the other half, his accident had been the dream, and he was still healthy and whole.

He slowly sat up and surveyed his surroundings. He lay on some type of raised, circular stone platform. Four three-foot-tall square stone pillars stood directly in front of him, with a pile of objects lying on the top of each. On the other side, in the very center of the platform, stood a twenty-foot-tall stone statue of a warrior. It held a sword in one hand, the blade pointing down, and a shield in the other. The warrior wore plate armor with a helmet on its head.

Morgan stood beside him on his right, her arms folded tightly across her chest. Trey sat beside him, and Caleb stood on the other side. Spence cautiously stood. His legs were weak, but they worked. He was a little unsteady, and his head and stomach swam.

The dais stood six feet above the surrounding ground, with a short flight of stairs leading down on each side. The land was flat and covered with short brown grass. It stretched fifty yards to each side and a hundred yards to the front and back until it reached a twenty-foot-high wall that enclosed the entire oval-shaped area. The sole break in the wall was a large, dark, arched opening on the side they faced. The vortex was gone, and there was no sign of Spence's wheelchair or backpack.

Spence experimentally squatted down and stood several times, working the stiffness out of his muscles.

"Oh my God! You can walk," Morgan exclaimed.

"I know! It's crazy," Spence said, grinning bigger than he had in months. "Where are we, anyway?"

"How should I know?" Morgan shivered visibly.

"You're the vortex expert. Is this a vortex thing?" Spence continued.

"No…I don't think so. I've never read of one transporting people somewhere else."

"This has to be a dream," Trey said softly. "I mean, Spence can walk again, and his chair isn't even here." He stood and slowly turned to survey their surroundings.

It was the first time Spence had heard Trey speak without cockiness and bravado. Trey was right, though. He had to be dreaming. Trey must have punched him in the back of the head or shoved him out of his wheelchair again, and he still lay unconscious in the desert clearing. That's why his head hurt, he was dizzy and nauseous, and he had been lying on a hard surface. But it was an incredible dream. He could stand again! So, he might as well enjoy it. Maybe he could even fight back in the dream. Perhaps he could hurt Trey badly.

A long, deep growl from the dark opening interrupted Spence's thoughts. He stared at the archway one hundred yards in front of them. The hole was at least fifteen feet tall and the same width. His mind raced as he slowly processed the situation. "Uh, guys, we'd better see if there are some weapons on those pillars."

"Why, ginger?" Trey said. "It's probably just a dog or coyote."

Spence was used to the "ginger" comments. He had pale skin, red hair, and plenty of freckles. That, plus being twenty pounds overweight, did nothing to help his high-school social standing. Spence ignored Trey reverting to being Trey. "That cave is a little sketch. I'm guessing whatever is growling will come out of that opening. Judging by the size of the hole, it will be something bigger than a dog. And we're going to have to fight it with whatever is on those pillars. We're in an arena." Spence suddenly felt confident. Although he was probably in a dream, this was his environment, even if he just knew it from online gaming.

"And how do you know that? Oh, wait. *Dungeons and Dweebs!*" Trey exclaimed.

Caleb walked over to one of the stone pillars and began rummaging through the items on top. He held up a three-foot-long, silver short sword, turning the blade side-to-side to examine it. He swung it experimentally several times. Then he began inspecting the remainder of the items. Spence and the other two walked over to stand beside Caleb. Each pillar had a different weapon on it, along with clothing and some type of pack.

"What are you doing, Rambo?" Trey asked Caleb.

"Since there aren't any guns, I'm upgrading my pocketknife," Caleb replied, not looking at Trey.

Trey grunted and surveyed the other pillars. He approached one with a giant, gleaming, silver battle-ax lying on top. He picked it up and swung it back and forth, like the way Caleb had wielded the sword. "I'd better take the manly weapon. I know none of you girls could handle this." The ax had a leather strap stretching from a hole in the end of the handle to a hole just beneath the head.

Spence's heart began racing again, and he forgot the cold. This dream was turning out perfect, other than Trey being there. They had teleported to a different world or land. The vortex did remind him of the portal's mages could create in *World of Warcraft*. Now, they were choosing fantasy-type weapons. When he spotted a staff on top of one of the pillars, he quickly walked over to it. He doubted any of the others would even know the purpose of a staff, but he couldn't take a chance.

Spence felt every muscle, tendon, and ligament move and contract in his feet and legs, from toes to hips. His legs quickly felt stronger and steadier, and he gained confidence with each step. He reached the pillar, grabbed the five-foot-long black shiny staff, and held it reverently. The staff was very lightweight, and he couldn't determine whether it was wood or metal. One end had a crystal orb on it. It was warm to the touch despite having been lying in the cold air and on cold stone. He experimentally pointed it at one of the walls, but nothing happened. He tried pointing it in various directions, but it appeared to be just a stick with a glass bulb. His excitement tempered.

"Nice choice, Spence. You'll do awesome if we encounter a baton-twirling contest," Trey said.

Spence gritted his teeth and squeezed his staff. If he could only break the bulb over Trey's head....

"None of this makes sense," Morgan said, hesitantly walking to the last pillar. She picked up a shiny black longbow. She experimentally held it in her left hand and pulled the string to the corner of her mouth with her right.

"No, it doesn't. But if Spence is right, there's not much choice but to try and defend ourselves," Caleb said matter-of-factly. "Let me guess, *Hunger Games* fan?"

"Yep. Plus, my father is an avid bowhunter. I refuse to hunt and harm animals, but I've shot targets with him since I was six. I can outshoot him without sites or aids."

Another growl interrupted their conversation, and the four stared at the opening. Something shifted in the darkness. "Hurry, guys!" Spence was the first to rummage through the remainder of the items on his pillar. He slipped on a black robe. Although thin and light, the material felt tough and provided instant protection from the cold. He fastened a wide black belt with a sheath hanging from one side around his waist and slid a silver dagger into the sheath. Then he removed his tennis shoes and changed into knee-high leather boots. Despite his staff being just a stick, he suddenly felt the part of a mage.

The others followed Spence's example and began donning clothing and gear too. Caleb put on a chainmail shirt, a pair of black leather pants, gloves, and tall leather boots. He also had a belt with two daggers and a sheath for his sword. Trey fastened on a shining metal breastplate, a metal helmet with a nosepiece, brown leather pants, a belt and dagger, gloves, and boots. Morgan slipped into a thick black tunic that came to midthigh. She pulled on dark gray pants, a belt with a sheathed dagger, black gloves, and black boots. She placed a quiver of arrows across her shoulder.

The transformation was quick and impressive. In five minutes, they went from a ragtag group of teenagers to a party of fantasy adventurers. Spence hoped he didn't wake up too soon. *This was awesome!* Then he heard a blood-curdling roar that ended in a howl.

26

"What the heck is that?" Trey asked. Nobody answered. They stood transfixed, staring at the dark opening.

"That's no coyote. I've never heard anything like it," Caleb said.

Two red glowing lights appeared at the cave entrance. Slowly the lights moved forward until a gray, hairy, doglike snout extended into the daylight. Then the entire head appeared, with the red orbs revealed as eyes. The head resembled a giant, mangy wolf's. As more of the creature emerged, Spence saw the rest of its body was some type of lizard or dinosaur. The beast was nearly as tall as the opening, and the body extended thirty feet, including a long tail ending with a spiked ball.

CHAPTER 5

"What kind of freakin' monster is that?" Trey finally broke the silence.

"We need to wake up. Now!" Morgan hissed.

"A wolfosaurus," Spence said softly. This creature was even too exotic for *Warcraft*. His body felt heavy, as if he were another stone statue on the dais. He watched as the monster raised its head and sniffed the air, swinging it slowly back and forth. Then its glowing eyes halted on them. It sniffed again and then emitted the bone-chilling roar. "Dream or not, that thing is going to try to eat us."

"He's right. We might as well end the dream fighting. They say you can't die in your dreams, so we should wake up soon," Caleb said. He strode around the pillars and statue to the edge of the dais.

"Well, I can't let Rambo outdo me," Trey said and walked over to join Caleb, swinging his ax.

Spence reluctantly joined the others, holding his staff tightly in front of him with the orb pointed at the monster. Morgan appeared on his other side, nocking an arrow on the bowstring.

The beast growled and then charged. It was a hundred yards away but quickly closed the distance. "See if you can hit it, Morgan," Caleb yelled.

"I don't kill animals," she replied.

"First of all, it's going to kill all of us. Second, that monstrosity isn't an animal. Third, you don't have to eat it. Now shoot it!"

Morgan pulled the string to the corner of her mouth. She paused for a moment and then released the arrow. It sailed high over the beast's back and stuck in the ground behind it.

"Nailed it, Katniss," Trey growled.

"Bite me, ogre. It's the first time I've shot this bow." She nocked another arrow. Now, the creature was just fifty yards away. She drew the string and shot again. The shaft struck the right side of the monster but bounced harmlessly off its rock-hard scales. "Damn it!"

Spence squeezed hard on his staff, but nothing happened. He thought his heart would beat out of his chest and kill him before the monster could. His entire body trembled now but not from the cold. He didn't know whether his legs were weak from lack of use or fear. The ground, including the dais, also shook from the thundering charge. They were no match for a creature like that; they probably couldn't kill a regular wolf, much less a dinosaur-size one.

"Let's spread out. If it attacks one of us, the others attack from the sides. Morgan, aim for its head. Shoot its eyes out," Caleb ordered. He rushed down the stairs to the ground and moved to the left of the platform.

Morgan ran down the stairs and scurried to the right. Trey strode down the middle and stood in front of the dais. Spence descended the first few steps and then stopped, well behind Trey. The creature slowed its charge momentarily as it analyzed its prey changing positions. It then resumed its charge straight ahead, toward Trey. Trey started swinging his ax back and forth, seemingly unfazed by the enormous monstrosity rushing toward him. Then he inexplicably lowered his ax when the beast closed to twenty yards. He stood motionless, staring straight ahead.

"Trey! Get ready! Morgan, now!" Caleb shouted.

Spence was still frozen, helplessly waiting to watch Trey get shredded by the foot-long wolf teeth. He was too frightened even to relish the prospect. He desperately wanted to move and tried to think what he would do if he were Anniswind—only Anniswind had powerful spells and a magical staff. He had a stick with a glass tip and a dagger.

The beast slowed as it neared Trey. It didn't want to trample him, Spence realized; it wanted to eat him. It issued a deep, long growl that vibrated in Spence's chest, despite it still being thirty feet away. The monster sniffed the air again, and its red eyes glowed brightly, transfixed on Trey. It walked the final steps, stopping a half dozen feet from the frozen teenager. It raised its head high—its mouth hanging open, drool oozing from between its teeth and striking the ground with a hiss. Trey still didn't move.

Caleb charged from the beast's right side just as Morgan loosed an arrow from its left. The shaft missed the eye but struck the beast's cheek. It roared in shock and pain and swung its head to face Morgan. Then Caleb's sword flashed and sank into its front leg. The monster howled and jerked its head to the right. Its snout struck Caleb before he could retreat, sending him tumbling backward. He landed ten feet away on his back with a dull thud but somehow still clung to his sword.

Trey finally came to life. He moved forward and swung his ax at the side of the beast's mouth. It sliced the lip open, instantly coating the gray fur with a stream of blood. The wolf head jerked around to face Trey. This time the monster retreated a few steps to reassess the three threats. It raised its head and emitted an ear-splitting roar, followed by a howl. Morgan used the pause to release another arrow. This time it struck its left eye, half the arrow embedding in its skull, with the other half still protruding.

The creature yelped loudly and spun to face Morgan, the greatest threat now. It swung its spiked tail, striking Caleb as he regained his feet. He barely managed to block the spikes with his sword but was tossed high into the air, landing on the grass twenty feet away. This time he lay still.

Trey charged forward with his ax, attempting a blow to the other side of the beast's face. Without looking, the monster raised its lizard leg into the charging boy. Trey managed to strike it with his ax, but the impact sent him crashing onto the stone steps just below Spence. His ax remained in the monster's leg. He moaned softly once and then fell silent, motionless.

Morgan retreated and desperately tried to nock another arrow. Spence finally realized he had to do something, or they would all be dead. It might already be too late for Trey and Caleb. He slowly moved, his limbs weak and heavy. "Come get me!" he shouted, his voice made louder from adrenaline and fear. *Dear Lord, please help us all survive this.* He hadn't prayed much since his prayers to walk again had gone unanswered. But now, since his paralysis was cured, it was as good of a time as any to find faith again. He tried to back up the stairs to the level surface of the dais, but his right foot caught the edge of the step behind him. He slowly and helplessly collapsed onto the stairs. He still clutched the staff with both hands and instinctively thrust it behind him to help cushion the fall.

As soon as the staff struck the base of the step behind him, a surge of heat and electricity raced up its length. The crystal tip glowed a bright white. Then part of the shaft slid open beneath his left hand, and his fingers touched three buttons in the exposed compartment. The wolfosaurus, distracted by the light from the staff, stopped its approach on Morgan and turned its massive head to face Spence. Spence's knees would have buckled beneath the evil red gaze if he still stood. The beast licked its lips and slowly walked toward him.

31

Spence lowered the staff and pointed the glowing tip at the creature's mouth. Hopefully, he could at least fend it off for a few minutes while Morgan hit it with another arrow. As he squeezed the staff tighter and braced his body against the hard stairs, his left forefinger pressed the top button. He heard a click, and then the staff began to vibrate violently. The beast had reached the bottom of the steps, almost to Trey's prone body. It stretched its neck out far enough for Spence to feel and smell its hot, reeking breath.

Then the lightning bolt surged out of the staff. The bolt and its many jagged forks of light struck the monster's head, shoulders, and chest. A huge roar of thunder erupted after the strike. The recoil pressed Spence hard into the stairs, with the back of his head striking the edge of the top one and the staff nearly flying from his hands. The concussion from the thunder knocked Morgan to the ground.

The beast staggered back a few steps while the lightning enveloped it and penetrated its tough hide and scales. Its body convulsed as it wobbled momentarily and then collapsed onto the ground. Once the lightning finally subsided, the creature slowly rolled over on its side. The red glow disappeared from its eyes, and its long tongue hung out the side of its mouth. The smell of ozone and burning hair hung over the arena.

***

"They made quick work of your wolfosaur," Artemis said.

"Impressive," Ra agreed.

"Interesting that the weak one chose the staff," Enki added. "The spinal repair went well too. It was good you could reverse the muscle atrophy in his legs."

"The weak shall inherit the earth...or Nibiru," Artemis answered, grinning. "I told you this group would have some interesting dynamics and skills."

"Perhaps we can finally find our champion out of this group," Odin said.

"Or possibly multiple champions," Artemis replied.

"Interesting. We have never believed that possible. That could offer the best results," Enki said.

CHAPTER 6

Spence slowly regained his feet and stared wide-eyed at the staff in his quivering hands. *Thank you, God.* The shaft had closed together, leaving no trace of the hidden compartment. The tip no longer glowed, and he didn't feel any electricity or vibrations. He realized the butt of the staff striking the stone stair must have activated it. He peered at the giant monster, which was obviously dead with thin tendrils of black smoke drifting up from its charred body. His body was weak and his legs shaky, but he suddenly felt vastly different. He had never experienced a similar feeling in his entire life. Despite unlocking the staff's power by his clumsiness, he felt confident. He felt in control. He felt…powerful.

"Holy shit!" Trey said weakly from the stairs below. He was still prone but propped up on his elbows with his head turned to stare at Spence.

Spence retreated up the last couple of steps and stood at the platform's edge. He leaned on his staff and watched the others below. With his staff, dagger, and black robe, Spence was now a mage. He wanted to run around the dais in victory laps on his newly functioning legs. Morgan stood and slowly walked toward the stairs. She appeared a little paler but unharmed. Spence hoped she hadn't seen how he had activated the staff. Caleb also stirred on the left side of the dais. He cautiously climbed to his feet and staggered toward the others, rubbing gingerly at his ribs. Trey rose to his knees and then finally stood.

"Like my baton?" Spence tried unsuccessfully not to sound smug. "I think I won the contest." Spence savored Trey's expression and lack of a comeback. This moment was the highlight of his life. He had his legs back, possessed a powerful staff, and had just saved his life and those of three others. He wished the moment could last forever and hoped the dream never ended now.

"You saved my life," Morgan said from the first stair. "You saved all our lives."

"Ah, don't mention it. You were good with your bow too. You did Katniss proud," Spence said, his chest unconsciously puffed out and shoulders drawn back.

"Thank you, Spence. Morgan's right. I owe you," Caleb said. He sheathed his sword when he reached the base of the stairs.

"Thanks, Caleb. You were the first one to attack, though. We'd all be dead if you hadn't begun the battle," Spence replied. "Are you hurt? That tail whacked you pretty good."

"Surprisingly, not bad. My ribs feel bruised, but this mail shirt is much tougher than it looks. I don't think anything is broken, at least. Trey, what happened to you? You'd have been wolfosaurus food if Morgan hadn't shot it."

Trey walked over to the beast and wrenched his ax free. He then paused and stared at the dead monster. Suddenly, he kicked it in the leg, paused, and then kicked it several more times. Then he began yelling obscenities and raining blows with his ax from the monster's leg to its head. It was soon a bloody mess. After several minutes, he finally stopped, panting. He gave it one last kick, wiped the ax head clean on the grass, and slung it over his shoulder with the leather strap. He joined the others, now all gathered at the top of the stairs, and sat down heavily beside Spence. He didn't meet anyone's eyes or speak.

Spence had watched Trey's tantrum in stunned silence. He wasn't sure if Trey was upset at having frozen in the battle or just at their situation and being out of his element. Spence heard sobbing from his right and turned to see Morgan sitting with her knees pulled to her chest and head buried in her folded arms. He was shocked that the confident Morgan was crying in front of them. He glanced back to the left and observed Caleb sitting on the other side of Trey, staring blankly at the wolfosaurus.

The gravity of their situation suddenly crashed down on Spence. His excitement over being bipedal again in a strange fantasy world and euphoria over his role in slaying the monster subsided. They were four teenage kids stuck in some type of nightmare. It couldn't be real. But if it were real…. He couldn't even force his mind to comprehend the possibility. Exhaustion overwhelmed him, and his limbs were leaden. He sat down on the cold stone between Trey and Morgan.

Morgan's soft sobs were the only sounds disturbing the eerie, suffocating silence of the arena. Spence wasn't sure how long they sat there, but eventually, the silence overwhelmed him. He had too many thoughts swirling around in his mind to focus on any for long. Wherever they were, and whether it was a dream or not, they had to do something. They couldn't sit here and mope and cry forever.

"Well, we did work together to kill that monster," Spence said.

"Yeah, and it looks like we scored some pretty cool bling," Trey said. "This breastplate and ax are sweet. They're light as plastic, but neither has a scratch."

"Mine too," Caleb said.

Morgan finally raised her head and wiped her eyes with her tunic. "Once I got used to it, my bow was pretty awesome too. It feels like a twenty-pound draw weight but hits like a sixty-five or seventy."

"It sounds like we all have magic weapons," Spence said, a little disappointed at not being the only one. But from what he could tell, his was by far the most powerful, and he had undoubtedly gained the most.

"Which makes even less sense. Monsters and magic? Where are we? What is this place? And what do we do now?" Morgan asked, her voice shaky.

Spence looked at the others and received two blank stares and a shrug. He then nervously scanned the dark opening, hoping and praying no more creatures emerged. Nothing stirred in the darkness. Then he heard a noise from behind them, in the center of the platform. It sounded like stone grating against stone. He and the others stood and turned to locate the source. The statue in the middle moved—or at least its head swiveled to face them. Spence stared in disbelief as the face transitioned from stone to flesh. The now black eyes stared at them. The mouth moved.

"Welcome to Nibiru, humans," a voice boomed from the statue. "I am Enki, one of the gods of this world. You have defeated a great monstrosity and threat to our peoples. You have proved yourself worthy of the quest with your bravery and skill."

"Where is Nibiru?" Trey blurted out.

The statue ignored Trey's interruption and continued, "Four races inhabit Nibiru—Nephilim, elves, dwarves, and Draconians. They each live separate from one another, kept apart by evil creatures. You must journey to each race and liberate them from these monsters. If you complete this quest, we will allow you to return to your world."

"That's bullshit! We don't care about your races or monsters or quest. Return us now," Trey demanded.

"Gather the remainder of the items on the pedestals; you will need them all. Then travel east across the Barrens to the Nephilim town of Argos. Seek out the one named Titus. He will aid you in your journey. Good luck, questers." The head of the statue rotated forward and once again reverted to stone. The oppressive silence returned, lasting over a minute before anyone spoke.

Chapter 7

"Wow!" Spence said. "Enki and Nibiru."

"What does that mean?" Trey demanded. "Who is Enki, and what is Nibiru?"

"Enki was one of the main gods of the ancient Sumerians. They believed their gods lived on a planet called Nibiru. It's supposedly in our solar system but just orbits the sun every thirty-six hundred years or so. Each time the planet passed close, the gods traveled back and forth from Nibiru to Earth. Enki allegedly helped create humans by splicing their genes with those of early man, *Homo erectus,* I think, to be the god's slaves. It's really a fascinating theory—"

"Why in the hell do you know all that?" Trey interrupted.

"They're called books," Spence retorted.

"I'm ready to wake up!" Morgan shouted.

Spence's mind reeled. He had read and been intrigued by the Sumerian theories presented in Zecharia Sitchin's books. Based on his translations and interpretations of ancient Sumerian texts, Sitchin wrote quite a few books about ancient astronauts, with *The 12th Planet* being the most famous. But Spence didn't believe in Sitchin's theories. After all, he was raised a Christian. But could Nibiru really exist, and they actually be on it? Could Enki have been the voice of the statue? "Guys, what if this isn't a dream? It's been going on for a while," Spence said.

"Then what is it? How did we end up in a different world, Nibiru, ruled by gods, with nightmare monsters and talking statues? Not to mention magical medieval weapons," Caleb said.

Spence enjoyed the others consulting him and not just ignoring or teasing. "In *Warcraft*, magical portals can teleport you to different places. That vortex must have been some kind of portal."

"That's a computer game, genius," Trey said.

"Then what is your jock-theory?" Spence replied, surprising himself with his tone toward Trey. He'd be seconds from receiving a punch or kick in the real world. But Trey just glared at him. Trey wasn't in his element now and was obviously shaken by it. Spence continued, "Some people also believe there are different dimensions from ours and parallel universes. I think the vortex was a doorway to a different dimension or planet."

"Like *Pacific Rim*," Morgan said softly.

"Yeah, or the *Narnia* books," Spence added.

"What about you walking again?" Caleb asked.

Spence thought for a moment. "I'm not sure about that. I wonder how long the journey in the vortex took or how long we were unconscious?"

"Hmmm. It was hard to tell. It seemed like I flew and then floated forever," Morgan replied.

"Maybe the gods fixed me before we woke up," Spence said. "In the Sumerian myths, they were very advanced."

"What about the Nephilim? Weren't they like giants or something in the Bible?" Morgan asked Spence.

"Yes. But Zecharia Sitchin, who wrote a lot about the ancient Sumerians, theorized that the Nephilim were the gods from Nibiru," Spence said.

"Were they giants?" Morgan said.

"I don't think so. The gods supposedly created humans by mixing their DNA and that of early man."

"What's a Draconian?" Trey asked.

Spence shook his head. "It sounds familiar, but I can't remember what it means."

"Did Enki and the Sumerians speak English?" Caleb asked.

Spence thought for a second. That was a good point. "No, the Nibiru gods taught the Sumerians their language and writing. I'm not sure why Enki would speak English."

The four didn't talk for several more moments. Morgan reached inside her black tunic and pulled out her cell phone. She held it up to the sky and frowned. "No service, of course."

Spence and Trey retrieved their cell phones from their pockets to confirm Morgan's statement.

"Siri, where the hell are we?" Trey asked his phone.

"You need cell service for that, stupid," Morgan said.

Trey scowled at her and then continued, "Damn, I could Instagram the hell out of some wolfosaurus pics." He then snapped a picture of the statue.

"It do beg for some selfies," Morgan replied, half-smiling.

Spence and Morgan also took a picture of the statue, and then Spence finally turned and walked over to his pedestal. A crude leather pack remained, which he slung over his right shoulder, on top of his robe. It was lightweight and didn't seem to be a problem for his legs to support.

"What are you doing?" Morgan asked as she and the others reached him.

"What the statue told us to do."

"Do you even hear yourself? What the statue told us to do?" Morgan said.

"Look, until I wake up, I'm assuming this is real. We're in a new world, and we need to find the way back to ours. The vortex is gone, so we must find another way. Our only clue is what the talking statue told us to do. Unless you have a better idea or want to sit here on the cold stone until some other monster finds us or we freeze to death, I think we need to finish equipping ourselves and find Titus in Argos." Spence had always been a follower. For the first time ever, he felt ready to lead, not simply fall in line with others.

The other three walked to their pedestals and retrieved different types of packs. Caleb had a backpack like Spence's. Morgan found two leather pouches that fit on each side of her belt. Trey had one large fanny pack-type pouch that fit on the back of his belt. Soon they all gathered at the top of the steps where they had fought the battle.

Spence examined his three companions—a warrior, a barbarian, and an archer. He, of course, was the mage. They needed a cleric or healer, though.

"Which way?" Caleb asked.

Spence felt the pride again when all three turned to him. "Let's see…the statue said to head east to Argos."

Caleb spun around in a circle, surveying the overcast sky. There was little evidence of a sun, but it was still possible to determine which way the light was traveling. "The light has been moving that way, which is west unless things are different in this world. So, I'd say let's go this way." Caleb walked down the stairs without waiting to see if the others followed. They trailed close behind.

At the bottom of the stairs, Trey ran over to the dead monster's body. For a moment, Spence thought he was going to attack it again. Then Trey turned, held his phone out, and took a picture of himself in front of the beast's head.

Caleb stopped and turned. "Seriously? You're taking a selfie?"

Trey returned to the group. "Hey, when we get back to Earth, I'll blow up the Internet."

Spence knew it was foolish and childish, but he quickly ran to the wolfosaurus and took a selfie. Morgan shook her head but still hurried over for her shot.

"You all are idiots. You were crying and throwing tantrums a few minutes ago, and now you're acting like you're back at school." Caleb turned and continued walking to the wall on their left.

"Well, at least I didn't thirst trap it," Morgan said, barely loud enough to be heard, and fell into line behind Caleb.

Spence followed Morgan, letting Trey bring up the rear. Spence was a little nervous having Trey behind him, but at least he could protect from an attack from that direction—he just hoped Trey wasn't the attacker. But Spence had his staff now. He wasn't scared of Trey—or at least, less than he had been an hour before.

When they neared the rock wall, Spence noticed the flight of stairs carved into its side. It had blended in perfectly until they were close. They ascended the steps single file. Once they reached the top, they saw the land was primarily open and hilly in all directions. The landscape was brown and bleak, with the ground covered in brown grass and something resembling sagebrush. A few dull green bushes, an occasional tree, and random rock formations broke up the landscape. The smooth hills were big enough to prevent them from seeing too far into the distance. A slightly worn path in front of them wound through the hills to the east. The hills were fewer and smaller in that direction.

"Wow, pretty," Morgan said.

"Kind of like the desert, minus the sun and heat," Trey added.

"It reminds me of the drive I took from San Francisco to Yosemite a few years ago. At least it's not one hundred degrees here, though," Spence said, walking onto the trail. The gray sky was dimming, and it would be dark within a few hours. "To Argos."

"Did any of your books describe Nibiru?" Caleb asked Spence.

"I don't believe so, at least not that I can remember."

They maintained the same single file order, with Caleb leading the way. They didn't speak much as they walked. Spence soon became used to walking again, and his mind focused more on the strange new world. He kept his eyes scanning from one side of the road to the other. The light was fading rapidly, and Spence didn't know what to expect in whatever world they were in. He knew good things typically didn't happen after dark, though.

He absently stroked the smooth shaft of his staff. He wondered what the other two buttons did. Maybe the staff shot fireballs and ice bolts too. He decided he would keep the technological secret of the staff to himself and let the others believe it was magic. He wondered about Trey's and Caleb's armor. The wolfosaurus should have seriously injured them, but neither was. He also didn't know whether Morgan's bow was special or if she was that good of a shot. But out of all of them, he obviously had the most dangerous weapon.

"I think I'll change my name to my *Warcraft* character's name. From now on, call me Anniswind the Great. Or just Anniswind for short," Spence said loud enough for all to hear.

"Anal Wind?" Trey asked. "That's your name?"

"Anniswind!" He couldn't believe Trey had already returned to his usual jerk self, even after he had saved his life.

"Anal Wind the Smelly. Or Silent but Deadly? Or, I know, Fart the Malodorous!"

Spence's cheeks grew hot. Just like that, Trey ripped away his newfound feeling of control and power. Morgan and Caleb laughing along with Trey made it worse. "How about I deep-fry you like I did that monster?" He turned and lowered his staff at Trey.

"How about I split you in two from head to toe?" Trey grabbed his ax off his back.

"OK, boys. That's enough. There will probably be plenty of ways to die in whatever godforsaken world this is, other than killing each other. Un-bunch your panties, and let's try to reach the town before dark," Morgan said.

Spence finally lowered his staff and breathed a few deep breaths. Someday, Trey would pay; he didn't rule this world. Trey slung his ax over his shoulder but offered no further taunts or comments. Spence turned around, and the four began walking again.

After a few minutes, Morgan slowed until she was just half a step ahead of Spence. She spoke quietly, without looking at him. "I saw your little fall, or should I say fail, on the stairs. You did save our lives but dial back the machismo a little bit. You could have just as easily gotten us all killed." She then picked up her pace and moved back in front of him.

Spence's anger rekindled. *Maybe they all needed to pay.*

Chapter 8

They followed the faint road for at least an hour. The landscape didn't change much, with just the reddish-brown grass and dirt, barren hills, and occasional trees the only scenery. Spence didn't see any animals or even birds flying. The light continued fading, with little evidence of the actual location of the sun. The air grew colder as the light disappeared. It seemed like a dreary December day in Colorado. Spence was used to the harsh Colorado winters, but he was prepared there with insulated boots and gloves, layers of clothes, hats, and ski masks. His robe and crude boots could only do so much. Having just come from a hot, sunny desert made it that much worse.

Caleb eventually stopped walking and turned to face the others. "It's going to be dark soon, and we have no idea how far the town is. I say we make some type of camp while we can still see."

Spence had been excited to reach the town, but now he was exhausted. The stress of the situation, plus the battle, had taken its toll. His legs were also tired and achy. He assumed it was from the lack of use over the past few months, but he hadn't exercised much since he had survived tenth-grade gym class. He nodded assent to Caleb. Morgan and Trey didn't protest.

"There are a couple of trees at the base of that hill," Caleb said, pointing to the south. "Hopefully, there is something useful in these packs." He strode toward the trees, with the others trailing close behind.

Caleb unslung his pack when they reached the trees, knelt beside it on the ground, and hastily rummaged through it. "Rope, tinderbox, tarp, pouch of coins, and a necklace with like a ruby pendant on it." Caleb withdrew the necklace and hung it around his neck.

Trey removed his fanny pack and searched through it while still standing. "A whetstone, something that looks like an emergency blanket, coins, and a necklace with a blue pendant. It seems kind of gay, but I might as well wear it. Maybe it's magic," Trey said and placed the chain over his head.

Morgan scowled at Trey and then searched through the pouches on her belt. "Bandages, two small, round containers, coins, a vial of red liquid, and an amethyst necklace." She, too, donned her necklace.

Spence placed his pack on the ground and squatted to peer inside. "Sweet!" He pulled out a silver chain with an emerald pendant. The pendent was warm and even seemed to vibrate faintly. He had no idea of its purpose, but judging by his staff, it might be powerful. He slipped it over his head and around his neck. "It looks like there is a tarp in here, rope, coins, and two vials of a white liquid. Dang."

"What?" Caleb asked.

"None of us have food or water," Spence replied.

"Fatty hungry?" Trey asked.

"Shut up, spaz," Morgan replied for Spence.

"Everybody focus," Caleb said. "Trey, let's take these tarps and ropes and make a shelter. Morgan and Spence, see if you can find some dry sticks. There won't be much wood, but hopefully, we can get a small fire going. Morgan, if you see something edible, shoot it."

"I don't kill animals," Morgan snapped.

"I hope you will if it's between that and starvation," Caleb said.

"I don't think any of us will starve tonight." She turned and walked toward the next closest trees.

Spence watched her walk away. He was a little disappointed he wasn't the leader after his shining moment of slaying the wolfosaurus. But he was tired and liked the thought of being away from Trey for a few minutes. He mostly forgave Morgan for her earlier comments since she had come to his defense. He left his pack, grabbed his staff, and hurried to catch her. She appeared menacing with her dark hair and tunic in the dim light. "Crazy day, huh?"

"I know, right?" she replied.

Sarcasm was something Spence did know about Morgan from school. "I don't think we're dreaming."

"We can still hope."

"Well, maybe we should just embrace it. I mean, we get to be on a quest in a strange world, full of monsters and different races. How many people can say that?" *And I can walk again.*

Morgan turned to stare at him. "Embrace it? We're four freakin' high school kids trying to fight monsters! We might have survived the first one, but there are at least four more. We're all not going to survive this—if any of us do. And don't take this personal, but I can't think of any three people I'd less rather be stuck with in this disaster than you three."

Spence swallowed hard. "That didn't sound personal at all."

They gathered sticks and small tree limbs from the few nearby trees and returned to the camp with two armfuls. Caleb and Trey had tied a rope between the two trees and placed Caleb's tarp over it. Then they had cut some stakes out of tree limbs and staked the backside of the tarp to the side of the hill and the front corners to the ground, leaving a doorway in the front and a protected shelter within. They had spread Spence's tarp over the floor inside the tent.

Spence and Morgan dropped the wood in front of the shelter. Caleb went to work with the flint from the tinderbox and his dagger and had a flame going in just a few minutes. He added more limbs to it and soon had a nice size campfire. The four sat on the ground around it.

"I guess this *would* be better with some food to cook," Caleb said.

"You think the statue would have packed us dinner," Trey replied.

"Well, hopefully, the town isn't far away. We have money to buy what we need," Spence added.

"I just thought of something else," Morgan said softly.

The other three turned to her.

"Where's the bathroom?"

Caleb laughed loudly, with Trey and Spence joining in. "Haven't been camping before, huh?"

"In a camper with a bathroom," she replied, glaring at the three boys.

"Just pick a spot and squat," Trey said. The three laughed harder.

Morgan glowered at them. "What about toilet paper?"

"Well, that's a little trickier. I guess hand or leaves. Oh, but you have to dig a hole and bury it, or wild animals can find it—and us," Caleb said.

"Or scoot your butt across the grass like a dog," Trey added.

Morgan stood. "You may all kiss my ass." She turned and stomped off into the darkness.

Spence chuckled. He was glad he wasn't the one getting teased, though he hated anyone had to. Of course, getting teased about using the bathroom wasn't the same as being teased for being a nerd or crippled. And Morgan could more than fend for herself.

"Shame we couldn't have gotten stuck with a hot chick," Trey said.

"I think she's pretty hot," Spence replied.

"You think your right hand is hot," Trey said. "What about you, Rambo?"

Caleb looked up and stared across the fire at Trey. "If you're addressing me, it's Caleb."

Trey glared and then flashed a slight grin. "What about you, *Caleb*?"

"I guess she's OK. I haven't really noticed."

Morgan's footsteps approached from the darkness, made darker by the light of the fire. She reappeared, sighed, and sat between Spence and Caleb. "Well, that sucked. And a tree limb almost became part of me."

The other three laughed. "You'll get used to it," Caleb said. "My dad and I camp all the time."

"You can piss standing, though. What's your story, by the way?" Morgan asked. "I hear lots of rumors."

"I wouldn't believe everything you hear. We enjoy camping and spending time outdoors. That's all," Caleb replied.

They didn't speak for a few minutes. Trey dug the whetstone out of his pack and began running it along the blade of his ax. It made a loud grating noise in the silent night, and occasional sparks leaped off the metal.

"I doubt it needs sharpening," Caleb said.

"Sounds cool, though," Trey replied.

The fire kept the cold away, although Spence guessed the temperature continued to drop just beyond its reach. He spent the quiet time reflecting on the events since they had teleported to Nibiru. The more he thought, the more he realized something wasn't right, other than the obvious. "Something doesn't add up about all this."

"So, you're saying something doesn't add up about getting transported from the desert to another planet, you walking again, fighting a wolfosaurus with medieval weapons, and being assigned a quest by a talking statue?" Trey asked.

Spence breathed deeply and tried not to let Trey get his blood pressure up. "Well, it's all weird. But someone brought us into an arena to kill the wolfosaurus as a test. Now, we must kill four monsters separating these different races. Why would someone from this world need four teenage kids from Earth to do that, especially one that's paralyzed? The Nephilim, dwarves, elves, and Draconians can't defeat them? Enki and the other gods can't defeat them? The Sumerian gods were very advanced in the myths and even created humans. They also had powerful weapons, including what sounded like nukes."

"It does sound like a pretty weak plot," Morgan agreed.

"Nothing makes sense about any of this. The only hope is we wake up in the morning in our own beds," Caleb said.

"I bet Mrs. Stephenson is freaking out," Trey said.

"And the school. And our families," Spence added.

"I hadn't even thought of that. However, we haven't been gone too long. They're probably just thinking we wandered off and became lost," Morgan said.

"You know, you're always hearing about people going missing across the country, and sometimes they're never found. What if they were brought here? Or other places like it?" Spence asked, a whole new group of thoughts racing through his mind.

"The Bermuda Triangle?" Morgan said.

"Hey, I bet we find Amelia Earhart," Trey said, laughing at his joke.

They fell silent again. Spence considered the possibility of never leaving this world. He assumed the others did too.

"Well, the quicker I go to sleep, the quicker I can find out if this is a dream. And I won't be wishing I had something to eat or drink. I'm going to bed." Caleb stood and disappeared into the shelter.

"Gee, sleeping in a tin can will be cozy," Trey said, following Caleb.

Spence and Morgan also moved under the tarp. They had to lie on the hard, cold ground with no blankets for cover, although the tarp on the ground gave them a little protection. They used their packs for pillows. The fire had warmed it up decently inside the makeshift tent, though. Spence tossed and turned and worried that he might not be able to go to sleep, but he entered a night of fitful dreams before he knew it.

CHAPTER 9

"Damn it!"

Spence opened his eyes at the sudden sound. It took several seconds for him to process where he was, then the hard ground reminded him. He wiggled his toes to confirm that he wasn't back in his bed on Earth. He lay on his side facing Morgan, who had also just woken. A dim light illuminated the tent. Caleb stood at the doorway looking out, and Trey sat on the other side of Morgan.

"Still not a dream," Caleb said in response to Morgan's exclamation.

"What time is it?" Morgan asked.

Caleb looked at his camouflage watch. "It doesn't look like time works right here, or we're not in the same time zone. It says ten o'clock. I'd say it's around six o'clock, although it's hard to know when you can't see the sun."

The four slowly rose and packed the tarps and ropes. They all took turns disappearing behind a nearby hill for bathroom duties. Spence's stomach hurt and burned from lack of food. His mouth and throat were also so dry he could barely swallow. This would be a short-lived quest if they didn't find the town soon or at least a stream.

They set out trudging down the old trail. Nobody wasted time or energy on talking. At one point, Caleb knelt and picked up a small stone off the ground and placed it into his mouth. "Suck on a pebble, and it will make you produce saliva and help thirst."

Spence found a small round rock and tried it. It seemed to help, but he wasn't sure if the effect was real or psychological. The landscape was just as barren and lifeless as the day before. The sky was also still gray and the air cool. No breeze stirred, though, which helped. They stopped at what they guessed was lunchtime to take a thirty-minute break beneath a tall tree. Spence's legs and feet were aching.

"Is this a cool adventure for you, Spence?" Trey asked.

"It's a little sketch at the moment. But it will get better when we find the town and get some food. And it beats the heck out of you pushing me around in my wheelchair."

They began walking again and hiked for a few more hours. Finally, when they crested a large hill they had been gradually ascending for some time, they saw a town in the flat valley on the other side. A square wooden wall surrounded the entire perimeter, with tall, square towers at the corners and on both sides of the gates in each sidewall. All the buildings visible were also wooden. The road led to the open gate in the front.

"Oh, now this is cool!" Spence exclaimed. He experienced a rush of exhilaration. It resembled a town from *Warcraft*. Spence fished his phone out of the front pocket inside his robe and snapped a picture. Morgan and Trey repeated the act. Caleb just scowled, shook his head, and continued walking.

The light had faded from the sky when they entered the gate. There didn't appear to be anyone in the towers. Lamp poles stood at regular intervals down the dirt streets, and Spence soon realized flames burned inside and not bulbs. The street they walked on was the widest and appeared to be the main road through town. Several other smaller streets bisected it, with fewer signs of foot traffic. Most of the buildings were two or three stories tall. Signs hung above many of the doors, indicating what kind of business they housed. They didn't see many citizens out. The ones they saw appeared human and were all dressed in similar drab, crude coats and cloaks. They did seem to be tall, though, but not giants. Some wore short swords and daggers, but no armor was visible. Most were male, and Spence didn't notice any children. They received many stares and some pointing and whispering, and everyone gave them a wide berth down the street.

"How do we find Titus?" Caleb asked the group.

"There should be an inn or tavern on this main street. That will be the place to start," Spence responded confidently.

"And how do you know that? Did I miss the directory?" Trey said.

"Six hours a night of online fantasy role-playing games," Spence responded.

Soon they came to the largest building they had spotted so far, a three-story square structure on the right side of the street. A lamp shone on the sign hanging underneath the roof of the long front porch. It read

Elysian Inn. Six stairs led up to the porch, which was lined with a half dozen empty wooden chairs.

"Weird. Elysian is out of Greek mythology," Spence said.

"You're weird," Trey replied.

Caleb ignored them and headed up the stairs; the other three followed close behind. Swinging double doors, like the saloon doors in the Old West, led into the building. Caleb pushed them open and entered the crowded, boisterous room within.

The interior also resembled an Old West saloon. A long wooden bar stretched down the left wall. Most of the stools were occupied, and two people served drinks on the other side. The remainder of the room contained a mixture of round and square tables. Chandeliers of candles hung around the room, and candle-filled sconces lined the walls. The air hummed with conversation and frequent bursts of laughter. The inhabitants all appeared human, except the ones standing were at least seven-feet tall and very broad. Trey looked small by comparison. Most dressed in plain clothes—shades of beige, brown, green, and gray—that appeared made of canvas or wool and looked a few hundred years older than Earth's current fashion. A few males wore leather armor shirts, and short swords and daggers were the only weapons visible.

"Half giants," Morgan whispered.

For a moment, Spence thought they could slip in unnoticed, despite their weapons and dress—but just for a moment. "Looks like the next quest has begun!" a grizzled old Nephilim behind the bar shouted when he spotted the party. He was closer to average height.

Somehow, the entire room heard the Nephilim's exclamation. The buzz stopped, and an uncomfortable silence ensued. All heads turned, and all eyes gazed upon them. Spence nervously surveyed the room. The faces were rough and weathered, and none appeared to be less than forty years old. There were a few women scattered throughout the room, most wearing long, faded dresses. Just the servers had colorful, low-cut dresses and wore makeup. The women were all well over six feet tall. No children were present. After what seemed like minutes, the heads turned, the conversations resumed, and the noise returned.

"Not exactly a hero's welcome," Trey said.

Caleb led the three to the bar and in front of the speaker, who still stared at them. "Excuse me, sir. What do you know of us and our quest?"

"Don't know nothing of your quest," the Nephilim grumbled, aggravated at being addressed.

"But you said something about the next quest beginning," Caleb continued.

"Aye. It has. And you are the questers."

"Then how do you know we're the questers?" Trey asked.

"Doesn't take a wizard to notice your height, clothes, and weapons." The Nephilim turned and began walking away.

"Wait! Do you know where we can find Titus?" Caleb called out.

"Far corner." The Nephilim disappeared through the door in the wall behind the bar.

"Seems nice enough," Morgan said.

"Told you he'd be here," Spence said. He turned with the others to examine the far corner of the room. Most of the tables were full, with four to six patrons each. A round table sat in the far-left corner with a lone person behind it. The person wore a gray cloak and a gray wide-brimmed hat pulled down close above his eyes. The shadows mostly hid his face, and he stared at a large wooden mug in his right hand. Spence immediately thought of Strider from *The Lord of the Rings*.

CHAPTER 10

Caleb led the party on a winding path around the many tables and chairs. They received some glances and sideways looks, but nobody acknowledged them. Finally, they arrived at the corner table. "Titus?" Caleb asked.

The Nephilim on the far side of the table didn't look up. Suddenly, the chair closest to Caleb slid toward him. The Nephilim must have kicked it beneath the table. Caleb glanced at the others and sat. Trey and Morgan sat in the other two empty chairs.

"Oh, that's just great! Nobody thinks about me needing a chair," Spence exclaimed, his voice high, as it became when he was upset. Then he was even angrier at losing his newfound cool.

"Go find you a chair, whiny ass," Trey responded. He then pulled off his metal helmet and set it on the table.

Spence huffed and glared at him momentarily and then spun away to find an unoccupied chair. He had to walk several tables away to find an empty one. Three large, rough-looking Nephilim sat around the table littered with a dozen empty mugs. "Excuse me, sirs," Spence began. "Could I borrow this chair?"

The Nephilim continued talking among themselves; none even acknowledged Spence. Spence's face instantly grew hot. Without thinking, he slammed the butt of his staff hard onto the wooden floor to get their attention. He was startled when the shaft came to life again, and electricity surged up his forearm and into his elbow. The crystal orb glowed brightly, and the secret panel slid open beneath his hand.

The Nephilim at the tables surrounding him suddenly fell silent after the sound of the staff striking the floor and the bright light. "I'm taking this chair," Spence stated loudly, his voice now deep and strong. He proceeded to grab the heavy chair and drag it toward the corner. His heart raced, and his sweaty palms made it tough to hold onto the worn wood. But he also felt energized. He would never have done that in the past, even before the accident. Since he had entered this world, regained the use of his legs, found the staff, and killed a dangerous beast, he no longer felt like a cowardly geek. He ignored the grumbling and whispering of the Nephilim behind him. The din in the room had returned to normal when he reached the others and Titus.

Spence rapped the butt of his staff on the floor and was relieved the compartment closed, the orb stopped glowing, and the heat and electricity ceased. He sat in the chair and slid in between Caleb and Morgan. The four continued their conversation, not acknowledging his encounter with the other table or his staff use.

"Who are these gods?" Caleb asked.

Titus's face was visible now—leathery, wrinkled, and covered in a week's worth of stubble. He was obviously tall, and all his features were larger than human. His eyes were deep blue and out of place with the rest of his appearance. "There are four—Ra, Enki, Artemis, and Odin."

"Those are mythological gods from four of our world's ancient civilizations," Spence said, eager to be a part of the conversation.

"Egghead told us who Enki is, and I think I've heard of Artemis. Wasn't she a Greek chick?"

"She was a Greek goddess. I believe she was the goddess of the wilderness and hunting," Spence said.

"I like her already," Morgan added.

"Who are the other two?" Trey asked.

"Ra is Egyptian, and Odin is from Norse mythology—Vikings," Spence replied before Titus could respond.

"Well, that's kind of random," Morgan muttered.

"Spence, you are a fountain of useless knowledge," Trey said.

"Not so useless now, though," Spence replied.

"I know the other gods didn't come from Nibiru, though," Caleb said.

"You're right. They all had different homes," Spence said.

"Ra is the god of my people; Artemis, the elves of the Forbidden Forest in the north; Odin, the dwarves of the Desolate Peaks in the west; and Enki, the Draconians of the Forsaken Swamp in the south."

"Inviting names," Caleb said.

"Another reason for the races not to seek out each other," Titus replied.

"Hey, Spence, you must come from the west," Trey interjected, grinning at Spence.

"Where is the land of obnoxious jocks?" Morgan asked, glaring at Trey.

Spence squeezed the handle of his staff and stared at Trey. Since the encounter with the three Nephilim over the chair, he felt almost confident enough to confront him. "What is a Draconian?" he asked Titus, finally turning away from Trey.

"They are lizard people. They walk upright like humans but are covered with scales and have the head and tail of a lizard."

Spence's mind raced. Now he remembered reading about people believing in reptilian aliens called Draconians. This world was getting stranger by the moment. "I think Enki was considered the god of water, so that makes sense he would be their God."

"Have you seen Ra?" Caleb asked.

"Yes—or at least images of him. The gods can appear anywhere and anytime."

"Like the talking statue?" Morgan asked.

"They can do that or appear as glowing images or in our dreams. We mostly see Ra, though, unless all the gods appear together."

"What does he look like?" Spence said.

"He wears a headdress with a mask covering part of his face, resembling a bird. His crown is a golden disc, with a serpent encircling the base. His skin is bronze-colored, and he wears colorful robes," Titus replied.

"What makes them gods?" Caleb asked.

"They each created their own people. They also created and control everything in this world," Titus answered.

"Why wouldn't the gods just get rid of the monsters themselves?" Caleb asked.

"It is hard to say," Titus said. "I am sure there is a good reason, though."

"They're all a bunch of cowards if you ask me!" a voice said from the table closest to them.

Spence and the others turned to seek the source.

A big Nephilim with a thick head of curly black hair and a matted, thick beard stared at them. His eyes were bloodshot, and he was obviously drunk. He held a mug in his left hand, and more mugs littered the table. His two companions stared at him with open mouths. "They never appear in the flesh—just send their images. They're afraid to come down and face their creations like Nephilim!"

"Seth, that's enough! You're drunk. It's time to call it a night," one of his companions said, laying his hand on Seth's arm.

"Are you afraid Ra will strike me down?" Seth continued.

"You know he will! Let's go. We'll walk you home."

A serving woman appeared carrying a silver tray of mugs. She placed one in front of everyone at Spence's table and then turned to Seth. "Here's a special brew for you, sir. It's on the house."

Seth grabbed the mug, stared at it, and looked up at the server. The blond woman smiled and then turned and headed toward the bar. Seth shrugged and gulped a large drink. "I'd like to see Ra appear in this bar. I say the gods have no real power. Our fear is all they have."

The color drained from the faces of Seth's companions. They both leaped up and made their way through the crowd toward the door. Seth set the mug down and opened his mouth to say something more. His mouth closed, and he peered into the cup. Suddenly, his eyes grew wide. He turned to the party of questers, his face twisted in fear and pain. Drool escaped his lips, and sweat glistened on his forehead. He tried to stand but lost his balance and fell face down onto the floor. He twitched for a few seconds and then lay still.

CHAPTER 11

"Too much to drink," Titus said softly, drawing their attention back to him. "Go ahead with your questions."

Spence exchanged a nervous glance with the others and then spoke. "Where is Nibiru?" Out of the corner of his eye, he noticed two burly Nephilim appear and half drag, half carry Seth through the crowd and toward the door.

"I don't know what you mean."

"Have you heard of Earth?"

"I know it is the land you come from. The last questers came from Earth," Titus said.

"And where is Nibiru compared to Earth?" Caleb asked.

"I am not sure. I just know the gods bring the questers to the arena. If they survive the battle, they come here."

"Does anyone complete the quest and return to Earth?" Caleb said.

"I do not know. I just escort the questors halfway to the Forbidden Forest. None have returned here." Titus sipped from his fresh mug and nodded for the others to do so.

"I hope ours are a little smoother than Seth's," Trey said. He peered inside the wooden mug and swirled the liquid. He sniffed it, shrugged, and then swigged a deep drink. "Ah! I'm starting to like this place a little better."

Caleb went next. He gulped deeply and let out a sigh when he came up for air. Morgan took an experimental taste and then swallowed a couple of bigger swigs.

"Uh, guys, we're not old enough to drink beer," Spence said, wrinkling his nose as he sniffed his. His parents occasionally drank wine and beer but didn't allow him to sample them.

"Spence, so help me, I'll hang you from the chandelier by your underwear with the wedgie I'm about to give you," Trey said, finishing a second drink.

Spence glared at Trey and then turned up his mug in defiance. The drink was slightly bitter and burned a little going down, but it wasn't too bad, and he remembered just how thirsty he was. He drank deeply.

"Our quest is to kill monsters that prevent each race from leaving their territory," Caleb said after emptying half of his mug. "Is that what the quest always is?"

Titus scratched his scruffy chin. "Usually some version of that, I guess."

"So is the purpose of our quest to unite all the races?" Morgan asked.

"Or to just grant them the freedom to leave their lands?" Spence added.

"It is hard to say. I am sure granting us freedom is part of it. I am not sure about the uniting, though," Titus said.

"What type of monster corrals you?" Spence asked.

"I am unsure. It has been a while since anyone from Argos has tried to travel to the other lands. As far as I know, no one has tried to reach us either."

"Then how do you know there is still a monster out there?" Trey said.

"I have heard enough horrible sounds when I escort the questers. And people do occasionally leave the protection of our walls. When they do not return, we can only guess their fate. I just do not know the specific monster."

"What do we do when we leave here?" Caleb asked.

"I will get you halfway to the Forbidden Forest. Then you must journey to the elven town of Sabekha and seek out Illexya. She will guide you to the path to the dwarves."

"Alexa?" Trey asked. "Cool, maybe she can play some tunes for us."

"Illexya, idiot!" Morgan said.

Trey grinned and flipped her the bird.

Spence tried to ignore them both. "And we'll fight another monster between the elves and dwarves?"

"Yes. And between the dwarves and the Draconians."

"How did you get appointed to help the questers?" Morgan asked.

"It is said Ra approached my father many years ago and appointed him leader of this town. As leader, one of his tasks was to escort the questers. He began taking me with him when I was a teen. After he passed away, I became the leader. Although being the leader does not mean much here." Titus abruptly stood. "Well, it is time for me to go. I will meet you at the general store down the street tomorrow morning. I suggest you eat and get some rooms here for the night. You can buy supplies for your journey at the store in the morning. There should be money in your packs. Good night."

The four watched him glide through the crowd and disappear through the door. "What do you all think?" Trey asked. He finished the rest of his drink and waved to the server halfway across the room.

"I'm in the longest and weirdest dream ever," Morgan spoke first.

"Or in the best dream ever," Spence said. His body was warm and tingly from the drink.

The three turned to Caleb. "Whatever this place is, it's bizarre— Nephilim, elves, dwarves, and lizard people; gods named after ancient gods on Earth; monsters and magic weapons…. Is it a mythical planet or another dimension? I guess we have no choice for now but to play along."

The server returned, and they all ordered more ale, as she called it, and dinner. She said she would bring them the nightly special. The mood of the four lifted as they indulged in more of the alcoholic beverage. The food arrived and consisted of meat similar to a beef pot roast, boiled potatoes and cabbage, and hard bread. The meat was not very flavorful, but they all realized they were starving. Morgan traded her meat away to the other three in exchange for extra potatoes, cabbage, and bread.

"Do you think our buddy Seth was poisoned?" Trey asked, chewing and talking with his mouth open.

"Of course," Caleb responded.

"By the gods?" Trey asked.

"By the bartender or server. I'm not sure what to think about the gods. It sounds like they're sending holograms or projections. But that must mean they exist in some form or another."

"Help me, Obi-Wan Kenobi. Help me, Obi-Wan," Morgan said, laughing. Her cheeks glowed red.

"Good one!" Spence said enthusiastically and slapped the table with his hand. He was impressed with the *Star Wars* reference.

"Looks like Hansel and Gretel are drunk," Trey said, finishing off his second mug.

"And you're still a bloated piece of refuse," Morgan said, trying to look angry but with a smile creeping into the corners of her mouth.

Trey began to retort but then shook his head and returned to drinking and eating. They finished the food and ordered another round of drinks. Caleb inquired with the server about rooms for the night. Spence was growing very tired, both from the ale and the crazy events of the past two days. He could see the others were too. It seemed like a week since they had been on their class field trip.

When the server returned with fresh mugs, she informed them that just two rooms were available. Caleb scrounged in his pack and found enough strange coins to pay for the food and rooms. The server just picked out the combination of copper and silver coins she claimed covered them. She gave them two keys and explained that the rooms were up the stairs in the corner. The keys were numbered ten and eleven. She mentioned a privy was at the end of the hall upstairs.

"What the hell is a privy?" Trey asked.

"A bathroom," Caleb replied.

"Oh, great, we get a communal bathroom," Morgan said, rolling her eyes.

"I'm betting it won't be nice either," Spence said.

"Hopefully, it will beat last night, though," Morgan replied.

"Well, Morgan, since there are two rooms and four of us, I guess you get to pick your roommate," Caleb said, his speech slightly slurred.

"Me and you, baby," Trey said, leaning toward Morgan and grinning widely.

"Not enough ale in this world or ours, Bluto," Morgan replied, sticking her finger in her mouth and making a retching sound.

"So, it's true that you're not into men?"

"Well, if I see a man, I'll let you know." Morgan turned away from Trey and stared at Caleb and Spence. "Spence, I guess I distrust you less than Rambo and Bluto. Let's go." Morgan stood, grabbed a key, and headed toward the stairs.

"You girls have fun. Don't do anything we wouldn't do," Spence said, scrambling up and following Morgan. Even though his head swam, and he was a little unbalanced, he managed to jump over Trey's outstretched foot. He was tempted to turn around and strike it with his staff but was in too good of a mood to let Trey bring him down. Between the ale, the battle, the encounter with the three Nephilim, being in a strange *Warcraft*-like world, walking again, and getting to room with Morgan, this was shaping up to be the best two days of his life.

Spence followed Morgan up the wooden staircase, both swaying slightly. At the top, a narrow hallway lined with doors on one side led to the right. Each wooden door had a number burned into it. Morgan stopped at door number ten and used the skeleton key to open it.

The room inside was minimally furnished: two twin-size beds, a wooden dresser with a large bowl of water on it and a small mirror behind, a high-backed blue cloth chair, and a nightstand between the beds with a burning oil lamp on it. The far wall contained a window with a ragged curtain hanging in front. Old, threadbare rugs covered most of the floor, and rough, unfinished boards made the walls and ceiling.

"I'm going to the bathroom," Morgan announced and abruptly left the room.

Spence walked over to the dresser and splashed some of the water from the basin onto his face. He removed his belt and robe and laid them at the foot of one of the beds. He gingerly leaned his staff against the wall beside the head of the bed and then sat, his head still swimming slightly from the ale. He was exhausted. He had no idea of the time, but his body told him it was late.

The door swung open, and Morgan entered. "Oh my God! The privy is basically the nastiest outhouse ever! There is just a wooden bench with a hole. Who knows where it leads—probably to the street below. There's an old bathtub with dirt rings a half-inch thick with a bucket beside it, but I have no idea where you would get water. And you will die if you breathe the fumes."

"I was afraid of that. Bathrooms and hygiene weren't the greatest before modern times."

"It just keeps getting better and better. Why don't you go take your turn, and I'll undress and get into bed?"

Spence nodded, stood, and walked out into the hall. He began heading toward the door at the far end when the door to room eleven opened. Trey staggered out, nearly bumping into him. Spence moved over just in time to avoid a collision and continued walking down the hall. Then Trey's large hand grabbed his left shoulder.

"Where you think you're going, nerd boy?" Trey shoved Spence hard against the wall, then brushed his way past him and walked toward the bathroom door.

Rage coursed through Spence's body. The exhaustion and the effects of the ale disappeared, and his head was clear. He clenched his fists and gritted his teeth tightly together. He wanted to charge Trey and shove him down or punch him in the back of the head. But he knew Trey could hurt him badly. He then considered running to get his staff and blasting Trey and the privy into oblivion. Spence didn't know if he could do that, though. He hated Trey worse than anyone he had ever known but didn't know if he could kill him in cold blood. Besides, he might need Trey and the others to complete the quest. Someday though…someday, he would pay Trey back for everything he had ever done to him.

Instead of waiting on Trey, Spence went downstairs and found another bathroom. It appeared the same as Morgan had described the one upstairs. Luckily, he could do his business standing. He held his breath and quickly finished. He returned upstairs and slipped into the room without seeing Trey again.

He was disappointed to find Morgan in the bed asleep, with the stained white sheet pulled to her neck. He had hoped to try to get to know her better. Oh well, there would be plenty of chances for that over the coming journey. He removed his boots and slid into his bed. He tried not to think of what else might have slept on that same mattress or about the laundry practices of the inn. He had planned to reflect more on the day, Nibiru, and their quest but was asleep moments after extinguishing the lamp.

CHAPTER 12

"Damn!"

The exclamation brought Spence fully awake. He opened his eyes and stared at the boards forming the ceiling. He slowly rolled over and saw Morgan sitting on her bed. A dim light shone from around the curtains and through the holes in them. Her hair was tousled, and her black lipstick was mostly rubbed off. She wore a black tank top, which must have been underneath her Earth clothes. The sheet lay over her thighs, but her calves and feet were exposed. Spence instantly wondered what she wore beneath the sheet. He quickly tried to suppress those thoughts. "What's wrong?" he finally uttered.

"I guess I need to give up on the dream thing," she answered.

"Yeah, I think you'd better. For better or worse, we're stuck in this world."

"At least you want to be here, though."

"I do enjoy the walking thing," Spence replied, again wiggling his toes and feet under the covers to ensure he still could.

"A lot of good it will do you in the belly of a monster," Morgan replied. "Well, I have to get dressed. You can either roll over the other way or go to the bathroom."

Spence would rather have gone to the bathroom, but he thought it would be best not to stand for a little while. He rolled over to face the wall and tried to focus on the events of the past two days and the upcoming quest, not the sounds of Morgan dressing. He was only halfway successful, with his thoughts bouncing wildly between the different subjects. When Morgan finally went to the bathroom, he rolled out of bed and dressed.

Soon all four were gathered in the common room below, seated at a round table. Their breakfast consisted of eggs, sausage, and toast. Spence was glad to learn they served coffee to drink. They ate in silence for the first few minutes.

"So, Morgan, did you get your nerd on with Spence last night?" Trey asked.

"As much as you did with Caleb," Morgan retorted, staring at her coffee. She ate the eggs and toast but gave her sausage to Caleb.

"What's up with the meat thing?" Caleb asked.

"I'm a vegetarian," Morgan replied.

"Why?"

"Is it any of your business?" Morgan asked, looking up from her mug.

"If it annoys me, it is," Caleb replied, returning the glare.

Morgan held the stare for another moment before finally speaking. "I don't think it's right how animals are bred and raised just for food. They're kept in tiny pens they can barely move in, fed steroids and all kinds of drugs, just to be slaughtered for us to eat."

"What else should they be doing? I don't think the cows and chickens would last too long in the wild," Trey said.

"They could at least be allowed to roam free on farms and ranches."

"What about animals that are hunted and killed?" Caleb asked. "They're living in the wild and have more than a fair chance of surviving."

"If it's truly sporting, like bowhunting with no sites or aids, I could possibly tolerate it. But it's not a sport when drunken rednecks sit on their fat, lazy asses in tree stands and shoot deer walking right below them with high-powered rifles with scopes. I'd like to see them use a bow like this and kill a deer."

"Well, you'll have to slay some game with your bow, and then we can all enjoy meat," Caleb replied.

"Only if there aren't other good options," Morgan said. "Next subject."

"OK. Spence, I've been meaning to tell you that you look cute in your black dress and necklace. Maybe you can find a wig and earrings at the general store," Trey said.

"Screw you, Trey!" Spence spat without thinking.

Trey's smile instantly disappeared, and he leaned forward. "I'll put you back into a wheelchair, loser!"

"Enough!" Caleb shouted. "Damn it, Trey, this isn't high school! You're just a teenage kid in some weird world of monsters and magic. Knock off your bully shit."

"Do you want to take it outside, Rambo?" Trey asked, turning toward Caleb.

"Spence and Morgan, I'm leaving and going to the general store. You can come with me or stay with the missing link. I'll kill him if I have to hang around him any longer," Caleb said, standing and slinging his pack on his back.

Trey stood too and reached out to grab or shove Caleb. Caleb caught Trey's right wrist with his left hand in a move nearly too quick to see. In another flash, Caleb's right hand held his dagger pressed to Trey's neck, just above his breastplate. "Give me a reason not to slit your throat!"

Trey's eyes bulged, and his lips pursed tightly. He moved his left arm slightly, and Caleb's knife pressed tighter against his throat. A thin trickle of blood ran beneath the blade and down to his collarbone. "OK," he whispered.

"OK, what?"

"I'm...I'm sorry," he croaked.

"I'm telling you, Trey, I'm done playing. You're either with us, on your own, or dead. Decide." Caleb removed his dagger, sheathed it, and strode toward the door. He dropped some coins on the bar on the way outside.

"I'll kill that freak," Trey said, rubbing the blood from his neck with his finger and staring at it. He left the table and disappeared out the door.

"Boys," Morgan said and also left the table and exited the inn.

Spence finished his coffee, grinning. Trey was out of his element here and outnumbered. Hopefully, his bullying days were nearly over. He was a little shocked at Caleb's reaction and did not doubt that Caleb would seriously injure Trey if necessary. He shouldered his pack and followed the others. It was midmorning outside, and the day was gloomy and cold once again. He spotted the three heading down the street to the right of the inn. Caleb led the way, with the others spread out behind.

Most of the buildings on the main street appeared to be warehouses and businesses. They saw some Nephilim walking up and down the road and in and out of the buildings. Spence noticed no signs of horses or wagons—just foot traffic. The general store was a large two-story building in the center of town with a covered porch on the front. The sign hanging above the door read Petros's Mercantile. Spence entered the building last.

The inside of the store was like a two-hundred-year-old Super Wal-Mart, with a little bit of everything stuffed onto its many shelves: weapons, tools, housewares, clothing, and food. Caleb was speaking to an old, white-haired, wizened Nephilim behind the counter in the store's back, and Trey and Morgan browsed through the weapons. Spence walked over and stood beside Caleb. He noted that the Nephilim wasn't much over six feet tall.

"Petros, we need food and water for four people for a few days. Can you help us?"

"Ah, yes. Time for another quest," the little Nephilim cackled. "I'm afraid my fare is kind of crude, but it'll keep you alive…long enough to get killed." He laughed and disappeared through a door behind him.

Caleb turned to Spence. "What do you think are in the vials?"

Spence was still getting used to playing a valuable role in the new world. "Potions. They're pretty standard in RPG."

"RPG?"

"Role-playing games."

"How do we know what they do?" Caleb asked.

"There's no way to know for sure. It appears someone packed our bags to match our classes, though. Mine are probably related to magic or energy. I'm not sure, but I'm guessing Morgan's are healing since she also has bandages and most likely salves."

Caleb shook his head. "This place is freaky. I've prepped all my life for surviving against marauding bands of humans. I never knew I needed to know about monsters, magic weapons and armor, and potions."

Morgan and Trey wandered over and joined them. Trey didn't make eye contact with anyone.

"That's where I come in," Spence said, grinning.

Caleb didn't return the smile. "What else do you think we need?"

Spence stroked his chin and scanned thoughtfully around the store. The truth was, he had no idea. His online games left out a lot of trivial details. He searched his memory for how the various character classes were typically equipped in *Warcraft*. "You could buy a small shield since your sword is just one-handed. Trey might find bracers for his arms, and Morgan could replace her arrows. I doubt they have anything for me, but I might check for rings or anything magical. We'll all need some type of bedroll and blanket too. Oh, and we'll need coats." Spence's robe was warm, but he knew he needed additional protection if the weather was going to stay cold.

The four split up and searched through the store. The weapons and armor pieces were crude compared to what they already had. Caleb found a small, round wooden shield with a metal ring around the outside and metal strips crossing the middle. Trey found bronze-colored bracers that snapped into place over his thick forearms. Morgan bought a dozen more arrows. Spence didn't see anything of use to him. They each found long, thick wool coats. Caleb selected a dull green color; Trey's was brown and resembled a western duster; Spence chose gray, and Morgan stayed with the black theme. They didn't find any bedrolls but bought coarse blankets instead.

When they returned to the counter, Petros was back with stacks of bags containing food and wineskins filled with water. They stocked their packs with the food and wineskins and paid for their purchases. After paying, Spence was the only one with more than a few coins left. They then donned their new coats, and Spence shoved Morgan's blanket into his bag since her packs were too small.

"Good luck, questers," Petros said as they headed toward the door. They heard his cackle as they left the store.

Titus waited for them outside, dressed in the same gray cloak and hat as the night before. He now had a brown canvas pack slung over one shoulder and a short sword hanging in a scabbard by his side. He was slightly over seven feet tall but leaner than most Nephilim. Spence couldn't guess his age but had a feeling he was younger than he appeared.

"Are you ready?"

"As ready as we'll ever be," Caleb replied.

Titus turned and descended the steps to the dirt street. The others followed, catching up and fanning out to both sides of him. His long legs allowed him to move faster than it appeared he walked.

"Do we get horses?" Spence asked. Although he enjoyed walking again, his legs were sore from all the walking over the past two days.

"Horses?"

"Big four-legged animals that people ride?"

Titus grunted. "We walk."

The buildings were smaller and spaced farther apart as they progressed down the street. A few narrower lanes branched off to each side. Spence found it strange walking in a town with no cars, horses, or wagons. Even in the old western movies, horses and horse-drawn buggies filled the town streets. This town only had Nephilim bundled up, scurrying here and there.

"Is it always cold here?" Spence asked. He didn't particularly care for silence, although he knew his talkativeness aided in getting him shunned by many at school and online. He tried to control it, but he usually found himself speaking before he had even finished forming the thought. He would have to try harder now that he was a real mage.

"Just depends on what Ra wants."

"You don't have seasons?" Spence continued.

"To some degree. But if Ra chooses to make it hot, it gets hot. Usually, it is some degree of cool, though," Titus replied.

The street ended at another set of towers and a gate similar to the entrance of the town. The road appeared even less traveled, though. They walked through the gate and followed the trail east. The terrain seemed the same as it had on the journey to the town.

CHAPTER 13

"Titus, what do the people in your town do for a living? I assumed you were farmers, but we've seen no sign of farms outside the walls," Caleb said.

"Everyone has a trade or job. We grow what crops we need and raise animals inside the town walls. It is too dangerous to be outside them."

"What's your main job?" Caleb continued.

"Just to make sure everyone is doing what they are supposed to be doing."

"I notice that many of your people don't have weapons," Spence said.

"Oh, we all have some. We just do not carry them often. Our walls protect us from the monsters, and the other races do not visit. We rarely journey outside the town. When we do, we usually carry weapons, but they are pretty useless against the beasts. We try to use stealth and discretion and avoid engaging them as much as possible."

Spence was surprised that even the huge Nephilim couldn't kill the monsters. They walked in silence for several hours. Spence's legs and feet ached, and his shoulders were sore from carrying the pack. He hoped the quest wasn't going to be all hiking in bleak fields. The distant sound of flowing water eventually broke the stillness of the day. The hills gradually decreased, the trees multiplied, and the ground and vegetation turned a little greener.

The roar of the water grew louder as they walked, and Spence saw the source of the roar half an hour later. A large river flowed in front of them, with a line of trees and green vegetation covering the bank in both directions. Spence judged the river to be at least fifty yards wide but couldn't determine precisely because the other side wasn't visible—a mist rose off the water. The fog wasn't thick close to them, but nothing was visible after fifty yards.

"The river Styx," Titus said.

"Of course, it is," Caleb replied.

"Why of course?" Trey asked.

"Do you ever pay attention in class? The river Styx was the river in Greek mythology separating Earth from Hades," Spence said.

"What's on the other side?" Morgan asked. She had been quiet, as usual.

"No one knows," Titus said.

"No one has tried to cross it?" Spence asked.

"Yes. A quester or two has. They do not make it. In addition to the distance and strong current, beasts live in those waters. You may try if you wish, but you will die quickly."

"Trey, let's see how fast you can swim to the other side," Morgan said.

"Why don't you bite me, Fright Night?" Trey grabbed his crotch as he spoke.

Titus turned and led them to the north, parallel to the river. The path now resembled an old game trail. Spence was hungry and, despite his coat, cold. Fantasy movies like *The Lord of the Rings* made it look so cool when the characters marched along during their quest. Living it sucked. His feet had long ago gone numb, and he didn't have gloves like the others. He frequently alternated which hand held the staff and withdrew the other hand inside his coat sleeve. His legs and shoulders throbbed, and he struggled unsuccessfully to pay attention to the alien surroundings instead of focusing on the cold and pain.

After another hour, Titus led them into the trees on the left and halfway down the steep, rock-covered riverbank. They used the trees to avoid slipping and tumbling into the river. Spence warily eyed the murky waters, searching for shadows beneath the surface. Titus continued leading them parallel to the river until they saw an opening between two large rock slabs. He led them up to the cave.

Once inside, Titus quickly lit a torch in a sconce by striking flint against his dagger blade. He returned the flint and dagger inside his cloak, removed the torch from the sconce, and led them further into the tunnel. The tunnel was just wide enough for them to walk single file. The cave walls were primarily smooth and wet, and the floor was flat but littered with various size loose rocks. A small stream flowed through the middle and out onto the bank and down to the river.

After sixty feet and a couple of bends, the passageway elevated slightly, opening into a dead-end circular room twenty feet in diameter. The room was dry, with the stream originating from somewhere underneath. Several boulders were arranged like chairs around the center of the room. Titus touched his torch to several others placed in sconces along the wall, soon brightly illuminating the room. He slid his torch into an empty sconce, sat on a boulder, and nodded for them to sit on the ones around him.

"Eat," he said gruffly and rifled through his pack to retrieve a sandwich.

The cave was like a warm living room compared to the outside. Spence could feel the heat of the torches, despite them being at least ten feet away. He removed his pack and eagerly peered inside. He hadn't paid attention to what Petros had given them for food. He saw several packages wrapped in what resembled brown wax paper. He unwrapped one and discovered flat, round pieces of bread close to the thickness of a tortilla. A second pack contained slices of dried meats resembling ham and beef, and the third held hard cheese slices. A canvas sack contained miscellaneous pieces of fruit.

Just seeing the fare—as unappealing as it was—brought home just how hungry he was. He had gone from not walking at all for several months to walking nonstop for two days and had eaten much less than his average daily intake. He placed a hunk of beef and a slice of cheese between two pieces of bread. He ate a big bite and was pleasantly surprised at how good it tasted. The meat was salt-cured, and the cheese tasted like sharp cheddar. The bread was dry but thin enough not to interfere with the flavor of the meat and cheese. He looked up to observe the others doing the same. Of course, Morgan's sandwich contained no meat.

Titus finished before the others. He washed his sandwich down with a big swig from his wineskin. "Once you eat, I will lead you a few miles farther north, and then I must return. I will leave you at a thick stand of trees where you can make camp. You do not want to be out in the open at night."

"Then what do we do?" Caleb asked.

"Continue following the river north. You should reach the Forbidden Forest in two days."

"Do you know when we'll encounter the monster we have to kill?" Trey asked.

"Not really. I would think soon after you depart the safety of the trees. That is why I do not go any farther. The Barrens are wild and filled with evil creatures."

"What kinds of creatures?" Morgan asked, biting her lower lip.

"It is hard to say. There have not been many survivors. I have heard tales of giants, enormous lizard-like beasts, and giant snakes. I have felt the ground shake and heard roars and calls but have not seen any monsters. You have weapons to fight them with and armor to protect you, though."

"Look, we cannot stay here long. I need to tell you something quickly, while the gods cannot hear or see us," Titus said, leaning forward conspiratorially.

"More about your gods? I hate to break it to you, bud, but they're not real," Trey said.

"I do not know about your world, but the gods here are real!" Titus's said forcefully. "They see everything. Even if they do not appear in person, they have helpers everywhere. What do you think happened to Seth? He is dead for merely speaking ill of them. There are only a few places in the ground, similar to this one, that they seemingly do not know of or care to watch. The gods created this world and the creatures within it. What monster did you face in the arena?"

"It resembled a giant lizard with a spiked tail and a wolf's head," Spence responded. He had scooted forward on the boulder and absorbed every syllable Titus uttered.

"Did it seem natural? They are all abominations, like the elves, dwarves, and Draconians. I do not know why they have created any of us or the purpose of the quests, but we are all just part of their whims." Titus glanced from face to face, making sure they heard his words.

"What about Argos? You all look like us—human—only larger," Caleb said.

"We look the part. But did you notice any children?" Titus spat onto the rock floor. "We cannot reproduce. There are a thousand of us in Argos. When one dies, another will soon appear—an adolescent male or woman will wander into the town. They have no memory of where they came from or their lives before. We take them in, assign them a role, and they stay until they die. My father was my adopted father. He trained me to be the leader like him."

"They did fix my spine," Spence said. He quickly explained his paralysis on Earth.

"Well, the gods must have. But trust me, there is a reason behind it. It was not out of the kindness of their hearts."

"Why are you telling us all this?" Caleb asked.

Titus stared at the stone floor. "There are those of us who are tired of living under the thumb of the gods. But as you saw with Seth, we are powerless. We have no way to fight or escape. The gods give the questers powerful weapons and armor. If you can survive long enough, you might figure out some way to help us."

"And fight against the gods?" Spence asked incredulously.

"Perhaps. Speak to the elves and dwarves and Draconians. I have not seen an elf or dwarf in ten years, and I have never met a Draconian. I do not know what they might know. I would think some of them might feel the same way we do. No one likes to be a pawn in another's game. Just keep in mind that the gods are always watching and listening. You will have to find a place like this if you wish to speak ill of them. Also, I doubt they intend for you to complete your quest. I have never heard of any surviving."

"What would you do if you were free from the god's control?" Morgan asked.

Titus stroked his chin. "Be free. We could travel where we wanted to go and settle where we wanted to settle. We could make our own rules and laws and not be controlled and live in constant fear."

"Well, if we complete our quest, you will be free to leave Argos," Spence said.

"Free to leave but still under the thumb of the gods. And what will be next? There will be something else. They will not grant us true freedom and allow us to do as we please. Ever."

"Aren't you worried they wonder why you bring questers into this cave?" Caleb asked.

"You are the second group I have brought here. Since I am still alive, I assume the gods are not suspicious yet. But we must go."

Titus repacked his pack, snatched the torch off the wall, extinguished the others, and headed back down the passageway. The other four repacked their belongings and hurried after him. Spence desperately wanted to talk to the others and discuss what Titus had revealed, but he would have to wait for another opportunity.

Titus extinguished his torch and returned it to the sconce at the cave entrance. He instructed them to fill their wineskins in the spring at the bottom of the cave and then led them out and along the riverbank until they reached a break in the rocks. Then he guided them up the bank and to the level ground above. The air seemed even cooler after the comparative warmth of the cave.

**

"I am glad you created these 'safe' places," Odin said.

"It is the only way to truly monitor our people. We have taught them all too well not to speak ill of us in public," Enki responded.

"Titus and the Nephilim are getting brave...or desperate. Attempting to incite a rebellion?" Ra said.

"Only to the questers, though. It is a shame that Titus and the other leaders lack intelligence, cunning, and bravery. Then we would not even need the Earthlings," Artemis said.

"True. Unfortunately, we cannot yet create some attributes in a lab," Enki replied.

***

As they walked, Spence's mind replayed every word Titus had spoken. He struggled to wrap his mind around the conversation. This world was strange enough, with monsters, magical weapons, and quests. But now, they had confirmed gods ruled Nibiru, and they created and actively interfered with the inhabitants. They had also fixed his broken back. And now, the four of them were just pawns in a greater game. His head hurt.

They trudged another two hours in the bleak landscape. Since Caleb's watch didn't match the time in Nibiru, and the sun never broke through the clouds, the time of day was indeterminable other than the degree of gloom. Nobody spoke. Spence didn't trust himself to talk and not mention things they shouldn't speak of in the open. He assumed the others had similar reservations.

Titus finally stopped when they arrived at a thick stand of pine trees. "This is where I must turn back. You can shelter in these trees until morning. I would keep your fire small and maintain a watch. You should be safe, but you never know. Head north at daylight. You will encounter your monster soon, so stay alert. By the day after tomorrow, you should reach the Forbidden Forest. I cannot tell you where Sabekha is, but I assume there will be a road or path leading through the trees. Good luck."

CHAPTER 14

Spence and the others thanked Titus and watched him turn and walk back the way they had come. Spence wondered if he would hike all night or camp somewhere with the coming darkness. Then he realized Titus would probably use the cave, and that is why the torches were in place, and the gods didn't worry about its purpose. *Clever.*

Caleb led the four into the copse of pines. The outer ring of branches nearly touched the ground, and they had to crawl beneath them. The inside gradually opened, with the trees there spaced farther apart and their branches starting much higher. In the center, ringed by tall, thin pines, was a round depression devoid of trees but filled with pine needles. They had found the perfect shelter. So perfect, Spence wondered if someone, or the gods, had created it just for the questers.

"Let's gather some wood and stones and get a fire going before dark," Caleb said.

"What about what Titus said?" Spence asked, suddenly thinking of what kind of monsters might be close.

"Other questers obviously have," Caleb said, nodding to the charred remains of a fire in the middle of the depression. "We can keep it small. Besides, between the sinkhole and these trees, I can't imagine anything being visible from the outside."

Nobody argued further, and they set about collecting dead pine limbs scattered on the ground. Luckily, plenty of dry wood and stones were available. When they all had returned to the middle of the depression, Caleb used pine needles for tinder and quickly built a small fire inside a ring of stones. He stacked the remainder of the wood close to the fire. He then had Spence help him set up his tarp, utilizing rope and stakes to create a perfect semicircular shelter, with the fire close enough to fill it with heat.

"Amazing," Spence said. "How did you learn to do that?"

"It's what I do," Caleb replied. "You can take your tarp and place it over the ground inside." The fire provided the only light now since it was fully dark outside the trees.

"How did you learn to do the forest stuff, growing up in the Rockies?" Spence asked, still fascinated by Caleb's skills.

Caleb grabbed one side of Spence's tarp and helped him stretch it out. "My dad owns a cabin near Asheville, North Carolina. It's been in his family for years. We spend most of his vacation time there—hiking, hunting, fishing, and camping. If something bad ever happens out west, we'll try to make our way there and live."

"Weird, but pretty serious skills, Rambo," Trey said. He had been reticent since the incident that morning at the inn.

The four sat on Spence's tarp, rummaged through their packs, and retrieved food. The meal was pretty much the same as lunch, but they were plenty hungry and glad to have it.

"Man, this walking twelve hours a day sucks! Everything I have is sore," Spence said. "But I'll take it over not being able to walk at all," he quickly added.

"Yeah, I would have played a sport if I'd known I'd needed to exercise," Morgan agreed.

"Figures," Trey said.

"What figures?" Spence asked, dreading the answer.

"You ladies not being able to handle a little exercise. This is nothing compared to two-a-days and running the bleachers a few times."

"Oh yeah, you're such a stud. Let's all bow down to Trey," Morgan said.

"Finally, we agree on something," Trey replied with a smug grin.

Spence tried to ignore Trey's comment, which was actually a little tame for him.

"Too bad all the running and training didn't stop you from freezing like a little girl in front of the wolfosaurus," Caleb said.

"Oh no, he didn't," Morgan said, laughing.

"Screw you, forest freak," Trey said. His hand moved down to the ax handle on the ground. "I can outfight you any day."

"Uh, huh," Caleb said, not even looking up at the incensed Trey.

Spence tried thinking of something he could do to diffuse the situation. While part of him would enjoy seeing Caleb and Trey fight, the outcome would hurt their party regardless. "Hey, what would you guys be doing at home right now? Let's say it's eight o'clock, and it's Thursday night."

The other three turned to stare at Spence with varying degrees of anger. Finally, Morgan's face softened a little. "I'd be on the computer, on all my social media sites, with the TV on *Teen Mom 2*. I know, the show's stupid, but it's like a train wreck, and I have to check out the carnage each week."

Spence laughed. Morgan had begun letting her personality peek through a little more lately. "Well, of course, Thursday nights are raid nights on *Warcraft*. I'd have the TV on, though, probably watching *Ancient Aliens* reruns."

"*Mountain Men* on the History Channel," Caleb replied, fishing around in his backpack for something.

Trey shook his head. "Thursday night football, of course. I think the fact three out of four of us wouldn't be watching football is even stranger than being stuck in this nightmare."

Just when Spence thought he had lifted the mood, Trey was there to deflate it. "I wonder what we'll fight tomorrow?"

"Titus mentioned giants, lizards, and snakes. We've already fought what was similar to a lizard. I'm betting on the giant," Caleb said, holding the apple he had retrieved from his pack.

"Gee, that should be fun," Morgan replied.

"Nothing us band of adventurers can't handle," Spence chirped. However, he searched his memory for various giants he had fought in *Warcraft*.

"And what a band of adventurers too—a geek, a Goth, and a psycho. I'm the only one even worthy of being in a situation like this," Trey said.

Caleb was now carving the apple with his dagger. He stopped to stare at Trey, the dagger tip pointing at him. "Seriously, what is wrong with you? Were you dropped on your head? Did you eat paint chips? What is your malfunction? We're not in high school, and you don't have any of your neckless, idiot jock friends here to laugh at your stupid jokes and bullying. We can walk away tomorrow and leave you to be the hero all by yourself."

Trey leaped to his feet and stepped outside the tarp, holding his ax in his hand. "I swear I'll cut your head off, you little wannabe mercenary! By the way, what do you and your dad do together all that time you spend camping in the woods?"

Caleb's sword was in his hand by the time he reached his feet. He also stepped outside the tarp, and the two squared off in front of the fire. Spence and Morgan scrambled to their feet and moved to flank Caleb.

Spence was sick and tired of Trey and trying to make peace. He couldn't take it anymore and also couldn't risk a chance of Trey hurting or killing Caleb. He struck his staff on the ground, and it came to life with a power surge. The crystal flared brightly, much brighter than the fire. "If you fight Caleb, you have to fight me," he said, his voice just slightly quivering.

"Not a problem, dork." Trey swung his ax back and forth several times.

Morgan pulled her bow off her back and nocked an arrow. She tilted the bow to the side and drew the string halfway back. "And me."

Trey looked at Morgan and then Spence and finally Caleb. His smirk faded, and his face suddenly reflected a rare uncertainty, if not a touch of fear. After a tense moment, he slung his ax over his shoulder. "We're done. You losers are on your own." He retrieved his pack from inside the canopy and headed to the fire's far side.

Spence struck his staff on the ground, extinguishing the glow, and the other two slowly put away their weapons, keeping a wary eye on Trey. They could barely see him through the flames and the darkness beyond. Spence and Morgan sat on the tarp, and Caleb joined them after throwing more logs on the fire.

"Tomorrow morning, we'll pack and leave without him. He's on his own. If he tries to join us, we ignore him and continue with our mission," Caleb whispered. "We need to keep watch tonight, both for monsters and Trey. I don't trust him. I'm not sure if he'd kill us in our sleep, but I could see him taking our weapons or packs. Since I wake up early, I can take the last watch. Who wants first?"

Morgan exchanged a look with Spence. "I normally stay up until one or two o'clock. I can take first," Morgan said.

Spence nodded. He fell asleep quickly, so he wouldn't have much trouble sleeping during Morgan's and Caleb's shifts.

Caleb lay on the tarp, using his pack as a pillow, and pulled his blanket over him. He left on his mail shirt and placed his sheathed sword close beside him. Spence watched and then emulated him on the opposite side of the tarp. The ground was pretty soft with the pine needles, and between the heat from the fire and the blanket, Spence was comfortable. Morgan sat in front of the fire with her bow lying across her knees. It didn't take long for Spence to fall asleep.

A rough hand shaking Spence's shoulder saved him from a marauding pack of monsters. He peered up to see Morgan standing over him. He blinked a few times and shook the images of his last nightmare from his mind. He sat up, grabbed his staff, and stood beside her. "Any trouble?"

"No, fairly calm. I heard some strange noises in the distance, but nothing close to the trees. And nothing from *our* ogre." Morgan lay down beside Spence's spot, using his larger pack for a pillow. She used her blanket, though.

Spence stood in front of the fire for a while. The size and heat of the fire indicated Morgan had added some more wood. He tried peering through the flames to verify that Trey was sleeping. He could make out a dark shape but could not determine his position and if he were under his blanket. Once, he thought he heard a wolf's howl in the distance, but it sounded miles away.

He finally sat on the edge of the tarp where Morgan had sat and laid his staff across his lap. Although his dreams seemed to have lasted all night, his body and mind felt like he had only napped for a few minutes. He was worn out physically and mentally from the past three days and dreaded the morning. He had been excited about being in a strange new world—one in which he had power. But the previous three-day hike wasn't fun, and he was confident tomorrow's march wouldn't be any better. Plus, they would have to fight something again. Even with weapons and armor, they could all die. All the previous questers had failed and died in the same strange new world, with similar weapons and armor. He also wondered about Trey and how that situation would resolve itself.

He stared at the dancing flames as his mind raced wildly between the uncertainty lying ahead to the certainty he had left behind. He did feel like he had a role to play now. They actually consulted and valued his opinion, despite some occasional teasing and ribbing. He had a weapon that had saved them all in the first battle. He was a nobody and confined to a wheelchair in the real world. He had no friends, and no one asked or wanted his opinion. He hated school and his teenage life. After his wreck, he lost hope of adulthood being better than adolescence. He would have to depend on others to help take care of him for the rest of his life. Here, in Nibiru, life was already better, despite the cloudless cold, hiking, and danger.

CHAPTER 15

Spence's eyes snapped open, and he experienced instant panic. His heart raced as his eyes frantically searched the darkness around him. The fire had mostly burned out, with only a few yellow flames flickering over the pile of red coals. The sky was already beginning to lighten. He glanced behind him and saw that Morgan and Caleb still slept. He peered across the fire but could just see the same black lump he'd seen before. He couldn't believe he had fallen asleep, sitting straight up. It must have been for a while, too, judging by the fire.

Once his heart slowed, he realized how cold it was without the heat from the blazing fire. He had to revive it before he woke Caleb. He slowly stood, giving his aching legs and back time to stretch and adjust to the movement, and walked to the right side of the fire to the stack of wood. Holding the staff in his right hand for support, he leaned over to grab a few medium-size sticks with his left hand. When he straightened up, he dropped the wood. He would have screamed except for the hand clamped over his mouth.

Trey stood towering in front of him, his left hand on the staff above Spence's and his right hand pressed over Spence's mouth. He leaned forward, his sour, hot breath bathing Spence's face. "Don't move a muscle, or I'll twist your head off right here," he whispered. His eyes darted past Spence to confirm the others still slept. He returned his gaze to Spence. Darkness mostly hid Trey's face, with the light from the coals barely illuminating the right side.

Spence couldn't stop his legs from shaking, and his heart tried to pound out of his chest. He was fully awake now, and his mind worked feverishly to formulate an escape plan. He could try pulling away and yelling for Caleb, but Trey was too strong for him to wrench the staff out of his hand. He couldn't let Trey have it. He knew Trey was a bully and often mistreated him throughout school, but he never thought he would seriously hurt or kill him. But now, Spence wasn't so sure. He wondered if he could knee him in the groin and then jerk the staff away. But if he missed, or Trey blocked or dodged it….

"We got along much better when we were on Earth, and you didn't have this magic stick. You were safe and sound in your little chair. It doesn't seem fair for the weakest one to have the most power. Do you think?"

Now, he knew what Trey wanted. If Trey had his staff, none of them could stop him. Spence didn't doubt he'd use it on Caleb and Morgan if he had to. Spence swung his left hand around and grabbed the staff below his right hand. He shook his head.

"Spence, be sensible. You were fine at home without this stick. You'll be fine here. I'm not going to use it on you. I'll make sure to keep you alive. I can't make the same promise for your two buddies, but I've got your back."

Spence had never heard Trey attempt to be nice to him, and he might have even been telling the truth. But Spence still couldn't voluntarily relinquish his only power. Plus, he couldn't do that to Caleb and Morgan. He shook his head again.

Trey stepped back and stretched to his full height. "I'm going to let go of your mouth. If you yell or scream, you'll be dead before your little friends can save you. We both know you can't shoot your lightning bolt without hitting the staff on the ground. And I'm not going to let you do that."

Trey pulled his hand off Spence's face and placed it on the staff below Spence's hands. He gave the staff an experimental tug, nearly pulling Spence into him. Spence knew he was no match for Trey's strength. He wondered how fast Caleb could help him if he yelled. But it would only take Trey a second to activate the staff. He might not have seen the panel open before, but it wouldn't be hard to detect it beneath his hands. Locating the buttons wouldn't be a problem, either. Caleb wouldn't stand a chance. Spence pulled back on the staff, barely swaying his larger foe.

Trey suddenly jerked hard on the staff. As Spence went stumbling forward, Trey's knee met his stomach. The breath rushed from Spence's lungs in a painful gasp. His hands released the staff, and he crumpled to the ground. He clutched at his stomach and gasped for air as he somehow managed to raise his head to watch Trey complete his victory.

Trey's mouth opened briefly in triumph as he stared at the staff and began to speak. Then suddenly, the crystal orb flared brightly. The staff hummed loudly and emanated a crackling sound. Trey yelled, and his hands and arms began shaking violently. His triumph crumbled into fear and pain. Somehow, he managed to throw the staff down in front of Spence and then toppled backward, landing heavily on the ground. He stared wide-eyed at his burned hands and shook uncontrollably while uttering a string of profanities.

Spence heard Caleb and Morgan rushing out of the shelter. The still lit head of the staff brightly illuminated the entire depression. They both held their weapons and stared back and forth between the gasping Spence and the sobbing Trey. Spence reached out and grabbed his staff. He was nervous for a moment that it might shock or burn him too. But as soon as he wrapped his hands around it, the orb's light extinguished, and the staff returned to normal.

"What the hell happened?" Caleb asked, holding his sword pointed toward Trey.

Caleb's tone surprised Spence. He carefully formulated his words, knowing he couldn't reveal the entire truth. "Um, the fire was dying out, so I came over here to get some wood. When I stood back up, Trey was there, trying to steal my staff. He managed to jerk it away, and then it lit up and began shocking and burning him."

Caleb glared down at Trey. Trey was now sitting, still staring at his hands. "Why did you try to take his staff, Trey?"

"I don't have to answer to you," Trey said, unsteadily climbing to his feet.

"No, Trey, you don't. And you just made our decision extremely easy. We're going to complete this quest and go home. You can do whatever the hell you feel like doing, but not with us. We're done. Good luck." Caleb turned to Spence and Morgan. "Let's pack. It will be light enough to walk by the time we leave."

"I'll do whatever I want to. If I want to come with you, I will," Trey said defiantly.

"No, you won't. If you follow, you'd better stay out of sight. You know you can't take us all on, and Morgan and Spence can kill you from fifty yards away. Don't mess with us, Trey." Caleb walked under the tarp and didn't look back.

Spence was excited. He wasn't sure why the staff had shocked Trey, but now he knew no one else could use it, and his tormentor was gone. He glanced at him, but Trey only spat, turned, and walked to his blanket. Spence joined Morgan and Caleb in packing the tarps and ropes.

Occasionally, he snuck a peek across the fire at Trey. The sky was light enough to see Trey was also packing.

CHAPTER 16

Soon the three headed out of the sinkhole and into the pines. Without a trail, Caleb just followed the path of least resistance out of the trees. The sky was already brighter than the previous three days and the air warmer. The clouds still prevented them from seeing the sun, though.

"Why didn't you wake me for my shift?" Caleb asked. The three now walked side by side out in the open.

Spence had hoped the incident with Trey was behind him. "Uh, I just wasn't very sleepy, and I figured you could use the rest. I was going to wake you once I had the fire going good. Of course, that's when Trey attacked."

"I always knew he was a bully, but I had no idea he was that evil," Morgan spoke for the first time that morning. "What a loser. I'm so glad to be done with him."

"Oh, I doubt we've seen the last of him. He'll follow us," Caleb said.

"How do you know?" Spence glanced over his shoulder but didn't see anyone behind them.

"Deep down, he's a coward. He has no idea what to do or where to go."

"Do you think he'll try to attack us?"

"Hard to say. If we stay alert, Trey won't be able to. You can fry him with your staff, or Morgan can shoot him in the head."

"I hate him but don't know about killing him," Morgan replied, also looking over her shoulder.

"Well, that's your choice. If you'd rather, you can let Trey kill you. But you'd better hope he doesn't try other things first."

"Ewww! OK. I'll kill him."

The mist rose from the river to their left, although they couldn't see the water. The land was still open but with more trees dotting the landscape. The bleak brown finally started transitioning to green. Spence kept his eyes roving, looking for their next fight. He noticed Morgan and Caleb did the same.

They all fished around in their packs and ate a quick breakfast while they walked. Spence was tired of eating the same food each meal, but he stayed hungry, and the fare was better than nothing. He washed it down with water and kept trudging along. Spence was still sore all over, but he was glad for the warmth. Everyone's mood was lighter than it had been the day before.

"What do you think they're saying about us back home?" Spence asked.

"Probably wondering how the football team will do if Trey doesn't return," Morgan said.

Spence smiled. He still wasn't sure how to take Morgan, but he assumed she was joking. "What about your parents?"

"I doubt they're shedding too many tears. I'm sure my father is off on some important business trip. Mother is probably at the spa."

"Oh, you're a rich kid," Caleb said.

"My father makes a lot of money, and my mother spends a lot of money. So, not much trickles down to me."

"Any brothers or sisters?" Spence asked.

"I have an older sister, Jade. She's studying premed at State. My parents were pretty much done when she went away to college. You know, she was super smart and super good—the perfect daughter. Then I come along and muck it all up."

Spence had forgotten about her sister, Jade. His sister, Kayla, had graduated with her. Jade was one of the first students to come out of the closet at their school. "My parents are probably pretty worried. They've taken much more interest in me since the accident," Spence said. He tried to envision how his parents might have reacted when they heard he was missing. Did everyone think they had been abducted? Or that they were lost in the desert? His father most likely still went to work. He was an aerospace engineer—a genuine rocket scientist—and loved his job. His mother might have found a substitute teacher for her for a day or two. "And my brother and sister, when they hear about it."

"What are they like?" Morgan said.

"Well, Andrew is twenty-six and is a nuclear engineer in the navy. We don't see him much. Kayla is twenty-four and is a schoolteacher in San Diego, so I don't get to see her much, either."

"What about you, Caleb?" Morgan asked.

"My dad will be missing me. Although he knows I can take care of myself. I assume they all think we're lost in the desert," Caleb said.

"I'm sure they know nobody would abduct a bunch of misfits like us," Morgan added.

"Or maybe no time has even passed there," Spence said thoughtfully. "Like in Narnia. This world might be in a different place in space and time."

"Interesting…it does seem to happen a lot in books, anyway," Morgan said.

The warmer air was much easier to breathe and hike in, but Spence's legs and butt soreness wasn't easing much. He cursed himself for not having exercised more since mandatory PE classes ended two years ago, before the wreck. If he'd known he'd be on a genuine quest and not just sitting at the computer guiding a character through a video game…. His feet were also blistered and hurting. The boots were rough and hard, unlike modern hiking boots on Earth. He began sweating beneath his coat and robe as he struggled to keep up with Caleb. Caleb seemed unaffected, even wearing the chain shirt, sword, and shield. Morgan was hard to read. She mainly kept quiet and trudged steadily along. If she suffered, she didn't show it.

Caleb eventually strode ahead of Spence and Morgan. Spence was tired of being lost in his thoughts and focusing on his discomfort. "So, Morgan, what is a Goth, exactly?"

Morgan turned and stared at him for several seconds as if gauging if he was making a dig or asking an honest question. Her face finally softened some. "Personally, I hate the term." She paused as they walked, gathering her thoughts. "People lump a bunch of kids into the Goth category. Having a class of Goths is like saying we're all the same and not individuals. I dress the way I do and act the way I do because I don't want to fit in with everyone else. I hate all the cliques and squads and class bullshit at school. But even when you want to be different, you're still thrown into a class."

"Yeah, tell me about it. If you look like me, you're a nerd regardless of any other traits you have," Spence said. Maybe they weren't so different. "What do most Goths believe?"

"Well, as I said, we're all different. I hate the class system of modern society. The rich get richer, and the poor get poorer. And nobody cares about the poor. Politicians use them for votes and to pass along their agenda, but no one genuinely cares about them. The middle class is only looking for a way to become the next upper class."

"What about racism?" Spence asked, a little nervous at Morgan's possible reaction.

"Oh, don't even get me going there! But that's a big part of our caste system. Who are the poor? Go to the poorest section of any large town or city and tell me what you see. It ain't a bunch of Spence's, Caleb's, and Trey's."

Spence swallowed hard. "Well, at least the United States is better than many countries. I mean, look at China and Russia and how they treat people," Spence replied.

Morgan rolled her eyes. "Debatable. But we should be much better. We call ourselves the greatest country in the world, so we need to back it up and act like it. I mean, we have the money and resources to do much more than most countries."

"Yeah, I guess. What else?"

"I hate we're destroying the environment and Mother Nature, yet nobody cares. And half the people are out there spewing lies and claiming it's not happening. Nobody has a true idea of what kind of world we'll leave behind when our generation is gone. It will be a wasteland. But somehow, the rich will still survive and thrive. The poor will suffer and die, and the middle class will become the new poor."

"Well, we have made a lot of changes in the past few years, with getting away from coal and pushing natural gas and alternative fuels. Cars are much more efficient, and electric vehicles are getting more popular. And the US can't do it all by themselves," Spence said.

"Now you sound just like the people I'm referring to," Morgan said, scowling. "Again, we should be doing much more. We can't worry about how expensive solar and wind power are. You can't put a price on saving the Earth. Big oil still has all the money, power, and influence. We must stand up to them and really change the status quo. Then we can lead the way and pressure the other counties that depend on us."

Spence realized that she wasn't looking for a debate, and he wasn't armed well enough to win it, anyway. "True. Is that all?"

"I don't know. I guess I just don't like conformity. Somehow, I want to make a difference and not be a sheep like everyone else. I'm just not sure how."

"I actually agree with a lot of that. Maybe I'm kind of a Goth, without the makeup and black clothes," Spence said. Hopefully, he could win some brownie points.

Caleb stopped walking and turned around to face them. "OK. I honestly don't care about either one of you or your beliefs, but you're both full of crap. Morgan, you say you are a nonconformist, don't fit in with society, and don't want to be classified as a Goth. Yet every day, you put on your Goth makeup and all your body piercings, dress up in your Goth clothes, and hang out with a group of Goth kids. If you were such a freethinking, nonconformist loner, you wouldn't hang out with any group and truly try to stand out in the crowd.

"Spence, you're the biggest pretender of all. You're not a loner or a freethinker. Before your wreck, you just wanted to fit in with any group other than the geeks. If you could be a jock, you'd be Trey's lapdog. If you could be a preppie, you would. Now, you're thinking about being a Goth. You're both as bad as Trey and all the other sheeple."

"So, should we just be loner freaks like you, with everyone scared we'll come into school and shoot it up someday?" Morgan said.

"At least I'm an original, baby. And if you are sincerely passionate about the evils you mentioned, you'd be doing something about it—protesting, writing Congress, writing to the newspaper, writing a blog, running for class office…something. Look at Greta Thunberg. I don't care for her, but she's at least doing stuff." Caleb turned around and continued walking.

"Don't pretend you know me like that! Fuck you!" Morgan shouted.

Spence fumed. Every time he began to feel good in the new world and his new situation, something or someone dragged him back down. This time it wasn't even Trey. Deep down, though, he wasn't sure if he was mad at Caleb for his words or because he had a tough time internally debating him. He didn't want to be like Trey! Although he couldn't deny how often he'd wished he could be the popular star athlete growing up. He hoped that he wouldn't pick on kids like himself, but he wouldn't mind the rest of it. He was changing, though. He felt it. He was gaining confidence and getting stronger. He would be his own person soon.

***

"You were right about this group," Odin said. "They are most acrimonious."

"I must confess, I was growing concerned," Artemis replied. "They were beginning to bond."

"It is time for some more action, though," Ra interjected. "They are in my realm now."

"What do you have for them?" Artemis asked.

"I have been working on something special. I call it the Guardian," Ra replied.

"It is not too powerful, is it?" Enki asked.

"It will be a tough battle and not won by one shot from the staff. But it is theoretically survivable."

89

"Well, let us introduce them to this Guardian."

CHAPTER 17

The three walked another few hours in contentious silence. Spence's legs and feet were numb, and his mind could not focus on anything for long. He sweated profusely beneath his clothing. Caleb finally halted them at midafternoon at a small clump of tall oaks. He leaned against a tree and drank deeply from his wineskin.

Spence leaned against another tree. The land still looked the same, only with a few more trees and bushes dotting it. The rolling hills continued, and the river was still nearby to the east. Several large hills lay parallel to them to the west, blocking the view of anything lying beyond. He peered back the way they had come—still no sign of Trey. Spence wondered if he was following or if he might have returned to Argos.

Spence searched through his pack until he located an apple—he needed a break from the meat and cheese. He then sat beside his backpack, laying his staff on the ground beside him. He sighed out loud with the relief in his feet and legs. He could lie down and fall asleep in minutes. Morgan followed suit and sat against the trunk of the tree beside him.

Caleb fished an apple out of his pack and turned, surveying the surroundings himself, lingering a little longer on the south, and then sat and leaned against the tree. They all ate the apples in silence.

"Morgan, is this world better than ours?" Spence asked, risking another interjection from Caleb.

Morgan had her head leaned against her tree. Her eyes were closed, and she appeared to be asleep. "With a few exceptions, actually, yes." She didn't open her eyes.

Spence began to respond when he heard a loud boom in the distance. It sounded like it came from behind the hills to the west. "What was that?"

Caleb put a finger to his lips and moved into a crouching position, facing the hills. Another boom and another. They sounded almost like single thunderclaps. The three wearily stood. Caleb drew his sword and threaded his left forearm through the back of his shield. Morgan grabbed her bow off her back and nocked an arrow. Spence clutched his staff with both hands.

The booms quickened, and the ground began shaking beneath them. Spence's stomach knotted tightly. Something huge was moving toward them, and it wasn't a thunderstorm. Without having to communicate, they each attempted to hide behind tree trunks. Spence tried not to breathe, but he wondered if the others could hear his heart pounding and his knees knocking.

An object appeared just over the largest of the hills and steadily grew taller. Spence was horrified to realize it was a giant head. The head rose higher, and then the shoulders appeared, followed by the chest, arms, and the rest of the enormous body. It paused on top of the hill, only some hundred yards away. The face was roughly human, but it only contained one large oval eye in the center of the forehead. It had prominent features, with thick lips, a bulbous nose, and ears that stuck out far to the sides. A few tufts of hair adorned the top of its head. The monster wore a furry, grayish-brown tunic hanging to its knees. Its arms, legs, and feet were bare. It held a massive wooden club or a small tree trunk in its right hand. The creature's size was hard to determine from this distance, but it was at least twenty feet tall and weighed a massive amount.

"A Cyclops," Spence whispered. It looked just like the ones in movies and described in books. *Dear Lord, please give us a little help with this one too.*

The Cyclops slowly rotated its massive head from side to side. It appeared to sniff the air through its deformed nose. Then the black eye landed on their hiding place. It opened its mouth, filled with yellow-stained teeth, and emitted a roar. It then started toward them at a distance-eating trot.

"Back up but stay behind the trees. Morgan, take a shot at its eye when it's in range. Spence, get ready for the lightning bolt," Caleb barked.

Morgan retreated a few steps, nearly to Spence's tree. Spence also backed up and then banged the butt of his staff against the ground. Once again, the staff came alive. His knees still shook, but as he lightly placed his finger over the first button, he was confident he could drop the monster with a single press. He decided to wait, though, and see how the battle progressed.

The Cyclops' huge strides quickly closed the gap between them. Small tree limbs and twigs dropped on and around them from the intensified ground shaking. When the giant was only thirty yards away, Morgan loosed her first arrow. It sped swiftly toward the monster but just grazed its left ear. She quickly nocked another. The Cyclops was on them in a few more steps. It swung the ten-foot-long club at the tree in front of Morgan. The top half of the tree exploded, sending limbs flying and falling in all directions. The biggest remaining piece of the tree landed twenty feet away.

Spence and Morgan frantically retreated. Caleb darted out from behind his tree and into the open. The Cyclops momentarily stopped and surveyed its prey. It then stepped forward and swung its club down on top of the tree Caleb had been behind. Again, tree limbs exploded all around, and the trunk split in two all the way to the ground. One half fell right before Caleb and the other in front of Spence and Morgan. Caleb held up his shield to deflect a few of the flying tree shards.

Morgan released another arrow. This time it struck just to the right of the eye. The monster used its left hand to scrape the shaft away like a thorn. A third blow from the club destroyed the third tree. Spence lowered his staff and pointed the glowing tip at the Cyclops' chest. *Get some!* He braced his arms and legs and pressed the first button. Once again, the bolt of lightning surged forth. The central fork struck the Cyclops in the chest, and dozens of other tendrils enveloped its entire body. A mighty thunderclap knocked Spence and Morgan to the ground.

Spence pushed up on his elbows, wanting to watch the monster topple lifelessly to the ground. But the Cyclops stood frozen as the lightning slowly disappeared. A black hole was in the material on its chest, and smoke rose from several places on its body, including the patches of hair on its head. It didn't fall, though. *Dang it!*

"Morgan, now!" Caleb's voice rang out from a distance.

Morgan sprang to life, regained her feet, drew the string to the corner of her mouth, held a deep breath, and released. The arrow sped straight and true and struck in the middle of the eye. Half of it disappeared into the monster's head.

The Cyclops roared again and swung its club toward Morgan. She staggered backward and barely managed to avoid the swing. Spence scrambled to his feet. His staff had returned to normal, with the tip no longer glowing and the buttons covered. He struck the bottom on the ground again, but this time nothing happened. Terror suddenly filled him as he stared up at the monster now towering over him and Morgan.

He frantically struck the staff another time, but again nothing happened. *It must need time to recharge!* He forced his legs to move and retreated further. Morgan released another arrow, this time striking the side of the Cyclops' nose. The beast turned slightly and swung the club straight down, striking just between Spence and Morgan. The force of the blow sent them both sprawling to the ground.

Spence desperately gripped his staff with both hands and thrust it out in front of his chest. The Cyclops was massive this close. The monster stood right before them, with Morgan lying ten feet to his right. Spence couldn't determine whether it could see with the arrow in its eye or was just going by sound or smell. It swung its massive head back and forth, either trying to decide who to kill or trying to *see* who to kill.

It raised the club high above its head. Spence braced for death. Maybe somehow, the staff would absorb the blow, but he doubted it. Or, even if the staff did, his arms and body couldn't take the force that would be transferred into him. The sole consolation was it would be over quickly. He wondered what would happen if he died in another world. Would there be a heaven or hell? Would his spirit return to Earth or be trapped here? He closed his eyes and waited.

The blow never came. Spence opened his eyes and saw the Cyclops had turned and swung its club at Caleb. Caleb had rushed in and attacked it from behind—a line of blood stretched above its right ankle. Caleb dove out of the way of the swing and scrambled back to his feet. Morgan also climbed to her feet and fired an arrow at the back of the monster's left knee.

Spence stood but was powerless. His staff wouldn't work, and his only other weapon was his dagger, which would be useless against a creature that size. He watched helplessly as Caleb rushed in, stabbed at the monster's right knee, and then darted away, narrowly missing another club swing. Morgan fired another arrow, this time into the back of the right knee. The wounds to its legs appeared to be taking a toll, and it plodded forward with a noticeable limp in the right leg.

But Spence knew the sword and arrows wouldn't be enough. Eventually, Caleb would get tired or trip, and it would be over. He said another quick prayer and once again struck the butt of the staff onto the ground. The staff vibrated, and the orb illuminated. Instantly, his fear and fatigue melted away. This time, he lowered the staff and placed his finger on the second button. The lightning didn't kill it, so he had to try something different.

Spence pressed the button. *Please!* The staff recoiled slightly and sounded like it had launched a Roman candle ball. A small flaming ball shot forth from the orb, also resembling a Roman candle ball. The sphere sailed slowly through the air, trailing a tail of sparks behind it. The monster swung again at Caleb, oblivious to the approaching projectile. Spence and Morgan watched breathlessly. Spence didn't know if Caleb saw the ball, but he assumed he didn't since he had just narrowly rolled away from another crushing swing.

Spence's heart stopped when the Cyclops moved a step to the right to pursue Caleb. Then he watched the flaming ball adjust and continue heading toward it. Caleb lunged and jabbed the monster's right knee again with his sword. He leaped back as he had been doing, but the Cyclops changed its attack. Instead of taking an overhand swing, it swung the club backhanded in an upward stroke. Caleb tried to spring to the side and extended his shield in defense, but the top corner of the club struck him, sending him twisting into the air. He collapsed heavily on the ground some twenty feet away.

Just as the Cyclops moved forward to finish Caleb, the flaming ball struck him in the middle of the back. The small ball flared into a massive fireball, momentarily engulfing the monster in flames. Spence watched in amazement at the power the small projectile unleashed. Then he stared in horror as the Cyclops turned to face him. The fire still burned its tunic, and the surrounding skin was melting, but the monster still lived. *Seriously?*

CHAPTER 18

The Cyclops slowly began walking toward him. The flames and Caleb's hacks had slowed it, but it still lived. A large piece of the tunic fell to the ground, exposing the creature's midriff. Patches of yellowish-brown skin had melted away, exposing wires and metal underneath. "It's a cyborg!" Spence exclaimed. "Run to the river!"

Spence turned and began sprinting. His staff had returned to normal, and he knew it would be at least several minutes before he could use it again. He was not a good runner and had little endurance but hoped the monster was slowed enough so he could reach the river first. He didn't have a plan yet, but if they could somehow knock it into the water, hopefully it would short-circuit and die.

Morgan quickly caught him, and they ran side by side. Spence didn't dare look back at the Cyclops. He was all too aware of the rumbling and ground shaking behind him. The river wasn't visible yet but was only a hundred yards away. The cyborg sounded to be around thirty yards behind. Spence didn't know if Caleb was still alive. Hopefully, he was and would follow them. He was the only one who could mount a melee attack against it. If Caleb didn't come, the only hope was the staff recharging in time.

"Do you have a plan?" Morgan panted.

Spence's chest hurt from the exertion, and his legs were leaden. He feared he would tumble to the ground at any moment and be squashed by a foot or crushed with the club. "No. We…have to…make it…to the river." He gulped air as fast as he could inhale. "Then…we have…to…get it…in."

At fifty yards, the ground shaking intensified. The Cyclops was closing the distance. "No matter what, keep running!" Morgan shouted.

"Huh?"

Morgan suddenly veered off to the right. Spence risked a glance and saw her nocking an arrow as she ran. He then turned around to focus on the ground ahead of him. His legs were burning, his chest tight, and an asthma attack was possible. The ground shaking intensified. At any moment, he would be within club range. The trees at the edge of the riverbank were close now, though. He was so close.

The steady thumping behind him paused as if the beast did a stutter step and then slowed. Morgan must have done some damage with an arrow. Spence reached deep inside for one last burst. He remembered grade-school gym class and trying to finish with a kick at the end of the six-hundred-yard dash. He always had one of the slowest times but usually finished strong. He ran at the brink of losing control, as if he were running downhill faster than his legs could move.

The thumping started again behind Spence, but Morgan had given him the distance he needed. He scampered into the trees and down the riverbank. He frantically decelerated, reaching out to grab and release several trees to slow his descent. Spence grabbed and held onto one of the last trees before reaching the water and swung himself around, facing up the bank.

The large shadow of the beast appeared just before he saw its monstrous head. It roared at the edge of the line of trees and swung its club into the nearest one. It used two swings and a shove to fell the tree. Spence jumped to the side as the tree crashed close to him, the upper half splashing into the river.

His mind raced, trying to figure out how he could get the monster into the water or at least survive the attack. He glanced behind him. The river flowed swiftly, and the water appeared deep. He considered wading into it, but the current would instantly sweep him away. He also had no reason to doubt Titus's stories of monsters swimming beneath the surface. But those were the two reasons he had to get the Cyclops into it.

The Cyclops descended the bank, smashing and shoving trees in all directions. Without thinking, Spence ran and leaped onto the felled tree trunk now sticking out over the river. The tree was around two feet wide at the bank and narrowed as it stretched out over the water. The tree limbs beneath the surface kept most of the trunk above the water. He turned around and backed down it, holding his staff with both hands to help him balance.

The monster had reached the bottom of the bank, only ten yards away. Its eye glared at him, with the arrow still protruding from it. It swung its club backhanded into the last tree standing between them. The tree fell sideways, landing at the water's edge, parallel to the river. The Cyclops paused momentarily and then straightened. Spence glanced past it to see Morgan at the top of the bank, nocking another arrow. Then the monster moved forward to the edge of the water and stopped at the base of the tree Spence stood upon.

Spence retreated further, wobbling and nearly losing his balance. The river rushed all around him, and the tree didn't feel stable in the strong current. The first branches were just behind him. He knew with one kick of the giant's foot or swipe of its club, he and the tree would be sailing down the river. He turned his staff vertical and struck the base against the tree trunk. Nothing happened. It was over. He retreated until his back pressed against the limb behind him. He wrapped his right arm around it and held his staff with his left hand. Maybe he could stay afloat...somehow.

The Cyclops raised its club overhead. It paused for what seemed like an eternity. Then Spence heard a yell and caught a glimpse of movement rushing toward the Cyclops. A silver blur streaked from behind and crashed with a dull thud into the back of the Cyclops's right leg. The blow knocked the Cyclops off balance. Its feet struck the tree it had felled just seconds before. It teetered on the edge of falling, its arms waving to regain its balance.

Spence realized Trey was the object that had crashed into the monster, running into it with his shoulder lowered as if he was making a tackle. In a blur, he tore his ax off his back and struck the Cyclops' lower back. The monster tumbled over the tree and fell face-first into the river. It thrashed its arms and legs, trying to fight the current. But the water was too swift and deep even for it. The strong current slowly pulled the Cyclops away from the bank and carried it downstream.

Its torso rose once, looking like it might regain its feet, then it suddenly lurched to the side. Something had struck it underwater. Then an unseen force rocked the Cyclops in the other direction. A flurry of splashes erupted around the beast, and multiple objects broke the surface. The club slapped at the water several times and then disappeared. After a moment, the Cyclops vanished too. Different body parts reappeared and disappeared as it moved too far away to see the remainder of the struggle.

"And the crowd goes wild!" Trey shouted, holding both arms above his head, his ax in his right hand. "Damn, no body for my selfie, though."

Thank you, Lord. Spence let go of his death grip on the limb and slowly shuffled up the trunk to the shore. Morgan had made her way down the bank to greet him.

"Wow, I never thought I would be glad to see you," Spence said.

"Well, you saved me from the first one. I saved you from this one. I guess we're even now," Trey said, slinging his ax over his shoulder.

"Well, there was the thing this morning when you tried to steal my staff...."

Trey's face stayed neutral. He stared at the ground and absently scratched his head. "Look, Spence. I just want to say—"

"This doesn't change anything, Trey," a voice said from behind them.

They all turned to see Caleb at the top of the bank. A tear stretched across his black pants on his right thigh. Blood was visible on the skin beneath, and the leather was wet down to his red-stained boot. The grass around his foot was also crimson. He was pale and leaned against a tree for support.

"Caleb, are you OK?" Morgan exclaimed, rushing up the bank toward him.

"I'm fine...it's only a scratch. Now, Trey, we still don't need you with us, despite you helping for some reason. So, you can just disappear again."

Spence observed Trey, waiting for him to erupt. In Caleb's condition, it wouldn't be a fair fight. But Trey didn't get angry. In fact, his face looked sad.

"You would have all died if I hadn't shown up, Caleb."

"Do you want a trophy? I think I'm all out," Caleb replied. Morgan stood close to him now, bending over and examining his mangled leg.

"I'm just saying we all need to stick together. We don't have to braid each other's hair and paint our toenails, but let's just get through this stupid quest and back to Earth."

"Caleb, you can't even travel like this. I dislike Trey as bad as you, but we need all the help we can get," Morgan said to Caleb.

Caleb looked down at her and opened his mouth to speak. Then his eyes rolled up into his head, and he let go of the tree and collapsed to the ground.

"Both of you, get up here!" Morgan screamed.

***

"A cyborg was your new creation?" Odin asked.

"Very careless," Artemis added.

"The fireball did more damage than I anticipated. I gave the cyborg extra-strong skin, and the tunic was like armor," Ra replied.

"Now they know all is not as it appears," Enki said.

100

"No matter. Gods can create technology too. We know the wizard realizes his staff is not magical," Ra said.

"Still, careless. This group is more intelligent and perceptive than the others," Odin replied.

"There is nothing to worry about, brothers and sister. If they do not figure out how to heal him, their leader will be gone," Ra said.

"I think we should proceed with setting the wheels into motion for phase two before we lose them all," Artemis replied. "They're already the strongest candidates we've had and may provide our last chance."

"I agree, and we have already sown the seeds with all the races. Odin, do you want to start with your barbarian while he is still an outcast?" Enki asked.

Odin grinned. "This might be interesting."

CHAPTER 19

Spence arrived just behind Trey. Morgan had already opened her packs and wrapped a bandage tightly around Caleb's upper thigh, right above the huge gash. The Cyclops's club had sliced it open before it sent him flying. She then drew her dagger and cut his pants open further, revealing the full extent of the damage. The skin and muscle were split open to the bone. The blood had slowed with the tourniquet, but it still oozed forth. His pants and boots were soaked in blood, as was the ground where he had stood and the trail he had made coming to the riverbank. Caleb's skin and face were ashen, and he was unconscious. His breathing was soft and shallow.

"Oh, God, what are we going to do?" Morgan asked.

Spence turned away from Caleb's leg. He was squeamish at the sight of blood and felt the familiar lightheadedness and nausea. He desperately tried to focus on something else, kneeling and rifling through Morgan's pouches. He withdrew one of the small, round containers. "It looks like you have the packs of a healer. I would try some of whatever this is on the wound," Spence said, handing her the container.

Morgan grabbed it, looking at him doubtfully. She finally shrugged and twisted off the lid. Inside was a thick, grayish-green paste resembling mud. She returned the cap. "See what's in the other one. The gash is too deep for that."

Spence hastily grabbed the other container. He screwed off the lid and saw it contained a white powder. He handed it to Morgan.

"I hope this works. He's not going to last long." Morgan sprinkled the powder back and forth over his wound like shaking salt from a shaker. She used all the powder and handed the empty container to Spence. She then used both hands and squeezed the incision shut. Caleb moaned softly.

"You're good at this," Spence said, screwing on the lid.

"I'm thinking about becoming a nurse. At least then I can help people."

"What about a doctor?"

"My sister is trying to talk me into following in her footsteps. I don't know if I can stand going to school that long, though. If college is anything like high school, I know I can't." Morgan eased the pressure with her hands.

"Wow, look at that!" Trey exclaimed, leaning over Spence's shoulder.

The three examined Caleb's leg. The cut was no longer gaping open and wasn't bleeding. The skin was fresh and pink, and the wound resembled a shallow slice, several days old. "Hand me the paste stuff," she said to Spence.

Spence handed the other container to her. She stuck two fingers into the paste and rubbed it along the cut. She repeated until she had used all of it to cover the wound and the surrounding skin. It began thickening and drying almost instantly. "He's still unconscious and pale."

"Here, try this," Spence said, handing her the vial of red liquid.

Morgan clutched the vial, staring at it skeptically. "In his mouth?"

"Yep."

Morgan pried the cork out of the end of the tube and opened Caleb's mouth with her left hand. Then she leaned over and slowly poured some of the thick red liquid into his mouth. She paused to make sure the liquid disappeared down his throat and then emptied the remainder. She then sat and observed with the others.

Caleb's breathing became deeper and slower, and color began returning to his face and exposed leg. He appeared more as if he was in peaceful sleep instead of at death's door.

"You have some amazing drugs," Trey said to Morgan, still leaning over Spence.

"Too bad I had to use all of them," Morgan replied. "Nobody else better get hurt."

Caleb's eyelids fluttered a few times and then opened. He stared at the sky for a moment and then slowly sat upright. He glanced at the three peering intently at him and then looked down at his ripped pants and exposed flesh. He traced his fingers along the dry, gray paste. "What happened?" he finally whispered.

Spence recounted the past half hour. Caleb just vaguely remembered trying to run and follow the footsteps of the Cyclops from where it had knocked him unconscious. He didn't remember seeing Trey sending the monster tumbling into the river or their encounter after.

"At least we know what one of the potions does. Thanks." Caleb slowly regained his feet. When he put weight on his right leg, the paste cracked and began flaking off like pieces of dried mud. He flicked the remaining bits off with his fingers. The skin underneath was pink and smooth. The gash had disappeared, and there probably wouldn't even be a scar. He then squatted and stood a few times to test it. "Amazing."

"Look, bro, I'm sorry for last night…and everything. I temporarily lost my head. I don't know. I guess this place just got to me. I mean, I'm way out of my element here. And it seems like all of you have adjusted better than me. Instead of being the star linebacker, I'm just a nobody here. But I've done a lot of thinking and have come to grips with it. I know the only chance we have is to stick together. Forgive me?" Trey extended his hand to Caleb.

Caleb stared at Trey's extended hand and then met his eyes. "To be honest, I still don't trust you. You had planned to take Spence's staff and probably kill all of us with it. It's not like it was just an accident or heat of the moment. I'm too tired to think about it now, though. We'll camp separately tonight. Maybe tomorrow we can discuss it."

Trey shrugged and then turned to Spence. "Forgive me, dude?"

Spence wasn't sure how he felt about Trey. He doubted he could completely change in only a few hours. He went ahead and shook Trey's hand, though.

"And you, sis?" Trey said to Morgan.

"I need more convincing." She turned away and repacked her bags.

"Well, I'll catch you guys' sometime tomorrow," Trey said and then turned and disappeared up the bank.

Caleb removed the bandage that had served as a tourniquet and retied it lower to cinch his ripped pants leg together. "All right, let's find a place to make camp. It will be dark soon, and we're all exhausted. We should stay in the trees and take our chances that the river monsters don't get out of the water." Caleb led the others out of the trees and into the open land.

Spence's eyes frequently scanned over and around the rolling hills to the west. The thought of another battle made his stomach flutter. He was disappointed his staff couldn't bring down the Cyclops, even with the lightning bolt and the fireball. He liked the fireball, which followed its target, but he would be dead if he had been alone. Hopefully, not all the monsters they faced would be that tough.

Then he thought about the monster being a cyborg. "What do you all think about the Cyclops being a robot or at least part robot?"

"Pretty weird," Caleb replied.

"I wonder if the wolfosaurus was a robot too?" Morgan asked.

"I don't think so. But it was something created or genetically altered—I mean a mammal head with a reptile body?" Spence said.

"So, one way or the other, everything in this world has been created," Morgan said.

"Just like our world, except we only have one god," Spence replied.

"Not according to everyone. There are lots of different religions and beliefs, and lack of beliefs," Morgan said.

Spence was too tired to get into a religious discussion. His legs were shaky, and he was physically and mentally spent. He was relieved when Caleb soon stopped at a clump of trees at the top of the riverbank. They set up camp, with one tarp tied to the trees as a roof and the other spread on the ground below as a floor. Caleb was certainly talented at making camps. Each setup was different, but he completed them quickly and decisively. They were also acclimating to their roles. Spence and Morgan collected firewood as Caleb built a fire pit and started a fire.

They all gathered beneath the tarp in front of the fire just as the sky released the last of its fading light. They ate the same meal for the third night—only the bread was tougher and drier, and the meat and cheese hard and greasy.

"If we don't reach the Forbidden Forest by tomorrow night, we might have to try to hunt. I haven't seen many animals, but there must be some rabbits or squirrels around. Morgan, do you think you can manage killing something?" Caleb asked.

Morgan looked up from her cheese and bread. "I guess," she said softly. "If we're truly out of other options."

"If you can find something else to eat, then by all means do it. But I haven't seen any nuts or berries or any plants I recognize as edible."

Morgan nodded. "What do you think about Trey?"

"I don't know," Caleb replied. "He did save us and is a good fighter."

"And you might have avoided getting hurt if he had been there hacking on the Cyclops from the beginning," Morgan added.

"He also tried to steal my staff and would have probably fried you two and possibly me as well," Spence replied. His heart raced at the recollection of the incident.

"There is that...." Morgan said.

"He's a bully and arrogant and an idiot," Caleb said. "But it seems he might finally understand we're not in high school anymore, and this is life and death. And it sounds like he realizes he is totally out of his element here and can't survive by himself. I'm sure he won't be able to build a fire tonight, and he has no tarp or shelter."

"Do we take a chance on letting him join us again?" Morgan asked.

Caleb turned to Spence. "Spence, you're the brunt of most of his abuse. What do you say?"

Spence stared at the fire. He definitely enjoyed Trey not being around. The whole mood was different with only the three of them. But Trey did save his life. They would likely face monsters as nasty or worse than the Cyclops. And now Trey knew he couldn't steal his staff. Maybe he could be a decent human being, at least until they returned to Earth. A night alone might help cement the change. "I guess, assuming he finds us tomorrow. But we have to always watch him and assume the worst."

"Morgan?"

Morgan sighed. "If we have to. He can be like our pet pit bull…cobra."

CHAPTER 20

With the air warmer and a blazing fire, the night was the most comfortable one they had experienced. Spence was exhausted but wasn't ready to sleep. He typically stayed up until midnight or later at home, playing online games. The exertion had made him fall asleep quickly for the first few nights. But now, despite his fatigue, his mind was reasonably alert. "I think I'm having Internet withdrawal."

"I know, right?" Morgan echoed. "Do you know how long it will take me to catch up on Facebook, Twitter, and Instagram? And no telling how much I've missed on Snapchat."

Caleb shook his head. "Then this is exactly what you two dweebs need—detoxing."

"You don't use the Internet?" Spence asked.

"Not for social media, anyway. I've never been on any of those sites or whatever they are. If people are your friends, you can talk to them and see them in real life. I use the Internet to keep up with the news and world affairs—"

"Let me guess, Fox News?" Morgan asked.

Caleb scowled but continued. "And, of course, shopping for camping, hunting, and survival gear. Now, eBay, Cabelas, and Amazon, I miss."

"Hey, let's play a game!" Spence exclaimed. He was excited talking to real people, not just participating in online game chat.

"Oh, God. We're not on a car trip, Skippy," Morgan said.

Caleb smiled and shook his head.

Spence experienced a surge of adrenaline that threatened to blossom into anger. He inhaled deeply and tried to control his emotions. Morgan flashed the slightest of grins, and he realized she might just be joking. "No, seriously. Let's take turns picking a category, and then we each say the one thing we miss the most."

"You know, if Trey were here, I'd say you'd be close to receiving a wedgie," Caleb said.

Morgan laughed.

"Come on, guys. What else do we have to do? It's like eight o'clock. Surely you aren't going to bed." He paused, reading their faces. They weren't entirely shutting him down. "OK. I'll start it. Food—I miss pizza."

"Eggplant parmesan," Morgan said.

"God, you're a freak," Caleb replied. "Give me a grilled cheeseburger and fries."

"Cool," Spence said. "OK. Morgan, you go."

"No one ever speaks of this game in the real world, or I'll hunt you both down. OK. We've already discussed the Internet. So, next, I'll say television—I miss *The Walking Dead*."

"Whoa, there's a shock!" Caleb said.

"Why don't you bite my walking dead ass?" Morgan responded.

Caleb grinned and bared his teeth, clicking them together. "*Doomsday Preppers*."

"You know, you two are both walking stereotypes," Spence said. Morgan and Caleb both turned to stare at him, but surprisingly they laughed. Spence laughed too. This night was shaping up to be fun, almost like a camping trip with friends in the real world. "*Ancient Aliens*."

"Oh, and you're not a stereotype? I think we need to play another game—guess what year or decade one of us will get laid," Morgan said. All three laughed.

"OK. My turn," Caleb said. "Person. Mine is easy, my dad. We do everything together."

Spence had to think on this one. He didn't see his older brother and sister much. His mother and father had been fawning over him since his accident but seemingly more out of duty than love. But when he was upset or sad, his mother was the one coming to his aid. "It'd be my mother."

"I'd say my sister, Jade. She's away at college, but we FaceTime or Skype twice a week. She gets me as good as anyone," Morgan said.

"Hobby—mine, of course, is *Warcraft*," Spence said.

"After social media, reading," Morgan replied.

Caleb was silent for a moment. "You know, other than being with you guys instead of my father and the existence of monsters and gods, mine is pretty much what we're doing."

"That's sad," Morgan said.

Caleb shrugged.

The three didn't speak for several minutes. Spence was out of ideas for missed things, and he didn't want the other two to tire of the game. So, he changed the subject. "Maybe we won't have to fight anything tomorrow. We should reach the elves before dark."

"Hard to say. The elves have a monster, too, but we don't know whether we'll encounter it before or after meeting them. Besides, who says the only things we fight are the monsters of the official quest? According to Titus, there are lots of creatures roaming around," Caleb said.

"Oh, yeah," Spence said. "Hey, you know what I just thought of?"

"Do share," Morgan said.

"Well, the gods here are named after mythological gods on Earth."

"Yep," Morgan replied.

"And they opened a doorway to bring us here. What if the gods visited Earth in our past, and are the gods the myths are based on? What if the Sumerian myths were true? Did you ever see *Stargate*?"

Morgan and Caleb both shook their heads.

"Well, to make a long movie short, a group of modern-day people finds a strange device, like a doorway, in Egypt. Once they finally crack the hieroglyphic code on it, it opens a portal leading to another world. It's a primitive world that resembles ancient Egypt and is ruled by Ra. But it turns out he uses technology instead of god powers to rule them."

"Hmmm...." Caleb said.

"Interesting," Morgan replied.

"Maybe all the gods from this world visited Earth in the past," Spence said. "Or perhaps this really is Nibiru, and it's passing close to Earth again. Instead of them visiting Earth, now they're bringing Earthlings here. Just something else to ponder."

"I'm tired of pondering," Morgan replied. "Well, boys, I'd better do my business before bed." Morgan stood.

"Hey, at least there should be some better toilet paper options. There are ferns on the riverbank and moss on the fallen trees and rocks," Caleb said, grinning.

"Gee, that should be wonderful! When we get back, I might go into the toilet paper business. Want to go green? Use Morgan's Finest. You can choose from soft moss, firm fern, or raw-and-bleed leaf."

Spence burst out laughing, followed by Caleb. Morgan finally joined them. She walked off into the darkness of the trees, still chuckling.

"What do you think of Morgan now?" Spence asked.

Caleb stared out into the darkness, where Morgan had disappeared. "Well, I'm not a fan of the whole Goth thing. I couldn't stand any of them at school, and I disagree with most of her philosophy, but I guess she's not too bad. A heck of an archer too."

"Would you do her?"

Caleb swung his head around and stared at Spence. "Do her? Did you actually just ask that?"

Spence laughed. In his usual speak first, think last way, the question didn't come out exactly as he had meant it. "Just kidding. But do you think she's attractive?"

"She's not ugly or anything. I'd like to see her without the black war paint and a few less piercings, though."

Spence heard crunching noises approaching them, and Morgan soon materialized in the glow of the firelight.

"Always a pleasure." She returned to her seat. "Your turns."

Spence and Caleb took turns disappearing and doing their business in the dark trees. Soon they all gathered back around the fire.

"I think I'm going to lie down. We'd better take watches again. I'll take last. Which one of you wants first?" Caleb said.

"I'll take first," Morgan replied.

Spence and Caleb moved further under the tarp, covered themselves with blankets, and used their packs for pillows. Morgan laid her bow across her lap and gazed out into the darkness. Spence stared at her, silhouetted by the flames. Now that her personality was showing, and snarky and condescending had become sarcasm and humor, he was beginning to really like her. He had found her physically attractive since the night at the inn, but probably mostly because she was the sole girl, and he had never had a girlfriend. But now, the feelings were more than just physical. He liked her personality too and enjoyed being around her. Although he didn't feel sleepy, his thoughts soon led him to sleep.

He awoke to something shaking his shoulder. He peered up and saw Morgan leaning over him.

"Get up, ancient alien."

Spence blinked a few times and slowly sat up as Morgan backed away. "No trouble?"

"Just some big splashes in the river. Something is moving around in the trees too, but hopefully just a deer or something. I gathered a little more wood for the fire."

Spence crawled out from under the tarp and stood by the fire. He stretched his back and legs. Sleeping on the hard ground definitely didn't help relieve sore and aching muscles.

"You don't stink, do you?"

Spence turned to Morgan. "Excuse me?"

"I don't feel like unpacking my blanket. I'll just use your bed if you don't care."

"Oh. Well, uh, not too bad yet, I guess. Although lack of deodorant, cologne, and hot water will take its toll on all of us."

"I'm sure it already has, and we're just used to one another's funk." Morgan smiled and lay where Spence had slept. She used his pack for her pillow and wrapped up in his blanket.

Spence sat by the fire, facing away from the tarp shelter. He knew he was stupid, but he was excited by the thought of Morgan wrapped in the blanket that was still warm from his body and her head lying where his had been. He tried to shut out the image of them both lying under the blanket, bodies pressed together and faces inches apart. He would have no trouble staying awake tonight.

Spence ended his shift after a primarily uneventful watch. He heard the big splashes Morgan had mentioned and some crunches and snaps in the trees, but nothing too close. As he walked under the tarp, he realized the flaw with Morgan's plan—now he couldn't use his bed. He studied Morgan, the firelight gently flickering across her face. Her brown hair was tussled about her head and her exposed cheek. Her lips were parted slightly, and she breathed deeply. He knew he couldn't wake her and risk her wrath. And, of course, sliding in beside her warm body certainly wasn't an option.

He walked over and touched Caleb's shoulder. Caleb instantly awoke, and his hand shot out and grabbed Spence's wrist before he could even react. After a few blinks, Caleb released his iron grip, and Spence backed away.

"Sorry, Spence. Any trouble?" Caleb grabbed his sword and rose to his feet.

"Just some fish jumping."

Caleb walked past Spence and to the fire. He then turned to see Spence still standing in the same spot. He looked at Morgan sleeping in Spence's bed. "I don't even want to know. You can use mine."

Spence sheepishly nodded and crawled under Caleb's blanket. It didn't take him long to fall asleep.

CHAPTER 21

After a quick and cold breakfast, they broke camp and headed out of the trees and into the open. The sky was overcast but brighter, as the day before. The temperature was still cool but manageable with the exertion of hiking.

Spence's soreness was easing some, despite sleeping on the hard ground. His right calf and left groin still ached a little, and, of course, his feet were blistered in his boots, but the pain was better than it had been. More trees appeared, primarily pines, scattered individually and with a few clumps here and there. He hoped that meant they neared the Forbidden Forest. He didn't look forward to fighting again, but he was tired of this terrain.

"Favorite movie of all time," Spence said after a few hours of walking.

"*The Hunger Games*, of course," Morgan replied.

"You do make a good Katniss," Spence complimented. He received a quick smile in return. "*The Lord of the Rings*—all of them."

"*Red Dawn*, the original," Caleb replied.

"You know what movie this reminds me of a little bit—minus the alternate universe, monsters, and gods?" Spence asked.

"*The Lord of the Rings*?" Morgan replied, eliciting a quick laugh from Caleb.

"Ha, ha. *Stand by Me*. Ever seen it?"

"Nope," Caleb replied.

Morgan nodded. "Oh, yeah! The four kids go to find a dead body. It does a little, except for no girl, and none of the kids dies in the movie. Not sure if ours will turn out the same way, though."

Morgan's statement brought Spence back into the new real world. Although their experience was like a book or movie and was an adventure, they had no guarantee any of them would survive it. They were four high school kids in way over their heads. This story wouldn't be regarded as fun or exciting unless they all survived intact. Maybe if they did survive, they could get together every ten years, like a high school reunion, and relive the memories.

"What is the deal with you and old movies?" Caleb asked.

Spence shrugged. "Friday night is movie night at the Underwood's, and my dad normally picks. He's stuck in the eighties and early nineties."

"Wow. That's terrible," Caleb said.

"You should hear what he listens to on Sirius XM in the car."

Caleb halted them after a few more hours at a small cluster of pines. They sat on the pine- needle-covered grass and dug out the remains of their food. When Spence finished eating, he realized he barely had enough food left—an apple and possibly one meat and cheese sandwich—for a meal. He knew the others had to be in a similar situation.

As if reading his mind, Caleb spoke. "Morgan, if you see anything furry and moving, you need to shoot it. We might reach the Forbidden Forest tonight, but I doubt we'll stumble right into Sabekha. You don't have to eat the meat if you don't want to, but I'd prefer not to starve or get weakened too much to fight from lack of food."

Morgan stared blankly at the ground. "OK," she responded.

Once they resumed marching, Morgan kept her bow in hand with an arrow nocked. The land was becoming more overgrown, with patches of weeds, briars, tall grass, and more trees. At the top of one large hill, Caleb pointed ahead. Spence followed his arm and saw a dark green line stretching across the horizon, still a few hours away.

"We should make it by dark," Caleb said.

Spence was lost in his thoughts an hour later when motion exploded in front of them. He looked up and saw two flashes of movement streaking out of a thicket of scrub. Then beside him, Morgan sprang into action. She drew the bowstring back and released the arrow in one smooth motion. That arrow flew to the left. Without waiting to see if it struck her target, she repeated the act and sent another one flying to the right.

"There's your stupid meat," she stated flatly.

"Wow, Kat, impressive," Caleb replied.

"It's easier to shoot when the target isn't trying to kill you."

Caleb hurried to the left and picked up a fat gray rabbit with an arrow sticking out of its breast. He then retrieved the other to the right. "Just remember, these are for our survival, and they had more than a fair chance. Few people could kill running rabbits with a bow. These aren't penned-in cows getting whacked in the head." Caleb handed the arrows back to Morgan.

Morgan wiped the blood off the arrowheads on the grass and returned them to her quiver. "I suppose."

Caleb drew one of his daggers and went to work, slitting their bellies up to their ribs and cleaning out the insides. Once they were clean and drained of blood, he stuffed them both into his pack.

As they resumed walking, Spence continued scanning the horizon. The hills began to flatten, allowing him to catch occasional glimpses of the dark green line that was most likely the Forbidden Forest. It reminded him of when he was a child and trying to catch glimpses of the ocean when his family drove to the beach each year.

"Have you all noticed anything?" Caleb asked.

"This world sucks?" Morgan responded.

"True. But there are no birds. We haven't seen one since we've been here. In fact, the rabbits and monsters are the only living things we've seen."

"What does it mean?" Spence asked.

"Maybe nothing. It's just a little weird."

"What isn't weird here?" Morgan asked. "There's also never any wind."

"Or sun or blue skies," Spence added.

"Very true. Interesting," Caleb replied.

The green line on the horizon expanded in thickness and height and eventually coalesced into a forest of tall pine trees. The sight of the trees and the rapidly fading light spurred them into a brisk walk. Spence tried to ignore his aching legs and feet and thought of lying beside a warm fire on a soft bed of pine needles. He anticipated the night would be warmer than last night and hoped the woods would be safer than the open land.

They reached the Forbidden Forest an hour later. The sun had presumably just set, and the sky was a faint gray glow. The three stood staring in awe. The pine trees averaged eighty to one hundred feet in height. The limbs started twenty feet up and were then thick to the tops. The trees reminded Spence of the sequoias in Yosemite, except the tops were thicker and stretched out farther. Pine needles carpeted the ground beneath the trees. Little underbrush was visible, just occasional smaller pines and some patches of ferns. The light was much dimmer only a few feet inside the woods.

"There's not much light left. I'll find a spot for camp while you two gather wood. It should be easy with all this pine." Caleb entered the trees and began looking for the correct configuration of trunks for a campsite.

Spence and Morgan entered the woods behind Caleb. The fading light gave the forest an eerie glow. The air was noticeably warmer under the protection of the trees. The forest was strangely silent and the stale air almost oppressive. Spence wasn't exactly afraid, but he was a little on edge. He couldn't help but wonder what type of creatures, mechanical or living, they would face next. At least something as big as the wolfosaurus or Cyclops would have a tough time maneuvering in the trees.

Caleb was right about wood being easy to find—there were plenty of dead, dry limbs scattered around the tree trunks. They soon had armfuls and used their hearing to locate Caleb, who was finishing creating a three-sided shelter. He quickly started a small fire. It soon illuminated a twenty-foot circle, meeting a wall of darkness that enclosed them. "We should keep the fire small. Someone, or something, could spot this from a mile away in this darkness. Grab me some big rocks and a couple of long, straight sticks, and we'll fry some rabbit."

Soon, Caleb had stacked the rocks on two opposite sides of the fire, skinned the rabbits, and cut them into pieces. He then sharpened the ends of two sticks and worked them through the hunks of meat, creating two kabobs. He then rested the ends of the sticks onto the rocks, some distance above the flames. The three sat in front of the fire, placing their weapons and packs behind them.

"Hmmm, smell that, boys? Screw the stale bread and molded cheese," Caleb said.

Morgan scowled at Caleb but still stared intently at the fire and roasting meat.

Caleb turned the kabobs several times until the meat was sufficiently browned. He bit a small bite of one of the pieces. "OMG, this is so good!"

"OMG?" Morgan laughed. "LOL."

"What's good?" a voice said from the darkness just outside the reach of the fire.

Caleb dropped the kabob and reached for his sword. Morgan and Spence likewise searched for their weapons on the tarp behind them.

Trey suddenly appeared in the light on the other side of the fire, grinning.

CHAPTER 22

"You guys are already losing your edge; you'd been screwed if I were a cyborg monster." He walked around the fire and stood beside Caleb. "So, can I rejoin you and have some of whatever meat you're cooking?"

Caleb released the handle of his sword and glared up at Trey for a moment. He then glanced over to Spence and Morgan. "Have you been following us?"

"Not really. But Titus instructed us to follow the river until we came to the Forbidden Forest. I had planned on camping alone again tonight, but I saw your fire as soon as I entered the woods. Turns out you weren't too far ahead of me."

Caleb sighed. "Have you learned anything?"

Trey stared at the ground. "Yeah. Like I said yesterday, I was a jerk. I just lost my head being in this hellhole of a world. I guess I didn't like not being in control or being the big man on campus, like at school. But as you said, this isn't high school anymore. This is our new real world, and we must stick together to get back to ours. You won't have any more trouble out of me."

Spence scrutinized Trey closely, searching for any hint of insincerity. He actually seemed…humble. He had saved their lives the day before, and now he had apologized for his actions twice. Could he have really changed? He looked at Morgan and saw the surprise on her face too. She met his gaze and gave the slightest of shrugs.

"Trey, I'm going to take you at your word. You did save our lives yesterday. You can join us. But if there is any drama, any drama at all, you're on your own for good," Caleb said.

Trey smiled and sat beside Caleb.

"Here, you two share this one, and Trey and I will take the other." Caleb handed a rabbit kabob to Spence.

Spence greedily grabbed the stick. He plucked a thigh and leg from the end and handed the stick to Morgan. His mouth watered even before the meat touched his lips. He had never eaten rabbit before, but it was now his favorite meat ever. The exterior was slightly crispy, but the meat inside was still juicy and succulent. It lacked salt or seasoning, but the meat was more flavorful than anything he had eaten in the past four days.

He turned to Morgan, who grasped the stick and stared at the meat as if it were rancid. "It's OK, bae. This is survival now. We can't fight the next monster on empty stomachs. Try it."

Morgan stared at Spence with her mouth hanging open. "Bae? Seriously? You think you know me like that?"

"Hey, we slept in the same bed last night," Spence responded, then ate another big bite of meat.

"Dork," Morgan said but flashed a grin. She gingerly removed the other thigh and leg, returned the stick to Spence, and grasped the meat with both hands. She slowly raised it to her nose and sniffed it a couple of times. She then cautiously lowered it to her mouth and bit off a tiny bite. She chewed experimentally with her front teeth and then swallowed. "Dang." She tore off a sizable chunk and chewed it much more vigorously.

"Wow, look at that," Caleb said. "Good job!"

"Woohoo! That a girl," Trey said.

"She even killed these, Trey," Caleb replied.

Morgan transferred the meat to her left hand and held out her right, extending her middle finger to Trey and Caleb. But she continued eating while doing so.

The four devoured the rabbit pieces and retrieved wineskins from their packs to wash them down with warm water. "We'll have to find more water tomorrow. Hopefully, we'll locate the elves early," Caleb said.

"Oh, how are your hands, Trey?" Morgan asked.

Trey held his hands up and showed his palms to the others. They were red but didn't appear severely burned. "Well, it hurt like a mother but turns out it was more the shocking than the heat. They're still a little sore, though."

The four relaxed against their packs, lost in thought for several minutes.

"Damn."

"What?" Spence asked Trey.

"I just thought how cool it would be to be able to post this adventure on Facebook. Yesterday would have been, 'OMG! Worst day ever! My buds got their asses kicked by a robotic Cyclops. I had to lay the smack down on it and send it floating down the river to be eaten by monsters. LOL.'"

All four erupted into laughter, and Morgan actually snorted a couple of times. "Well, you know it didn't really happen unless you post it on Facebook."

Spence had to admit that Trey wasn't completely brainless—just most of the time. "And we could have blown up Instagram and Snapchat with our selfies with the wolfosaurus!" Spence added.

"Hashtag, worst week ever," Morgan said.

"Of course, we would have had to post pictures of the rabbit before we ate it too. Because you know the social media rule of posting pictures of your meals whenever possible," Trey added.

"You know one thing good about this world?" Morgan said when the chuckles had faded. "Look around. No pollution. No bottles, beer cans, and trash littering the riverbank or the woods. And there is no smog in the air or even jet contrails."

"But also, no Internet and television," Spence replied.

"I'm starting to think it's not a bad thing, either. I mean, what would we have all done the past four days at home? Go to school, come home, surf the net, watch TV," Morgan said.

"Porn."

"I really don't want to know what you would be doing, Sticky," Morgan said to Trey.

"Hey, they have Goth porn too!"

"Idiot," Morgan replied.

"What if we never get to go home again?" Spence asked.

"That probably means we'll be dead," Caleb answered. "I think this is pretty much an all-or-nothing deal."

The mood instantly sobered. Despite Spence having already faced death twice, listening to Caleb speak about it so matter-of-factly was strange to hear. They were just four kids in a strange world fighting monsters on a convoluted quest. How could they even survive, much less succeed? Spence wanted to lighten the mood again. "Hey, Trey, we've been playing a game, with one of us asking a question and everyone having to answer it."

Trey shook his head and turned to Caleb. "Is he for real?"

Caleb nodded. "Yep. We're on one big road trip…to hell."

The others all laughed. Spence wasn't upset, though. He knew or strongly believed they were only busting his chops. "Middle name. Mine is Eugene."

Trey laughed. "Spence, ole buddy, I'm honestly trying hard to be good here, but now you're just poking the grizzly bear with a stick."

Spence's heart skipped a few beats, but he was determined not to be a spaz. He breathed deeply and grinned. "Hey, it's a family name. It belonged to my grandfather, a Vietnam War vet. He's my hero."

"OK. I'll let it slide, Spence Eugene Underwood," Trey said, shaking his head and hiding his mouth behind the back of his hand. "Mine is Ethan. Trey Ethan Morrison—a studly name, any way you slice it."

"I'll tell mine, but keep in mind, any laughter will result in someone getting skewered and roasted over the fire. "Nicole. Morgan Nicole Turner."

"Nicole? That's pretty sexy," Spence said.

"Come here, Spence," Morgan said, reaching out for him.

Spence scooted away, nearly bumping into Caleb, and everyone laughed. He was proud of himself for suggesting the game. It was working better than he had hoped at lifting the mood.

"Caleb Jackson Stone," Caleb said.

"Family name too?" Spence asked.

"My mother's maiden name. I've thought about changing it over the years, but she did give birth to me."

The four fell silent again. It seemed like most subjects led to awkward, painful moments for at least one. Then Spence suddenly realized he was still hungry. The rabbit had been fantastic but didn't fill him. He sat up and rummaged through his pack for a snack. He hadn't been genuinely full since Argos. His pack of bread was nearly empty. Then he found another, smaller package at the bottom, which he hadn't noticed before but assumed was more dry bread. He unwrapped it and found small, yellowish squares resembling cornbread. He didn't bother sniffing and took a bite out of one. The square was denser and moister than cornbread and was slightly sweet. It might have been because he hadn't eaten sweets since entering Nibiru, but the new food tasted unbelievably delicious. He finished the square, and it satisfied his hunger and seemed to replenish his energy. He suddenly felt like he could fight another monster.

"Have you all tried any of this?" he asked excitedly, holding one of the squares up in the firelight.

The others searched their packs but didn't find any of the strange bread. Spence gave them each a small square, which they devoured. In a few minutes, they were all raving about it.

"Wow, that's the best thing I've ever eaten!" Morgan exclaimed.

"Right up there with pot brownies," Trey said.

"How many of those do you have?" Caleb asked.

Spence examined the package. There were three, but he didn't want to reveal that for some reason. He rewrapped the package and returned it to his pack. "Just one."

"What, you get the magic staff and the magic food too?" Trey asked.

"Hey, I can't help what was in my pack. And I shared it with you guys," Spence said defensively. But he realized how important something that seemingly nutritious was. "Besides, when my staff is recharging, I'm defenseless."

"That stuff is like drinking a 5-Hour Energy combined with a Monster," Caleb said. "I could hike all night or fight something."

"Well, maybe it will give Spence enough energy to stay awake tonight." Trey rummaged again through his small pack.

"Stay awake? When did he fall asleep?" Caleb asked, sitting upright.

"He was sleeping sitting up two nights ago. I got cold, woke up, and realized the fire was almost burned out. Then I saw ole Spence sitting straight up sound asleep on the other side. He finally woke and got up to throw more wood on the fire. That's when I decided to see if I could borrow his cursed staff."

Caleb's gaze swung from Trey to Spence. "Is that true?"

Spence's heart pounded as fast as it had while clinging to the tree above the river with the Cyclops preparing to send him into its deadly waters. His hands began sweating, and his face felt flushed. "Uh…I…well—"

"Damn it, Spence! You freakin' idiot! Our first night in the wild, and you couldn't stay awake for a few hours?" Caleb shouted. His voice sounded even louder in the silent forest.

"I…I…didn't mean to!" Tears welled up in Spence's eyes. He couldn't cry. Not here. Not now. "And I stayed awake last night."

"What if it hadn't just been Trey? What if it had been the wolfosaurus, the Cyclops, or any monster? We would have all died in our freakin' sleep!" Caleb's hands balled into fists on the ground.

"No wonder you don't have any friends," Morgan said. She didn't hide her disgust. "Friends don't let each other down like that. All you had to do was stay awake. You didn't try to get up and walk around? Rub water on your face?"

First Caleb and now Morgan. Spence had foolishly thought they had become friends. He had felt like he was part of a group, part of something bigger than just him. Now, they were just as mean as Trey. This was like his supposed friends kicking him out of the guild in *Warcraft*, except this was real life. He was back in gym class, being pummeled in dodgeball. Surprisingly, Trey wasn't jumping in. He just sat there, taking it all in with a smug look. Tears pooled at the corners of Spence's eyes and threatened to race down his cheeks in seconds.

He slung his pack over his back, grabbed his staff, and stood. "Screw you, Caleb! Screw all of you! I've saved all your butts twice with my staff. And this is the thanks I get? Sure, I messed up. I'm sorry; I'm not used to fighting monsters and hiking twelve hours a day! I hope none of you ever makes a mistake. Good luck on your quest without me!" Spence turned and stomped into the darkness.

CHAPTER 23

Spence was so upset and angry that he shook all over. He hadn't intended on leaving when he first stood. He had only been going to the opposite side of the fire. But now, he found himself walking into the dark forest. He struck the butt of his staff on the ground, and the glowing crystal provided a ten-foot radius of light around him.

"Spence, come back!"

Spence recognized Caleb's voice. He couldn't just return now, though. He had to keep going. He might rejoin the group tomorrow, but he had to spend tonight on his own. He had to make them regret being so cruel. He quickly walked away before they could follow, or he changed his mind.

"Spence!" Morgan's voice yelled.

Hopefully, they'd learn a lesson. Spence's fast pace caused his staff to bob up and down, and the effect of the light was somewhat disorienting. The light bleached out all color from the trees and ground, making everything shades of black and gray. Shadows danced on all sides. It appeared like he was in one of those low-budget camcorder horror movies. *The Blair Witch Project* immediately came to mind. That movie had always creeped him out. Now, he was in a dark forest, possibly housing real horrors.

He thought he might be out of sight of the camp by now, but he wasn't sure with the darkness of the forest and his bright staff. But he didn't want to go too far away in case he decided to rejoin them in the morning. He stretched his right arm out and wrapped his hand around the crystal, which was surprisingly cool. The light now shone out between his thumb and forefinger, creating a flashlight-like beam. He could still see, but the light wouldn't be as visible from a distance.

He soon spotted a thick bunch of what resembled laurel bushes growing around a huge pine tree. The bushes were the only nonpine vegetation he had seen other than ferns. He made his way to the foliage and poked his staff inside, ensuring no creatures hid within. The bushes' limbs were thick, but they opened inside and around the tree's base. He dropped to his hands and knees and slithered inside.

He crawled into a perfect, human-size hiding spot. He would be impossible to spot from any distance outside. He struck the base of the staff against the tree trunk, and the pitch-black returned. He slid his pack off and leaned it against the bottom of the tree. He then scooted down so he could use it for a pillow. He clutched his staff in his left hand and placed his right hand on the hilt of his dagger. The burst of energy from the cake had waned, probably from a mixture of burning rage and his brisk walk. He was tired—both from the physical exertions of the day and the mental stress of the recent encounter.

He felt safe in his shelter. Nothing could get to him, at least not without making a lot of noise in the process. The space was warm and cozy, with pine needles providing a bed beneath him. Hopefully, he would hear the others approaching in the morning. They would be loud in the solitude of the woods. Despite a mind jumbled with thoughts, he closed his eyes and slept.

He awoke after an undetermined amount of time. A bright light shone in his face. He blinked several times and struggled to remember where he lay. When he recalled his sheltered sleeping place in the strange forest, he sat up and held his staff pointing in front of him.

He couldn't discern the source of the light somehow knifing its way through the thick laurel leaves. It resembled sunlight, but he could see the forest was still dark. Then he thought it might be a flashlight or spotlight. He considered staying hunkered down in the bush. Maybe whatever created the source of light couldn't see him. He waited for what seemed like minutes, but the light stayed fixed on him. Reluctantly, he crawled on his hands and knees out of the thicket.

He stood and shielded his eyes with his right hand. The light was coming from above, shining down at an angle to him. Despite no noise, Spence's first thought was of a helicopter or UFO. The light slowly moved off him and retreated until it shone straight down to the forest floor. A humanoid figure suddenly stood bathed in the golden beam, looking like an actor on center stage. The light was too bright to make out the facial features of the being, and he could barely discern the silhouette.

The figure walked or moved toward him, and the bright light followed. Spence clutched his staff tightly but didn't activate it. Somehow, he knew if the being meant to hurt him, it would have killed him while he slept. His legs shook, nonetheless.

The entity stopped six feet away. Now that it was much closer, Spence could see that it was male and wore a long white robe. His facial features were young and flawless. White hair cascaded out from beneath a golden horned helmet, falling to his shoulders. His eyes were black. The light bleached out the details of his other features and made the being's skin look very pale. He crossed his hands before him, the long robe sleeves coming to his wrists.

"Hello, Spence from Earth," the being said in a deep but not loud voice.

"Uh…hello…sir," Spence stammered. His voice sounded high-pitched and weak.

"I am Enki, lord of water and lands of the South."

"The talking statue?"

"That was I."

"You rule the lizard people?" Spence asked. Curiosity slowly replaced his fear.

"They do not like that term; they are the Draconians or reptilian humanoids," Enki replied. His face was expressionless as he spoke.

"What do you want with me?"

"We brought you here to complete a quest, the quest of liberating the races from the creatures separating them. If you are successful, we will allow you to return to your world. However, I know others do not respect you in your world. In fact, your fellow questers do not even respect you. You will also lose the use of your legs again and must depend upon others to care for you for the rest of your mortal life. If you complete the quest and return to Earth, what is your future there?"

Enki's knowledge of his situation shocked Spence. He recalled having those same thoughts since coming to Nibiru. Although high school had sucked, Spence hoped to graduate, attend a good college, and find real friends and groups he could fit in with. Then maybe after he graduated and was in the real world with a real job, the bullying and teasing would stop. That was before his accident. But confinement to a wheelchair crushed all those dreams. It would be hard to go to college without his parents hiring someone to take care of him. And even if he could attend college and graduate, what job opportunities would there be for him? Who would care for him after his parents were gone?

"There is a very good chance your future will be no better than your present, and you will never fit in with your people or find meaning and purpose."

"What are you saying?"

"The four races of Nibiru have coexisted for many years. For the most part, they have kept to their own territories and minded to their own affairs, mainly due to the creatures roaming between the lands. But in their hearts, they would like to expand outside their homes—first to explore and then to settle. Just think of your world and the great explorers and conquerors of old.

"My siblings and I believe once you have freed them from their unnatural constraints, they will encroach on each other's territories. Nibiru is not a big world. Unfortunately, it is not in the nature of any species to maintain a peaceful existence for long. The resettling will lead to conflicts, eventually leading to war. One race, or perhaps all of them, will inevitably want to rule the others. It is not so different from your world. Peaceful coexistence is hard to maintain for long."

"Why?" Spence lost all fear and absorbed every word Enki uttered.

"There is always a reason—politics, religion, resources, power. Again, think of the great wars in the history of your civilization. How long does peace ever last? Look at the Middle East on Earth. The people there have been warring for thousands of years. For what? We gods have tried to put measures in place to separate our peoples."

"Like the monsters?"

"Yes."

"Then why remove them? Just keep them penned in."

"After much deliberation, we have determined each race deserves its freedom. In your world, the citizens of each city and land may travel to any other. Would you enjoy being confined only to your town or city or country for eternity?" Enki asked.

"Oh, yeah. I guess not," Spence said, his mind still struggling to process the flood of information. "But why don't you and the other gods just kill or remove the monsters?"

"We could, of course, but we try to avoid meddling directly in the affairs of our peoples. And true freedom must be earned. We had hoped the races would have the courage to defeat the monsters themselves. Alas, they are weak and lack leadership. Therefore, we leave the task to the questers and assess their courage and skills."

Spence swallowed hard. "What do you think will happen when all the monsters are slain?"

"As I said, a war—a useless war. Four races will all be fighting each other. All lack direction and purpose. There will be many deaths, but nothing truly gained. No race is strong enough to defeat the other three and achieve a lasting peace."

"How do I come in?"

"An all-out war can only be avoided in one way. One race needs to stand up and take dominion over the others. True power is the only weapon that can reign in chaos. Democracy might work within one race but not between the races. There has to be governance and guidance."

"You think I could be that leader?" Spence asked incredulously.

"You have proved your worthiness. You have the power of your staff, and you have courage and intelligence. I could give you additional powers, and I could remove the limitations of your staff. If I presented you to the Draconians, they would follow you."

Spence trembled again, but not out of fear. This had to be a dream within a dream. "What would I do?"

"You would have to strike quickly and decisively against one of the other races—subjugate them to the Draconian rule. The others would then mostly likely obey your leadership. If not, you would have an army comprised of the Draconians and the race you defeated. It would just be a matter of time before you and your people rule Nibiru. It would be quick and, hopefully, relatively bloodless. Then you could establish true, lasting peace. All would be free within their new society."

Oh my God! Spence let his mind run wild with the fantasy. He could be the leader of an entire world? No one would ever tease him again, and he would never have to return to the wheelchair. He would put the Treys of the world to death or into hard labor or banish them to live among the monsters. "You honestly think I could do that?"

"I have seen power and courage within you. My people are strong too. The Draconians are the sturdiest of the races—strong, fast, and cunning. They combine the best of Nephilim and reptiles. I offer you something you could never even dream of in your world. And someday, I could possibly make you a god."

Spence swallowed hard. "What about the other gods? Don't they rule the other races?"

"They do. But they do not know I am here. If you agree to this, we will have to strike quickly before they can react. I am sure they will, or even have already, approached your *friends* to champion their peoples."

Spence was overwhelmed. His mind went from racing wildly to feeling sluggish and numb, and his body was weak. He only wanted to lie down and sleep. "I don't know what to say," he whispered, unsure if Enki even heard.

"You may consider my offer while you continue your quest. I just hope you do not take too long and get slain, or one of your companions accepts their offer first."

"How will I let you know?"

"Your pendant. If you are in a private place, squeeze it tightly and say my name, and I will appear. Or you can press the gem hard and be transported to Abzu, the sacred town of my people in the Forsaken Swamp."

Spence reached inside his shirt and touched the smooth, warm stone. He remembered the others had pendants, too, probably with the same powers. "OK."

"Think hard, human. This decision will be the biggest you have ever made. Until we meet again."

The light suddenly disappeared. Enki still stood there for a moment, glowing white in the pitch black of the forest. Then he abruptly disappeared too, leaving Spence standing in the total, silent darkness. He was too overwhelmed to attempt to sift through his thousand conflicting emotions and thoughts. He dropped to the ground and crawled back into his sleeping spot. He closed his eyes and miraculously fell asleep.

CHAPTER 24

The sounds of voices awoke Spence the second time. He lay on his left side, facing the forest where he had entered his shelter the night before. He knew it must be dawn by the dim light filtering through the green laurel leaves. He sat and strained his ears. Sure enough, he heard voices, still distant but moving in his direction. He grabbed his pack and staff and crawled out of the bush. He darted behind a nearby pine tree and waited.

He assumed the voices were from the others, but he wasn't sure what to do. Should he go his own way or rejoin them? It probably did make more sense to stick together, and he at least needed his tarp for shelter. His staff was powerful, but it had to recharge between each use, leaving him defenseless during that time. And if he had to fight multiple opponents, he wouldn't stand a chance. He needed to learn how to use his dagger and fight hand to hand. Maybe he could learn from Caleb or Trey. The thought of asking Trey for anything made him cringe. However, he did seem a little more civil since he rejoined them yesterday.

Then he suddenly remembered the encounter during the night. His heart instantly raced as he recalled the details. He reached inside his shirt and fingered the pendant. *Was it a dream?* Or had he actually met the god, Enki? Then he thought about the offer. He could lead the Draconians and rule Nibiru! Even the name, Draconian, sounded cool. What would they call him—emperor, king, lord, or God? An entire world to rule by himself. Nobody would ever tease or pick on him again. He recalled the *Narnia* books, where the kids from Earth had become the rulers of Narnia. The books were almost exactly like this.

Then he remembered the remainder of the conversation with Enki. He thought of the pendants each of the others wore. Each pendant probably represented a different race. They would receive a similar offer from one of the other gods. *What if they already have?* Nobody would know if they had a visitation during the night or even in their dreams. He wondered how the others would view the offer.

He could see Trey wanting the power and glory, although Trey also had a pretty good deal on Earth. He was already popular and enjoyed high school. He was the type of person who would somehow succeed in life despite being a jerk and a bully.

Morgan hated high school and life in general nearly as much as he did. But would she lead a race into a war and try to conquer and rule the world? He didn't see that. She was antigovernment. She would not be one to support the subjugation of the other races.

Caleb was a wildcard. He could undoubtedly fill the role and lead, but he seemed too much of a loner to want to be a permanent leader.

Did the choice only come down to him? If he did accept the offer, what would happen to the others? Could he help them get home? Or would he offer them positions in his army or government? Or enslave them….

The voices were close now. Spence peeked around the tree and saw the other three following pretty much the same path he had last night. He forced his mind to temporarily bury the thoughts of power and strode purposely forward to intersect them.

"Spence, where have you been? We thought we might find you dead," Morgan said.

"Dead? I'm a mage," he replied with as deep and steady a voice as he could muster. "I scouted ahead and spent the night over in the bushes. I've been waiting for you to catch up."

"Look, Spence, I'm sorry about snapping at you. But we all have to have each other's back. Some mistakes can't happen. Understand?" Caleb asked.

"Yeah, sorry, Spence. We're all just tired and stressed," Morgan said.

"Ditto," Trey added.

Spence felt a little better at hearing their apologies. It still didn't excuse how quickly they had turned on him, but it was better than nothing. At least this way, he could rejoin them, for now anyway, and save face. "No problem, guys. It won't happen again. You know I have your backs," he said. *Or will stick a dagger in them.* "You guys go ahead. I'm going to fish out some breakfast and eat as we walk."

"I'll wait on Spence. You two go ahead," Morgan said.

Spence was surprised but good with the company. He wished he could tell Morgan about his encounter last night, or at least find out if she had had one too, but knew he couldn't. He slapped together a meat and cheese sandwich out of the remaining scraps and washed it down with most of his remaining water as they walked. Hopefully, they were close to finding Illexya. Caleb and Trey were still in sight in the dim, eerily lit forest. "This is a strange place," he said.

"The Forbidden Forest and the entire world. I'm just constantly on edge, waiting for the next battle. It's not like we can get lucky and avoid it either. We know there will be something in here we have to fight."

"Yeah, you're right. I wonder if we'll ever get used to it?"

"Probably about the time we die," Morgan said, flashing the slightest grin. "Hey!"

"Hey, what?"

"You'll never guess what Trey confessed last night!" Morgan was as excited as Spence had ever seen her.

"He's a bully, jerk, loser, and male ho? Oh, we already know that. Closet transsexual?" Spence hadn't spent much time around Morgan, but he was strangely comfortable with her. That was unusual, considering she was female and a Goth to boot.

Morgan laughed. "Hmmm…scary thought…. No, Caleb came out and asked him why he was so messed up and had to pick on and bully everyone."

"Love or hate him, you have to admire Caleb's balls. I mean that figuratively, of course."

"Another scary thought." Morgan laughed again. "Yeah, he doesn't pull any punches. Trey actually broke down and cried!"

"No way!"

"Way! He was all up in his feelings. He finally told us his father is an alcoholic. After his mother died of breast cancer, his dad began drinking all the time. He's abusive when he is drunk—physically and mentally. Nothing Trey does is good enough. His dad also compares him to his older brother, Tyler, the all-state running back who received the football scholarship to State. So, Trey is really insecure and feels like he must be the best at everything to please his dad. If he can't be the best, he tries to tear down the ones who are better."

The revelation amazed Spence. He reviewed everything he knew about Trey to see if it made sense. "Why does he pick on me so much?"

"He didn't say specifically. I'm guessing because you're smarter and have a relatively normal family life. And you're OK with not being a jock."

"And you and Caleb?"

"Well, Caleb is obvious. He doesn't need the approval of others and is brave. He has no self-doubt, and Trey is filled with it. I'm not sure about me—probably just because I don't try to fit in with the popular kids and don't take any crap from him. I think he fears people who are different from him, and we're all three very different."

They walked in silence for several minutes. "I guess that makes sense," Spence finally said. "Although, I still think people have a choice in life. Not all poor people are thieves or druggies or murderers. Trey doesn't have to take his issues out on others."

"Yeah, true. But you do hear that many kids raised in abusive homes also abuse their kids or spouses. Trey doesn't have kids or a spouse, so he takes it out on his peers. But it does make me feel a little pity for him," Morgan replied. "You never know what people go through behind closed doors."

"True dat. I guess we'll see if Trey tries to improve since he's opened up."

"It seems like he *is* trying."

After several glances from Caleb and Trey, Spence and Morgan quickened their pace and caught them. "Where are we going?" Spence asked Caleb.

"Good question. For some reason, I'm just assuming we should head west. The river is to the east, and we just came from the south. So, we only have two choices. It looks thicker to the north too." Caleb said. "Oh, and here's your tarp."

Spence stuffed the tarp into his pack, as well as his coat. The others had removed theirs, and the day would be warm enough not to need them. He then turned to the left and saw the trees did appear thicker in that direction. The branches stretched lower, making visibility much less than east and west. The forest was lighter now, with occasional bright spots on the ground. They weren't precisely rays of the sun but just the more radiant glow of the sky fighting its way through occasional gaps in the thick branches above.

An hour or so later, the trees in front of them suddenly opened into a pine-needle-covered clearing. The area was at least a thirty-yard circle and the only completely open space they had encountered since entering the Forbidden Forest. The clearing was devoid of tree stumps or evidence of trees ever standing there. Bushes grew thick on both sides of the clearing and stretched out of sight in each direction. It would take a lot of effort to hack through or find a route around the clearing.

"This is strange," Caleb commented.

"I wonder if it's an elven meeting area?" Spence asked.

"I'm not sure. There are no seats or signs of foot traffic," Caleb replied. He scanned up in the surrounding trees. The tree branches mostly covered the sky despite the distance between tree trunks. Only a small circle of bright light was visible directly above the clearing. The light was as close to seeing the sun as they had come in Nibiru, although it still couldn't entirely penetrate the clouds. "This looks like a trap, though. Keep your eyes open."

Spence scanned the ground for trip wires and ropes—standard traps in *Warcraft*. But the land was flat and smooth with pine needles. The surrounding trees also appeared unaltered. The clearing was definitely out of place, though. He began to think they should just go around it despite the time and effort it would take.

They were close to the middle of the clearing when the trap sprung. The ground simply fell away beneath the party. Spence inadvertently yelled and grabbed his staff with both hands instead of flailing wildly. His body was shifting backward, and he braced to land on his butt and back. The others emitted various sounds of dismay, with Morgan screaming the loudest. The pine needles swirled around them, adding to the chaos and confusion.

CHAPTER 25

The fall was a quick one, however, and the landing soft. Spence dropped onto a springy surface that at first felt like a trampoline. He bounced up and down each time one of the others landed nearby—except his body didn't leave the surface. He was stuck to it from head to toe. The only body part free was his right arm, which was folded across his chest, grasping the staff in his right hand. It only took a moment to recognize the surface.

"It's a spiderweb!" Morgan shouted the obvious.

A giant spiderweb was terrifying enough—but not even being able to look around made it worse. Spence also realized his staff was useless here even if he had full range of motion. "Can any of you move or get to your weapons?"

Spence heard some grunting and felt a slight shaking of the web. "My hands and arms are stuck to the web. I can't get any leverage to pull them free," Trey said.

"Same here," Caleb added.

"Stuck fast," Morgan said.

Spence was the only one who could move at all. He also suspected the spider that had spun the giant web would be there at any moment. He said a silent prayer, fought to control his panic, and forced his mind to think. He had been in similar situations in *Warcraft*, which usually resulted in his party wiping a time or two. This was real, though, and the party couldn't wipe. He had to be brave. He had to be the hero without using his staff.

Spence carefully released the staff with his right hand, still clinging to it with his left, and slowly slid his hand toward his side. He knew he couldn't let any part of his arm touch the web, or it would be stuck. He moved his hand gingerly along his robe and down to his belt. Finally, he felt the cool metal of his dagger hilt. He carefully removed it from its sheath as he debated where to cut first. He needed to be able to see. He raised his arm and lowered his hand until the blade was beside his face, and he began sawing around his head with the dagger. He was relieved the blade could cut the web and not get stuck too.

In a moment, his head was free. He raised it and surveyed the scene. They had just fallen twenty feet onto the web, which appeared almost like a white fiberglass floor. It formed a circle, matching the opening above, and funneled down to a huge hole in the middle. Morgan lay the closest to him, only a few feet away; Caleb and Trey were on the other side of her. Movement caught his eye in the darkness beneath the hole at the web's bottom.

He sawed at the web around what he could reach of his right shoulder and side. Then he rolled hard to the left, breaking the remaining strands on that side of his torso. He then cut around his left shoulder, arm, and side. His torso fell back beyond where the web had been, hanging in the space, but his lower body was still held fast. He managed to cling to his staff with his left hand. He strained and finally rose, like doing a sit-up. He paused to sneak a peek at the hole. He saw a massive, dark shape just beneath it with two large red orbs visible.

"What's going on?" Caleb asked. "Are you free, Spence?"

"Working on it." Spence debated on how to proceed. If he just cut his legs free, he would fall through the web. He couldn't determine what lay beneath or how far the fall might be. Then he had an idea. He reached behind him, jerked the pack from his back, and laid it on his legs. The web coated the outside of it, and he had to use his dagger to cut the strands so he could reach inside. He pulled out the tarp and flung it out behind him, holding one edge and letting it spread out onto the web. It covered the hole where his torso had fallen through and stretched over to Morgan on one side. He tossed his staff onto it.

He peered into his pack and spotted one of the vials of white liquid. He had no idea what the liquid did, but now was the time to use it if it was magic. He pulled the cork out and turned the vial up. He managed to swallow the thick, bitter liquid without gagging. He tossed his pack on the tarp behind him and began cutting the web around his hips and legs. He slid back on the tarp as he freed sections of his legs until his entire body was entirely clear of the web and safely on the tarp.

The monster that emerged through the hole was even more terrifying than just a giant spider. The lower half of the body was that of an arachnid. The upper portion was the torso of a praying mantis. Six spider legs touched the web, and the upper two, those of a praying mantis, extended out in front of its body. The monster was the size of a grizzly bear, and its legs were twice the length of the body. The creature moved slowly, turning its triangular head, with its two huge red eyes, to survey its prey.

A spider mantis! Spence hated spiders, but praying mantises had always terrified him. He remembered growing up when Andrew had captured one and fed it grasshoppers. The praying mantis would grasp their bodies with spiked front legs and then rip their heads off. It then quickly devoured the head and then the remainder of the body. His brother's friend caught one too, and they placed the two together in a cage. The two fought to the death, with the winner brutally dismembering and eating the other. Spence had always thought how terrifying a praying mantis would be if it were giant. And now, he faced a giant one combined with a spider.

Spence froze for a moment, and his heart beat wildly. But then he began feeling something else. The fear quickly melted away, and he suddenly experienced a rush of energy and strength course through his body. He crawled over to Morgan and cut her left arm free.

"Grab your dagger and cut yourself loose. Move onto the tarp so you don't fall through the web." Spence felt alive in a way he never had before. He stood on the tarp. The spider mantis's entire body was on the web, and it moved steadily toward Trey, the closest to it. It tentatively touched Trey's feet with its two long, barbed front legs.

"Get off me!" Trey roared.

The creature withdrew its legs momentarily and then moved its entire body closer. Spence could imagine it quickly ripping Trey's head off and devouring it. He waved his arms and jumped up and down. "Hey, Shelob!" Despite it being a grotesque mutation of a spider, he still couldn't help but think of the giant spider from *The Lord of the Rings*, "I'm free of your little web! Come get some." He realized his newfound energy and courage must have come from the potion.

The spider mantis sensed the vibrations on the web and skirted around Trey and Caleb. It moved purposely toward Spence in case he sought to escape. Spence glanced down and saw Morgan was mostly onto the tarp and finishing freeing her legs. She was skilled with a dagger.

The potion also made Spence's mind razor-sharp. He had no doubt or hesitation. He slipped off his cloak and tossed it on the tarp beside Morgan. "Place this on the web as a walkway to Trey and Caleb. Free their hands so they can start cutting themselves loose. Then you can shoot some arrows into the monster."

Spence didn't wait to see if Morgan followed his instructions. The spider mantis was ten feet away, or a front leg's length. He flipped his dagger around and grasped it by the blade. Somehow, he now knew how to throw a dagger. His mind communicated to his arm and hand exactly how hard to throw it and how to spin it so it would strike and stick into the beast's face. He let the dagger fly. It rotated several times and struck the spider mantis in the middle of its large head. The monster hesitated a moment and then continued toward Spence.

Spence bent over, grabbed his staff, and stood just in time to jab the orb toward the spider mantis. It reached its long front legs out and tried to knock the staff away. The barbs on the underside of the legs resembled curved daggers. The tips were sharp and long enough to stab through him. If the monster grasped him firmly with those legs, it was over. Spence used his newly gained strength and swung the staff side to side, striking each leg. After a moment, the beast retreated out of the range of the staff. It paused and stared at its prey with its unblinking eyes.

Spence realized its plan just in time. He crouched and pointed his staff straight above him. Then the spider mantis leaped. Its massive girth flew high into the air and then descended onto Spence. Its two front legs stuck him, nearly knocking him down. Somehow, he avoided impalement. He held his ground, though, and jabbed his staff up to meet the creature's underside right before it landed on him. The orb and top of the staff penetrated its abdomen, just below the praying mantis portion of the body. Still, the mass of the beast bore down on Spence, knocking him to his back on the tarp. The spider mantis pushed itself up on its long rear legs, extending Spence's arms that still clung to the staff. Then it managed to lower its head toward Spence's face while keeping its torso elevated so Spence couldn't drive the staff any deeper.

The compound eyes glowed evilly, and the two antennae on top of its head twitched. The mandibles surrounding its mouth eagerly worked back and forth, and its mouth opened and closed. Its pointed front legs reached out toward the sides of Spence's head, and its mouth emitted a steady hissing sound. Spence had to release his staff and move his hands in front of his face. He would have to try to defend himself with his bare hands.

Spence's mind was still perfectly clear and unclouded by fear or panic. His brain calmly analyzed the situation and searched for possible solutions. Time seemed to flow slower, and he was in control, not the spider mantis. A flash of silver caught his eye. He noticed his dagger handle protruding from between the eyes. The legs grasped the sides of his head now, and its mandibles were only a foot away. The hissing blocked out any other sounds around him. He extended his hand with blinding speed, grasped the dagger hilt, and jerked it free, barely avoiding the mandibles in the process.

He deftly slashed both legs, deeply cutting one and nearly severing the other. The hissing stopped, and the spider mantis pulled its head away. It raised its injured legs and poised them to impale Spence with the sharp tips. Then he heard a dull thunk followed by another. Two arrows protruded from the side of the monster's head. The spider mantis lifted its weight off Spence and twisted its head to face the new source of pain.

Instead of sliding out from beneath the spider mantis, Spence slid further beneath it. *Surprise!* He plunged his dagger into the top of the creature's abdomen, below his staff, and sliced halfway down it. The spider mantis recoiled, and Spence just managed to grab his staff with his left hand as it leaped back, sending blood and entrails spraying onto Spence and the tarp. It landed ten feet away, swaying weakly on the web. Two more arrows struck its eyes. The spider mantis collapsed, drawing its legs close to its body. It didn't move again.

CHAPTER 26

Thank you, God, for the potion. Spence sat up and turned to his right. Morgan stood on Spence's cloak and had another arrow nocked. Behind her, Caleb and Trey were still cutting themselves free from the web. "Never mind, guys. We've got it." Spence couldn't resist a dig. He wiped his dagger on the tarp, sheathed it, and stood. "When you get free, walk on my cloak over here. We must find a way out. There might be more of those beasts down there."

Morgan arrived first. Caleb freed himself next and crawled onto the cloak. He then stood and walked over to them. Trey arrived a minute later.

"Dang, that was a freaky monster! Like giant spiders aren't scary enough." Morgan reached inside her tunic and brought out her phone. She snapped a picture of the dead spider mantis. "Shoot, I can't get over to it for a selfie."

Trey pulled out his phone and looked down at it. "Damn it! Battery dead." He slid it back into his front pocket. Spence quickly checked his phone and ascertained it was also dead. Caleb just glared at all three of them.

Trey turned to Spence. "What in the heck got into you? You were like a freakin' superhero."

"Yeah, ole Spence was flexin' all up on that beast!" Morgan said.

Spence considered lying about the potion, but they would know something had to explain his newfound prowess. "I drank a white potion. It did give me strength, but the main thing is what it did to my mind. I can pretty much remember everything I've ever seen and read. I remembered all the fight scenes from movies, TV, and books, and my body just knew what to do without thinking. It's like in the movie *Limitless*."

"Damn, why do you get all the good stuff?" Trey asked.

"Because I'm a wuss without it," he said without argument.

"How are we going to get out of here?" Caleb asked, looking at the opening above.

The effects of the potion were already wearing off. Spence's mind became a little cloudier, and mundane fears and doubts started returning. He had to figure out how they could escape before the effects were totally gone. The opening was twenty feet above them. The sides were dirt with some roots sticking out here and there, but not enough to climb up with. He scanned around them and only saw the tarp, cloak, spider mantis, and web. Then he noticed something else move beneath the opening at the bottom of the funnel. "Guys, there's more."

The three turned and saw the movement Spence stared at. There was more than one shape but smaller than the dead spider mantis. "And, of course, it has babies," Caleb said.

"Caleb, take your rope out. Tie your dagger to the end of it and then cut loose a patch of web with your sword and wrap the top few feet of the rope with it. Then throw the dagger out of the opening. The web should stick to the ground, and we can climb out." The idea came to Spence in a flash. "Morgan, keep an eye on the spider mantises. Trey, can I use your back to activate my staff?"

Caleb went to work preparing the rope as Spence had instructed. Morgan walked to the edge of the tarp and nocked an arrow. Trey turned his back to Spence, and Spence struck the butt of his staff on the middle of Trey's breastplate. Trey had to step forward but didn't lose his balance. The staff activated, and the orb lit the sinkhole. At least half a dozen spider mantises gathered at the web entrance. The first one was just crawling through the opening.

Spence considered using the fireball, but it could set the entire web on fire. He didn't want to experiment with the button he hadn't tried yet. So, he chose lightning bolt. "Brace yourselves. This will be loud." He leveled the staff at the head of the first monster and pressed the button. *Fryin' time.* The staff recoiled and unleashed the bolt of lightning. The bolt struck the lead spider mantis and continued to spread to the ones behind it. A loud burst of thunder followed the loud crackle and sizzle. The entire web vibrated violently. Caleb was already on his knees, but the other three fell onto the canvas. Trey's leg slid off the edge, instantly sticking to the web.

"Nailed it," Spence said. As the last effects of the potion wore off, fatigue rushed in. He was suddenly exhausted, mentally and physically.

"Hey, I can use that," Caleb said and used his sword to cut and peel the web away from Trey's leg and wrap it around the rope.

Caleb coated the first four feet of the rope thickly with web strands until it resembled cotton candy. He then stood and began swinging the dagger over his head like a cowboy roping a calf. He let out more slack and then let the rope fly toward the edge of the opening. The dagger sailed high above the rim and disappeared. He pulled on the rope and slid several feet of it back until it stopped moving. "I'm not sure about this."

"If we can just get one of us up, then they can tie the rope to a tree to support the rest of us," Spence said.

"Then we should go with the lightest first. Morgan, you feel like climbing?" Caleb asked.

"Oh, great. It's tenth-grade gym class all over again."

"Except without Coach Perv," Trey said.

"Oh, don't remind me. I think he liked the boys better, though. OK. But catch me if I fall." Morgan slung her bow on her back and walked over to the thick rope. Her gloves provided a firm grip and protection for her hands. She reached up and grabbed the rope with both hands and tugged experimentally. The rope held. She pulled herself up and wrapped her legs and feet around the rope. She then began inching her way up, pulling with her arms and gripping with her knees and feet.

Spence cut his cloak free of the web and stuffed it into his pack. Morgan was only a foot from the surface when the rope began slipping, and she started sliding back. She removed her right hand off the rope and reached out and grabbed the lip of the hole. Morgan teetered momentarily but then slowly began moving again. She eventually managed to pull herself over the edge and out of sight. A few minutes later, she yelled for the next one to come up.

Caleb went next, having little trouble with the rope. Trey took a little longer, but his strength made up for his size. Spence stared dubiously at the rope. The potion had worn entirely off, and he faced the reality of his actual physical prowess or lack thereof. He remembered the rope climb in tenth grade. He had made it six feet and then clung there for five minutes before sliding back down, burning his hands and the insides of his thighs in the process. He hadn't gotten appreciatively stronger since then, had gained a few pounds, and the battle had drained him.

"Guys, you'll have to pull me up," he said weakly. He dreaded the response.

"Hold on tight," Caleb called down.

Spence looped the rope around his staff a few times and held tight with both hands. "OK." He then wrapped his legs and feet around the rope. The rope began moving, and he was slowly pulled to the edge. At the top, Trey and Caleb reached down and hauled him up. He received no teasing, comments, or even sneers. Maybe he had finally earned some respect. They helped him to his feet, and then Caleb pulled up the remainder of the rope. He cut off the web-covered end Morgan had tied to a nearby tree, returned the coil to his pack, and sheathed his dagger.

"Oh crap!" Caleb said.

***

"So much for your pets," Odin said.

"I am a little surprised they didn't slay any of them," Artemis replied. "The praying mantis modification greatly increased the creatures' ferocity and lethality."

"I think you gave the party too much power," Odin interjected.

"No more than any other group," Artemis said. "Besides, the weapons are nothing without the questors having the courage and wisdom to properly wield them."

"True. They *are* special," Ra said.

"You have chosen well, Artemis," said Enki. "I think they are too young and naïve to give in to fear and despair as the other groups have."

"But unless one heeds our call, they still have to make their way through the dwarves and the Draconians," Odin replied.

"We only need one," Enki replied.

CHAPTER 27

They were surrounded by beings appearing roughly human. They were tall, with broad shoulders tapering down to skinny, short, bowed legs. Their arms were muscular and unusually long, hands probably hanging nearly to their knees if extended. Their faces were pale, with high cheekbones, broad noses, and large ears. They all had dark hair and eyes, and most had varying degrees of thick facial hair. They appeared to be half-human and half-ape.

Many held drawn bows and others raised spears. At least a dozen were on the ground surrounding them, and that many or more were in the tree limbs overhead. They wore brown leather clothing, with shirts of leather armor. Their feet were bare, exposing long, hairy feet with long toes.

An exceptionally tall one approached them. He wore a green cloak over the brown leather and had a green circlet of leaves around his head. The four teens moved close together, facing away from each other. They kept their hands on their weapons. Caleb met the apparent leader.

"You must be the next group of questers," the humanoid said. He didn't hold a weapon.

"And you must be the elves."

"And you just slew the spiders?" he asked, ignoring Caleb's comment.

"Spiders? If you're referring to the evil mutations in the web, then yes. We fell into their web and either had to kill them or be their food. Were they your pets?"

"They guarded the edge of the Forbidden Forest. We let them be, and, for the most part, they did not bother us. A pity, but an impressive feat. No questers have survived them."

"So, no questers have made it this far?" Spence asked, looking over his shoulder at the speaker.

"I did not say that. The others were wise enough to avoid the clearing."

"Burn," Morgan said, also risking a look at the speaker.

"We're supposed to seek out Illexya in Sabekha," Caleb said.

"We will take you to Illexya."

"And who are you?" Caleb prodded.

"Seker. I am the captain of the forest patrol." Seker waved his hand, and the elves lowered their spears and released their bowstrings.

"What do you patrol against?"

"You ask too many questions. Follow me and try to keep up." Seker turned and began walking in the direction they were heading before they encountered the spider mantis lair. The elves in the trees swung and leaped from limb to limb overhead. The others flanked them on the ground in a wide circle.

"I loved *Planet of the Apes*," Trey whispered.

Spence was still exhausted. The potion wearing off made him even more tired than he would have been without it. It was probably only early afternoon, but it felt much later. He wanted to eat a good, hot meal and sleep. At least they were seemingly safe, though, surrounded by the elves. The elves looked like a genetic mutation of the gods, like the monsters they'd faced, and not naturally occurring beings. "I don't think they're taking us to Rivendale," he whispered, referring to the elven realm in *The Lord of the Rings*. Trey actually chuckled. Spence was surprised he understood the reference.

The pine forest soon transitioned to hardwoods. The spider mantis pit was close to the boundary. The pines must not have been officially part of the Forbidden Forest. The elves scurried up and down the trees effortlessly. They just reached up, grabbed a low-hanging branch, and swung onto it in one smooth motion. Spence couldn't count how many were around. Leaves covered the hardwoods, like the middle of summer, which was strange considering the bleak, winter-looking Barrens they had trudged through from Argos.

The woods were much brighter than the pine forest. The forest floor had a few bushes here and there but was mostly clear except for leaves and fallen branches. The tree branches overhead joined together, forming a mostly solid canopy.

The elves had their own language and exchanged short barks and grunts, like gorillas communicating in the zoo. Seker didn't speak to them anymore, and they decided not to bother him. Spence hoped Illexya would be more like Titus.

They began spotting more elves on the ground and in the trees as they walked deeper into the Forbidden Forest. They also heard more barks and grunts. Spence noted that although they weren't the elves of Tolkien, they did move effortlessly and could quickly blend into the woods. He also didn't doubt they knew how to use the bows and spears. If they had any of the strength of the apes they appeared to be mixed with, they would be very formidable. He recalled his conversation with Enki. The Nephilim were big and strong but seemed disorganized and not overly aggressive. He doubted they would provide much of a fight. Taking the Forbidden Forest would be tough, although he hadn't seen the Draconians yet. Then he realized he was daydreaming and tried to refocus on the current situation.

They eventually arrived at a cluster of massive trees, appearing out of place with the rest of the forest. They were as large as redwoods but were hardwood and not pine. A dozen or so grew close together. Seker halted the small entourage at the largest tree and turned to face them. "If you build a town on the ground, it is both easy to find and hard to defend. We chose a different option." He turned, looked up, and made a few barks and hand gestures.

Spence followed his gaze up the massive tree and high above saw the underside of wooden platforms encircling the trunk. He studied the surrounding trees and spotted similar structures. A moment later, a rope ladder came tumbling down the trunk in front of them. The top end disappeared through an opening in the platform some one hundred feet above.

"Elves do not need the ropes. We use them when we have guests. Follow me," Seker grabbed the ladder and began scampering up.

"Whoa! Wait a second! I don't know if we can all climb that," Caleb said.

Spence was proud Caleb considered him but also embarrassed. Despite it being a long way to the top, the rope ladder would be easier than an actual hanging rope.

"I will have some of my elves follow. No one will fall." Seker continued climbing.

Caleb went first, followed by Morgan and then Trey. Spence stared dubiously up the ladder. He slid his staff beneath the straps on his backpack and then grabbed each rope tightly and placed a foot on the first rung. The ladder seemed a little more stable than he thought it would be, probably because of all the weight on it above him. Then he wondered how much weight it would hold. An elf behind him grunted. He shook his head and began climbing.

His arms were weak and legs shaky, but he slowly and steadily scaled the ladder. He didn't look down and just pretended he was climbing a regular metal ladder, as he had many times at his house. He didn't let himself think that those ladders were only eight or ten feet tall, not one hundred. But after what seemed like an hour, he finally crawled through the square opening, and Trey and Caleb hauled him to his feet.

Spence quickly stepped away from the opening. The platform was twenty feet wide and curved around the tree like a deck. A waist-high rail was attached to posts along the edge. Despite the rail, Spence's stomach fluttered at the distance to the forest floor below. He never realized he had a fear of heights, but he had also never been one hundred feet high on a wooden platform in a tree.

Tree limbs stretched out in all directions beneath the platform, meeting with branches from the neighboring trees. Spence glanced up and saw the network of limbs continued until they blurred into the green canopy. Other wooden platforms and structures were both around the trunk and scattered on the larger limbs. Ropes stretched in random patterns from rail to rail and limb to limb. Elves swung and climbed in every direction he turned, adding to the sense of vertigo.

"Welcome to Sabekha, home of the elves," Seker spoke.

"Tell me we don't have to climb any of those ropes," Spence stammered. He couldn't. He wouldn't.

"They are much quicker, but I realize you humans are not as…adept. There is another way." Seker walked past Spence to the trunk. A narrow wooden ramp spiraled up the tree to the next platform above them, resembling a spiral staircase except with no stairs. Spence had no idea how it was crafted. It appeared to be one smooth board, somehow attached to the tree and curved around it, and at the same time gradually elevating the entire way up. It had a raised lip on the outside edge, providing the sole protection from an accidental step off the side.

"How far do we have to go?" Spence asked wearily. The ramp didn't look much better than the ropes. He wanted to throw up.

"Only two levels. There we will find Illexya." Seker began ascending the ramp with ease.

"Sounds easy enough," Trey said, walking past Spence and onto the ramp.

Morgan walked over to Spence. "Come on; you can do it. This is a lot easier than killing spider mantises and climbing ropes. Just hug the tree and don't look down." She followed Trey.

"I'll be right behind you," Caleb said, standing beside him.

The climb wasn't quite as bad as Spence thought since it started at the platform. He kept one shoulder, arm, and hand against the tree, stuck his staff's end inside the lip, and used it as a hiking stick. He occasionally paused and risked a glance out on the limbs to some of the other platforms and structures. They resembled children's treehouses with small platform-like porches in front of the doors—the elves' homes. He saw other, larger open platforms here and there that appeared to be gathering areas.

They passed through an opening in a second platform, which also encircled the tree. This platform was like the first, although it held a large wooden structure supported between two huge tree limbs. Seker led them past it and onto the next ramp section, and they continued climbing. Spence's legs burned, and his arms and shoulders were weak. He had officially surpassed his lifetime exercise output over the past few days.

Finally, as the last light faded from the sky, they ascended through the opening onto the third platform. This one was slightly smaller than the others but had more elf activity. Lights on poles were spaced along the rail. Spence glanced around and saw other lights gleaming all around the tree limbs and platforms. He couldn't discern what they were, but they weren't flames. They resembled light bulbs shaped similarly to the tip of his staff.

Seker led them around the side of the platform to a large wooden hut built against the tree trunk. There was a break in the railing at the platform's edge, and a walkway extended to a huge circular platform suspended on top of several thick limbs. Ropes on both sides served as railings. A large group of elves milled about the structure, which was illuminated by a light glowing in the middle resembling a fluorescent fire pit.

Seker pointed toward the opening in the hut. "Illexya is waiting." He then turned and walked back the way from which they had come.

CHAPTER 28

"Bubbly guy," Morgan said.

Spence followed Trey and Morgan into the structure, with Caleb entering last. The inside appeared more extensive than it had from the outside. The floor was soft and covered with a blanket or carpet. The surface was spongy, as if there might be leaves or pine needles underneath. Glowing bulbs attached around the walls and ceiling provided adequate lighting. Built-in shelves in the walls held various housewares. Thick pillows were strewn across the floor and were the only objects serving as furniture. It reminded Spence of the treehouse his neighbor had built growing up, except that one didn't have the lights and shelves.

An elf reclined on a pile of pillows in front of the tree trunk, which formed the rear wall. Her body was much different than the male elves. Her face and arms were hairless, and she had long black hair and dark skin. Her dark eyes rested above high, sharp cheekbones. Her nose was flatter and broader than humans, but her lips were pink and human-like. Her body also appeared much leaner and slimmer than the males. She wore a red cloak over the leather clothing beneath. "Sit." She spoke in a husky voice.

The four selected pillows around the elf and sat. Spence found it surprisingly comfortable with the soft floor and thick pillows, especially with his weariness. He studied Illexya's face and features. She seemed to have a royal air about her that demanded respect.

"The next group of questers.... I have heard about the spiders. While it saddens me a little, slaying them was an impressive feat. You are the first group to arrive with all its members intact."

"Part of our quest was to kill the spider mantises. You didn't want them slain?" Spence asked.

"We did lose an occasional elf when the creatures wandered out of their hole, but they were more of a defense from anyone entering our forest from the east than a hindrance to us."

"Then why did we have to kill them?" Spence said. He wondered if Illexya didn't know about the god's plot to remove the monsters and set the stage for a race war.

"We do not question the gods' wishes," Illexya replied.

"Have you seen a lot of groups?" Caleb asked.

"Every few months, some will pass through. But it has not been long since the last—two males and a female were all that remained. I assume they did not make it too far into the mountains if you are already here."

"Do you ever hear of what happens to them?" Spence asked.

"No. We do not interact with the dwarves or have not in years. We do not leave our forest, and they do not leave the mountains," Illexya replied. Her eyes moved to each of them, studying them in detail.

"Because of the monsters?" Caleb said.

"Yes. It is too dangerous to be worth it. There are the wastelands between the Forbidden Forest and the Desolate Peaks roamed by beasts, just as there are between the Nephilim and us. My people will escort you to the edge of the forest. Then you will be on your own."

"Can you tell us anything about what we do when we reach the mountains?" Caleb asked.

"Only that you must seek out Thordr in the dwarven town of Kaldrfell. I assume there will be a path or trail leading to their town. He will inform you of the next part."

"This is like the worst scavenger hunt ever," Morgan said.

"I will see that we fill your packs with food and water before you leave tomorrow. Now, if you will follow me, we shall feast. You may leave your gear; you will sleep here tonight."

Illexya led them out of her hut and to the large gathering across the plank. Female elves crowded the platform, holding plates of food and mugs of drink. Some stood, and others sat in small groups. There wasn't laughter or boisterous talk as there had been in Argos, but just a steady hum of conversation. Wooden tables stood at the far side of the platform, filled with trays and plates of food like a potluck dinner. Tall glass containers held a red liquid resembling wine.

Illexya led them through the crowd to the tables, greeting and speaking to many elves along the way. They each grabbed a wooden plate and loaded it with food. The fare consisted of several types of meat, vegetables, and bread. They didn't fully recognize anything, but they hadn't eaten their fill since Argos, so they piled their plates full. They each poured themselves a wooden cup full of the red liquid and then followed Illexya to one of the few areas open enough to sit.

Spence didn't realize the extent of his hunger. His body had begun adapting to the small, bland meals of meat and cheese he forced down three times a day. Now, they had hot and flavorful food. He wanted to savor the myriad of flavors, to let the food melt in his mouth. But he didn't have the willpower and shoveled it in. The others, except for Illexya, did the same.

The red liquid was a thick, sweet wine. Spence had never actually tasted wine, but this was really good. It tasted like grape juice, other than being warm and burning slightly on the way down. He drank as if he hadn't had water in days. He knew he shouldn't drink wine so fast, but again, he was weak. Several male elves made rounds through the crowd and ensured his plate and cup stayed full.

"Meat again, Morgan?" Trey asked.

"Nope."

"Why not? You loved the rabbit," Caleb said.

"Because there are other, delicious options," Morgan said, devouring another piece of bread resembling a traditional yeast roll.

"Hey, Spence, you digging all the hot elf chicks?" Trey said, grinning with his mouth full of food.

Spence studied the female elves. They all closely resembled Illexya. They were slimmer than the males and had bare faces, but they still had short legs and long arms. They were definitely more feminine than the males, but he doubted any humans would classify them as attractive. "Uh, let's just say I don't think they're my type."

"You all are pigs," Morgan said, glaring at both of them.

Spence quickly turned to Illexya before Trey or Morgan could speak again. "So, Illexya, I've noticed most of the elves on this level are female, and most of the ones in the forest were male," Spence said. "Are the women in charge?"

Illexya eyed him for a moment, then laughed. "Well, I have been the ruler of the elves for some time. But that does not mean the females rule the males. I prefer the companionship of the females, and they inhabit more of the upper levels of Sabekha. The males stick more to the lower levels and also patrol the forest. It just occurred naturally over time." She paused for a moment to sip some wine. "I suppose once my rule is over, the next leader could have different ideas."

"I personally love it," Morgan chimed in, grinning. "Keep them boys out of our tree. Can you make my companions go down a level or two?"

Illexya turned to Morgan and returned the smile. "Not tonight. You will all sleep in my hut."

They ate and drank steadily for the next half hour until they finally began to slow. Illexya had eaten leisurely and gracefully, watching the four with a slightly amused expression. She finished her first plate around the same time they had completed three or four. "Tell me of your adventures in our world," she finally said, handing his plate to one of the serving elves.

Spence's stomach was stuffed to bursting, and his head had begun to swim. He felt good, though. The wine had even more effect than the ale had in Argos. He also felt talkative. He started narrating all the details since they had entered this world. He left out the part of the cave by the river, though, and everything Titus had told them. He also didn't reveal his encounter with Enki, of course. Caleb scowled at him several times as if he were saying too much, but Spence ignored him. He didn't reveal anything he considered a secret.

"Very impressive," Illexya spoke when Spence finally finished with them killing the spider mantises. "As I said earlier, you have fared better than the others."

"Tell us about your god, Artemis," Morgan said suddenly with a slight slur. Her cheeks were red from the wine.

Illexya stared at Morgan for a moment, with a flash of anger almost too quick to perceive. Her face then resumed its normal, stoic expression. "She is a good goddess and provides for my people. She created the Forbidden Forest and us–she is the goddess of the wilderness and hunt. If we obey her, she keeps us safe. She also keeps the other races away from us."

"Is that good?" Morgan asked.

"Is what good?"

"That the races are all separate. Why couldn't you all just intermingle and live in peace?"

Illexya clenched her teeth together for only a second. "It is not for us to decide. It is the business of the gods. But we do not trust the other races. We believe we have the best life here in the Forbidden Forest. The Nephilim live in the unprotected open plains; the dwarves in the harsh, rugged mountains; and the Draconians in the hot swamp. They would all probably love to live in our safe, temperate forest."

"So, even if the monsters are removed, you would just stay here?" Caleb asked.

"Most likely. We have everything we need."

Spence watched Morgan intently, surprised that she asked about Artemis. She had shown little interest in the gods until now. What if Artemis had spoken to her, just as Enki had to him? It might make sense since she was female and ruled the elves. And Artemis was the goddess of the hunt and usually illustrated with a bow. *That must be it—the elves might be her future followers.* He would have to watch her closely.

"Does she visit you?" Morgan continued.

"We see her occasionally. She can appear and disappear at any time. But mostly, she speaks to us in our dreams." Illexya studied Morgan intently.

"What does she look like?" Morgan asked.

"She wears a green tunic, embroidered with gold, that comes to her knees and a golden crown with a half-moon symbol. Her hair is golden, and her body is muscular."

"And what does she tell you?" Morgan pressed.

"She can tell us the future or give us tasks to do. But we never speak to each other regarding what she chooses to enlighten us with." Illexya suddenly stood. "I know you are exhausted, and I can see the wine is thick in your veins. It is time to go and sleep. Your quest resumes tomorrow." She walked through the slightly diminished crowd of elves who acted a little happier and livelier since they had eaten and indulged heavily in the wine. She didn't look back to see if they followed.

CHAPTER 29

The four slowly stood, all swaying to some degree, and followed Illexya across the plank and into her hut. Spence entered last and shut the wooden door behind him.

"I assume it's safe to remove our armor?" Trey asked.

"Of course. You could not be anywhere safer than here," Illexya replied.

Trey and Caleb removed their armor, and all four of them stripped down to only their Earth clothes. "Ah, it will feel so good not to sleep in that soup can," Trey said. Caleb nodded in agreement.

Once they had made beds out of the pillows, Illexya touched each of the crystals, extinguishing the light and immersing the room into total darkness. Spence had hoped to stay awake and talk with the other three, but he didn't feel comfortable with Illexya there. Then the exhaustion overcame him. He settled into the thick carpet and pillows, and their warmth instantly enveloped him. He fell asleep before he could even fight against it.

Spence didn't remember dreaming. He just awoke when a hand shook his shoulder. He opened his eyes but saw only darkness. He was groggy, and the room felt like it was moving. He tried to swallow to wet his dry throat and struggled to remember his location. It didn't feel like the forest floor or anywhere outside. Then he slowly recalled the trees and the platforms. He began to speak, but a hand covered his mouth. The hand was soft and feminine.

The hand was removed, and he was pulled to his feet. Someone led him forward toward the tree trunk, with him nearly tripping over some of the pillows strewn across the floor in the process. After a few seconds,

Spence was confused—they should be at the tree trunk by now. The hut was only so big.

The hands released him, and he heard a sound like a cabinet door shutting. Spence blinked several times as light suddenly blinded him, and then he peered through squinted eyes. Morgan stood in front of him, with Trey and Caleb sitting on each side in seats carved out of the inside of the tree. Illexya sat straight ahead, a glowing light mounted above her. They were inside the trunk of the enormous tree. "What—"

"Please, be seated, quickly," Illexya whispered.

Spence sat in a carved seat beside Caleb, and Morgan sat on the other side beside Trey. The space was small, and they were packed tightly together. The others looked half-asleep and half in shock. None of them dared to speak.

"I brought you here because I do not think the gods can hear or see us. As you probably know, or the Nephilim told you, the gods see and hear almost everything in this world." Illexya paused long enough to indicate she expected a response.

"Titus…told us some things," Morgan said. Caleb glared at her from across the small room.

"Did he take to you to a protected place?"

"Yes. A cave by the river," Morgan continued.

"Tell me what he said," Illexya said, her voice forceful.

Morgan glanced at Caleb and then Spence. Spence wasn't sure if Morgan should tell him everything. But if Illexya went to the trouble of bringing them to this secret room, she was most likely trustworthy. Spence nodded at her. His eyes met Trey's, but he couldn't read Trey's serious face.

Morgan recounted the conversation in the cave with Titus. She also included the story of Seth in the tavern. Illexya nodded slowly as she spoke.

"Titus is wise for a Nephilim. The gods are indeed real, and they created the world and everything in it. Look at my people and me. We are unlike you and the Nephilim. We are not…natural. We are like Nephilim mixed with beasts. Like the Nephilim, we cannot reproduce. We die, and others appear. Our number stays at one thousand."

"Why?" Caleb spoke this time.

"Why what?"

"What is the point of the gods creating this world and the races?"

Illexya's eyes trailed off Caleb, and she stared at the floor, the inside of the tree trunk, which was ancient judging by the number of rings. "We have all wondered that. We thought it was simply to serve them. But lately…lately there is something else."

"What do you mean?" Caleb continued.

"I did not exactly tell the entire truth when I said we do not speak of our visions of Artemis. Some of us occasionally meet here, only for a few minutes, in the middle of the night like this. Artemis has spoken to some regarding dark clouds coming. And a war…a war between the races."

"Has he spoken to you about this?" Spence suddenly asked, a little more anxious than he meant to sound.

Illexya stared at Spence as if debating how much to reveal. "Just that there will be an outsider, a leader, who will lead the elves. And one day, we will rule this world. He said I needed to be ready and that I would be important to this leader."

A chill raced down Spence's spine, and he nearly gasped aloud. He glanced at Morgan. She stared at Illexya with wide eyes and mouth slightly open. He was sure his face was similar to hers. Trey leaned forward in his seat, looking intently at Illexya, but his face didn't indicate the shock Morgan's did. Again, he was unreadable.

"Is this the reason for the forest patrol?" Morgan asked.

"Yes. We have to be watchful," Illexya replied.

"Do you think the leader might be a quester? Or one of us, even?" Spence hesitantly asked. He didn't want to draw any attention to himself or his secret knowledge.

"It would seem to reason. There are no other outsiders. Have any of you spoken to Artemis?"

Cold sweat joined the chills coursing down Spence's spine. He turned to Morgan, and she briefly met his eyes and then lowered hers. Trey still stared at Illexya, and Caleb remained silent. Spence wasn't going to dare say anything. He wondered if one of the others would reveal if the gods had contacted them.

The elf's gaze traveled from one face to the next. Each ended up looking down or away after meeting Illexya's eyes. "Then perhaps it will be another quester. We had better end this meeting. Just remember, the gods are always watching and listening. And learn what you can from the other races. Something is afoot. There might be more to your quest than meets the eye. Now, leave and return to your beds. I will wake you in the morning."

Morgan stood and grabbed the small knob on the back of the door, and Illexya touched the light to return them to utter blackness. They carefully navigated through the small doorway and felt their way to their beds. Illexya emerged last and closed the door behind her.

Spence's mind wanted to race, to comprehend the ramifications of what Illexya had revealed. But his fatigue and sleepiness returned. He fell fast asleep and didn't wake until the morning.

CHAPTER 30

They slept past daybreak. Spence awoke to see Trey and Caleb already up and moving. Morgan was just starting to stir.

"Where are our packs?" Trey asked, kicking loose pillows around the room.

Caleb was likewise searching. "Looks like our host stole them."

Spence sat up and was relieved to see his staff still beside him. The others had their weapons, too—only packs and pouches were missing. He stood but didn't join the others in the search. Morgan rose too, awakened by the voices. "I'm sure she didn't steal them," Spence said.

The door opened before the others could respond, and Illexya stood in the doorway, silhouetted in the morning light. "Breakfast is ready. We are stocking your packs with good food and drink, not the scraps the Nephilim gave you. Please dress and follow me."

The four dressed into armor and adventuring garb and trailed Illexya. She led them again across the plank and to the circular platform. The tables were loaded with breakfast foods: scrambled eggs from animals that probably weren't chickens, something like hash brown casserole, meat resembling venison, some type of orange fruit, and pitchers of a liquid that was either ale or apple cider.

Other elves were eating, mostly female again, but fewer were present than the night before. The four piled their plates full and followed their host to a clear seating area. Despite the feast last night, they were still hungry this morning. Spence couldn't officially recognize anything he ate, but it all tasted delicious. The elves definitely cooked better than the Nephilim. The liquid did taste like a thick apple cider. He didn't think it contained alcohol, but he couldn't be sure. Surprisingly, he didn't feel hung over from the night before. He actually felt better than he had since entering Nibiru. His legs, feet, and shoulders were barely sore, which was surprising considering the long climb up the tree. He was getting accustomed to the walking, carrying the pack, and the battles. It felt like he had been in the Forbidden Forest for a week instead of only two days.

They didn't speak much during the meal. When they finished, four elves approached and handed them their bags, stuffed full of supplies. "You will have plenty of food to last you until you reach the dwarves. You should be going, though, to take advantage of the daylight. You should reach the Desolate Peaks by dusk tomorrow, assuming you…make good speed. Spence, we managed to clean the web off your cloak, and we gave both you and Caleb new tarps."

Spence knew what Illexya had almost let slip—assuming the next monster didn't eat them. The four stood and situated the packs onto their backs and belts. They had brought their weapons with them from Illexya's hut.

"Morgan, here are more arrows. You will find ours much more exquisitely crafted than the crude sticks of the Nephilim." Illexya handed her a handful of black, shiny arrows.

"Thank you, Illexya," Morgan said, and she placed the arrows in her quiver. "Would there be a place around here where we could bathe? It's been close a week since any of us have showered, and I think we're all a little ripe."

"Ah, forgive me. My people do not worry about such things. A few miles from here, a small stream will cross the trail. Follow it north, and you will find a large pool of water that should be suitable."

"Is there a shortcut down?" Trey asked.

"Oh, there are many, depending on how brave you are. Follow me."

They followed Illexya off the back of the platform and across another long plank. It ended at a smaller square platform. A rope tied to a thick limb overhead stretched down at a forty-five-degree angle until it disappeared between the limbs and wooden structures. The section of the railing was missing beneath the rope. On a rail on the far side of the platform hung at least a dozen thick sticks, polished slick and bent like boomerangs. Illexya lifted one of them off the rail and handed it to Trey. "Place this over the rope and hold tight."

Trey carefully examined the piece of wood. He glanced up at the rope and then peered down its length. He then turned to Illexya. "I'll be going one hundred miles per hour by the time I smash into the ground."

Illexya gave an ever-so-slight smile. "I am not sure how fast that is, but you will not die unless you let go too soon. We elves do not mind climbing, but sometimes we take the easy way down. You will also be heading in the correct direction. I would have Seker lead you out, but you will be safe until you leave the woods. Simply follow the trail west. Good luck, questers."

Caleb grabbed one of the pieces of wood and tested it by trying to break it in his hands. He shrugged after a moment. "I'll go first." He placed the piece of the wood over the rope and grabbed it tightly with both hands. "You only live once." He lifted his legs and began sliding. At first, he moved slowly, but his speed increased once he cleared the platform. He let out a whoop and shot downward like riding a zip line.

"Well, I'm going next. If Caleb splats at the bottom, at least he'll break my fall." Trey followed Caleb's lead and was soon rushing down the line. He, too, bellowed loudly. Various elves paused to watch from the platforms and limbs he passed.

"This whole adventure is like Disneyland in hell for fat geeks," Spence said to Morgan.

Morgan laughed. She reached out and rubbed his head. "You've graduated from being a fat geek. You're doing just fine, Spence."

It felt like the hairs on his head stood beneath her soft touch. "I think you're coming along well too, sis." He tried to rub her head, but she pulled away.

"But you're still last!" She placed her handle over the rope and screamed, "YOLO!" as she plunged over the side.

Spence didn't want to zip line hundreds of feet to the ground, which wasn't even visible. But he also didn't want to walk back down the ramps and climb down the rope ladder. He ensured his staff was secure under the straps on his pack and then cautiously placed one side of a wooden handle over the rope. He wiped his free hand on his pants, grasped the handle with it, and then wiped the other hand. He grabbed the other end tightly and slowly raised his legs.

The handle slid slowly at first, at a speed Spence could tolerate. Then once he cleared the edge of the platform, the rope dipped. He felt like he was traveling as fast as riding the Tower of Doom. Tree limbs, leaves, platforms, and huts zoomed past. The rope bounced up and down occasionally, threatening to loosen his grip. He screamed, but not the fun scream of the others; he screamed because he was going to die.

He tried closing his eyes, but not knowing what was coming was even worse than seeing it. He opened them again and just prayed for it to be over. He could barely make out the blurs of elf faces staring at him from the platforms and limbs he rushed past. Eventually, he cleared the last tree limbs and could see the ground below. He screamed again as it rushed up to meet him. Then, when his legs were a few feet from impact, the rope angled up and significantly reduced his speed and leveled his descent. He saw the rope tied to a tree limb straight ahead. The others stood in front of him.

"Drop and run," Caleb yelled.

Spence didn't like the idea, but the thought of rising farther away from the ground was worse. He reluctantly let go of the handle and dropped to the ground. The drop was only two feet, and his speed was manageable. He hit the ground and ran to match the speed of his slide. He slowed and stopped just as he reached the others.

"Nice landing!" Morgan said, rubbing his head again.

"Never thought I'd see it," Trey said.

"See what?" Spence asked.

"Flying nerds."

Spence's euphoria and exhilaration from both the ride and surviving it began to wane. Had the old Trey returned? He glared at him.

Trey suddenly smiled and playfully slapped his arm. "Just kidding, bud. You did good."

Spence sighed in relief and then smiled. "You're a flying turd," he said and laughed.

Trey stared at him for a moment and began to reply. Then he smiled, followed by shaking his head and laughing. Soon Morgan followed. Even Caleb chuckled and shook his head. They had been under so much stress for the past few days and would be soon again. It just felt good to enjoy some lighthearted fun. It felt good to be teenagers again, even if only for a few minutes.

CHAPTER 31

Spence dug his cloak out of his pack and put it on, more for show than the cool air. Random rays of light fought their way through the canopy, the beams appearing solid in the damp air. The forest consisted of mostly mature hardwood trees, though not nearly as large as the ones the elves lived in. The ground was level and the walking easy. The woods were still, with only the noises of water droplets plopping onto the ground from leaves high above and the sporadic rustling of forest creatures scurrying across the forest floor. Occasionally, they heard a sound in one tree or another and even caught a rare glimpse of movement that wasn't a small animal. They knew the sounds were from elves, either keeping a watchful eye on them or merely watching in voyeuristic curiosity.

"Morgan, I'm surprised you're not staying here. I mean a goddess, a female leader, and the women seemingly ruling the men," Trey said.

"Don't tempt me. I'd have all the boy elves sleeping on the ground. And the girls would rule from the biatch tree."

They all four laughed. Spence was always amazed at how Morgan could handle Trey, from joking along with him one time to getting in his face and giving it back to him another. Then he thought about his theory that Artemis had contacted Morgan to champion the elves. Had Trey been smart enough to make his statement to judge her reaction?

"I need a cigarette," Morgan said after the laughter had stopped.

Caleb laughed. "We're walking in a pristine, ancient forest on a beautiful morning, as far away as we could be from modern civilization, and this makes you want to smoke?"

"When did you hear me say I'm not screwed up?" She laughed. "I don't know. Mornings like this remind me of September mornings after school starts back from the summer. When I was little, my dad used to walk Jade and me to the school bus stop. He'd always be puffing on a Marlboro, with the smoke hanging around our heads in the thick, damp air. God, I loved that smell of fresh smoke. Of course, when I was older, and he no longer walked us, me and Jade would take a quick puff on a stolen cigarette before the bus arrived."

"And you continue to this day in the school parking lot, huddled with the Goths behind bus fifty-six," Trey added.

"Sounds like we need another hiding place," Morgan said, but not giving Trey her usual dagger gaze. "I suppose it just reminds me of a happier, more innocent time when we were a closer family."

"A nasty habit—especially from someone who wants to save the earth from the evils of mankind," Caleb said, this time not smiling.

"We all have our vices," Morgan said. She brushed a spiderweb out of her hair. "Besides, it wouldn't be fair if I were too perfect. What about you, Survivor Man? Tell us something about you."

"Like what?"

"Like, what do you do that reminds you of your childhood? Or what vice do you have? You're a survivalist, right? I'm sure there is something you do or some habit you have that doesn't fit in with wanting to live alone in the wilderness surviving off the land."

Caleb grunted but didn't respond.

"Look, we're trapped in some type of make-believe world, fighting monsters and swinging in trees with elves. We've all saved each other's lives and will again. There's a fairly good chance one or all of us will be buried here. I seriously doubt that we are returning to high school and our cliques. I think it's time we tear down some walls," Morgan said.

Spence was pleasantly surprised with the exchange. He thought Morgan might have been the last to open up. But she was as emotional and animated as he had seen her. They had been going full speed, like at the start of a James Bond movie, since they had arrived. Now, for the first time, they had time to breathe. Illexya had also assured them they would be safe for at least a day or two. Their stomachs and packs were full, the day was beautiful, and the mood was as light as it had ever been.

"Beer for me," Trey said.

"Are you ordering one or what?" Morgan asked.

Trey chuckled. "My vice and what makes me think of childhood. It's kind of ironic. As I told you, my dad is an alcoholic. He's an angry drunk too. I can't count the times he's beaten the shit out of me with one hand while holding his beer in the other; the son-of-a-bitch never spills a drop, either."

"So, beer is a *good* memory?" Spence asked.

"Not those memories. But when I was a kid, my dad was my little league football coach every year. He wasn't as bad back then, when Mom was still around, and Tyler was home. Sure, he still drank, but he kept it under control. But when I smell beer, I think about when we'd sit on our front porch after a practice or game. He'd always drink a beer or three, and we'd talk about football—little league, high school, college, pro." Trey paused for a moment, and his eyes turned ever so glassy. "He was a tough coach and father, but every now and then, while he sipped on an Old Milwaukee, he'd give me a compliment or two and talk about my future. When I turned twelve, he'd even give me a little sip occasionally."

"I'm guessing all that changed after your…mom…." Morgan said softly.

"Yeah. A lot changed."

"What did Tyler end up doing?" Spence asked.

"He blew his knee out his junior year at State and ended up dropping out. He went to truck driving school and is now an over-the-road truck driver. We don't see him often."

"OK. Caleb, Trey stalled for you. You're up, big boy," Morgan said, shattering the awkward pause after Trey's revelation.

"I can't believe I'm sharing anything with you band of misfits." Caleb turned and gave a slight, crooked grin. "Prepping is my biggest love…and my biggest hate. My father began prepping after 9/11. Of course, I was too young to remember when it began. He was convinced the terrorists would hit us with nukes, taking out the power grid. If not the terrorists, then China, Russia, or North Korea would take it down with a cyberattack or an EMP. Once the grid was down for a couple of weeks, the country would spiral into irreversible chaos. If we didn't kill ourselves, Russia or China would take over. Either way, we had to learn how to survive off the grid."

"That sounds a little crazy," Spence said hesitantly.

"Crazy? Really? How long does it take for looting to start after a hurricane or tornado? Hours. Every grocery store and Wal-Mart would be empty in a week without power. Sure, the police, military, and National Guard would try to keep order. But what about when their families run out of food and water or the neighbors are threatening them? Once the authorities leave their posts, it's on. People revert to savages very easily when it comes down to survival. You can argue the premise of the grid going down but not what would happen after."

Spence had never thought about it, but Caleb made a lot of sense. He nodded for Caleb to continue.

"Well, when I was old enough to participate, my dad became even more obsessed with prepping. He spent every free moment buying and storing supplies and building an underground bomb shelter and numerous bug-out hideouts, including the cabin in Asheville. And we constantly trained with weapons and practiced hand-to-hand combat. He tried to make my mom participate. She did, but as little as possible. She never said it, but I could tell she thought we were crazy.

"When I was twelve, my dad and I went on a camping trip in the desert. We used to go on survival outings that would make Bear Grylls, the king of survival, cry. I mean, a pocketknife and piece of flint and two days in the desert? Well, when we returned, Mom was gone. She left a note that Dad read and promptly shredded. He never told me what it said. He just said she didn't want to be with us anymore." Caleb's eyes turned glassy now. He paused for several seconds.

"I knew the prepping made her leave. I used to wonder if she'd come back if we stopped. Or if I stopped, would she return for me and take me with her. But she never came back to give me the option."

"She never contacted you again?" Morgan asked.

"I get a card in the mail every year for my birthday and one for Christmas. There's no return address. She usually writes a line or two and says she loves me and hopes to see me again someday soon. She sends a pic at Christmas. That's all. So, Dad and I keep prepping for doomsday. But the longer we go without it coming, the more I wonder about my mom and how things might have been different. So, prepping is both my love and hate."

"Did your mom get remarried, or do you know?" Morgan asked.

"Oh, yeah, a year or two after she left. And I have a four-year-old stepsister, Abigail, or Abby as Mom calls her, who I've never met. She always looks adorable in the Christmas pictures, though."

Spence was amazed at the revelations coming out today. He realized this was really the first time they had gotten to talk without drama or conflict. Since Trey had seemed to mellow, the tension had eased. "My turn?"

"You're up," Morgan said.

"I don't have a good story like you guys. I have a mom and dad, who I assume love me. They never really took an interest in me until my wreck, though. I heard all the stories from Kayla and Andrew of all the fun things they did growing up. But once they graduated and left the house, it felt like my parents forgot they had one more to raise—like they were too old and tired to be concerned with me. I used to beg my dad to go out and play with me—riding bikes, shooting basketball, throwing a baseball, hiking…anything. But he was busy with his job, yard work, or just too tired. Mom was always grading papers and making lesson plans.

"There weren't any kids my age in our neighborhood. When I was twelve, Dad bought me an Xbox. He never played it with me, though, so I taught myself how to play. I discovered a whole online community of kids to play games with. My parents weren't shy about spending money, so they gave me any game I wanted, as long as I was quiet and didn't bother them.

"After my accident, my parents became a lot more attentive, like they felt guilty or something. But I just immersed myself into online role-playing games, mainly *Warcraft*. I suddenly had *friends* and found something at which I was rather good. No one knows what I look like or that I'm crippled, and I can play characters that not only can walk but are superhuman. So, computer games are my biggest love and hate. I love them because they're all I have, but I hate them because I'd like to have so much more."

"Did you ever try to play sports?" Trey asked.

Spence swallowed hard. "Yeah, I begged to play Little League, every sport, like Andrew and Kayla did. But my parents said I'd get hurt, that I was different from my brother and sister. I guess because I was pudgy, weak, and uncoordinated. They also didn't have time to run me to practices and watch games. And I didn't have any kids to play with outside in the neighborhood. So, by the time I got to high school, I was overweight, socially awkward, and friendless. And of course, it only got worse after my accident."

"Jesus, could Nibiru have picked a better quartet of screwed-up misfits?" Morgan asked.

Spence laughed with the rest of them. It helped to prevent tears from appearing in his eyes.

"Maybe that's what they wanted. Maybe the gods have a sick, sadistic sense of humor," Caleb said.

"Yet it seems we've made it further than any other group," Trey replied.

"I guess the moral of the story is, don't screw with crazy," Morgan said.

"OK. Team, bring it in." Trey stopped walking and pulled the four into a tight circle. "Hands in the middle. Crazy on three." Trey stuck his hand into the middle of the circle. Caleb placed his on top, then Morgan and Spence. "One…two…three…crazy!" They all four shouted the word *crazy* loudly and threw their hands high into the air.

"Hey, guys, does this mean we're a squad now?" Spence asked.

171

Trey laughed. "Well, Spence, I reckon it does. In this world, we're now the Earth Squad."

CHAPTER 32

They walked along in silence for the next hour. Spence noticed all four of them soon returned to good spirits despite the earlier conversation regarding their messed-up lives. He thought getting everything out in the open was cathartic. For the first time in Nibiru, the quest actually felt like an adventure—like being in Narnia or Middle-earth or Azeroth, the *Warcraft* world. He was a little nervous about how long it would stay that way, though. He didn't know whether one of them would ruin the peace or if it would be the gods and their creations.

"It's strange how far away Earth feels. We've only been here for a week, and now this feels normal." Spence broke the silence.

"Yeah, the body and mind do adapt quickly. I guess it's how soldiers deal with being in combat or prisoners of war for years," Caleb said.

"I used to have nightmares about being away from the Internet during a power outage. Yet somehow, I'm not detoxing," Morgan added.

"I wonder if we'll ever see home again?" Spence asked, a little more somber.

"I would have bet a lot of money against it when we first saw wolfy and during each battle. But somehow, we keep surviving. The question is, even if we complete the quest, will the gods honor the bargain and let us go?" Trey replied.

"Hey, there's the stream!" Caleb exclaimed.

Spence spotted the small clear stream cutting its way through the woods and crossing the trail in front of them. They all rushed off the path and headed up the incline to their left. The vegetation was thick and green on both sides of the water. When they crested the top of the hill, they saw the pond. The pond was small, around thirty feet in diameter, and nestled bowl-like in the surrounding ground. The front side was open, but bushes surrounded the back. The water was murky but had a bluish tint, not brown or green like most of the ponds he had seen on Earth.

"Oh my God! A bath!" Morgan squealed and sprinted past the others toward the water.

Spence hurried behind her, flanked by Caleb and Trey. They all instinctively headed for the bushes to disrobe.

"No peeking, boys," Morgan said from a nearby clump of vegetation.

Spence tried avoiding looking in her direction, although he saw her flinging clothes out of the corner of his eyes. Then thoughts of seeing Morgan naked were replaced by the dread of getting naked in front of her. "I say we all run and jump in the pond at the same time," he said as he shed his clothing.

"On three. One…two…three!" Caleb counted.

All four pushed through the scrub and charged toward the water. Spence leaped as far as he could and then pulled up his legs like doing a cannonball in the town pool. The others made similar splashing entries. The water was cold but so refreshing. His feet contacted the bottom, which was smooth and soft. He realized they hadn't considered the depth or what might be in the pond, but at this point, he didn't care.

"Oh, wow!" Morgan said. "This feels so good!"

"That's what she said," Spence said, again speaking before thinking.

Caleb and Trey roared with laughter. "Damn, Spence, you go, boy," Trey said. He even reached out and gave Spence a high five. Caleb slapped him on the back of his right shoulder.

Spence laughed too and enjoyed the reaction of Caleb and Trey. He suddenly felt like one of the guys.

Then Morgan turned to stare at him, her mouth hanging open. "I cannot believe you just said that!"

Spence's heart skipped a couple of beats at the possibility he had offended Morgan. He began to apologize when she shoved him playfully. "But actually, pretty darn funny."

Spence breathed a huge sigh of relief and splashed water at Morgan. Then the four of them had an all-out splash fight for several minutes. Finally, they separated and did some actual bathing.

"This seriously does feel like the best bath ever, even without soap and shampoo," Spence said after approaching Morgan again.

"I know, right?" Morgan replied. She submerged beneath the surface and appeared a few seconds later, rubbing her face and hair. "I never thought I would go this long without a bath."

"I'd say our funk will destroy this pond for the elves," Caleb said.

Spence remembered the elves they had caught glimpses of following them through the forest. Did they watch now? He scanned the trees but didn't see any movement. Oh, well. He was enjoying the water too much to care. He ducked under the surface and rubbed his hair as if shampooing it in the shower.

"We could play Marco Polo," Trey said, swimming over to the group.

"Umm, you boys knock yourselves out. I'll be over here not touching or getting touched by any of you," Morgan said.

"So, does that mean the lesbo rumors are true? Are you gay like your sister?"

Morgan glared at Trey. "You're an idiot! First, leave my sister out of this. Second, what if I am? Third, seeing or touching your body would definitely drive me to it if I weren't."

"Oh, snap," Spence said, laughing. Spence had tensed when Trey first asked the question. The morning had been good so far, but it could all change on a wrong word from any of them, especially Trey. He had heard the rumors about Morgan in school. Supposedly, she'd been spotted kissing a girl at some big party, which, of course, he hadn't been invited to. And she wasn't known to have dated any guys. Her older sister was a confirmed lesbian too. But only Trey would come out and ask. Her answer did little to clear up the mystery, though.

Trey only laughed and swam off in the other direction. The four swam, frolicked, and bathed for some time. Spence did his best to avoid catching glimpses of Morgan's olive, bare skin and tried not to stare at the tops of her breasts. He did notice her black lipstick and eye makeup were gone. They had been fading and disappearing in places but now had vanished entirely. The transformation, although minor, was amazing. She appeared younger and much more innocent. Her lips were pink and full not covered in black, and her brown eyes were more noticeable. Her hair spread out and floated about her shoulders.

Spence swam over to Morgan when he caught her away from the other two. "I probably shouldn't say this, but I like your non-Goth look."

Morgan stared at him for a moment as if preparing a stinging rebuke, but then her face softened. "The war paint is gone?"

"Yep."

"I guess that's good. Somehow, it didn't feel right here. Besides, I think I stand out enough, don't you?"

"Definitely! No other hot chicks in Nibiru." The words left Spence's mouth before he could stop them. He cringed as he waited on a response.

"Aww, thank you, Spencey. Hey, it looks like you're changing too. This quest has buffed you up some."

Spence peered down at his exposed upper torso. His body *had* already begun changing. The lack of food, hiking, climbing, and fighting monsters, had taken a good toll. His belly was flatter, and his arms and chest were more defined. He knew his legs were firmer and more muscular. He wasn't big and buff like Trey or chiseled like Caleb, but he was better than the old Spence. "Gettin' swole." He laughed. "I wonder if that is in the brochure?"

Morgan laughed loudly. "I think your personality is blossoming too."

"Hey, all my online friends think I'm hilarious. You guys have just been missing out on all this."

"Looks like it."

Morgan stared into his eyes for several seconds, instantly making him uncomfortable. The verbal exchange had been good, and he had made her laugh, so he needed to go out on a high note. "Race you to the other side!" He turned and began splashing hard, not seeing if she followed.

They played in the water for another half an hour before agreeing to run to their clothes simultaneously. They used their coats, which they hadn't had to wear in the forest, to dry and then dressed. Soon they once again looked the part of fantasy questers.

"Now, if we only had deodorant, perfume, and cologne," Morgan said.

Spence glanced at Morgan and noticed that all her piercings were gone except for a diamond stud in each ear. She must have removed them while drying and dressing. She turned toward him, and their eyes met. He smiled, nodded, and gave a thumbs-up. She returned the smile and then turned away to place her bow and quiver across her back.

"Hey, look, Morgan is de-Gothed," Trey said.

"Wow, you look like a different person," Caleb said, noticing for the first time. "In a good way."

"Well, you boys just keep in mind that although I might look all sweet and innocent now, I can still kick your asses," Morgan replied with the thinnest of smiles.

Spence didn't doubt it. But it would be the best butt-kicking he'd ever received.

CHAPTER 33

They followed the stream back to the trail and resumed hiking, feeling refreshed. They walked for a few hours through the seemingly endless Forbidden Forest before stopping for lunch in the middle of a cluster of four oak trees. The elves had done well packing their bags, and they ate a combination of meats, cheese, and fruits. The elves had also replaced the tarps with thinner and lighter ones that folded up much smaller in Spence's and Caleb's packs.

"Hey, Caleb," Spence said.

"Yes?"

"Can you train me in hand-to-hand combat? I'm dead in the water when my staff is charging, at least without using my potion."

"This ought to be good," Trey said.

"Sure. Why not?" Caleb stood and walked into a large clear area outside the tree cluster. "Hands or daggers?"

"Daggers. But let's use sticks instead." Spence searched the ground until he found a stick around a foot long. Caleb found a similar one.

"OK. Let's see what you've got. I'll instruct as we go."

Spence studied Caleb, who stood still with his hands hanging by his sides. He slowly closed the gap, but Caleb still didn't move. Spence raised the hand with the stick beside his right ear—still no movement. Then he charged. He was nervous he might actually plunge his stick into Caleb's head or shoulder if Caleb didn't defend himself.

Then Caleb moved. He smoothly switched his stick to his left hand, stepped to the side, grabbed Spence's right wrist with his right hand, and spun him around to face the other direction. He placed his stick against

Spence's throat. "You're dead. You can't project your intentions so far out. Try again."

Trey and Morgan applauded and laughed. "Nailed it," Trey said.

Spence's cheeks warmed slightly. He had to learn this, but he had a lot to learn. He paced away a few steps and turned around to face Caleb. He approached cautiously, this time holding his stick in front of him. Again, Caleb stood there calmly and watched. When Spence was three feet away, he suddenly lunged forward and tried to stab the stick into Caleb's belly.

Caleb stepped to the right and grabbed Spence's wrist again. This time he pulled Spence toward him. As Spence fell off balance and tumbled forward, Caleb slapped him on the back with his stick, sending him sprawling onto the ground. Spence landed with a heavy thud. "Better. But you always have to maintain your balance. Try again."

"I bet that spider mantis feels stupid," Trey said. Morgan cackled loudly.

Spence regained his feet and shot Trey a glare. Trey might have changed some, but he was still good at hurling insults. Once again, he faced off against his adversary. Spence held his stick in front of him again and approached in the same manner. This time, instead of lunging, he jabbed his stick forward.

Caleb stepped to the side and struck Spence's stick with his. Spence managed to withdraw his stick without losing his balance. "There you go," Caleb said encouragingly.

The two circled each other and jabbed and swung their sticks. Caleb continued instructing Spence as they went. He taught Spence how to parry, sidestep, and use his free hand to punch, push, grab, and pull. Soon Spence was sweating profusely and puffing hard, while Caleb was barely winded. Spence kept going, though. Caleb was still much quicker, but Spence had come a long way by the end of the session. He couldn't get a kill shot on Caleb, but he could keep him on the defensive for a while and somewhat defend against Caleb's attacks.

They finally sat with Morgan and Trey. Spence drank deeply from his wineskin. Caleb sipped on his. Spence felt a little better now. He knew he needed more training, but he had gained some confidence. Morgan asked Caleb to train her next, and Spence lay on the ground with his head on his pack and watched the two. Morgan was surprisingly quick, and her slight frame presented a smaller target to an enemy. She could never overpower a big man, but she could carve one up pretty well with a sharp knife.

"Think you could take her?" Trey said, elbowing Spence.

"Whoever fights her better take her out fast. She could de-boy you in the blink of an eye."

"True dat."

After the impromptu training sessions, they packed and continued the journey. The afternoon was a perfect temperature, and the walking was easy. The trees were old and mature where they walked, but the forest became thicker and more tangled to the north, just as it had in the pine forest.

They all remained lighthearted and in good spirits. Spence didn't hear as many rustles in the trees as they distanced themselves from the tree city. Caleb said he thought at least one or two elves still tailed them, but he didn't know for sure. They saw an occasional deer and turkey, in addition to the squirrels.

"So, Morgan, you want to be a nurse, right?" Spence asked.

"Yeah, or possibly a doctor if I can stand college that long."

"How about you, Caleb? Any plans after high school? Or just prepping?"

"I don't know. My dad has always been convinced the world as we know it would be over by now. I've never really thought much about what I'd do if it didn't end. Prepping doesn't pay the bills."

"Well, what do you like besides the outdoors?"

"Nothing. Well, I wouldn't mind being a forest or park ranger. Then I could be outside and still train and prep for something bad."

"That's a good idea," Spence said. "What about you, Trey?"

Trey flexed his left bicep and kissed it. "This body was built for two things. One of them is football."

"Oh, God!" Morgan exclaimed, rolling her eyes.

"Oh, and that would be what the ladies say about the other thing," Trey replied.

Morgan bent over and made a loud retching sound.

"And that would be the next thing the ladies say," Caleb said.

Spence and Morgan erupted in laughter. Caleb's personality was also starting to show. He had a dry sense of humor and a surprisingly sharp wit. Trey only scowled at all three of them.

"So, you're going to play football, and then what?" Spence continued.

"Well, if my NFL dream doesn't work out, possibly physical therapy. Then I could be a football team trainer or strength coach. Working for a pro or college football team would be pretty sweet."

"What about you, Spence?" Morgan asked.

"Well, after my wreck, I gave up on the idea of going to college. I mean, I wouldn't be able to do it without a helper unless it was online.

But if I did go to college, I'd think about computer science. That's something I could do even paralyzed, and I've always loved computers and programming. It would be awesome to create computer games. Maybe I could make the next *Warcraft*. Or…I know, the next Nibiru! I'll call it…*Fantasy World!*"

The other three laughed. "You know, that ain't a bad idea. The game starts on Earth, and then the party is teleported to a fantasy world. They have to complete a quest to get back," Caleb said.

"Dang! We might be on to something!" Spence exclaimed.

"And we would be the gods, creating the world and the quests. Each quest would be unique, with different monsters and challenges," Morgan added. "Oh, but we're featuring some powerful women in our world."

"As long as they're scantily clad," Trey said. He grinned at Morgan's scowl and continued, "That would be a good movie or book too…or a series of books and movies. Every book would feature different people going into the fantasy world."

Caleb stopped walking, and the others halted too. Spence began to say something and then saw the look on Caleb's face. He didn't need telepathy to know they all shared the same thought simultaneously. "Holy crap," Caleb whispered, his lips barely moving.

"Do you think?" Spence asked. "Just for entertainment?"

"Why not?" Caleb replied.

"Makes a lot of sense," Morgan added.

"We'd better keep going," Spence said, looking nervously around them. They had probably said too much already.

"Yep, that's a heck of an idea. When we return to Earth, we can work together making a game and a book," Caleb said, and then he turned and continued walking. The others followed him.

***

"They are very perceptive, indeed," Artemis said.

"Yet still wrong," Odin replied.

"But should we be concerned with how much they have already deduced?" Ra asked.

"It is of no consequence. They will never construe our true intentions. They think this is merely a game. And in the end, they have no choice but to do what we need them to do. They can theorize as much as they wish," Enki said.

CHAPTER 34

The rest of the day was uneventful. Spence desperately wished they could find a safe place to discuss what they were all thinking, but the woods didn't provide any privacy. Maybe when they reached the mountains, they could find a cave to hide in. If this was just some type of entertainment, who was the audience? Just the gods? Or were they in an alien reality TV show? It would sure beat the heck out of *Survivor*. What did that mean for his visit from Enki? Would the war only be more entertainment—a war between the races? Or was their theory wrong and everything Enki had said true?

The sky was dimming when Caleb found a small clearing ringed by tall trees. They quickly worked together to set up camp and were soon sitting around the fire, talking and laughing. Since they were in the protection of the forest, they all removed their armor and weapons and relaxed in their Earth clothes. Then they enjoyed another meal of elven food. They also discovered they each had a flask of the thick, red wine they had drunk with dinner the night before.

"Well, guys, this is probably the last night we're not going to have to worry about fighting something. That deserves a drink," Caleb said.

They retrieved their bottles, uncorked them, and touched them together. "Bottoms up," Trey said.

Spence had lost all reservations about drinking alcohol. They were too young to drink, but they were also too young to fight monsters and perform quests for gods. The elven wine was much smoother than the Nephilim ale. The pleasant, warming feeling blazed a path from his mouth to his stomach. It had been a good, relaxing day, and the night was shaping up to be even more fun.

Soon they were all giggling and laughing and acting stupid. Then they decided to try a cappella karaoke. Morgan went first and sang a medley of Miley Cyrus songs, using a stick for a microphone. Only knowing half the words didn't hurt the performance; she filled the missing gaps well with her own words. The finale was an attempt at twerking that nearly sent her tumbling into the fire. Spence and Caleb guffawed loudly. Trey smiled but had a strange, intense look and seemed more focused on the drinking.

Surprisingly, Caleb went next. He sang "Friends in Low Places" by Garth Brooks. His voice was remarkably strong, and he had the country twang down. The song seemed fitting for the group of adventurers. He finished to loud applause and handed the stick microphone to Spence.

Spence had never even sung in the shower. But the wine had him feeling invincible, and Caleb and Morgan had already come out of their shells. He didn't listen to music, other than the radio in the car, and didn't even have a music-streaming account. But he made his voice as high as possible and attempted, or butchered, Selena Gomez's "The Heart Wants What It Wants."

Morgan rolled on the ground laughing until tears soaked her face. Caleb hooted, hollered, and laughed harder than they had ever heard him. Trey glared at Spence, not even cracking a smile. Spence stepped closer to Morgan and sang to her. She tried to watch but struggled through the fits of laughter and tear-filled eyes.

"His heart wants you, Morgan," Trey called out. He had finished his entire bottle of wine.

Spence turned and walked toward Trey. He leaned down and sang to him: "No, it wants you, big boy," he said in his best female voice. This time Caleb laughed even louder than Morgan.

"Get away from me, you fucking fruit!" Trey shouted, shoving away Spence's hand that held the stick. Spence stumbled back a few steps.

"Geez, someone can't handle his liquor," Spence said—something he would have never said sober.

Trey stood, swaying slightly. "What did you say?"

"I said you need to go to bed and sleep it off." Spence saw Trey had his fists balled tightly. Caleb and Morgan had stopped laughing.

"First, you try to hit on me, and now you try to tell me what to do? I think you've forgotten your place." Trey walked a few paces toward Spence.

"Trey, don't do this," Caleb said, also standing.

"Shut up and mind your own business, Rambo. Me and Spence are just going to practice hand-to-hand combat." Trey slurred his words slightly.

Spence considered retreating further, but he felt good enough not to fear Trey. His head swam slightly, but he was also loose and relaxed. Plus, now he knew some fighting techniques. Spence placed his left foot in front of his right and braced himself. He still held the stick in his left hand. He had hoped Trey had changed for good, but now he had reverted to the old Trey. The alcohol had awoken the beast.

"So, Mr. Mighty Wizard. Who was it? Fart Wind?" Trey shoved Spence in the chest, sending him backpedaling a few steps. "You think you're all bad since you helped kill a couple of monsters. And now you're a freakin' comedian singing your little gay song, trying to make me look gay too." Trey closed the distance between them again. "I think you need to return to being a scared little girl."

Spence saw the punch coming and stepped to the right. He swung the stick down and struck Trey hard with the pretend microphone in the forearm. Trey grunted as he staggered past, nearly falling to the ground. He whirled around, wobbling for a second, and charged back toward him.

Spence ducked the next swing and jabbed the stick into Trey's stomach. The end of the stick was blunt, so it didn't penetrate, but it caused Trey to double over and gasp for air. Spence guessed it left its mark. He didn't want to fight Trey but knew Trey would keep coming if he didn't. Just as Trey began to straighten up, Spence hit him with an uppercut with his right hand. The blow caught Trey in the chin and sent him staggering backward.

Trey caught himself from falling once again. His eyes were wild with rage. "I'm going to kill you, you sniveling little piece of shit!"

Spence braced himself again. Then he heard a loud crack, and a piece of wood went flying past him. Trey's eyes rolled up into his head, and he collapsed face-first onto the ground. Morgan stood behind where Trey had stood, holding the other half of the tree branch.

"Nighty night, little girl," Morgan said.

Caleb walked over to Spence and stared down at Trey. "Dang, I hope you all didn't kill him." He knelt beside Trey and placed his fingers on his neck.

"Wouldn't be a great loss," Morgan replied.

"He's alive," Caleb said, standing. "It's just the alcohol. It must make him like his dad."

"Or just brings out the real Trey," Spence said. He grinned at Morgan, who returned it and dropped the branch.

"Let's tie him up so he can sleep it off and not try anything else tonight," Caleb said. He walked over to his pack and cut a length of rope into two pieces. They rolled Trey over and hog-tied his feet and hands. "By the way, Spence, nice fighting."

"Well, looks like the party's over," Morgan said. "That's another reason he deserved a blow to the head."

The three left Trey where he lay and returned to the makeshift shelter. "Do you think we need to set watch tonight?" Spence asked.

"Hopefully, Illexya spoke the truth when she said we would be safe. I think we can chance it and all try to get a good night's sleep," Caleb replied.

The night was comfortable, so they weren't concerned with the fire burning out. Spence lay wide awake for a while. As he listened to Trey start snoring, he experienced a mixture of emotions. He was proud of how he had fought and stood up to Trey. However, it might have turned out differently if Trey had been sober. But still, he had come a long way. Even though it had only been a week, Spence had transformed. In addition to not being paralyzed, he was stronger, mentally and physically. Spence wasn't completely fearless, but he also wasn't afraid of everything. He had faced death several times now and had done things he had never dreamed he could. He was no longer the insecure, nerdy wimp he had been on Earth. He had grown.

He wondered about Trey. He had thought Trey had changed since he rejoined them in the pine forest. But after a bottle of wine, he returned to the old Trey, or even worse. Who was the real Trey? Could he trust him again? He knew alcohol changed some people, and some were mean drunks. But in others, it just brought out their true selves, like a truth serum.

He thought of Enki and his offer. Earlier, when they were all sharing and bonding, he had mostly forgotten his encounter with the Draconian god. He had been committed to the quest and his friends—his squad. Now, he wasn't so sure. He figured the gods had contacted the others by now too. They sure acted guilty when Illexya asked them. Could they all be having the same thoughts? He finally drifted off to sleep, the wine subduing his racing mind.

CHAPTER 35

"What the hell?"

At Trey's angry yell, Spence slowly opened his eyes. As usual, it took a moment for him to recall where he had fallen asleep. He pushed up onto his elbows and saw the woods were lightening with the predawn glow. He caught a glimpse of movement outside the shelter. Then he remembered Trey, all tied up. He was finally stirring from his unconsciousness.

"Why am I tied up?

Spence slowly stood, followed by Caleb and then Morgan. The three walked to where Trey lay on the ground, trying to pull his hands free of the ropes.

"What happened? Damn, my head hurts!"

"You got drunk and then tried to assault Spence. He and Morgan beat the crap out of you and knocked you out. I tied you up so you wouldn't try to cause any more trouble," Caleb said.

Trey's eyes moved from Caleb's face to Spence's and then Morgan's. "Really? Oh, I'm sorry, Spence. It was just the wine. Can someone untie me?"

Spence stared at Trey and tried to determine his degree of sincerity. He did seem like he meant it, but Spence still wasn't sure. Either way, he could never trust him. Caleb bent over and untied Trey's hands and feet. Trey sat up and laid his head on his arms, which he had folded over his knees.

"Who hit me in the back of the head? And with what?"

"Oh, that was me," Morgan chirped. "And it was a big ole tree branch. Broke it in half on that melon."

"Gee, thanks," Trey said, giving her a sideways glance. "And I thought the only head injuries I had to worry about were in football." Trey slowly stood, rubbing his head. He then lifted his shirt and revealed a red circle surrounded by a deep purple bruise. He looked up at Spence. "Your work?"

"My microphone," Spence said with a slight smile.

"Damn. I guess I must have deserved it, though. I'll have to watch the drinking. I should know better after having my father beat the shit out of me once a week for most of my life."

The four ate a quick breakfast, packed, and donned armor and weapons. Soon they headed west again. The day was gloomier since the forest didn't have the same glow as the day before, and the air was also cooler.

"What is the deal with the sun here? I mean, we haven't even seen it yet," Spence said, longing for a warm ray of sunlight to touch his skin.

"Maybe it's winter in this world," Morgan replied.

"We should reach the Desolate Peaks before dark. That means we probably get to fight something again. Back to the new, real-world," Caleb said.

Spence noticed everyone was more subdued today. He didn't know if it was dread over having to fight some unknown monster again, the incident with Trey, or something else. He guessed a little of each. He tried envisioning what the next adversary might be. They had faced a huge wolfosaurus, a giant robotic Cyclops, and enormous spider mantises. Then he remembered the type of monsters typically inhabiting mountains in books and games. Surely they didn't have to face a dragon! But he wasn't so sure. They hadn't encountered anything flying yet, so why not a dragon? *Great.*

They walked for several hours without speaking. The woods had begun thinning around them, and the trees weren't as mature. They also noticed more large boulders and slabs of rock. They no longer heard any rustling in the trees. Caleb said he didn't think they had escorts or watchers today.

"Guys, what if we have to fight a dragon next?" Spence finally asked.

The others were silent for a moment. "A week ago, that would have sounded crazy. Now, it kind of makes sense," Caleb said.

"Our weapons aren't going to help us much. I'm not sure if my lightning bolt or fireball would do much against it, even if I could hit a fast-moving target," Spence said.

"What about my arrows? I probably could hit it if it were close enough," Morgan said.

"Unless it's like Smaug from *The Hobbit* and has a weak spot in the scales over its heart, they will be useless too."

"It's hard to plan a strategy if we don't know what we're facing and the terrain," Caleb said.

"Well, we know it will be mountainous. Judging by these boulders, I'm picturing rocky. So, it will probably be fairly open, hopefully with some cover and hiding places," Spence said.

"But if it's fire-breathing, we'll be screwed regardless," Caleb said.

"Do you think the gods could create a fire-breathing dragon?" Morgan asked.

"In this messed-up world, who knows? Spence, how do we kill a dragon?"

"Well, in most games, it takes magic. All our weapons seem to be magical or at least special. But you and Trey can't do much damage from the ground. We need to figure out a way to get it to land."

They spent the next two hours strategizing as they walked. They discussed different scenarios for different terrains and whether the dragon could breathe fire or had any other special attacks. Spence thought it might all be for naught if they didn't even face a dragon. But it was a good sign that they were at least trying to plan. And some of the strategies could work for any foe. Caleb had a quick mind and thought like a general in the military. Spence knew it was from the training with his father. Caleb also said they watched a lot of the History Channel, and he loved military history. That was good for the quest, but Spence also thought Caleb might be more of a threat than he had first believed in accepting a god's proposal to lead a race into battle. Caleb could probably do it better than any of them if he wanted to. Spence's mind was almost as sharp at high-level strategy but not as good with the minute details.

The land became hillier and rockier as the day wore on, and the trees thinned further. The air also continued to chill as they gradually left the confines of the forest and its protective canopy. The day was indeed more overcast, with the clouds appearing to threaten rain, or snow if it cooled enough.

The hills soon transitioned into one huge slope, with the high side to the west. They had emerged from the Forbidden Forest halfway up the incline. The boulders transitioned to larger rock formations, and stones littered most of the ground, from pebbles up to the size of basketballs. Ahead they saw the land stretched into tall, rocky peaks, and the trees all but disappeared save for a few stunted pines. The range of mountains resembled sharp, jagged teeth.

"Guys, we'd better be looking for a place to camp. There might not be many good areas once we get further into the mountains. Maybe we can find a cave or at least a good alcove and have time to gather some wood before dark," Caleb said.

The four fanned out and began searching for shelter. The light was rapidly fading, although Spence couldn't tell whether the sun had set yet or if the clouds were just thickening.

"There might be some shelter at the base of that rock formation," Caleb said, nodding to their left.

Spence followed his gaze to a vast collection of boulders, some thirty feet tall. The face of the largest slab of rock sloped outward from the ground, leaving a natural shelter at its base. They could completely enclose themselves if they could somehow fasten the tarp to the rock face and then to the ground. They were also still close enough to the trees to gather firewood quickly.

They all began heading that way…until they froze in their tracks. A high-pitched shriek rang out from somewhere up above. It sounded like an eagle, only much louder.

"Gee, wouldn't you know I'd be right for a change," Spence said.

The four turned until they located the source of the screech. The monster approached swiftly from directly behind. It looked more like a pterodactyl than a dragon. Its wings resembled a bat's and were at least twenty feet long. Its body was skinny, almost bony, and was around thirty feet long, with a tail stretching another twenty. It had large, muscular hind legs and short, stubby front ones, all tipped with long, curved claws. A long thin neck led to a narrow head with big nostrils and wide-set almond-shaped eyes. Ridges of bone ran up both sides of its nose and over the top of its head, appearing like horns. A pair of sharp, bony ridges, resembling curved teeth, ran down the neck, back, and tail. Overlapping, roughly octagonal scales covered the entire body.

"Get down!" Caleb yelled.

CHAPTER 36

The dragon swooped down like a hawk after a rabbit. They all dropped to their stomachs as the beast dove low and stretched its forelimbs down, attempting to rake or grasp one of them. The dragon missed, but the wind from its powerful wings stirred pebbles and dirt. It shrieked again, so close that Spence's ears rang, and then it flapped its wings harder and soared high into the air.

The four scrambled to their feet and drew their weapons. The dragon quit flapping high above and slowly rotated its body to face them again. It hovered for a moment, sailing like a vulture on a warm current. "Head to the trees! Morgan, see what you can do to slow it down. Spence, get your staff ready. Trey, you know what to do!" Caleb shouted.

Trey pulled his ax off his back, turned, and sprinted toward the sparse line of trees, some one hundred yards behind them. Caleb, Morgan, and Spence slowly retreated behind him. Morgan pulled her bowstring to the corner of her mouth and aimed an arrow at the soaring dragon. Spence struck the butt of his staff on the ground and instantly experienced the comforting surge of energy. The tip shone brightly in the rapidly vanishing daylight. Caleb held his shield before him and gripped his sword in his right hand.

The dragon suddenly stretched its wings out wide and flapped a few times, stopping its forward momentum and causing its body to rise. It opened its mouth, filled with long, sharp teeth, and screamed. Then it lowered its long neck and head and dove toward them, flapping its wings several times to gain momentum.

Morgan stopped moving long enough to let the first arrow fly. The dragon ducked its head, and the arrow flew along its back and disappeared behind it. She nocked another arrow and released it as the beast closed to fifty feet. This time she aimed for its chest. The dragon somehow managed to roll its body and pull up. The arrow appeared to graze its rear left leg but didn't penetrate. However, it disrupted the dragon's dive, and it had to sail harmlessly overhead and flap its wings to regain altitude. Morgan turned and continued jogging with the others toward the trees.

"That thing doesn't appear to be a robot," Caleb called out. "Nor does it seem magical. It looks like a dinosaur."

"Which means it can be killed with regular weapons, even though I'm sure those scales are tough to penetrate," Spence panted.

"If we can survive one more dive, we should be able to reach the trees," Caleb said.

The dragon circled overhead, beating its wings to spiral higher and higher as the three continued retreating. Spence was trying to decide when to attack and which button to use. Despite it resembling a dinosaur, it could be a magical dragon in this strange world. If so, he wasn't sure if the lightning would have much effect. And despite the fireball having a homing ability, he thought the creature, magical or not, might be able to avoid it. He still hadn't tried the third button, but he had an idea what it might do. One logical attack remained for something based on technology and not magic.

Once again, the dragon paused in midair, arched its body, screeched loudly, and entered its deadly dive. Morgan had two arrows nocked this time, with the thumb on her bow hand sticking up and bending forward to separate the tips. She waited until the dragon was thirty yards away and then released. The dragon flapped its wings and tried to pull up from the dive. The lower arrow sailed harmlessly past, but the upper arrow struck it in the middle of its stomach. The arrow found its way between two scales and half its length buried into the beast.

The dragon screeched but didn't continue climbing. It resumed its dive, although at a significantly reduced speed. Spence and Morgan dropped to the ground. Caleb crouched with his shield raised on his left forearm and his sword cocked behind his head. The dragon targeted him since he was the tallest target. The dragon's mouth opened, revealing the six-inch-long teeth. Its front legs stretched forward with the clawed toes spread wide. It tried to snap Caleb's head from his shoulders, but Caleb swung his shield up and struck it just under the chin, pushing its head upward and causing the bite to miss. Then he swung his sword into the beast's right front leg, slicing deeply into the flesh above the clawed toes. The blow also knocked the leg to the side, causing the claws to miss him.

This time, the dragon's shriek sounded different, mixed with either pain or rage. It flapped its wings and once again ascended high overhead.

Spence scrambled to his feet first. "You two run to Trey. It's my turn now. Tell Trey to get ready."

Caleb and Morgan turned and sprinted the remaining fifty yards to the trees behind them. Spence retreated another twenty yards and then stopped, watching the dragon complete its attack ritual. He gripped his staff tightly and pointed it at the beast, hovering his right forefinger over the third button and bracing himself.

The dragon changed its attack run slightly. It had apparently learned from dodging Morgan's arrows on each pass. It flew far out over the rocks and boulders and reduced its altitude considerably. Spence realized the dragon was going to come in at a much lower trajectory, which would give it more opportunity to dodge arrows and still attack. It would also make it nearly impossible for him to just drop to his belly and avoid the claws at least raking him, if not getting scooped up and carried away. His quest would be over if his new attack didn't work, or work well enough.

Despite Spence's recently discovered confidence and bravery, his legs shook. The dragon was enormous. It could probably kill him in many ways—a glancing blow from a wing, a leg, or the tail, not to mention the claws and teeth. The dragon began flapping its wings, propelling itself swiftly toward him, this time much lower in the sky. From a distance, it appeared to be coming straight at him. Spence then worried about when to unleash his attack. The failing light made it much harder to judge speed and distance. Everything had to go perfectly.

Two hundred yards…one hundred fifty…one hundred…. Spence gripped his staff even tighter and braced his shaking knees the best he could. He squeezed the third button at what he guessed to be fifty yards. *God, please let this one work!* The staff recoiled hard, sending him sprawling to the ground despite bracing for it. A sound like a sonic boom roared and instantly deafened him. He raised his head to see what had issued forth from his staff. To his horror, he saw nothing, and the dragon continued toward him, its mouth open and front talons stretched wide. Then, only twenty yards away, the dragon's entire body shuddered violently and then went limp. The beast still sailed toward him but was no longer flying.

Spence's mouth opened, but no scream issued forth. He watched in terror as the massive beast careened toward him like a crashing jetliner. First, the head passed over him, drooping down with its mouth hanging open, then the long neck, chest, front legs, and stomach, with Morgan's arrow still protruding. The arrow was so close he could have reached up

191

and plucked it out if he had wanted. Then he realized the tail wasn't going to sail harmlessly past him. He rolled to the side and kept rolling. The tail struck right beside him just as the ground shuddered from the dragon's body landing hard behind him.

Spence rolled onto this stomach and raised his head to observe the rest of the plan unfold. He still couldn't hear anything except for an intense ringing inside his head. The tallest tree in the thinned-out woods slowly began falling in his direction. The dragon had skidded another twenty yards past him, right in line with the tree. The tree toppled over and landed directly on top of the monster. Trey stood behind the newly created stump, his ax still in hand. Morgan and Caleb stood to either side of him.

Spence sat up and watched his three companions rush toward the pinned dragon. The dragon began moving again, slowly at first, and then thrashing violently beneath the tree's weight. Its tail moved the most, only restrained by the topmost and thinnest of the tree's branches. But the trunk securely pinned the dragon's head and neck beneath it. Its legs stuck out from either side, and the dragon began alternating pushing up from each side, trying to either roll the tree off or pull its body free.

Morgan stopped ten yards from the dragon's head and sent an arrow flying straight into its left eye. Trey and Caleb rushed in from either side of the trunk and began hacking at its neck. The creature opened his mouth and, Spence assumed, shrieked loudly. Trey chopped at the neck as he had at the tree trunk, sending blood spattering in all directions. Caleb alternated hacks with jabs, also covering the ground with bright red blood. Morgan shot an arrow into its other eye.

The dragon's body writhed desperately beneath the tree, and its tail broke limbs and slapped hard at the ground. But the beast was helpless to defend itself from its brutal attackers. Its mouth snapped open and closed and strained to reach an arm or weapon. Its armored hide was tough, but Caleb's and Trey's weapons were exceptionally sharp. After ten minutes, the pair had separated the dragon's neck and head from its body. Its body continued writhing and flopping like a decapitated snake. But the dragon was dead and just didn't realize it yet.

Thank you. Spence stood, brushed off his clothes, and rejoined the others. Trey and Caleb cleaned their blades on the dragon's hide, and Morgan retrieved the two arrows from its eyes. "Got to love it when a plan comes together," Spence said, grinning. His hearing was slowly returning.

"Simply having a plan makes a big difference," Caleb said, sheathing his blade.

"I just want one of those damn staffs," Trey commented, slinging his ax over his back. "How many more freakin' tricks does it do?"

"I think that's it," Spence said.

"What the heck was that one?" Trey asked.

"I'm not sure. I guess some kind of sonic shock wave."

"How do you have it make different attacks?" Trey continued.

Spence's heart skipped a few beats. He still hadn't revealed his staff contained buttons and not magic. It probably wouldn't matter, but for some reason, he didn't want the others to know, especially Trey. "A wizard can't give away all his secrets."

"We'd better make camp," Caleb said, saving Spence from further questioning. "It will be dark soon, and there might be more of those things around."

***

"Now the dragon," Ra said.

"Their working together has turned out to be a good thing. That has greatly increased the odds of at least one surviving. They only have my pet standing before them and completing the quest. Then, whether they accept the offers or not, it will be time for phase two. This group is definitely the one we have been waiting for," Enki said.

"I have another bit of good news," Odin said.

"And?" Enki replied.

"I have located the missing human."

"Did you have him eliminated?" Ra asked.

"No, not yet."

"Why not?" Artemis said.

"Our questers will do it for us," Odin replied.

"They will not kill one of their own!" Ra exclaimed.

"There are ways…."

CHAPTER 37

Caleb led the others past the dragon and fallen tree and toward the rock formation they had spotted earlier. It was dusk when they reached the boulders. Spence struck the butt of his staff on the ground and provided enough light for them to complete their camp tasks. The base of the largest rock provided a sheltered and dry space.

Caleb soon had a lean-to built against the stone and a fire blazing outside one end. The four ate in silence inside the warm shelter. The elven food was still fresh and flavorful. They drank water instead of wine this time, and they were much less lively than the night before. Once they had eaten their fill or as much as they allowed themselves, they all settled into various reclined positions on packs and gear. Trey pulled out his whetstone and sharpened the blade of his ax.

"Are you afraid of dying?" Spence asked Caleb. He often wondered what the seemingly fearless loner thought about during battles.

Caleb lay on his back with his knees bent and his head resting on his pack. "I'd rather not die…but no."

"Why not?" Spence continued.

"Why should I be?"

"Because you won't be alive, and you don't for sure know what comes after," Spence said.

"Well, the way I figure it, there will either be nothing or something. So, either I won't know I'm dead, or my spirit will still be doing something," Caleb said matter-of-factly.

"You don't believe in a heaven or hell?" Morgan asked.

"Maybe some type of heaven or eternal life…but not a hell."

"Why not a hell?" Spence said.

"Our lives are a blink in the eye of eternity. What could we do in that brief time to warrant burning and suffering forever? And what about the millions of people throughout history that were never exposed to the Bible and Christianity? Do they have to burn too? And the people raised in other religions? Shouldn't the punishment fit the crime? Other than a few exceptions, you couldn't do enough evil in fifty years of adulthood to deserve trillions of years of torture." Caleb raised his head to look at Morgan. "What about you? You don't strike me as the religious type."

Morgan sat leaning against her packs with her arms clasped around her knees. "My family is loosely Christian, I guess—we're part of the Christmas Eve and Easter morning crowd. I bounce back and forth— between atheist, agnostic, Wiccan, and spiritual."

"Where are you bouncing now?" Spence asked.

"Well, getting transported to another world, or rogue planet, ruled by four gods from our mythology kind of puts some wrinkles in the Bible story. I think I've found another category…'who the hell knows.'"

Spence and Caleb laughed. "What about you, Spence? I bet you're a good Christian boy, and you and your parents go to church every Sunday," Morgan said.

Spence scanned the faces of the other three. Caleb had returned his head to his pack. Trey sat with his back against the base of the rock and stared at the fire, still sharpening his ax head and seeming to pay scarce attention to the conversation. "Well, before my wreck, I was. My family is Catholic, and we went to church pretty much every Sunday all my life."

"And after your accident?" Morgan asked.

"I prayed hard day and night that I would be able to walk again. After a couple of months, I stopped praying and going to church. If there was a God, I hated him for doing that to me. I had already been dealt a bad enough hand."

"And now?" Morgan said.

"I'm back to being a good Catholic boy. I realized that maybe *this* is his answer. I mean, I know this is a messed-up world that makes no sense, but I can walk again."

"Nothing about this experience has shaken your faith?" Caleb asked.

Spence thought for a few seconds and shook his head. "Actually, it's probably strengthened it."

"Why?" Morgan asked.

"Because this is the first time I've faced death, and I stare it in the face pretty much daily. I don't like the thought of there being nothing after this. Or worse, I could go to hell for not believing. So, I'm believing and keeping the faith and hoping there's a heaven with golden paved streets and singing angels waiting on me. Plus, I've prayed before each battle, and we've survived, against all odds."

"I think the Bible left out the part about Nibiru. How do you explain that?" Morgan said.

Spence thought for a moment. "Well, the Bible says God created the heavens and the earth. It doesn't specify what all the *heavens* consist of. Maybe early man wasn't ready for the full scope of creation. Even the pope has said that discovering aliens wouldn't change anything. They would just be more of God's creations. So, Nibiru must just be another world he's created."

"And what if the gods here are actual gods? Then what do you do?" Morgan persisted.

Spence rubbed his hand through his hair. He wasn't sure if they should be talking openly about the Nibiru gods. Although so far, the gods of this world hadn't demanded worship. "Well, then God created them too. So, even though I will respect the gods of this world, I'll keep worshipping my God. Nothing changes as far as I'm concerned."

"What if we return to Earth, and you're paralyzed again?" Caleb asked.

Spence was silent for a moment. That was something he didn't want to think about. "I guess I'll just go on with life the best I can and have faith there is a reason for it all."

"Hmmm…. I wish I had your faith," Morgan said. "Life would probably be simpler."

"Why don't you? Just have faith, I mean?" Spence asked.

"You can't fake faith. If there were an all-powerful god, he'd know the difference. Maybe I'll get there someday. Besides, if we survive long enough, this adventure is likely to create or destroy faith in all of us anyway."

Spence had wondered if something in their quest, in Nibiru, might shake his faith. *What if the Nibiru gods are real? What if they have a different creation story than the Bible?* But as of now, he had no reason to doubt his faith or beliefs again. He would deal with faith-shaking revelations if and when he encountered them.

"What about all the other religions, Spence?" Caleb asked, continuing his prior conversation. "Are all of them wrong? If so, how do you know they're wrong and you're right? There is Islam, Buddhism, Judaism, and Hinduism, all with millions of followers. Some of them believe in reincarnation too. Maybe we all just keep living life over and over again, as different forms or people, and never even know when we die. Or at least not until we get it right and then pass on to the afterlife."

Spence inhaled deeply. He hadn't counted on getting into this deep of a religious discussion. He was a Christian, but he wasn't a Bible scholar or one to go out and preach to others. "I don't know, guys. I just have faith my religion and God are real and true. It's what I know and believe. Maybe the other religions are valid too. Or they might all be misguided and will have to answer to God when they die. But I only know what works for me. I'm not trying to convert the rest of the world."

Morgan turned to Trey. "And you, stud?"

Trey continued staring at the fire for a few seconds and then slowly turned his head to the others. "Well, we came from a screwed-up world to a seriously screwed-up world. I'd say if there's a God, he's either very hands-off or has a sadistic sense of humor. Guess that makes me agnostic, huh?"

"Sounds like it," Morgan said.

Spence watched Trey as he returned his gaze to the fire. He was different since his drunken attack the night before—different than he had ever been. Trey wasn't being obnoxious and bullying or fun-loving and happy-go-lucky. He was quiet and reserved…almost thoughtful. Maybe he was still embarrassed over last night. Or perhaps something else was going on with him. But Spence was especially wary of this Trey. At least with the other two, he knew what to expect.

"We had better take watches again," Caleb said. "This isn't the Forbidden Forest anymore. Three hours each should take us to morning. We'd better sleep in our armor with weapons nearby too."

"I'll take first," Trey called.

Spence recalled Trey talking about his staff just a few hours before and remembered the night he tried to take it from him. He wasn't too tired and thought he could stay awake during Trey's shift. Then Morgan and Caleb could watch Trey the rest of the night while Spence slept. "I'll take second," he said.

"Third," Morgan replied.

"Guess I'm last."

CHAPTER 38

The three stretched out and used packs and pouches for pillows and covered up with blankets. With the waves of heat from the fire and the protection of the tarp, the night was comfortable. Trey put away his whetstone and held the ax shaft in his hands with the gleaming head resting on the ground between his feet.

Morgan lay closest to Trey, then Spence, and then Caleb. Spence closed his eyes and pretended to sleep. He occasionally slightly opened one to see if Trey was still at his post. Each time he was, but several times it appeared he looked over at him, or possibly at all of them, sleeping. Slowly fatigue crept over Spence, and he caught himself dozing, waking with a start each time and checking to confirm Trey's whereabouts. He turned his entire head to the side when he didn't see him from the corner of his eye. The panic eased when he saw Trey outside the tarp placing more limbs on the fire. Spence closed his eyes before Trey returned to his seat.

The next time Spence opened his eyes, a face stared down at him. He caught the gasp in his throat as his eyes focused to see Trey leaning over him. His right hand instinctively clutched at the smooth handle of his staff lying beside him. Trey's expression was unreadable. Spence's body tensed from head to toe, involuntarily preparing for some type of blow.

"Your watch." Trey straightened and returned to his spot. He lay on the tarp, placed his ax beside him, and rested his head on his pack.

Spence exhaled his held breath and inhaled deeply. He slowly stood and walked past Morgan and Trey to step out of the shelter. He walked a few feet away from the fire to let his vision grow accustomed to the darkness. The night was cloudy as usual, although he saw a faint glow behind the clouds that could be a moon. He had never considered if Nibiru had a moon or more than one. Or was it Earth's moon? Sometimes he forgot this wasn't just a strange place on Earth. He had no idea if Nibiru was actually a planet passing by every thirty-six hundred years, somewhere else in the galaxy or universe, or in some other dimension altogether. The thoughts made his head spin.

The light was too faint to see anything except the clouds. The night was eerily silent. Spence thought he had shed most of the fear he had brought from Earth. But being in nearly pitch dark, in a strange land where they had just recently fought and killed a dragon, made him a little nervous. He had a powerful staff, but a quick attack at night could kill or incapacitate him before he could even activate it. He threw some sticks on the fire and made his way inside the shelter.

Spence didn't fall asleep on this watch; he would never do that again. He was still mad at himself for dozing off earlier, but he had been lying down and should have been sleeping, anyway. Now, Spence was sitting up and alert. He glanced at the others periodically. Caleb hardly ever moved. Morgan turned from side to side several times. Trey had occasional bouts of snoring, which only ended when he rolled over in the other direction. Spence's watch was uneventful other than a distant howl of either a wolf or coyote. He woke Morgan when he estimated his three hours were done. He stayed up with her for a few minutes to ensure she was awake and alert and then crawled into his spot. He trusted Morgan, and this time he slept soundly.

When Spence awoke again, daylight filled the shelter. Morgan lay beside him, but Caleb and Trey were not visible. He stood, clutching his staff, and headed toward the side with the fire, which still smoldered with red embers. Caleb stood a short distance away. His sword was in his hand, and he slowly swung it in different motions. Spence realized he wasn't fighting but doing some type of practice or elaborate calisthenics.

Trey appeared from around the side of the rock and walked toward Spence and the shelter. "Had to drain the python. Mr. Miagi's been going at it for a while." Trey walked past Spence and into the shelter.

That seemed a little more like the old Trey. Spence walked around the side of the cliff to relieve himself and then approached Caleb. In slow, steady swings, Caleb continued waving his sword back and forth and up and down. If he saw Spence, he didn't acknowledge him. Spence continued approaching. Suddenly, Caleb turned, and in a flash of silver, the blade's tip was almost touching Spence's throat. "And you're dead before breakfast."

"Jesus! You could have stabbed me in the throat!" Spence backed up a step and rubbed at his neck to make sure the sword hadn't nicked the skin. Even though they recently sparred, Caleb's quickness was frightening.

"Only if I wanted to, or you deserved it."

Spence inhaled deeply and let his anger and fear subside. "I want to learn how to fight with my staff."

Caleb lowered his sword and wiped his brow with his other hand. "I think you're pretty good with that."

"No, not with the magic. I want to be able to defend myself and attack if my staff is recharging. My dagger should be last resort."

"Ah. Good idea. Wait here." Caleb sprinted fifty or sixty yards away. He used his sword to chop off a low limb of a hardwood tree. A few more chops made it into a straight stick of comparable size and shape as the staff. Then Caleb walked over to another tree and hacked a stick to use as a sword. He sheathed his sword and sprinted to Spence, carrying the two limbs.

"Drop your staff and use this. I'm afraid to chop your staff with my metal blade. We'd probably both end up fried."

Spence gently laid his staff down and grasped the stick, which was thicker and bulkier than his staff but similar in length. Caleb swung his new weapon back and forth a few times.

"OK. Let's go," Caleb said after a minute.

Spence swung his stick in a quick overhand blow at Caleb's head. He thought the sudden attack would take Caleb off guard. But Caleb's stick flashed up to block Spence's. Then Caleb's left foot extended and stopped when it brushed Spence's stomach. "That would have hurt," Caleb said.

Spence pulled his stick back, and he and Caleb began circling each other. The process was like the dagger training, except at a further distance. Spence started on the offensive, and Caleb effortlessly blocked or dodged every blow. After several tiring minutes, Caleb went on the offensive. Spence thought he was doing well, blocking and sidestepping. Then Caleb continued to increase the intensity of his attacks until Spence was helpless to defend himself. Luckily, Caleb was careful to stop short of hitting him too hard with his stick.

They paused, allowing Spence to catch his breath and wipe the sweat from his face and head. Then Caleb began instructing him on offense and defense. He taught him how to gauge the opponent's stance, where his enemy's center of gravity was, and when his weight shifted. He explained how to anticipate typical attacks and typical defenses—and how to exploit them. Last, he taught him how to use his free hand and legs to take the enemy by surprise. Most people in a sword fight or knife fight just expected to have to watch the blade and defend from the waist up. Most attacks to the legs and groin were unexpected.

After an hour of training, Spence felt a little better. He still wouldn't have a chance against a Caleb, but he might be able to survive against an average foe. They returned to the shelter and joined Trey and Morgan for breakfast. Then they all packed, with Caleb taking down the tarps and returning them to his and Spence's packs.

They donned their coats and headed down the slope to where they had exited the Forbidden Forest. A wide path, almost like a small road, wound between the rocks and boulders. They followed it south and soon reached the rocky area they had seen the day before. It was devoid of trees except for a few small pines growing around the bases of some rock formations and on ledges on the side of cliffs.

The path narrowed to three feet wide as it steadily ascended farther up the rocky slope. After a few hours, the land transitioned to complete stone until the path appeared carved out of the side of the mountain. The drop-off to the left was steep, and, in some places, the trail was entirely missing, leaving gaps they had to step or leap over. The path ended late in the afternoon on top of a large, flat stone plateau. Standing in front of them in a semicircle stood a dozen dwarves.

CHAPTER 39

At first glance, the dwarves resembled the dwarves in movies like *The Lord of the Rings*—short, stocky, sporting thick beards and long hair. They wore shiny breastplates similar to Trey's, and most held battleaxes, also like Trey's, or long spears.

At second glance, they weren't exactly movie dwarves. Most of them had visual deformities: an arm or leg too short, a gnarled hand or clubbed foot, an eye too low or mostly closed, a thick protruding brow, a receding chin, a bulbous nose, or a cauliflower ear. *More creations.* Spence heard a shuffling from behind them, and a glance over his shoulder confirmed more dwarves were on the trail behind. He had no idea how they had gotten there or how long the dwarves might have followed them.

The largest dwarf, with thick, curly black hair and a matching beard, strode forward and stopped just a few feet in front of Caleb. He walked with a limp due to his left leg being shorter and thinner than his right. He had dark, weathered skin, and his eyes were squinty, almost giving him a Mongolian look. He held a spear twice his height. The top of his head came to Caleb's chest.

"Welcome, questers. I am Thordr, king of the dwarves of the Desolate Peaks." The dwarf spoke in a deep, gravelly voice. Despite being a foot and a half shorter than Caleb, he probably weighed more than Trey. "I have heard you slew the mighty dragon. For that, we are grateful. It has killed many of my people over the years."

"It was nothing," Caleb said.

"You shall stay with us tonight and eat and drink like conquering heroes," Thordr said. He then turned and walked through the other dwarves and toward the mountain face at the back of the plateau that stretched at least one hundred and fifty feet high.

Caleb turned and glanced at the others, shrugged, and followed Thordr. Once they had passed through the line of dwarves, the dwarves closed in on the sides, escorting them. Spence noticed various openings cut into the smooth stone as he neared the mountain face. He soon realized they were windows, most likely set on different levels inside. There were two huge wooden doors at the base, fifteen feet high and ten feet wide.

Wooden posts lined the perimeter of the plateau, with torches mounted on the top of each. Several dwarves moved around, lighting the torches in the fading light. The front of the plateau ended with a cliff. Spence couldn't see what the view consisted of in the fading light, but they were definitely high in the mountains.

The doors slowly swung open, creaking loudly, as they approached. They were at least a foot thick and had strips of metal bolted across both sides. Once they had walked through, the doors groaned shut behind them with a loud boom. The inside opened into a vast room, with the ceiling lost in the shadows high above. The room was illuminated by lamps on tables, torches mounted to the walls, and a fire burning in a massive fireplace in the far wall.

Spence surveyed the cave with his mouth hanging open. Stairs were carved into the stone on both sides of the door and wound up to a wide ledge above, which encircled the entire room. Then he saw additional ledges spaced out evenly higher and higher above. It looked similar to a hotel he had stayed in years ago in Florida, except the hotel wasn't carved out of stone or lit with torches.

Two dozen huge wooden tables were arranged around the center of the room, with lamps spaced evenly in the middle of each. Thick, short wooden chairs surrounded each table. Many dwarves sat around the tables, and more scurried in and out of passages opening off the main room. The ones entering the room carried trays of food and drink; those disappearing carried empty trays and plates.

Thordr led them to the head of the table closest to the fireplace. "Sit," he instructed them. He sat at the end of the table, and Spence and Morgan sat on one side and Trey and Caleb on the other. Dwarves brought them thick wooden plates and metal goblets. Others served roasted meat, potatoes, and thick pieces of bread and filled the goblets with a dark, amber liquid. "Did the Nephilim serve you ale?"

"Yes," Caleb said.

Thordr turned his head and spat on the floor. "This is real ale. Enjoy." He turned his goblet up and drank deeply.

Caleb raised his goblet and tasted an experimental sip. He nodded his head and swallowed another. Morgan followed suit. Spence sniffed his and then took a small drink. It tasted similar to the ale in Argos but was thicker, more bitter, and definitely contained more alcohol. The ale was good, but he knew they would have to pace themselves.

"OK. Let's go easy on this," Caleb said as if reading Spence's mind. Caleb gave a lingering glance to Trey. "We don't want to make a scene in front of our hosts."

"Well, since you all are staring at me, I get the point. I'll behave," Trey responded flatly.

The roast meat—mountain goat, Thordr informed them—was a little fatty and greasy but flavorful. The potatoes were good, too, and soaked up the juice-like gravy of the meat. The bread was thick and hard, like sourdough, but was as dark as pumpernickel. The elven fare they had eaten for the past two days hadn't been bad, but hot, fresh food was hard to beat. The food and drink kept coming.

"Have you hosted other questers?" Spence asked as the eating wound down to just nibbling.

"Three recently made it to the edge of our kingdom, at the border of the Forbidden Forest. They never made it this far, though."

"What happened to them?" Spence asked.

"A half-wolf, half-lizard beast just appeared and ate two of them. It roamed the mountains for a few days, terrorized my people, and then suddenly headed off into the Barrens," Thordr said, sucking the meat off a bone.

"We found it," Caleb said.

"The wolf beast?"

"Yep."

"And slew it?"

"Yep."

"Impressive," Thordr said, his eyes wide.

"What about the third?" Spence asked.

Thordr hesitated. "We are not sure. He must have separated from the other two before their demise. We have not seen him since, so I assume he has met his fate somewhere in these mountains. I cannot imagine one quester surviving alone for long. I assume the dragon ate him. Now, tell me of your other adventures and how you have survived while so many others have perished."

205

The four worked together to describe all the events that had transpired since they arrived in the strange world. They left out the troubles with Trey and Titus's cave and Illexya's hollow tree. And, of course, Spence left out Enki's visit. They shared everything else. Thordr listened with fascination, his eyes widening and mouth hanging open with the battle tales. All the other dwarves within earshot were similarly mesmerized.

"That is some story indeed. You four have great courage and skills," Thordr said, leaning back in his chair.

"Do we just travel south from here to the Forsaken Swamp of the Draconians and slay the last monster?" Spence asked.

"Almost. But first, you must defeat one more creature in my kingdom. Then you can continue to the Forsaken Swamp."

"What monster?" Caleb said wearily.

"There is a cave several miles south of here, not far off the trail. Inside is some type of monster that can turn dwarves, or anything for that matter, to stone."

"Medusa?" Spence asked.

"I have not heard of a Medusa. No one is sure what the beast looks like. I have been told it is wily and cunning, though. It can take the form of anything it wants. It seeks to deceive and lure its prey close, and then it turns them to stone."

"Have any of your dwarves seen it and survived?" Caleb asked.

Thordr leaned forward, his eyes darting back and forth to the other tables, and then spoke softly. "No. No dwarves have encountered it yet. I only learned of this beast a few nights past. Odin came to me in a dream and told me of it."

"You just dreamed this?" Trey asked.

"Not a real dream. It is the way Odin communicates with us during the night. He also left special helmets in my room you can wear to face the monster. He said they will allow you to see the beast's true form and protect you from its power."

"This isn't part of our quest. Why shouldn't we just skip it and continue to the Forsaken Swamp?" Caleb said.

"For some reason, Odin wants the monster slain. He told me that you must slay it before continuing and completing your quest. And I want it killed too. I do not need something turning my dwarves to stone. Since the dragon is dead, we will be free to roam or even leave our kingdom at will. We cannot have a…Medusa locking us in."

The four and Thordr fell silent and sipped at the goblets of ale. The dwarves at the other tables grew steadily louder and more boisterous.

Soon, several disappeared down various tunnels and returned carrying instruments. Some had stringed instruments, ranging from banjo to cello, others bore crude clarinets and flutes, and a few had stone jugs. The musicians set up around the fireplace and began playing music. Other dwarves left their seats and danced in the open space between the tables in front of the musicians. The music was rousing and fast-paced, almost like the square-dancing music Spence and the others had to dance to in gym class. Even the dances resembled square dancing.

Spence paced himself on the ale and observed that the other three did too. They were all a little subdued. He didn't know whether their mood was due to the prospects of yet another battle or just being on a seemingly endless quest. Thordr showed no such restraint, though, and downed tankard after tankard. He stomped his feet, clapped along many times during the songs, and called out frequently to the dancers and musicians.

Spence studied the dwarves in more detail. He estimated at least eighty gathered in the dining area, with others peering off the ledges stretching out of sight above. As with the elves and Nephilim, no young dwarves were present. There also weren't many females. Although the few he saw appeared and dressed like the males, so there might have been more than he thought.

Thordr finally looked at the four of them as if just realizing they did not appreciate the festivities as much as he did. "What is the matter? Do you not enjoy the hospitality of the dwarves?"

Caleb glanced at the other three briefly and then at Thordr. "I apologize. You are very hospitable. We're just tired from our quest. Slaying monsters and dragons is hard work. And tomorrow, we must face a creature that can turn us into statues. If it doesn't offend you, I think we'd like to get a good night's sleep."

"Ah, it is I who must apologize to you. I am sure you are weary. I have some comfortable sleeping arrangements for you. However, first I want to show you the heart of the mountain. Then I will lead you to your sleeping quarters."

CHAPTER 40

Thordr pushed his chair away from the table and stood, rubbed his full stomach, and turned and walked toward the right wall. The others stood and followed, with Caleb in the lead as usual. They left the loud and raucous celebration hall and entered one of several tunnels in the wall. The arched tunnel was only seven feet high and four feet wide. The floor was smooth and mostly flat, as were the walls and ceiling. Spence couldn't determine whether the passage was hewn out of the mountain or was a natural lava tunnel.

The tunnel had torches spaced on each side at thirty-foot intervals. The flames danced as they passed, causing shadows to leap wildly. The tunnel led downhill on a gradual slope. After a couple of hundred feet, they came to a thick, locked wooden door. It had an old worn bronze handle with a lock underneath. Thordr fished inside his breastplate and brought forth a chain of keys. He chose the correct one on the first try and unlocked the lock. They all walked through, Thordr grabbing a torch off the wall on the near side and then locking the door behind them.

This tunnel didn't have any torches, and the grade was much steeper. Thordr's torch barely illuminated the entire party. Another door blocked the tunnel after a hundred feet. Thordr chose another key on the chain and unlocked it. Once again, he allowed them all to pass through, and then he entered and locked the door behind him.

On this side of the door was a smooth, circular room twenty feet in diameter and with a ten-foot-high ceiling. There were no other entrances or exits. The walls, floor, and ceiling were so smooth they shone like obsidian in the torchlight. A chain with a sconce attached hung from the middle of the roof, six feet off the floor, where Thordr placed the torch.

A half a dozen solid wooden chairs sat in a circle beneath it. Thordr sat in one and beckoned the others to do the same.

"This is the heart of the mountain?" Caleb asked.

"As far as the gods are concerned, this is a place where dwarves can meet without fear of being heard or seen. Or at least we assume so since the gods have not struck us down for what we discuss here."

The room reminded Spence of Titus's river cave. That encounter seemed months ago.

"We do not have much time. Tell me everything you know of this world and the other races. Did they have similar safe places?" Thordr said.

Caleb glanced at the other three and received a combination of shrugs and nods. He told the entire story, including their secret meetings with Titus and Illexya. Spence and the others inserted comments here and there. Thordr leaned forward and listened attentively, stroking his thick beard absently.

Thordr finally leaned back in his chair when they finished. He stared up at the torch in silence for a moment. "Well, as you can see, we too are the gods' creations—abominations if you ask me. We also cannot reproduce, and new dwarves just show up on our doorstep to replace our dead. There are one thousand of us."

Spence thought the tunnels must go deep inside the mountain to house a thousand dwarves. "What is the point of it all?" he asked.

"I do not know. Although Odin has appeared to me in dreams and mentioned we too would receive a leader who would lead us into a great battle for control of our world."

"When did Odin mention the leader and battle?" Spence asked, leaning forward.

"Very recently. But I think it is only another game of the gods. Perhaps they are bored with our world or the quests and just want to have the races fight and kill each other for entertainment," Thordr replied somberly.

Spence exchanged glances with the others at the mention of 'entertainment.'

"What does Odin look like?" Trey asked.

"He is stocky and muscular like us but much taller. He wears armor similar to yours, with a horned helmet, and has long blond hair and a blond beard," Thordr said.

"So, you think the gods are real?" Caleb asked.

Thordr laughed half-heartedly. "Unfortunately, yes. Like the Nephilim you mentioned, we have had our share struck down for speaking out against them. Odin also placed the special helmets in my chambers last night while I slept. They are real, like it or not."

"What will you do if this leader appears?" Trey asked.

Thordr tugged on his beard in a way that appeared painful. "We will not have much choice. We will have to follow him into battle."

"Why, if it's all just for the gods' entertainment?" Caleb asked.

"It might be their entertainment, but it is our lives and deaths. If a leader comes to us, chances are the other races will have one too. There will be a war. We will have to either fight or surrender. Dwarves do not surrender. We will win or die fighting," Thordr said.

Spence made a mental note of Thordr's words. He didn't doubt the sincerity or that all his people probably felt the same. He didn't sense the same resolve in the Nephilim of Argos. The elves had been harder to read.

"What do you think about the Medusa?" Morgan asked.

"I do not know," Thordr replied. "There is bound to be something in that cave. It *is* strange the gods want to aid you. No party has made it this far, and other than the initial equipment, the gods have never seemed interested in the welfare of the questers. In fact, it seems they make it impossible to succeed. I would just say to keep your eyes and minds open. You cannot trust the motives or intentions of a god; that much I know for sure."

"Do you know what weapons or other abilities it might have?" Spence asked.

"No. It does not sound like anyone has made it past getting turned to stone."

"What do we do after we defeat the Medusa?" Caleb asked.

"Continue south out of the mountains and into the Forsaken Swamp. Seek out Qishti in the town of Abzu. I do not know them well, but they are a strange bunch—stranger even than the elves."

"And then?" Spence asked.

"You will have to defeat some type of beast when you reach the Forsaken Swamp. But after that, if you survive, you should have completed the gods' quest."

"And we'll get to go home?" Morgan asked, a tinge of excitement in her voice.

"As I said, I would not trust the gods. Just keep your eyes open and try to stay alive." Thordr stood and removed the torch from the hanging sconce. "I will lead you to your sleeping chambers. In the morning, I will ensure your packs are full of food and drink and give you the helmets."

CHAPTER 41

They followed Thordr up the tunnel and back to the main hall. There might have been fewer dwarves dancing and singing, but the party was still going strong. He led them up a flight of stone stairs in the back of the room and to the balcony encircling the great room below. Wooden doors were spaced at even intervals. Several dwarves leaned over the stone railing, watching the activities below.

He led them up three more flights of stairs to a similar fifth level and then led them halfway down the balcony. He removed four keys from his keychain and handed one to each.

"We don't have to share?" Morgan exclaimed.

"Not tonight. I will also have hot water brought to you in the morning to fill the tubs within so you can wash before breakfast. If you leave your clothes outside your door, we will clean them and return them to you in the morning. They look like they could quest by themselves."

"Oh, thank God!" Morgan squealed. "I mean Odin," Morgan said when Thordr stared at her.

"Good night, my guests. I will see you in the morn."

Spence entered his room and shut the thick, arched door. The walls were smooth stone, like the tunnels they had just come from. The room was oval-shaped, twelve feet wide and twenty feet long, with a seven-foot-tall ceiling. A twin-size bed in a wooden frame sat against the far wall. There was what appeared to be a stone toilet wedged into the corner. A metal tub sat on the left side, and a metal basin was attached to the left wall with a mirror mounted above. A small round table stood against the opposite wall with a wooden chair in front and a burning lantern on top. A thick oval rug, resembling a bear's skin, lay in the middle of the floor.

Spence set his pack on the table, removed all his clothing, stiff and reeking, and placed it in a pile outside the door. He then leaned his staff against the wall beside the bed and sat on the edge of the mattress. The room reminded him of a jail cell, complete with a toilet. He wearily stood and walked over to the basin. He scooped his hands in the water inside and splashed it onto his face. He then peered into the mirror. It seemed forever since he had seen his reflection. He had begun growing a scraggly beard, and his face appeared more weathered than it should have from only a week in the wild. It looked gaunter and more chiseled too. He still had some extra puffiness in his cheeks and neck, but he certainly didn't look like the weak, nerdy ginger he used to. His hair was tussled and had a windblown look. He looked rough…and he liked it.

He inspected the stone object in the corner and verified it was indeed some type of toilet. He used it, glad not to be in the bushes. There was no way to flush it, and he wondered if there were pipes underneath or if it was just like a port-a-john. He extinguished the lantern on the table and fell into the bed. The mattress was very firm, but the bed had a pillow, clean sheets, and a clean blanket on top.

He was a little disappointed they had separate rooms. If they had had to share, he would have probably gotten to room with Morgan again. As the fatigue and sleep tried to overwhelm him, he couldn't help thinking of her lying in her bed. Then he thought about her taking a bath in the morning. He felt the sleep receding and his mind and body becoming much too alert. He forced himself to think of other things—the infrequent baths and lack of deodorant and perfume, the monsters they had fought, the blood and gore he'd seen, and the Medusa they had to fight the next day. Finally, the bad and disgusting thoughts won out, and sleep took him.

Spence opened his eyes sometime later. An unnatural white light bathed the room. He shot up in the bed, expecting to see someone entering with a lantern or torch. Instead, he saw Enki standing several feet in front of the bed. He wore the same white robe as before, with the golden-horned helmet on his head. No beam of light shone on him this time, though. His entire body glowed, mostly translucent, like a hologram or ghost.

"Hello again, Spence the Wizard," Enki said in his deep voice.

Spence swallowed hard. His entire body trembled and shook in the bed. "Hello," he finally stammered.

"You have not used your pendant yet and summoned me or joined my people. I assume you have not decided on my offer?"

214

Spence's mind raced, though he couldn't move his body. He had thought less and less of Enki's offer over the past couple of days. Their party had worked well together, except for Trey's drunken rampage. They seemed to grow closer with each battle. He recalled his last conversation with Enki. It had been a tempting offer then, but he had figured the group would never accept him, and it would be an easy decision. Now, he felt part of something. And he had been instrumental in every battle. The group couldn't have survived without him. "I have considered it."

"There is not much time left. If you defeat the creature in the cave, you will be off to the Forsaken Swamp of my people. Then there will be only one more creature to defeat in the swamp."

"And then we will be free to return to Earth?" Spence interrupted.

"That was the promise of the gods. But know that we will have to undo the procedure we performed on your spine. You will be bound to your mechanical chair for the rest of your days. You will also return to disrespect, ridicule, and live a short, meaningless life. Or you may stay here and lead the Draconians. Would you not rather be healthy and revered and worshipped as a great wizard and ruler of all Nibiru? Can you even imagine having all four races bow down before you?"

Spence also hadn't thought much lately about what would happen when they returned to Earth. Would the four stick together once they were back in high school? Spence thought he knew the answer. Without quests and monsters to fight, they would return to their prior lives and prior roles. They wouldn't even be able to tell anyone of their adventure for fear of being deemed insane and shunned by all. He doubted they would pursue their book and game idea either. Sure, maybe he and Morgan would try to be friendlier, at least for a while, but it probably wouldn't last. But the biggest issue would be returning to being a paraplegic. How do you choose to return to that fate?

"And I can grant you a life much longer than a mortal on Earth," Enki said, with slightly more emotion than he had shown before.

"You can make me immortal?" Spence asked, leaning forward.

"Not exactly immortal. But I can slow your aging process, and I can ensure you are free from sickness and disease. Neither exists in this world."

Spence was silent as his mind reeled from Enki's words. "Can I let you know once we complete the last quest?"

"You may. But keep in mind it might be too late."

"Why?"

"I have confirmed my siblings have made similar offers to your friends. They all have the same opportunity. But the one who accepts it first will have a great advantage. If one race can subjugate a second one quickly and force them to fight with them, the other two will have no chance to stand before them. You have met the Nephilim, elves, and dwarves. Imagine my Draconians, the fiercest fighters of them all, combined with one of them. It will be over soon for the remaining two."

If Spence hadn't been sitting, his knees might have buckled. He could be an almost immortal ruler and shape and mold the world any way he wanted. Maybe he could bring technology to it or even travel back and forth to Earth! He didn't want to kill the other races, but they might surrender easily to the might of his staff and the fierce Draconians. It might be a relatively bloodless war. Perhaps he could even ally with another race instead of conquering it and then force the other two to surrender. He could make Nibiru a peaceful, blissful world.

Then he thought again about his friends. The other gods had approached them with the same offer. Was that why Trey was quiet and moody recently? Most likely. Trey had a good life and future in front of him on Earth, but he had to be intrigued by the possibility of ruling a world and living forever. And he could be free of his father. Trey also loved power and dominance. He'd probably make each race a football team and play on a big field in the Barrens.

Caleb was always hard to read. But he had lived his life preparing for the modern world to end and seemed to prefer camping and living primitively. He anticipated no future at all. Here in Nibiru, he would have a future. He might not want to be a ruler, but he could have someone else run it for him and live by himself in the woods or mountains. He also might enjoy training a race how to fight. Maybe he could even bring his father into Nibiru with him.

Then his thoughts turned to Morgan. She hated the modern world, with its pollution, intolerance, and injustices. She also had a very uncertain and potentially unhappy future on Earth. Here, she had no factories or labs or things to protest. She could create a world that would not allow industrialization, discrimination, mistreatment of animals, or any of the evils of modern society. After Enki's first visit, Spence wasn't too concerned with his friends being possible rivals. Now, he had a tough time imagining any of them turning down the offer. Yet so far, nobody had accepted it.

"What is your answer?" Enki asked.

"I am very interested, but I have to see our quest through. My friends cannot make it without me. I will let you know when we've completed the quest," Spence finally said.

"I hope it will not be too late."

Enki disappeared, leaving the room in pitch black again. Spence remained sitting for several minutes, his mind decompressing all the thoughts, before finally lying back down. Surprisingly, he soon fell asleep.

CHAPTER 42

A knock on the door awoke Spence the second time. The door opened before he could respond, and a stocky female dwarf entered, carrying two wooden buckets. The light from outside the door illuminated half the room. She flashed a mostly toothless smile at him, walked over to the metal tub, and poured the water. She then went to the table and lit the lantern. She exited, and an older, burly male dwarf entered and dumped two more buckets of water into the tub. A total of six dwarfs came in and poured two buckets each. The first one returned and laid two towels on the foot of the bed and his clothes, neatly folded. She then approached the tub and shook the powdery contents of a stone vase into the water. She smiled again and left the room, shutting the door behind her.

Spence rolled out of bed and hurried over to the tub. He swung a leg over the edge and dipped in his foot. The water was surprisingly hot. He placed the other foot in and slowly sank into the tub, the water coming to his chest. The powder the dwarf had dumped in had foamed up like a bubble bath and had a sweet, flowery smell. He had considered the elven pond a bath, but it didn't compare to actual hot water in a tub. His body tingled from head to toe. *I have to start taking baths more often if I return home.*

Although he was adapting to the hiking and fighting, his body still carried various aches and pains. The hot water massaged them all and allowed the tension to drain out of his tight muscles. He closed his eyes and just enjoyed the caressing of the water. He stayed there for at least thirty minutes, until the water was totally cold.

He climbed out of the tub and stopped in front of the mirror. Like his face, his body had changed. He now saw what Morgan had seen in the pond. He wasn't skinny yet or ripped, but he was getting toned. Spence had lines of definition in his arms, chest, and legs he had never seen before. He wasn't the pudgy geek who had stepped out of the shower a week ago and tried to avoid staring at his reflection in the mirror. A few more weeks like this, and he would be truly transformed.

He dressed in his soft, clean clothes, slung on his backpack, grabbed his staff, and left the room. Morgan exited her room at the same time.

"OMG!" she exclaimed. "The best bath ever!"

"And clean clothes that don't reek of BO and feel like sandpaper," Spence said.

"I know, right? We all bougie now."

Spence laughed and tried to reel his mind back from visualizing Morgan's bath. "Now, it's time for some hot food."

They made their way down the many flights of stairs to the great room below. Caleb and Trey sat with Thordr, and dwarves occupied half the room. They were much quieter than they had been the night before. Spence and Morgan sat down to plates already loaded with food: flat cakes resembling pancakes, fried eggs, and meat looking like pork chops. Stone mugs contained a hot, black liquid resembling coffee.

"Wow, you girls enjoyed a long bath, huh?" Trey asked.

Thordr actually laughed, as well as Caleb.

"Unlike your odor, ours washes off," Spence replied. He, Morgan, and Thordr all laughed.

Spence was surprised to discover the cakes almost tasted like pancakes, only a little tougher and with no syrup to cover them. The meat was juicy and tender, and the eggs were good. The liquid tasted like coffee, except a little thicker and more bitter. While the four ate, Thordr let a few dwarves take their packs and disappear into a tunnel.

By the time they finished, the dwarves had reappeared and returned their packs to them. Another dwarf brought four masks and set them on the table. They appeared to be fashioned of black rubber and resembled diver masks, except with two small circles of dark glass in the middle. Two straps ending with oval tips hung off each side.

"Take these with you. When you find the cave, place them over your faces before entering," Thordr said. "Tuck the side pieces into your ears. It is said the monster can beguile enemies with its voice too."

"A Medusa and Siren combined?" Spence said.

The four each grabbed a mask and placed it in their packs. Thordr explained how to find the cave as he walked them through the hall and out of the massive doors leading to the plateau. It was late morning of another cool, cloudy day.

"Fare you well, my friends. I hope you complete your quest."

They each shook Thordr's hand and then walked across the plateau to the trail on the other side. The path was similar to the one they had traveled the day before. It ranged from three to four feet wide, and the mountain once again rose steeply to their right, stretching high overhead. A sharp decline fell away to their left, littered with gravel, boulders, and sparse vegetation. It led hundreds of feet below to some type of rocky ravine. A smaller row of rocky peaks lay on the other side of the gorge, and the Barrens were visible in the distance beyond.

The four walked in pairs where they could, with Caleb and Morgan in front and Spence and Trey in the rear. They didn't speak for the first mile or so. Caleb finally broke the silence. "We need a plan for our next battle. At least we know it's in a cave, and we have to put our masks on outside it."

"And then?" Trey asked.

"That's as far as I've gotten. We have no idea what the creature is or what type of weapons or attacks it has," Caleb replied. He rubbed his head for a moment. "I guess me and you can go in first. I'll have my shield raised, and you can hold your ax in front of you. Morgan, you and Spence need to space yourselves behind and flank us so you can get clean shots. We'll provide defense, and you two hit it with everything you have. Spence, I would think your fireball would be devastating in a closed area, and it won't have the shock wave of your other attacks. Once you two attack, Trey and I will charge and finish what's left."

"Sounds simple enough," Trey said.

Spence considered the next monster and the masks. Something didn't seem right. The gods had never helped them, other than giving them weapons and armor at the start. If this monster was so tough to deal with, why didn't they just provide them with another one to fight? Or was there something else? Was this monster something the gods created and then couldn't control? Thordr also didn't learn of its existence until Odin told him about it a few nights before. Did it just appear in the cave, or where did it come from? Did the cave protect it from the gods, since supposedly at least in some caves they couldn't see or hear—although Enki visited him in his cave-like room the night before. Like the first visit, he couldn't be sure if Enki had been there in person or was only a projection. But Enki still had known which room he was in. So, not all caves were protected.

He wanted to discuss it with the others but knew he couldn't risk the gods' hearing. He wondered if they should even kill a monster that threatened the gods. But killing it was now part of the quest, and the quest was their only chance of returning home. They would have to slay whatever it was. Unless…. If the gods couldn't see in the cave, they wouldn't know the battle's outcome.

After another mile, the trail began to wind its way downhill, following the curvy contour of the mountain. Like yesterday afternoon, the angle of the cliff beside them lessened. Soon the cliff ended, and the trail spilled into a flat valley. It resembled the plateau, except the ground here was rough and littered with rocks and scrub.

Caleb led them to the far edge of the flat area. The ground below still dropped off steeply and was dotted with huge boulders and rock formations. A few stunted pine trees grew just below the edge. He removed his pack, dug out the rope, and tied it around the base of the closest tree. Although the tree was short, the trunk was thick. He threw the length of the rope down the slope. "I'll go last and keep an eye on the rope and make sure the tree holds."

Trey walked to the edge and placed the mask on the top of his head but didn't pull it over his eyes. He then turned and began backing down the slope. The incline wasn't steep enough to repel down but would be difficult to descend safely without the rope. He kept looking over his shoulder to guide himself around the boulders and stunted trees. He angled toward a large rock formation some one hundred feet below. He worked his way around the side of it and disappeared.

When the rope went limp, Caleb motioned for Morgan to go next. She grabbed the rope and nimbly backed down the decline, disappearing around the rock much quicker than Trey. Spence stepped forward next.

"I would have tried so much harder in PE if I'd known climbing ropes would become a major part of my life," Spence said. He slid his staff underneath the straps of his pack and then put the mask on his head, grabbed the rope, and began his descent. This wasn't as bad as the other rope adventures. However, he took his time and avoided tripping over a rock or tree root. He finally made his way down beside the large rock face and joined Morgan and Trey.

They stood on a slim flat stone outcropping attached to a tall rock face. A dark cave opened in the middle, just ten feet high and the same width. Trey already held his ax, and Morgan had her bow in hand, an arrow nocked. Spence freed his staff, and Caleb arrived a few minutes later.

Caleb clutched his sword in one hand and his shield in the other. "Spence, you'll need to light the way with your staff. Hopefully, the flames from the fireball will keep it bright enough for us to finish the job if we need to." He led them to the edge of the opening. "Masks on."

CHAPTER 43

Spence placed the mask over his eyes. It felt like a snorkeling mask he had used a year or two at the beach, except this one let in a lot less light. He placed each of the earplugs into his ears. They almost totally blocked out all sound. As he adjusted the mask on his face, his finger grazed some type of bump on the right side, over the temple. He placed his finger on it again and realized it was a button. Without hesitation, he pressed it. The lenses suddenly lit up like night vision goggles. The light was too bright, though, and he pressed the button again. The mask went dark, but he saw spots in front of his eyes.

"We won't need any light," he said, pulling the mask up so he could make sure he wasn't temporarily blind. He also removed one of the earplugs.

"Why?" Caleb asked.

"There's a button on the right side. These things are like night vision goggles. Don't press it out here in the light, though."

"Damn it!" Trey said. He clutched at his mask and snatched it off his head.

"Uh, what part of not pushing the button out here confused you?" Morgan asked.

"I've got a button you can push," Trey responded. He rubbed at his eyes with the backs of his hands.

"OK. Let's focus. Whatever's in there is bound to know we're out here now. Put your masks on, with the earplugs in, step into the cave and then press the button. We won't be able to talk after that," Caleb said. He didn't wait to see if the others followed. He stepped into the dark confines of the opening, hesitated as his finger located the button, and then disappeared further inside.

Spence watched Trey follow Caleb, and then he and Morgan went. He said his prayer as he stepped into the darkness and pressed the button, just before almost running into Trey. The masks made everything look bright white instead of green like the military night vision did in the movies. He stepped to the outside of Trey and clutched his staff tightly. The cave stretched straight ahead fifty feet. The tunnel was just a straight tube, but the walls, floor, and ceiling were rough, unlike the smooth dwarven tunnels. Small loose rocks littered the floor, and some stalagmites rose from it. The roof narrowed overhead and disappeared out of sight as a large fissure.

Spence didn't see a monster or Medusa or any other creature. Caleb and Trey began walking forward, their weapons before them. Spence followed, and he knew Morgan was beside him, slightly outside Caleb. Spence didn't activate his staff yet, afraid the light would blind them all. He hoped he would have time to activate it and fire before the monster attacked—if they encountered an actual monster

Spence realized the tunnel didn't end but made a ninety-degree right turn as they neared the cave's back wall. Caleb and Trey slowed just before the bend. Spence and Morgan stopped and waited nervously. He could hear his heart pounding in his ears in the oppressive silence of the earplugs. He wiped his palms one at a time on his pants. Caleb leaned around the corner of the wall for several seconds. He finally pulled his head back. He removed his earplugs and motioned for the others to do the same.

"It opens into a chamber at the end of the tunnel, and it appears to be a dead end. If the monster is in here, it's in there. When Spence activates his staff, close your eyes. As soon as the fireball launches, his crystal will go dark, and you can open them and attack. Spence, you shouldn't have to aim too closely with the fireball. Last time it locked on like a missile."

They all reinserted the earplugs. Caleb and Trey walked around the corner and halted until Spence and Morgan joined them. The tunnel ended one hundred feet away and opened into a round room. Nothing was visible in the room, but it glowed brighter than the tunnel and appeared to contain a light source.

Spence saw Caleb hold his hand up with all five fingers extended. He slowly lowered each one. When he was down to just a fist, his mouth opened, and he yelled something toward the distant room. The yell was so loud Spence could hear muffled sound through the earplugs, although he couldn't make out the words.

A thought struck Spence as Caleb counted down to his yell. A creature that turned everything living to stone was supposed to be this cave. Yet they hadn't seen any statues outside or inside the cave or any broken statue pieces on the floor. Movement within the distant room interrupted his thoughts. Only a shadow appeared first. Then a shape began to emerge. He struck the butt of his staff on the floor.

He closed his eyes for a second, but he was still nearly blinded when he reopened them. He squinted and tried to discern the distant shape. It did resemble the Medusa out of the movies. It had the lower body of a giant snake and a human torso. Except this one was a male. Spence couldn't discern many details due to the distance and the mask. The brilliant orb on his staff made it worse.

He lowered his staff beside Trey's left arm and pointed it at the monster. He placed his finger on the second button. He paused and waited for action from the Medusa. It slowly slithered fully into the doorway of the chamber. It held a bow in its hand and wore a quiver of arrows on its back. But it hadn't drawn its bow. Was it trying to turn them to stone with its gaze? Its mouth opened and closed, but no sound reached them. It could be talking or casting a spell.

Trey turned around and moved his mouth.

Spence read his lips and knew he was telling him to hurry up and shoot it. He stroked the raised button. He wasn't sure why he hesitated, but something just didn't feel right. First, the gods warned them about what they were to face and gave them the magic masks. Then, they had seen no evidence of statues or dead creatures. He suddenly removed his finger from the button and grabbed the left side of his mask. He slowly peeled the corner up. He hoped he was right. Of course, he'd never realize if he weren't.

It took a moment for his exposed left eye to adjust to the darkness. The light of the staff illuminated the tunnel almost to the monster. The room behind it did have a light source, too, silhouetting it. Spence lifted the other side of the mask and blinked hard with both eyes. There wasn't a half-snake, half-human in front of him. There was only a human. It did appear to hold a bow but wasn't a monster. He removed both earplugs.

"Stop!" the man yelled. "I'm not going to hurt you! I'm from Earth too!"

Spence remembered Thordr saying the monster could beguile people with its voice. Was this part of the trap? Or was it all a lie? He glanced over at Morgan. She had her bow halfway drawn. Caleb and Trey were tensed to charge and attack. He wondered if they still had their eyes closed.

"Who are you?" Spence called out.

"I'm Tom. Tom Marshall."

"We were told you were a monster that could beguile us with your voice and turn us to stone with your gaze."

The man laughed a loud but hoarse laugh. "The *gods* told you that?"

"Well, the gods told a dwarf," Spence said. He kept both hands on his staff but lowered it some.

"Figures. I hope you have learned at least a little bit about the nature of the gods by now," Tom said.

"You looked like a Medusa with this mask. Just so we can be sure, turn around. I will have my friends remove their masks and earplugs."

Tom laughed again and slowly turned. "More handiwork of the gods. Sure. Just talk the girl out of putting an arrow into my back."

Spence covered most of the staff tip with his left hand and tapped Trey and Caleb on their shoulders with his right. As they turned, he moved over and tapped Morgan. They all faced him now. He motioned for them to take off their masks and remove the earplugs. Each of them turned to look at the monster and then slowly lifted their masks.

"What's going on?" Caleb asked.

"See for yourself. It looks like a man to me. His name is Tom Marshall," Spence said. "From Earth."

Caleb pulled his mask down and then raised it again. Soon all three of them pushed the masks up. Morgan lowered her bow but kept the arrow nocked. Trey and Caleb slightly relaxed their offensive stances.

"It could still be a trap," Caleb said.

"I doubt it. I realized before we saw him that there were no stone statues anywhere around. And what is more likely, the masks making a man look like a monster, or taking off the masks making a monster look human?" Spence asked.

"How can we trust you?" Caleb called out.

Tom turned around and stared at the four. "Well, I could have just turned you all to stone."

"Good point," Morgan whispered.

"We could keep shouting back and forth and waving our weapons around, or you could come down here, and we can compare notes on this screwed-up world," Tom said. He then turned and walked into the room behind him.

CHAPTER 44

Caleb looked at the others. "Let's go, but don't let your guards down."

He led them down the passageway to the chamber at the end. The room was similar in size and shape to Thordr's safe room, except this one was rougher and obviously natural, not carved or smoothed by hand or lava. A fire burned in one corner, and a burning torch was wedged into a crack in the wall on the other side. Wood and logs littered the floor, and a tarp lay in the center, with a pack like Spence's lying on it.

Tom introduced himself as he shook each of their hands. He then sat on a thick piece of wood against the wall at the far edge of the tarp, laying his bow and quiver of arrows in front of him. "Pull up a log and have a seat."

The others grabbed various pieces of wood and sat in a rough semicircle in front of Tom. Spence struck his staff on the ground and extinguished the light. Caleb sheathed his sword, and Trey and Morgan slung their weapons on their backs. Spence kept his staff in his hands before him, with the butt resting on the floor.

"So, where are you from? I mean, on Earth," Tom said. Tom appeared to be in his mid-forties. He had unkempt black hair and a shabby, thick beard, both clearly results of living in the wild for a while. His face was tanned dark and weathered. He wore a studded leather vest with a black shirt underneath sticking out from the sleeves, black pants, and knee-high boots.

"Colorado," Caleb said. "We were on a school trip in Sedona, Arizona, when we encountered what we thought was a vortex. And the next thing we know, we were fighting a half-wolf, half dinosaur."

"Ah, classic. We began with something resembling a porcupine the size of an RV. It launched spear-length quills. Luckily, we only lost one in that battle. I shot arrows through both eyes and into its brain while another guy hacked and stabbed it with a sword." Tom leaned against the wall with his hands behind his head. "How did just you four come to the vortex?"

"I think we all just heard or felt like a humming or buzzing sound and followed it to the source. Morgan said it was the energy from the vortex," Spence said. He had wondered about how they were the only four out of the class to end up there. "Maybe we were the only ones that felt it."

"So, the gods somehow influenced and chose us four on earth?" Morgan asked.

"Sounds like it," Spence replied.

"Interesting," Tom said.

"Tell us your story," Caleb said.

"Where to begin…." Tom closed his eyes for a few seconds. "I was on a business flight on a chartered Cessna, flying from Los Angeles to San Francisco. We flew straight through an intense electrical storm, and the winds and turbulence were crazy. We lost one engine, and the pilot announced he would try to crash land in the ocean. Well, we never hit the water. It felt as if a tornado had sucked the plane in or hyperdrive from a science fiction movie. The next thing I know, six of us awakened lying on the ground. The plane was gone, and we weren't in the ocean…or California."

"Missing flight 1603!" Spence exclaimed.

"We made national news?" Tom asked.

"All over it," Spence replied, recalling the story's details.

"Oh, God! They didn't find our bodies, did they?"

"Nope. They never found the bodies or the plane. They said the plane was so small and the ocean so deep that if the batteries in the black box went dead, it could take years to find, if it ever was."

"Well, hopefully, that means I'm still alive, and this isn't hell. I've wondered about that a lot since being here."

Spence had never considered that alternative. He shuddered at the thought.

"There were six of you?" Caleb asked.

"Well, for a few minutes. We saw the giant porcupine around the time we had all gained our feet and most of our senses. We were on a stone dais in the middle of an arena. A statue stood in the center, and six pillars stacked with piles of gear were spaced around the edges. We all scrambled to gather weapons. But we were all middle-aged businesspeople: four men and two women. We didn't know what we were doing. Luckily, I had bow-hunted a little before, and another guy had some martial arts training. I grabbed the bow, and he picked a sword. And, as I've already told you, we managed to slay it."

"And then the statue spoke to you?" Morgan asked.

"Yep."

"Argos, the Forbidden Forest, and Desolate Peaks?" Spence asked.

"I see you've played the game too. Yeah, we lost one fighting a fire-breathing lizard in the Barrens. Then a giant snake in the Forbidden Forest claimed another."

"Then there were three left?" Trey asked.

"Yeah. Marty and Brenda decided to hole up at the edge of the Peaks. She had injured her leg in a bad fall, and he didn't want to leave her. I think they had something going between them too. So, I left them there and set out on my own."

"What happened to them?" Caleb asked.

"I'm assuming they were killed somehow, if you haven't heard about them, and I haven't seen them."

"The wolfosaurus," Spence said, recalling Thordr's words. "Thordr said it killed two people and then headed to the Barrens. Then we faced it in the arena."

"Ah."

"Then what did you do?" Morgan asked.

"I was tired of playing. I decided not to seek out Thordr and Kaldrfell. From meetings with the other races in their secret places, I assumed the gods couldn't see in most of the caves. There are a lot of caves in these mountains, so I figured this area would be easier to survive in than others. I live in one cave for a while and then scout around a little at night until I find another. Their night vision must be limited. Oh, they've sent a monster or two to find me, but I manage to escape or kill them," Tom said matter-of-factly.

"How long have you been in Nibiru?" Spence asked.

"Nibiru?" Tom said.

"Yeah. This world. That's what the statue, Enki, called it," Spence replied.

"Interesting."

"What's interesting?" Spence asked.

"When the statue spoke to us, it identified itself as Odin. And it called this world Asgard."

"Asgard?" Spence exclaimed. "The mythical home of Odin and the Norse gods." His mind reeled, trying to understand the implications.

"So, the gods each have different names for this world?" Morgan said.

"It would seem so," Spence replied. "Enki spoke to us, and he called this world his home planet's name of Nibiru. Odin spoke to Tom, calling it Asgard, for his home world."

The five were quiet for a moment. "I wonder if a different god meets each group of questers? And each god calls this world his own? Artemis would be Mount Olympus. I'm not sure what Ra's home world is, though," Spence said.

"History nerd doesn't know something?" Trey said.

"I know you're an idiot," Spence retorted.

"You know, come to think of it, none of the races' leaders referred to this world as Nibiru. They answered our questions about it, but they didn't call it by any name," Caleb said.

"Strange. But I don't suppose anything should surprise us here. To answer your question, it's hard to say. I guess a month or two. I hunt and trap enough animals to stay alive. I've found some of the local vegetation is edible too. I also had the rations from the rest of the party as they died off."

"What's your plan?" Caleb asked.

"To stay alive for now, and I've been hoping to find the next party. Although, the gods are getting tricky with trying to convince you to kill me. They must not like people not playing along with their games." Tom rose briefly and threw another stick on the fire. "Now, tell me how you've managed to get all four of you to this point."

CHAPTER 45

The four told their story, revealing everything except Spence's Enki encounters. None of the others volunteered if they had had similar contact. Tom listened with his face unreadable. He didn't appear surprised or shocked by any of it. He only raised his eyebrows when they spoke of Spence's cured paralysis.

"That's pretty amazing. I'm sure having four young people knowing how to play helps. Our 'wizard' never did get the hang of his wand. The others were mostly ineffective with their weapons too. I've gotten fairly good with the bow and my daggers. You guys have worked well together, too, and began planning your battles. We stuck together traveling but were more every man and woman for themselves in the fight scenes."

"Have you figured out what this place is? I mean, different races, monsters, gods, and quests…." Spence said.

"Well, I had similar secret conversations along the way with the races' leaders. They didn't speak of a war, though. That must be new. But I think it's pretty easy to see the gods or someone created the races and monsters. It looks to me mostly through genetic manipulation. I mean, even on Earth, I bet scientists could create some pretty freaky stuff if they didn't have rules and ethics holding them back," Tom said.

Spence suddenly thought of something. "Hey! That could be why the races don't have any children! They could be like mules on earth and can't reproduce. Then the gods just create another one anytime one of them dies."

Tom scratched his beard. "Good point. Or the gods just made them sterile for population control."

"Do you think the gods might be scientists?" Caleb asked.

"Everything here reeks of technology and not magic. I mean, our party's wand had push buttons in it, as does Spence's staff, I'm guessing."

The others all turned to Spence, expressions ranging from surprise to anger. Spence considered denying it but now wasn't the time. This was the first chance they had to really try to figure out the true nature of Nibiru. He struck the butt of the staff on the ground. Once the compartment slid open, he turned the staff to show the others.

"Why haven't you told us about this?" Trey asked angrily.

"Uh, you didn't ask?" Spence stammered.

"Why did it shock me when I tried to take it?" Trey said.

"The wand did the same thing. Probably fingerprint recognition, causing a loss of grounding and electric shock if the prints don't match." Tom turned from Trey to Spence. "Three powers?"

"A small ball that locks onto the monster and explodes into fire on contact, a lightning bolt, and a shock wave," Spence said, looking away from the glowering Trey. He struck the staff on the ground again and deactivated it.

"See, none of that is out of the realm of technology. The military has already experimented with lightning weapons and shock waves made from sound. I'm sure they could make a similar fireball—possibly a miniature heat-seeking drone with napalm or C4."

"What about the monsters?" Morgan asked.

"Well, you discovered the Cyclops was at least part robot. The wolfosaurus was most likely the cloning of a dinosaur and then further splicing with wolf DNA. The spider mantises, other than being massive, are obvious. I think these gods are more advanced than the scientists on Earth. But look how far we've come in fifty years. They wouldn't have to be that far ahead. I'm sure fixing spinal injuries is not too far in our future, either.

"The gods appearing are probably simple holograms. They could have cameras and listening devices everywhere to keep an eye on everything. On Earth, we've already created insect-sized drones with cameras in them. You know what this reminds me of?"

"*The Hunger Games*," Morgan said, her eyes wide with the revelation.

"Exactly. The Capitol could watch and influence everything in *The Hunger Games* books and movies."

"But why?" Caleb asked. "Why would the gods do all this?"

"The same reason…entertainment. You bring a bunch of strangers in, give them weapons, and let them fight monsters. It's like *Survivor* on steroids," Tom said.

Spence and the others all leaned forward. He recalled their conversation in the forest regarding Nibiru possibly being a game. "But who is the audience?" Spence asked. "It doesn't seem like the races are in on it or have any devices to watch it on."

"I'm not sure. But I have realized something." Tom got off his stump and went over to a nearby pile of branches. He broke off several handfuls of sticks and then gathered some small rocks off the ground. He returned to the center of the tarp and dropped to his knees amid the four.

"OK. Follow along. Here is the arena." He placed a rock on the tarp. "We headed east to Argos, here." He set another stone for the town. "Here is the Styx River. You cannot cross and go further to the east." He laid down several sticks, making a straight line beside the rock. "We headed north to the Forbidden Forest. The forest was too thick to pass further north." He placed another line of sticks on that side. "Then we headed west to the Desolate Peaks. The mountains also become impassable further west." He made a line with small stones on that side. "None of us has been there, but here is the Forsaken Swamp to the south. I'll bet all our lives it becomes impassable further south." He laid the remaining sticks on that side.

"Dang," Caleb said. "I thought something was weird."

"What?" Trey asked, staring at the shapes on the floor.

"This world is completely boxed in. Or possibly a circle, since we don't know the exact border shapes," Caleb said.

"And a fairly small one too. Think about how long it took you to travel each edge. What would you say, Caleb, twenty or thirty miles on each side?" Tom asked.

"Pretty close, depending on how far the actual border is," Caleb replied, still studying the layout.

"Then what's outside the borders?" Trey asked.

"Oh my God!" Morgan said. "Think of *The Hunger Games* again. They were in a circular arena with an invisible dome over it. The rest of the world lay outside. The Gamemakers could change the environment inside for each game."

"So, we could just be in one big arena, and the rest of the world, Nibiru, is watching all the questers and us on TV at night!" Spence exclaimed.

"Or something like that," Tom said.

"Then that would explain why there is no wind or birds and how the sky is always overcast, but there hasn't been any rain or snow. Maybe you could see the dome with blue skies and sun behind it," Caleb said.

"And I bet they somehow heat the forest and swamps, like the tropical habitats in the zoo," Spence added.

"Good points," Tom said.

"I wonder if the Styx runs beneath the dome, or what happens to it?" Spence asked.

Tom appeared thoughtful for a moment. "The Forsaken Swamp! I bet it forms the swamp."

"I wonder why everyone speaks English?" Caleb asked.

"Good question. And have people other than Americans been here?" Tom said.

"How do you think we got here?" Morgan asked.

"Not sure. A lot of scientists have speculated that there are multiple dimensions. And there are wormhole theories. As we've said, these beings are more advanced than we are. They must have some way to see into our world and open doorways to bring people into this one," Tom said. "Hey, before we talk all night, you wouldn't have any food to share with a fellow earthling, would you?"

***

"They have been in there for a while," Ra said.

"What if the masks did not work, or they removed them?" Enki asked.

"They would have no reason to doubt the terrible monster facing them. I am sure the wizard ended it quickly. It is nearly dark, and they are just spending the night inside," Odin said calmly.

"How have you allowed these places in your mountains where we cannot see or hear?" Artemis asked.

"The last earthquake must have opened some long-sealed passages. Somehow, the rogue human managed to stumble upon a few. But it is no matter now. They will have to come out eventually. And we have finally pinned down where the missing one is hiding, so he will not sneak out in the dark again."

"Has anyone had any luck recruiting their champion yet?" Enki asked.

"I think mine is close to breaking. We shall soon see. And if he goes, then so will go the others. No one will want to be last."

CHAPTER 46

They dug into their packs and spread out a meal for all to share. Thordr had packed bottles of the ale and refilled wineskins with water. Tom was obviously famished, and the five ate in silence. A half-hour later, they finished and repacked the remaining food.

"Tom, there's something else I haven't told anyone," Morgan said, staring at the ground.

"What's that?"

"We told you…told you about each of the races mentioning waiting for a champion to…to lead them in a war," Morgan stammered.

"Yes."

"Artemis visited me in a dream—twice, actually. At least, it seemed like a dream. She's trying to convince me to lead the elves in this war. She says I could be their queen and rule Nibiru."

If Spence had still been drinking, he would have spewed it across the room. His heart skipped several beats. He sought the faces of Caleb and Trey. They both appeared as shocked as he probably did.

Tom leaned forward on his log. "Artemis? Spoke to you?"

"Yes," Morgan said, avoiding the others' gazes.

"How are you supposed to contact her if you want to lead the elves?" Tom asked.

Morgan fished inside the top of her tunic and withdrew the amethyst pendant. "Artemis said I can squeeze this and say her name, and she will appear. Or I can press the gem and teleport directly to Sabekha."

Tom whistled. "Interesting. Teleportation? They're even more advanced than I thought. What about the rest of you? If she is the champion of one race, I'm betting you are the champions of the others."

Tom's eyes met Spence's and stopped. Spence's heart pounded as if he had to fight Tom. He swallowed hard. He knew his face gave away the truth. He reached inside his shirt and pulled out his emerald amulet. "Enki and the Draconians."

Spence followed Tom's gaze to Caleb.

He withdrew his ruby pendant. "Ra and the Nephilim."

Then all eyes were on Trey. Trey appeared even more agitated than the others, even looked embarrassed. He finally reached inside his breastplate and fished out the sapphire amulet. "That only leaves Odin and the dwarves."

Tom leaned back against the wall, placed his hands behind his head again, and whistled. "Sounds like the gods have really changed the game. Perhaps that's why you all have survived. They want a war—a world war. What a show it would be to have all four races fighting against each other, led by humans from Earth. Of course, there might be monsters thrown into the mix too. And if a race is wiped out, or all of them for that matter, they'll just start over again at the beginning."

"Or we could all be wrong, and this could be an actual world, ruled by real gods. And if one race defeated the others, it would rule the world," Trey said.

The others sat without talking for a moment. "Well, it's all just theories, but I think we hit on what made the most sense earlier. Anyway, surely none of you would take the bait and try to lead a race into this war," Tom said, shaking his head and chuckling. "You might have defeated a few mutated animals, but none of you are warriors or generals."

"From what I've seen, it wouldn't be much of a war," Trey said. He met each pair of eyes now staring at him. He coughed and then grinned. "Of course, none of us would be that crazy. We just want to get back home."

"What are you going to do?" Caleb asked Tom. "We'll have to leave here in the morning and head south to the Forsaken Swamp. Hopefully, the gods will honor their bargain and let us go home once we defeat the Draconian monster."

"I'm not sure. I know the gods have been searching hard for me and even sent you here to kill me. I doubt they'd let me live if I appeared out in the open. Plus, they would be upset you didn't kill me. I think the best bet is for me to stay here and have them assume I'm dead. Then maybe in a day or two, I can slip out and find another hiding place."

"That's not a long-term plan. You can't live the rest of your life hiding in caves," Caleb said.

Tom frowned. "True. I don't know. This race war thing has me intrigued. I might just try to stay alive long enough to see what happens."

"The race war won't happen. None of us will betray the squad," Caleb said.

Tom smiled. He stared at them, his eyes lingering several seconds on each. "Squad, huh? But you never know. You were strangers before this began. You can't say for sure what the others will do. And whoever caved first would have a huge advantage. Besides, you might slay the last monster and the gods decide not to return you to Earth. They might force you to participate in the war, stay here forever, or die. Then what?"

"It's really a genius plot," Caleb said solemnly.

Spence felt dizzy and nauseous. Tom might be right. If the gods wanted a war, they would have a war. If they all ended up having to lead a race anyway, why not be the first? And now they all knew the gods had contacted the others. Now, they had to try to read one another's minds. Tom was also right about them only knowing each other for a week. Even though they had been through a lot, did any of them truly know what the others would do if their lives depended on it? As Caleb had said, people reverted to savages very quickly when it came down to survival. The game had just changed. They were now in a very high-stakes poker game.

The silence dragged on for at least five minutes. Caleb finally broke it. "We'd better get some sleep. Tom, I assume we should set watches?"

"Probably. The gods might even send something to investigate if you're only spending the night here after killing me or if you figured out the ruse. I'd say the watch could stay at the bend in the tunnel. You could even use those masks to see in the dark. Just don't trust the appearance of whatever you see."

"OK. There are five of us and ten hours to cover. So, only two hours each," Caleb said.

"I'm kind of tired. I'll take the last watch if that's OK," Trey said.

Spence thought that was a little strange. But with this setup, with the sentry being a reasonable distance away and the other four sleeping in the small room, he wasn't too concerned. "I'll take first watch."

"Second," Morgan said.

"Third," Tom replied.

"That makes me fourth," Caleb said. "Let's get set up and go to it. Each watch should put a little wood on the fire to maintain the warmth and light."

The cave was warm enough not to need the blankets, so they each used them for pillows. Spence laid his pack next to Morgan and headed down the tunnel. The cave felt cold compared to the warmth of the small room. He found a dry rock right at the bend where he could see the slightly lighter opening at the end of the main tunnel and the flickering light in the room at the end of the other.

He kept the mask up on his head and thought he could detect anything significant entering the cave from the dim light coming from outside. He periodically slid it over his eyes to ensure something small hadn't slipped past his watchful eye. He used the time to replay their earlier conversation in his mind many times and his discussions with Enki.

The returning to Earth part was what bothered him. He'd already decided they couldn't tell anyone of their adventure. Who would believe them? They also probably wouldn't stick together in the real world, at least not for long. He was sure Trey would return to playing football or whatever sport was in season when they returned and hanging out with the jocks. Caleb would return to being a loner and prepping with his father. Morgan would still be protesting all her perceived ills of the world and hanging out with the counterculture group. Then, they would all graduate high school in the spring and go their separate ways.

Then, of course, there was the returning to the wheelchair part. Here, Spence had grown and changed as a person. He was strong and confident now. He was brave and bordering on fearless. He was whole. Yet on Earth, he would just be a disabled nobody. He wouldn't have a magic or high-tech staff to use. There would be no monsters to slay, and he wouldn't have people to fight with sticks and knives. He would return to being an ordinary, or slightly less than ordinary, paraplegic teenager. *Dang.*

Motion at the cave's entrance drew Spence out of his thoughts. He had just seen a small, dark shadow move. He stared but couldn't detect anything else. He slid the mask over his eyes. Something small flittered through the air and headed in his direction. Either a bird or bat flew directly at him. He thought it strange since they hadn't seen any birds or flying creatures other than the dragon. He gripped his staff and prepared to swing it like a baseball bat, but the object suddenly reversed direction, headed back toward the entrance, and disappeared into the night.

Once he estimated two hours had passed, he headed down the tunnel and woke Morgan. She roused quickly, and Spence wasn't even sure she had been asleep. He considered keeping watch with her, but he was a little tired and still had a lot on his mind. He assumed she and all the others did too. He lay on the tarp with his head on his blanket and eventually drifted off to sleep.

Spence awoke to movement and loud voices all around him. He lifted his head and saw Caleb and Tom standing at the entrance to the chamber, speaking loudly. Morgan stood beside him, her face revealing shock. He saw no sign of Trey or even Trey's belongings.

"Where would he go?" Caleb asked.

"Where do you think?" Tom replied.

"Surely not."

"I suppose there's a chance he went out to gather our breakfast. You know your friend better than I do."

"That's not Trey," Morgan said softly.

"What's going on?" Spence asked, climbing to his feet.

"Trey's gone," Morgan replied.

CHAPTER 47

"Gone? Where?" Spence knew the answer before the words cleared his lips.

"What do we do?" Caleb asked.

"Judging by the light outside, it's a couple of hours past the end of his shift. Depending on when he left, he should be close to the dwarves by now," Tom said.

Spence walked over to join Caleb and Tom. Morgan followed behind. "He probably just used his amulet to teleport to them. As soon as he arrives, they'll be preparing for battle. The question is, which race will they attack first?"

"And if that race has no warning, they won't stand a chance," Morgan said.

"Thordr didn't seem too gung-ho on a battle, though," Caleb replied.

"But he also said they would fight to the death. If Trey tells them one of us or all of us has gone to champion the other races, I think Thordr will be up for it. It sounded like he'd rather attack than defend, too," Spence said.

"What if we just went south and finished our quest?" Caleb asked. "Maybe the gods will let us return home, and Trey can play warlord until his heart's content."

"You could leave all the races to be slaughtered or enslaved by Trey?" Morgan asked.

"Yep. It's not our fight or world."

"I doubt the gods will honor their word at this point. It sounds like it's a war they've been pushing for. If they keep you here, you'll have to choose sides. Or hide in caves with me," Tom said.

241

Caleb rubbed his face. "Well, if I can't go back to Earth, then I'm not going to watch Trey become king. He'll try either to rule us or to kill us. I'll go to Argos and prepare the Nephilim for war. The dwarves will probably not attack them first since they would have to bypass the elves or Draconians, so I should have a little time. Lord knows they need all the help they can get."

"You're saying we should all just join our chosen people and then fight a big war against one another?" Morgan asked.

"Maybe not," Caleb replied.

"What else can we do?" Spence said.

"Lead all our people against Trey. Stop him and the dwarves."

"Then what?" Spence asked.

"Go after the gods," Tom said softly.

"Huh?" Morgan asked.

"With thousands of armed beings, what could the gods do? We could find a way out of this dome—if it is a dome—and go after them. The monsters wouldn't be a challenge with a small army behind us. I bet the gods are just flesh and blood if we could get past their technology. Then we'll figure out how to open a portal back to Earth," Tom said.

Spence shook his head. "That's crazy." He remembered Titus's words regarding fighting against the gods.

"I like it. What part of this isn't crazy? If the gods aren't going to let us go home, what choice do we have? We can all die in a war, hide in caves, keep fighting monsters until we die, or break out of this place and see what's on the outside," Caleb said.

Spence felt as if his brain could literally explode and destroy his head in the process. He could lead the Draconians into battle, with the Nephilim and elves as allies, against Trey and the dwarves. None of them knew anything about battles or wars or leading armies. He and Caleb had studied a lot of military history and famous battles and strategies, but this was real. Was there another option? "I suggest a slight modification to the plan," Spence finally said.

"What?" Caleb asked.

"I think Morgan, Tom, and I should head south to the Draconians. As soon as we leave, you can use your amulet to join the Nephilim. You can gather them together and head north to join the elves if Trey attacks them first. We can complete the quest and find out for sure if they're going to honor their bargain. If they don't, then I'll be there to take leadership of the Draconians. I'll be ahead of Trey and the dwarves even if he heads south first. Morgan can teleport to the elves. Then we can follow your plan. If the gods do honor their bargain, I'll ask them to teleport you to join us. Then Trey can stay here and fight to his heart's content."

Caleb scratched his cheek for a few seconds. "Not bad. Although the more I think about it, the more I'm not sure I could leave this world for Trey to conquer."

"Me either. He would create more atrocities and oppression than we even have on Earth," Morgan said.

"Well, I think we should at least see the quest through, just to know for certain," Spence said.

"Then I'll just go with you. If I can teleport, it'll only delay me getting to Argos by a couple of days. I doubt the dwarves will be the most mobile army. Besides, you might need my help."

"I'm not sure the gods will be happy to see me," Tom said.

"I don't think you have a lot of options," Caleb replied. "It's getting ready to hit the fan. What are they going to do? Send a monster after us?"

"True. I suppose this is what I've been waiting for. Let's go kick some ass."

The four ate, packed their possessions, and headed out of the cave into the gloomy daylight.

***

"Most unexpected," Enki said.

"Seems you were wrong, brother," Artemis added.

"That group is somewhat vexing. But no matter. My dwarves have their champion," Odin replied.

"What do we do with the others? We need to at least eliminate the one that has eluded us for so long," Enki said.

"I say leave them alone. They still must defeat the last beast, and my dwarves are readying for war. If they complete the quest, we will make them lead their races, or they will never be able to return home. The other one can go with whomever he wants. If they chose to do nothing, their former ally will conquer Nibiru and deal with them as he sees fit," Odin said.

"Then we have officially initiated phase two?" Ra asked.

The other three nodded one by one.

"So it begins," Enki said.

***

They used the rope to ascend to the top of the plateau. Caleb started to lead them toward the next section of the trail, but Tom motioned for him to wait. He walked toward the cliff at the rear of the plateau.

"What are you doing? The trail is over here," Caleb said.

243

"I think I see a mountain goat at the top of that cliff. It's a long shot, but if I hit it, it should fall, and we can butcher it. Keep an eye on my arrow. If I miss, I want to know which way." Tom walked until he was thirty feet from the cliff. He grabbed an arrow, nocked it on the string, and pulled the string to the corner of his mouth.

Spence was puzzled. He couldn't see anything at the top of the cliff and definitely nothing white like a mountain goat. He peered, blinked, and peered again—still nothing. He shrugged and just stared at the arrow. Then Tom released it. For a moment, Spence lost it against the white rock of the cliff, but then he picked it up again as it cleared the top. The arrow from the powerful bow soared high above, threatening to disappear out of sight. Then the arrow suddenly stopped. A distortion, or rippling, appeared in the gray sky as if a stone had struck water. The arrow hung in the air for a moment and then began falling back. It flipped over and fell tip down, landing somewhere out of sight on the other side of the cliff. The ripples decreased, and then the sky returned to normal. Spence and Morgan were right—an invisible dome covered Nibiru!

"Missed it. Not even close," Tom said. He turned and walked over to them. He spoke again before Caleb or Morgan could talk out of their open mouths. "I thought I was a better shot. Guess we'd better get to the trail."

Spence realized what Tom was doing. He didn't want to draw attention to the fact they had discovered the great secret of the gods and Nibiru. He wondered if the gods would be suspicious that they hadn't noticed the dome or that there wasn't a mountain goat. Hopefully not, or they assumed the party would have reacted with shock and amazement if they had. Oh well. The four had no way of knowing and couldn't do anything about it either way. At least now they knew for sure about the dome.

***

"Very astute," Ra said.

"That is not good. Now they know about the dome," Odin said.

"They must have already theorized about its existence. Besides, they cannot surmise the true purpose of it. And there is no way to escape. They will not leave the dome until we are ready for them too. Then it will be time to initiate phase three," Enki replied.

"I hope you are right," Artemis said. "They continue to overachieve."

***

The trail continued, similar to the prior sections, except now it led on a downhill grade. The mountain on their right and the ones around them gradually decreased in height, and the drop-off on the left wasn't as far.

They hiked fast with little talking for most of the morning. Spence knew they were all dying to discuss the arrow, but they couldn't. Nothing else was worth speaking of.

They stopped for lunch in midafternoon and then continued hiking out of the mountains until the light was fading from the sky. They chose an area to camp where the rocks transitioned to a mostly open space with bushes and clumps of plants. They found a small rock outcropping resembling their previous shelter. Spence and Caleb hung the tarp and gathered wood for a fire. Morgan and Tom went hunting for some of the rabbits they had seen on their trek.

Soon they were all gathered around the fire and roasting two skinned rabbits. Tom had also dug up some thick plant roots like white sweet potatoes. They roasted those on sticks too. Even though the food of late hadn't been bad, fresh meat was always good. Morgan once again ate the fresh, wild meat, apparently distinguishing it from meat not harvested from hunting. Spence tried the roots and was surprised they tasted like roasted chestnuts.

"I can't believe Trey accepted Odin's," Spence said after they had finished eating.

"Yeah, we all know he's an idiot, but he certainly kicked it up a notch or two with that move," Caleb replied.

"I always thought he had a fairly good deal on Earth. I mean, he's the big man on campus and will probably get a scholarship to play football somewhere," Spence continued.

"I'd say it's one of two things," Morgan chimed in. "Either he doesn't think we'll return to Earth, or things at home are even worse than he indicated."

"Well, I only briefly met him, but I guess you never truly know what's in anyone else's head. And we don't know what Odin might have told or promised him. Maybe the gods all offer different deals," Tom said.

"Good point," Spence said. Perhaps the gods were using different tactics and promises to sway each of them. Enki had threatened him with reversing the repairs to his spine. Now, he had to wonder even more about Morgan and Caleb. "Did your gods promise you anything special other than ruling Nibiru?"

"Like we'd tell you if they did!" Morgan said. Then she laughed, right before Spence's pulse elevated too much. "Nah. Just me getting to be queen—with you as my serving wench." She cackled again.

"You wish," Spence retorted weakly.

"Yeah, just ruling the world and the other races," Caleb said.

They stared at the fire in silence for the next few minutes. "I wonder what the last monster will be?" Spence finally asked. He figured it was pointless to discuss the gods or their offers further. Although Morgan had been joking, it was probably true that Morgan and Caleb wouldn't reveal if they had received special offers or were considering leaving.

"Hard to say," Caleb said. "I imagine something big and nasty. Not much good comes out of a swamp."

"You might have to take a little more heat without Trey here. You're the only melee we have," Spence said, referring to the term of a close-range fighter in *Warcraft*.

"True. So, you and the archers better get the job done quickly," Caleb replied.

"You missing the goat was crazy, huh?" Morgan asked softly.

"Yeah, appears we were right...." Tom said. "I can't shoot very well."

"Yep. It was good to see the fail firsthand, though," Caleb replied.

The four stared at the fire for some time, lost in thought. The air was a little warmer since leaving the mountains, but Spence still liked the comfort and warmth of the flames. "Well, hopefully, we'll be going home soon. We only have to defeat the last monster to complete the gods' quest. Then we'll be free," Spence said without much conviction.

"Yeah, won't be long," Caleb agreed.

"Do you have a family back home, Tom?" Morgan asked.

"Yep—a beautiful wife and two little boys, Zach and Isaac, six and four. They're the main reason I've tried so hard to stay alive. I hope I can at least see them again someday. Of course, they probably thought I died a month or two ago. Hopefully, the old lady hasn't remarried yet," he said, chuckling. He wiped at the corner of his left eye.

"I guess a place like this makes you appreciate what you had," Spence said.

The four didn't speak again for some time; the mood was somber and tense. Finally, Caleb said, "Well, we'd better set up watch again. Hopefully, nobody will leave during the night. I'll take the last watch this time."

Spence volunteered to take the first watch, followed by Morgan and Tom.

CHAPTER 48

The night ended without incident. The four ate a quick breakfast, packed, and were soon marching again. Before long, they had left the mountains and rocks behind and found themselves walking on soft, spongy ground. Small pools of water appeared first, followed by larger ponds. The vegetation grew thicker and larger, ranging from reeds to thick bushes. They passed a few cypress trees growing out of the water and occasionally spotted a willow and black ash.

The marsh eventually transitioned to a swamp, with many more large cypress trees. The thick canopy mostly blocked the sky. Soon, Caleb had to slow to pick a dry path through the expanding muck. They each had their share of accidental stepping into mud or water. The swamp was thicker and mostly water to the west. Spence recalled the map Tom had made on the cave floor. This was yet another impassable border—keeping them from reaching the side of the dome or whatever substance enclosed Nibiru. The swamp gradually forced them further south and east, which wasn't as thick and watery.

The four reached a dead end after a narrow trail they followed south ended on a small peninsula, surrounded by black water on the other three sides. Spence surveyed his surroundings. This swamp section was primarily devoid of trees and consisted of fairly open water with several islands and patches of growth. The air hung thick with the smell of rotting vegetation. The temperature was getting hot, and when they caught glimpses of it, the sky was bright, despite the sun not being visible. The humidity was much higher, too, similar to a greenhouse or the rainforest habitat in a zoo. They didn't encounter bugs or mosquitos, though, and they also hadn't seen snakes, alligators, or crocodiles. In fact, they hadn't seen any wildlife.

"Well, this place sucks," Caleb said. "But we might as well stop here for lunch."

The others agreed, and they soon sat in the middle of the circular patch of land at the end of the peninsula. With having to feed an extra mouth, most of the dwarven food was gone. Hopefully, they would go home soon, or the Draconians would provide more.

"It will be hard to go much farther without wading or swimming," Caleb said.

"Um, I vote no," Morgan said.

"Then you can stay here," Caleb replied.

They heard a splash in the water to the east, and all four heads swiveled together. There was an expanding circle of ripples on the surface but no sign of what had caused the splash. "I have a bad feeling we're fighting a giant gator or croc," Caleb said.

"Or snake," Spence replied.

"What the heck?" Tom stood and grabbed his bow off his back. He stared intently at another patch of water where the ripples still expanded.

The others stood and turned to stare too. "What did you see?" Caleb asked.

"Something moving through the water—something long and black," Tom answered.

Spence stared intently at the water but saw nothing but the ripples. He clutched his staff tightly.

"Over there!" Morgan shouted. She pointed to the south side of the peninsula.

Spence spun in time to see something black disappear below the surface. Ripples spread in that section too. He instinctively turned to the west. In a moment, he saw the object appear on that side. It was a long, black ridge, undoubtedly the back of something huge. "Over here," he said. Then it disappeared again. The strip of land that led to the island was behind them, so he knew the creature couldn't completely circle them.

"Watch the south," Spence said, turning to that side. Sure enough, the object appeared again. This time they all saw it, and it lingered above the surface longer. It was at least ten feet wide, and the portion they could see was twenty feet long. It disappeared yet again.

Caleb drew his sword, and Morgan and Tom both nocked arrows on their bowstrings. They all turned to the east side. The black shape appeared again. This time it rose even further out of the water, revealing its body was indeed ten feet wide and shaped like a tube. It disappeared again.

"What is that thing?" Caleb asked.

"It looks like a whale's back," Spence said. He struck his staff on the ground, the orb illuminating.

"Or a giant black snake," Morgan added.

They looked to the south, but nothing appeared. They then turned together to the west—still nothing. The four spun to the front again.

"Maybe it was just a swim-by, and it moved on," Morgan said.

Suddenly, the water exploded in front of them. A giant, black cylindrical shape stretched high out of the water until it towered thirty feet above them. Its skin was solid black and shiny like a seal. The four stood frozen in shock. Then the creature began folding toward them. The head tilted down until they saw a vast, gaping round mouth, lined with jagged teeth, descending toward them.

Spence stumbled backward, not even having time to press one of the buttons on his staff. He continued backpedaling even as he was falling. *Lord, please give us the strength and wisdom to survive another battle.* He fell hard onto his butt and quickly looked up to see if he was out of the path of the enormous monster's mouth. Morgan and Tom had scattered to both sides, out of harm's way. Caleb retreated, heading between Spence and Morgan as he held his shield and sword stretched out above him. The giant worm's teeth missed Caleb, but the top of the mouth struck his shield and sword. Luckily, the blow only sent him sprawling past Spence, and he wasn't crushed beneath the massive weight of the beast.

Spence watched in amazement as the worm's mouth struck the ground, shaking the peninsula and denting the surface. Then it slowly slid into the water. He clambered to his feet and rushed over to Caleb. Caleb had come to rest flat on his back. He stared up, obviously dazed. Spence helped him to his feet.

Caleb leaned over, with his shield braced on his left knee and sword tip pressed into the ground. He inhaled several deep breaths, shook his head, and stood straight. "Everyone spread out! If it comes after you, get out of the way. Everyone else attacks. Spence, we can use some techno-magic on this thing."

"Well, that's random. It looks like a giant worm or leech," Morgan said.

"Something created in the gods' lab, I'm sure," Tom replied.

Spence stood near the rear of the peninsula, hoping he would be free to fire a lightning bolt. Morgan stood to his right, Caleb in front, and Tom to his left. They all waited, bodies tensed and barely daring to breathe.

The water was calm, with no signs of the earlier ripples or the black back of the worm. But Spence knew it would return; it was only a matter of when and where.

The water erupted in front of Caleb. This time, instead of soaring high into the air, the worm launched straight out of the water toward him. Spence could only see the massive gaping mouth and rows of huge white teeth. Caleb managed to take two steps and dive headfirst toward Tom. The outside of the worm's mouth only grazed the bottom of his boots. Morgan and Tom both shot arrows into the side of the beast's head. Spence lowered his staff and depressed the first button. *Come on!* The lightning surged forth as the monster began sliding back into the water. The lightning struck just as its monstrous mouth disappeared into the depths.

After the thunderclap roared, Caleb leaped to his feet. "Did you kill it?"

"I hit it. But just a quick hit before it disappeared into the water," Spence said. His staff had gone dark, and the compartment closed shut.

"What about the arrows?"

"Mine hit, but I doubt it did anything. I mean, look at the size of it," Tom called out.

"Same here," Morgan said.

"Maybe Spence fried it," Caleb replied.

A giant splash debunked the theory. This time the worm came at Tom. Tom paused to fire an arrow into the dark mouth and then tried to roll away to the side. He wasn't quite quick enough, though. The right side of the beast's mouth crashed across his legs. Tom screamed but nocked another arrow and fired it point-blank into the side of its head. The worm lifted its mouth and then lowered it on top of Tom, totally enveloping him. Spence saw the mouth close together from all sides, sealing completely to resemble a typical worm's head.

CHAPTER 49

"No!" Caleb shouted and rushed over to slash the worm's body right behind its head. His sword sank deeply into the black flesh, causing a thick, dark liquid to ooze out of the gash and onto its skin. The liquid appeared either black or dark red on his sword. Morgan fired an arrow close to Caleb and struck the worm's head; the arrow disappeared into the blubbery flesh.

Spence couldn't attack, but he rummaged in his pack and drew out the other vial of the white liquid. If his staff didn't recharge in time, or its attacks weren't effective, he might have to drink the potion and at least regain the mental powers he had used against the spider mantis. The lightning hadn't worked, and he doubted the fireball would have time to strike before the worm submerged into the water. The shock wave would only push it further into the swamp and most likely not kill it. The worm once again disappeared beneath the surface.

"Tom!" Morgan shouted. The only thing remaining of Tom was a large amount of blood smeared across the grass he had laid on moments before.

"Damn it! How do we kill it?" Caleb yelled.

Spence tried not to think of Tom's gruesome fate. He forced his mind to recall everything he had studied on worms in advanced biology. "If it's like a real worm, it has a tiny brain just above the mouth and seven small hearts along the esophagus. Anything past that area won't hurt it at all. You know, like earthworms. You can cut them into pieces, and they still live."

"So, we have to hit its brain or all seven hearts?"

"Pretty much."

"We'll never stay alive that long," Caleb said.

The worm appeared again, arching high into the air and coming down on Morgan's side of the peninsula. Morgan shot an arrow into its hungry mouth and then sprinted forward, angling toward the water to the monster's left. She passed underneath the colossal mouth and emerged on the other side of its neck as the head smashed into the ground. She nocked another arrow and shot it in the neck.

Caleb rushed in from the other direction and hacked at its neck on the right side. Spence tapped the butt of the staff on the ground, but it didn't activate. The worm disappeared into the water once more.

"We need some ideas, people," Caleb yelled.

"I'm aiming for its eyes, but I have no idea where they are!" Morgan shouted.

Spence had a thought. "Caleb."

Caleb turned and stared at him.

"Catch." Spence tossed the potion high into the air toward Caleb.

Caleb had to drop his sword to catch the vial of liquid. "What's this?" he shouted angrily.

"The potion I drank when we fought the spider mantises. Drink it," Spence said.

Caleb scowled but pulled the cork out and downed the liquid. He tossed the vial to the side and grabbed his sword. He assumed his defensive stance facing the water.

Spence scanned the water on all sides. He wondered if they could retreat the way they had come. But here, the peninsula was at least wide enough to maneuver. The neck was a very narrow strip of dry land. If the worm could reach them, it could easily smash them all or knock them into the water. If they were in the water, they wouldn't have a chance. Plus, this was probably the monster they had to defeat to complete their quest. Fleeing wasn't an option.

If the worm had a pattern, it would attack Caleb this time, as it had at the start. The wait seemed longer than between the last two attacks. Spence wasn't sure if their attacks had slowed it. The arrows Tom and Morgan shot inside the mouth could have struck a heart or two. He doubted anything on the outside of the body hurt it.

Caleb tossed his shield and sword to the ground and drew his daggers.

"What are you doing?" Spence called out.

"Your potion is working. I have a plan," Caleb said without turning around.

Before Spence could ask another question, the water spewed again. The worm did appear in front of Caleb. This time it shot high out of the water, as it had on the first attack. It soared at least thirty feet high. Then the head tilted and fell toward the ground, its mouth open and sharp teeth exposed. It plunged straight toward Caleb.

This time Caleb didn't move. Morgan fired an arrow into the side of its head. Spence just watched in horror as the monstrosity descended on Caleb. Spence knew Caleb was quick, but the worm was too close for a dive or roll to safety. Closer and closer, the gaping maw of death rushed toward Caleb. Caleb stared up, his arms still hanging by his sides, each hand clutching a dagger. Morgan screamed from Spence's right, but Caleb still stood motionless.

As the mouth lowered around Caleb, he suddenly leaped into it, his arms now raised above his head. The mouth hit the ground and closed shut with Caleb inside. The trunk of the worm fell to the ground behind the head with a ground-shaking thud. Spence watched in shock as the worm slid back into the black water. Like Tom, Caleb was gone.

"No!" Morgan shouted and rushed to the water's edge. Spence joined her there a few seconds later.

"Caleb!" Spence yelled. The ripples gradually subsided, and the water stilled. He saw no sign of the worm or Caleb.

"Why did he just stand there?" Morgan asked. Her voice shook, and tears rolled down her cheeks.

"He said he had a plan," Spence said softly. "It was the potion."

They stood staring helplessly at the black, still depths.

"What do we do?"

"I can try my staff again. If that doesn't work, we'll have to run back the way we came, regroup, and figure out how to kill it," Spence said.

Bubbles eventually appeared on the surface, small at first and growing steadily larger. Soon the water churned white with them. Then the water exploded in all directions, and something erupted from the depths, soaring into the air. Morgan instantly had her bow drawn, and Spence stood in a defensive stance with his staff held before him. But this time, the disruption was not the giant worm. Caleb splashed down in front of them, gasping for air. Spence extended his staff, and Caleb grasped it. Spence then hauled him to the bank, and Morgan helped drag him onto dry ground.

Caleb rolled over on his back, gasping deeply. He still clung to both daggers. He closed his eyes and continued to breathe deeply for several seconds. Spence scanned the water, but the bubbles had subsided, and he saw no sign of the worm. He glanced at Morgan, who only shrugged and turned to stare at Caleb. Finally, Caleb sat up and gazed at the other two.

"Well, that was stupid. Did you kill it?" Morgan asked.

Caleb nodded silently.

"How?" Spence asked incredulously.

Caleb swallowed hard. "Well, to answer Morgan, it wasn't stupid and was the only chance we had. After drinking the potion, I remembered everything I had ever seen or heard about worms. I could visualize exactly where its brain and hearts were. I knew if I could get past the teeth without getting shredded, I could do some serious damage inside. I was tossed around a bit by the impact of it hitting the ground and sliding into the water, but I stabbed like crazy into the roof of its mouth, where I thought the brain was. I held my ground to avoid getting swallowed and jabbed and sliced where all the hearts should have been."

"Then what happened?" Morgan asked.

"Well, I killed it, but the worm began sinking rapidly, nose down, to the bottom of the swamp. The one thing I didn't count on was its mouth being sealed shut. So, I had to cut my way out of its esophagus to reach the water. When I opened the side, all the air inside it rushed out, carrying me to the surface. This swamp is deep, and I might not have made it up without the bubbles pushing me."

"That's incredible," Spence said.

"Tom?" Morgan asked.

Caleb shook his head grimly. "There's no time to cry for him, though. Spence, do you have any more of those potions? Those might be really helpful in the future."

Spence shook his head. "That's all I had."

"That sucks." Caleb stood, his face pale and his body swaying slightly. "Let's get off this island and find the Draconians. I don't want to risk encountering another one of those."

CHAPTER 50

They made their way back to the main trail, if it could be called that, and continued southeast into the Forsaken Swamp. The going was slow since they wanted to stay on dry land. In some spots, they had to leap from island to island. They had to wade occasionally but only where they could see weeds and vegetation sticking out of the water. They avoided the sections of water without any visible growth.

Soon the land, trees, and vegetation mostly disappeared. Small islands were scattered to the east and south but with no land connection from where they were. The islands had structures on them resembling beaver dams on stilts. Some islands had trees and bushes, and others were bare other than the structures.

"Well, crap," Caleb said. "Can everyone swim?"

Spence's heart leaped into his throat. He remembered a week of swimming lessons when he was twelve years old in the hell that was 4-H camp. But he spent more time trying to avoid being held underwater and flipped with wet-tipped towels than learning to swim. He had never really tried since then. "I can't," he croaked.

"And that's a shock," Morgan said.

"Like you can?" Spence retorted, his face getting warm.

"Well, most Goth girls don't spend a lot of time at the pool. They'd burn their fair skin. I can't use that excuse, but I guess I just never got into it," she said, grinning weakly. "I could possibly tread water for a few minutes."

"Great. Now what?" Caleb asked.

Before Spence could respond, they saw some disturbances in the water just before them. The three turned and readied their weapons.

255

Instead of a giant worm, three creatures emerged from the water. They were man-shaped but green and covered with scales. Spence, Morgan, and Caleb retreated to give the creatures room and to determine if they were monsters or the Draconians.

The creatures slowly climbed to their feet. They were at least six and a half feet tall. Their heads resembled lizards, with large green eyes with thin, vertical pupils and two slits for nostrils. They had small ears on the sides of their heads and a ridge on the top disappearing behind. They wore tight-fitting black sleeveless shirts and black pants coming to their knees. Their clothes were slick and shining with water, resembling spandex swimming suits. Exposed arms and calves were muscular, like those of the Nephilim. Their hands ended in long, bony fingers, and their feet were flat and wide, ending in short, webbed toes. Long, thick tails somehow extended through their clothing and nearly touched the ground behind them.

"Welcome, questers," one of them spoke. His voice was raspy and hissed on the esses.

"You must be the Draconians," Spence said, stepping up beside Caleb. He marveled at the lizard men. These were the best and most realistic of all the gods' creations—half-human, half-lizard. They appeared stronger and sturdier than any of the other races too. He wondered if they had to stay close to water, though.

"We are," the first one replied. "I am Sinnashi. Welcome to the Forsaken Swamp."

"We are supposed to meet Qishti. Can you take us to him?" Spence asked.

"He is expecting you." The three Draconians turned around to face the water. "Enter the water and straddle our backs," Sinnashi said.

The Draconians waded into the water until only shoulders and heads were above the surface. Caleb glanced at the other two, shrugged, and waded in. He straddled his legs over the back of Sinnashi, and the Draconian submerged beneath the surface and swam rapidly through the water. His arms, legs, and tail didn't break the surface or splash. It appeared Caleb magically skimmed across the surface. Spence couldn't tell whether Sinnashi's tail aided in swimming or functioned as a rudder to steer. Morgan followed, mounted the second one, and soon sped through the water behind Caleb. Spence nervously strode into the water and clumsily climbed onto his escort. He leaned forward, grabbed the creature's shoulders, and instantly sped across the water like riding on a submerged jet ski.

Spence grinned despite having just survived the battle with the giant worm and losing their newfound companion. He was amazed at how effortlessly the Draconian sliced through the water. It felt like he imagined riding a dolphin or giant seal would. Spence studied the small islands they rushed past. The mounds of sticks were indeed wooden huts, raised at least six feet above the islands on stilts. Draconians occupied most of the islands, either inside or outside the huts. They saw other Draconians swimming through the water, too, heading here and there.

The islands and lizard people became more numerous the further they traveled. Then after five minutes of swimming, the small isles disappeared, and they were in an open patch of water. A massive island lay in the center, covered with numerous wooden structures, some towering three stories high. Smaller islands ringed the three visible sides with wooden bridges connecting them to the main island. Large wooden structures and walkways also covered the smaller islands.

Caleb and Morgan already stood with their escorts on the edge of the closest island. Spence's escort angled toward them, and they soon joined the others.

"We will cross the bridge to Abzu, where we will find Qishti. Swimming directly to it is forbidden. Follow me," Sinnashi said. He led them onto a wooden walkway that ascended several feet above the ground. The other two Draconians trailed behind. Spence realized all the wooden structures on this island were also elevated on posts. The walkway branched several times, leading to various buildings on either side. They passed other Draconians; some nodded, and others ignored them.

Spence observed most of the Draconians had long, curved daggers hanging from their belts. Others stood guard at various locations, armed with spears and tridents. The walkway skirted around the largest round building in the island's center and continued on the other side. It then descended to the shore and intersected the bridge spanning a hundred feet of water to the main island.

Many more heavily armed, guard-looking Draconians were on the other side of the bridge. Sinnashi led them past more significant buildings on this main island and finally to the center's largest, three-story square building. Two guards flanked the double doors, holding tridents. They opened the doors and ushered the party through.

The lighting inside the huge room was dim, with only a few lamps and lanterns augmenting the gray light spilling in from windows spaced along two walls. The room contained many wooden tables and chairs and appeared to serve as a dining hall. It was currently devoid of Draconians.

Sinnashi led them across the room and through a door in the far wall. The room beyond was small and square, with no windows. Shelves lined the two sidewalls, and two small tables with lanterns on them sat in each of the near corners. Four chairs sat in front of a large desk straight in front of them. On the other side of the desk was an oversized, high-backed chair occupied by the largest Draconian they had seen.

The Draconian glanced up from studying some type of paper on the desk. "Welcome, questers. I am Qishti. Please be seated." Qishti nodded to their escorts, and they disappeared through the door and shut it behind them. "I have heard you defeated the swamp beast. Very impressive." Qishti had a slight lisp, but not as bad as Sinnashi.

The four sat in the chairs in front of the desk. "We did. And that was the last part of our quest. So, we should be able to return home," Caleb said, leaning forward in his chair.

"Ah. You are the first to complete the quest. Well done."

"Then where are the gods to return us to Earth?" Caleb continued.

"No one can summon the gods," Qishti said, staring at Caleb. "They will appear if and when they are ready. We do not question their ways."

"We can summon them," Caleb retorted, returning Qishti's stare.

"What do you mean, human?"

Spence wanted to catch Caleb's attention and stop him from doing what he was about to do. They should at least wait and hear what Qishti could tell them. But Caleb reached inside his mail shirt and retrieved his amulet.

"We each have one of these and can summon a god with them," Caleb said.

Qishti's eyes widened as he stared at the amulet. Spence and Morgan pulled theirs out too. "Why did they give you those?"

"Caleb," Spence hissed.

Caleb ignored him. "No, Spence, I'm tired of playing games. We can summon them or transport ourselves to their peoples and lead them to war."

"A war?" Qishti leaned forward in his chair now. "Then it is true...."

"You know about this war?" Spence asked.

"I have heard rumors. I did not think it would be this soon, though."

"Is that the reason for the armed guards?" Spence said.

"Yes. We have been preparing just in case the rumors were true." Qishti replied. "Which one of you has Enki's amulet?"

Spence's heart began racing, and his palm sweated on the stone in his hand. He cleared his throat. "Umm...I do."

"So, you can summon him now?"

"Uh…yeah…I guess."

"Do it, Spence. Let's have a chat with Enki about where the doorway leading home is," Caleb said.

"I don't know," Morgan said softly.

"Why the heck not? We at least need to know the options, right?"

"Qishti?" Spence asked.

"I am unsure," Qishti said, sitting back in his chair.

"He told you to do it anytime, right?" Caleb persisted.

"At least when I was ready to lead the Draconians," Spence said.

"Well, he shouldn't have given it to you if he didn't want you to use it. Try it."

Spence looked at Qishti again. Qishti's face was unreadable. But the scaly lizard face would be impossible to read at any time. Spence thought it odd that none of them found it strange talking to lizard people as if they were regular humans. But in this world, strange was relative.

Spence stood and walked to the door. He then turned and faced the others. Caleb and Morgan twisted in their chairs, watching him intently. The stone was unnaturally warm in Spence's moist hand. He cleared his throat and inhaled deeply. He squeezed the pendant and said, "Enki, please appear."

CHAPTER 51

Spence wasn't sure what to expect. After all, he wasn't even one hundred percent sure he hadn't dreamed both encounters with Enki. But since the others admitted to similar dreams, and Trey had disappeared, Spence thought they had a decent chance to see the god again or at least an image of him.

The silence was palpable. If anyone breathed, Spence couldn't detect it. Finally, after what seemed hours but was probably minutes, the air shimmered to Spence's right. At first, it looked like heat waves rippling in the desert air. Then the waves became more substantial. Eventually, they coalesced into a human shape. Enki appeared, a glowing white image. The image was obviously a hologram, although the figure did turn its gaze from each of them as if he were actually in the room.

Qishti stood from his chair and then knelt on the floor on one knee, leaning forward in a bow. "My Lord Enki! I am honored by you gracing my humble home."

"Thank you, my loyal servant. You may return to your seat." Enki then turned to Spence. "Greetings, Spence the Wizard," Enki said, his voice sounding like it came from the glimmering image.

"Spence the Wizard?" Morgan said softly to Caleb but loud enough for the others to hear.

"Does your summons mean you are ready to lead my followers?"

"Uh…well…not exactly," Spence stammered.

"Then why have you disturbed me?"

"Well…um…we killed the last monster in our quest." Spence inhaled deeply and steadied his voice. "When we came to Nibiru, you, through the statue, said if we completed the gods' quest, we could return home—to Earth."

"Ah, yes."

"So, please open up a doorway or vortex or whatever you call it, and we'll be on our way," Caleb said.

Enki turned to Caleb. His brows knotted together in a slight scowl, then quickly relaxed. "Caleb the Warrior, I would enjoy nothing more than to allow you to return to your home. However, things have changed."

"That's a shocker," Caleb replied.

"If your entire party were here, the quest would indeed be complete. However, Trey, the Barbarian is not with you," Enki said.

"Of course not. He's with your god pal, Odin, leading the dwarves into war," Caleb said.

Caleb's tone stone shocked Spence. But Spence had noticed a change in Caleb since Trey's disappearance. He had known they wouldn't get to go home and was obviously tired of being a pawn of the gods.

"It is true Trey has joined the dwarves. But the decision was his. Even as we speak, the dwarves are preparing for battle. That battle threatens the very fabric of our world. If they come this way first, I cannot allow the dwarves to slaughter my people. They must have a leader and prepare for war."

"What about the other races?" Morgan asked.

"Morgan the Archer, the other races need their leaders too, and also to ready for war," Enki said.

"What are the other three races to do? Attack each other or stand together and fight the dwarves?" Spence asked.

"It will be up to their leaders. But without some alliances, there won't be many survivors in an all-out war of the races."

"We don't know anything about war or leading people into a battle," Morgan said, her eyes glistening in the lamplight.

"Any more than your companion, Trey. There has never been a war in Nibiru, so none of the races have experienced battle, other than defending themselves against roaming creatures," Enki stated.

"What are you telling us? Now we *have* to lead a race into this battle?" Caleb asked, glaring intensely at Enki.

"We cannot force you to do anything. However, we cannot open a passage back to Earth as long as there is war in Nibiru. Also, without leaders, the other races will inevitably be eliminated or subjugated by the dwarves. So eventually, you will have to answer to your former friend and his army. How do you think that encounter will go? Do you think he will allow you to return to Earth?"

"Fuck you and all the gods!" Caleb shouted, standing and nearly knocking his chair over in the process.

Morgan grabbed his arm and stopped him from moving further.

"I would channel your anger, Caleb. Use it to prepare and lead the Nephilim into battle. Stop your former friend from his plan to rule our world. If you restore peace to our land, we will allow you to return to Earth."

Spence saw Caleb's mouth open to speak again, but Morgan stomped on his foot. He finally dropped back down hard into the chair.

Enki turned to Spence. "Spence the Wizard, you are here with the Draconians. If you choose to be their leader, then simply let my faithful servant, Qishti, know, and you can prepare your plans." Enki looked at Caleb and Morgan. "You two only have to use your amulets to travel to your peoples. Good luck to each of you, and I hope you choose well." Then Enki disappeared.

Spence returned to his seat. He exchanged a glance with Morgan and then Caleb. Neither of them spoke. Qishti finally broke the silence. "You should show more respect for Lord Enki," he said, staring at Caleb.

"He doesn't deserve my respect. He's just a—"

"Caleb!" Spence said. He remembered Seth in Argos. He knew the gods couldn't strike them dead directly, but Enki could easily have a Draconian stick a dagger in his back. "We are sorry, Qishti. It has been a tough quest. We're just disappointed we cannot return to our homes."

"I understand, but you still must show the gods respect. If not, they will punish you."

Another stomp from Morgan stopped Caleb from speaking again.

"Qishti, is there a place we can speak—where nobody can overhear?" Spence clarified, "We can't have our battle plans leak out before we're ready." Caleb and Morgan nodded in agreement.

"Ah, that is prudent. I do have a place we use when we require secret counsel. Stay here, and I will return momentarily. Then we shall have our meeting." Qishti stood and disappeared through the door behind his desk.

"Definitely a good time for a secret meeting," Caleb mumbled.

CHAPTER 52

Qishti returned a few minutes later with three white disks in his hands. He handed one to each of them. "Put these in your mouths when we enter the water. They will allow you to breathe. Just do not breathe through your nose."

Spence examined the device. It had a protrusion on one side—like the tip of a toy flute or recorder—which he assumed went into the mouth. The rest of it, the size and shape of a hockey puck, would remain on the outside. His heart raced at the prospect of swimming. He had no clue how even to start. But at least with this device, he wouldn't drown.

"You can leave your weapons and armor here—you will be safe. I would also advise leaving your boots," Qishti said.

Caleb stared at Qishti with raised eyebrows.

"No one will touch your items," Qishti said.

The three removed everything except shirts, pants, and daggers and followed Qishti outside the building.

"We are going for a swim," Qishti said to the guards outside the door, who straightened when they walked past.

He led them on the wooden pathway around to the rear of the large building. He then guided them through several forks until the path finally ended at the water's edge. "I trust you can all swim?"

Spence glanced at Morgan and then at Qishti. "Morgan and I cannot."

Once again, Qishti's face was unreadable. "Simply paddle your arms and legs and follow me. The water is murky but will not hurt your eyes."

Caleb placed the breathing device in his mouth. "How do I look with a toilet mint in my mouth?" he asked Morgan and Spence.

Spence laughed, glad to see Caleb's sense of humor make a rare appearance. He put the small tube into his mouth and closed his lips around it. The disk was lightweight and didn't feel as awkward as it looked. He hoped he could keep the mouthpiece firmly in his mouth.

"Spence, I'm so glad your cell phone is dead. This would blow up the Internet," Morgan said, placing hers in her mouth.

Qishti waded into the water until he was chest-deep. Then he arched his back and dove beneath the surface. Caleb followed him, with Morgan going next and then Spence. Spence had trouble getting his entire body submerged below the surface. He flopped and splashed on top of the water for a minute before finally using his arms to guide his body down. He kicked his legs hard to keep himself from rising to the surface.

He could barely detect movement straight ahead at the far range of his sight. Then he accidentally breathed in through his nose and momentarily panicked. He flailed in the water and nearly resurfaced before blowing the water out of his nose and breathing deeply through his mouth. After a few seconds, he had the hang of it and began kicking his feet, placing his arms together in front of him, and then spreading them wide with his palms turned out. It took a few minutes to learn how to maintain the same line in the water and not go too deep or float to the surface.

The water soon deepened to what he estimated to be ten or twelve feet. He gradually began catching the others and could soon make out Morgan's body in front of him. They must have slowed for him to catch them. Morgan appeared almost as unsteady as he felt. His face was right behind her bare feet a few minutes later. The water at this point was too deep even to discern the bottom.

Soon Spence saw a landmass materialize in front of them. It sloped down from the surface and disappeared into the depths below. He saw the others start angling down in the water, and he tilted his head down and brought his body into the new trajectory. They swam down the angle of the landmass at least thirty feet until they came to a round, black opening.

Qishti entered first, followed by Caleb and Morgan. Spence's heart accelerated as he swam through the hole barely wider than his shoulders. The water inside was nearly pitch black. He could only see Morgan's feet and nothing of the others in front of her. He followed Morgan as she angled up, and half a minute later, his head suddenly broke the water's surface.

***

"Where are they going?" Artemis asked.

"I do not know," Enki replied.

"How do you not know of this place and have it monitored?" Odin demanded.

"My Draconians spend most of their time in the water. I cannot watch the entire swamp. Besides, no questers have even made it close to here before," Enki responded.

"This could be a fatal oversight," Ra said.

"Nonsense. What are they going to do? They are just discussing their theories on Nibiru and our intentions yet again. If they do not depart to lead their races soon, we will force their hands," Enki replied.

***

Dim light shone from high overhead but not bright enough to illuminate the details of their surroundings. Then Spence heard steel striking stone and saw a flash of sparks. A few seconds later, he saw Qishti holding a burning torch. They were inside a dome-shaped structure with a small opening in the top. Water filled half of the space. Qishti stood on the shore of the other half, which was sand and rock.

Spence swam to the shore and wearily crawled onto the dry sand. He hadn't realized how badly his arms and legs burned. Caleb and Morgan already sat on the beach. Qishti lit another torch in a sconce on the near wall and placed his on the far one. Most of the domed space was still dark, but they could see each other well enough. He sat on a rock in front of the others.

"Private enough?" Qishti asked.

Caleb peered up at the opening in the top. "As long as nothing can look down the hole. Where is this place, anyway?"

"It is the inside of one of the islands. The opening is in the base of a hollow tree trunk, so there is no danger of someone reaching the island or fitting inside the trunk. The hole lets the smoke out and keeps the air fresh."

"And you know why we wanted the privacy?" Caleb asked.

"I assume so the gods cannot see or hear," Qishti said.

"Bingo. The other races each led us to secret places and told us things about the gods and this world. The gods must be unable to hear or see, or we would have died long ago."

"This place is safe, or I, too, would be dead."

"So, you speak badly about the gods?" Spence asked.

Qishti hissed. "The gods created all the races. But you have seen them and us. We are all monstrosities. They made us into walking and talking lizards and keep us confined to this swamp. We cannot reproduce or bear children. A replacement shows up when one dies, keeping us at

267

one thousand strong. We are their playthings. We have always wondered what our purpose is—why they created us. Now, I think we know."

"The war?" Caleb asked.

"Yes," Qishti said with a long hiss at the end. "I do not know their objective, but I doubt it is only to stop your former companion and the dwarves. What has Enki told you?" he asked Spence.

Spence thought momentarily of lying. But at this juncture, keeping secrets was pointless. "He wants me to lead the Draconians and conquer and rule Nibiru. He said we could subdue one of the other races and make them join us. Then we can take out the others one by one." Spence turned to Caleb. "Is that what Ra told you?"

"Pretty much."

"And the same for Artemis," Morgan added.

Qishti hissed again. "So, they do not want you to join together to stop the dwarves?"

Caleb rubbed his chin. "They probably do initially or don't care if we do. Then they will produce a reason to force us to fight each other."

"Why? Our world has never had war. The races exist in peace," Qishti said.

"For entertainment," Morgan said.

"Entertainment?"

Morgan glanced at Spence and Caleb, who both shrugged. She then told him the theory they had developed with Tom. Spence and Caleb chimed in here and there. The four sat in silence as Qishti absorbed their words for a few moments.

"I do not fully understand some of this technology you mention, but your theory does have merit, especially with the arrow hitting the sky."

"What about your land? What is south of the Forsaken Swamp?" Spence asked.

"There is a wall of impassable vegetation," Qishti said.

"What's underneath the vegetation?" Spence continued. "Is the water blocked too?"

"We have swum a little way beneath it. The vegetation and tree roots extend far beneath the surface. If you swim deep enough, you can go underneath. But we can only go so far until we run out of air," Qishti said.

"What about with these devices?" Caleb asked, holding up his disk.

Qishti scratched the side of his face absently. "We have not tried them there. We have enough land and did not see any reason to push further. We figured the water would become impassable at some point."

"Are you thinking the water could go underneath the dome?" Spence asked.

"Possibly," Caleb said. "Or at least go directly up to it. Maybe the gods didn't account for every scenario, especially since no questers have even made it this far."

"How would we get through the wall even if we reached it?" Morgan asked.

Caleb dragged his fingers through the sand. "Good question."

"If it were on land, I would suggest my lightning bolt or fireball," Spence said. "But I'm thinking neither would be a good idea in the water."

"Spence, you're almost a genius!" Caleb exclaimed.

"Almost?"

"How about the third attack—the shock wave? When the arrow struck the dome, it rippled like water and became solid again. What if your shock wave at close range could temporarily open a hole?"

Spence's mind raced through the possibilities. "It's possible. We don't know if the shock wave, or even my staff, will work in water, though. Or if it does, would it open a hole or just cause a bunch of ripples?"

"Maybe you could touch your staff to it and push the button. The dome can only be so thick. And if it can move like water or plasma, I'm thinking you could blast right through it. It would most likely close shut quickly, but it might stay open for a brief time, depending on the viscosity of the material."

"Viscosity? Someone paid attention in Mrs. Rhodes's A-P chemistry," Morgan said.

"Do you really want to try this? Should we not be focusing on stopping your friend Trey and the dwarves?" Qishti said.

"Will it take long to get there?" Caleb asked, ignoring the question.

"It would if you tried to swim from here. If we went by boat, it would take two hours or so. It is hard to know how long it would take underwater, assuming the way is not blocked at some point."

"Is there a time limit on these breathing devices?" Caleb asked.

"Around an hour, depending on how fast and deeply you breathe."

"The gods will see if we're in a rowboat for hours and wonder what we're up to," Spence said.

"True," Caleb replied. He rubbed his head thoughtfully. "Maybe we could make up an excuse to have to go that way. Any ideas, Qishti?"

Qishti stared past the four at the black water. "There is a flower growing in some parts of the swamp my people use to heal wounds. There would most likely be some in that area."

"But that only gets us to the overgrown part," Morgan said. "We still have to have a reason to dive underwater."

"Maybe not," Caleb replied. "We can just announce we want to see what's below the surface. I doubt the gods would have any clue of what we're planning. And even if they get suspicious, we'll know one way or the other within an hour. If we break out of the dome, all bets are off anyway. If we fail, we swim back, get in the boat, and go with the war plan."

"What do you hope to accomplish if you get outside this dome?" Qishti asked.

"I honestly don't know. I guess just discover what type of world we're actually dealing with. Maybe we can confront the gods without their monsters. They might save them only for the dome, and they live in a normal world," Caleb said.

"But they could have police or a military," Spence replied.

"Well, we've seen what our future is here. The gods are not going to let us go home. They want a war between all the races. If we defeat Trey and the dwarves, they'll find some way to make us fight each other until just one race remains, or at least until one is victorious. Then what? There will be something else. If it's not possible to win the game, then we need to change the rules."

"What about Trey and the dwarves? They have to be marching by now—either north to the elves or south to here," Qishti said.

"Well, if we cannot leave the dome, we'll only lose half a day."

"And if you escape?" Qishti asked.

"Then hopefully, we can stop the gods and their war. If they control things here, maybe we can force them to do what we want them to. Or intervene ourselves. In the end, we're all doomed if we just stay here and play the roles of pawns in their game."

"You are brave," Qishti said. "I guess that is why you have survived the quest."

"Sometimes you just get to the point you're tired of being afraid. I think we're all at that point."

Spence and Morgan nodded.

"Are we all in agreement then?" Caleb extended his hand in between Morgan and Spence.

Spence reviewed the options in his mind. The temptation of leading the Draconians into battle no longer appealed to him. Defeating Trey would be good, but he was now too close to Caleb and Morgan to want to fight against them. Caleb was probably right, too, about the gods wanting only one victor. They were making the rules, and he and his companions had no choice here but to follow them. If they could get outside the dome, anything was possible. Perhaps they could find other ways back to Earth or recruit allies to help them.

Part of him was glad that going back to Earth now was not an option. He wouldn't be forced to make that decision. Maybe they could find a way back that didn't involve losing his walking ability. He placed his hand on top of Caleb's.

Morgan didn't hesitate and placed hers on top of Spence's.

"For Earth!" Caleb roared.

"For Earth," Spence and Morgan repeated simultaneously.

"For the squad," Spence said, grinning.

"For the squad," Morgan and Caleb repeated, also smiling.

"I can take you there by boat, but I cannot leave my people or this world," Qishti said.

"Understood," Caleb replied.

"We will set out in the morning."

CHAPTER 53

"Domino's Pizza," Spence said when Morgan answered the door. They had eaten a fresh fish and vegetable dinner when they returned from the secret meeting. The Draconians were a stern race, and there hadn't been any drunken revelry at the meal. Then Qishti showed them to three rooms on the third floor. Spence was tired but too wired for sleep. He hoped Morgan might be awake too.

"Oh, boy! I hope it's a Pacific Veggie!" Morgan said, smiling.

The rooms had bare wooden floors and walls. A window was set in the wall across from the door, overlooking the waters they had swum in earlier. The room was furnished with a small bed, table and chairs, washbasin, nightstand, and two worn rugs on the floor. Two candles on the table and a lantern on the nightstand provided light. The layer of dust covering everything indicated that the rooms were not used often as sleeping quarters.

Morgan sat on the bed, and Spence pulled a chair out from the table and turned it around, facing her. "What's up, Spence the Wizard?"

Spence laughed. He had really grown fond of Morgan during their quest. She was the steady one and his sole source of comfort. She was so different from the Goth persona she played on Earth. "Some wizard. I have a staff with three buttons. You are the Archer, though."

Morgan smiled again. "Hey, you were pretty good with the spider-thingy. And shooting the bow is easy. I get to stand back and let the boys take the beating while I fire away. Now, what can I do for you?"

"Back rub? Foot rub?" Spence grinned. A few weeks ago in high school, he wouldn't have even dared to speak to Morgan. Now, after risking his life daily, he was a different person. Talking to a girl didn't compare to fighting horrific monsters that wanted to eat him.

"Umm, I don't think a swim in swamp water constitutes a bath. And no offense, but I ain't touchin' that body if it ain't squeaky clean."

"Yeah, there is that." *Would she touch it if it were clean?* "No, I was just in the mood for conversation. No talk of monsters and wars and death—only teenage stuff. I'm tired of playing grown-up."

"A little homesick, huh?"

"A little. I'm sure my parents are panicking by now and blaming themselves for letting me come on the trip. I wonder how freaked out everyone at school and in the town is? I mean, four kids missing for a week. I bet we've been all over the news and Internet."

"Yeah, we have to be doing some trending. Although, we might have been gone long enough to drop out of the headlines. You know how it goes. You're only news for so long until they push you to the side for something more interesting—probably a Kardashian or politics. All about the ratings," Morgan said.

"It's weird thinking about high school after all we've been through," Spence said.

"Yeah, constant fear of death changes your perspective. Somehow, studying, grades, sports, and cliques don't seem as important."

"Could you have imagined any scenario a few months ago where a geek like me would be hanging out in a bedroom with a Goth like you?"

"Not unless it involved chloroform and duct tape," Morgan laughed. Spence scowled at her, and she stuck her leg out and nudged his knee with her bare foot. "Heck, you would have kicked my butt even if I had chloroform and duct tape." Spence smacked her foot lightly.

"Oh yeah, I would have. However, you might take me now. You're not the same dough boy you were back then."

"Hey, if we survive another couple of weeks, I will be rocking the beach bod." They both laughed loudly.

"Yeah, we'll all look good for our burials."

"No death talk, remember?"

"Oh, yeah. Hey, I just thought of something! I still have some elven wine left. Want to share it?"

Spence's heart skipped a few beats. "I have some too!" Since Trey's meltdown, they hadn't drunk it again. "I'll be right back."

Spence returned with his bottle and joined Morgan on the bed. The move was a little forward, but he didn't care at this point. Morgan had extinguished the candles, so the lantern provided the sole light. "To surviving our quest," Spence said, holding his bottle out.

Morgan tapped hers against his bottle, and they both drank. "To kicking everything's ass in Nibiru and getting back to Earth." They clinked bottles and drank again.

"Should we invite Caleb over?" Spence asked.

Morgan wrinkled her brow. "Nah, let's let him sleep. I like him and everything, but he's not exactly a jolly soul."

They continued drinking and talking. They each had less than half a bottle of wine left, but both soon felt the effects. Spence didn't know whether their mood was just the release of a lot of pent-up stress or teenagers being teenagers, but they were soon laughing and acting silly— acting like kids and not hardened adults.

"What would be your first meal back on Earth?" Spence asked. His cheeks were warm from the laughter and wine.

"Well, since you mentioned pizza, veggie pizza, followed by chocolate ice cream, of course. You?"

"I like the pizza idea. I need the supreme, though. You need to get over the vegetarian thing."

Morgan punched him lightly in the arm. "Hey, I've eaten rabbit— that's pretty extreme. But you need to stop trying to eat every animal!" She slurred her words slightly.

At one point, Morgan retrieved her phone from her pants pocket. "Well, it's on one percent. Let's take one last selfie, buddy." She held the phone out, leaned her head against Spence's, and snapped a picture. "And...it's dead."

They continued drinking as they talked, and soon the bottles were empty. Spence's head was spinning some, and he noticed Morgan's eyes had that alcohol-induced glassy look. He scooted back on the bed and lay on his back, his head on half the thin, hard pillow. To Spence's surprise, Morgan lay beside him, her head beside his.

"Get the hell out of my bed," she said and then burst into laughter.

"I am the ruler of the Draconians, and this is my house and thus my bed," Spence said, laughing as hard as Morgan.

"Oh, yeah, I forgot. You are a wizard and king now. Well, I'd better get my butt up north to my elves. I will be the elven queen, ruler of Nibiru."

"Nah, my lizards will kick your monkeys' butts."

Morgan elbowed Spence in the ribs. "You wish. I think my monkeys' arrows reach further than your little tridents and spears. You won't get near us."

"Hmmm.... OK. So maybe we can team up and kick Caleb's and Trey's butts and rule as king and queen."

275

"Deal!"

They lay in silence for several minutes. Spence wanted to stay awake and continue enjoying the special moment, but his eyes were closing. He rolled over on his side, facing Morgan. She turned her head to gaze at him.

"I guess I should go back to my room and go to bed," he said softly.

"You could. But you're drunk. And you know the laws against drunk walking." She cackled.

"Good point."

"So, you can stay here. Better safe than sorry." Morgan rolled over, facing the other direction, and leaned over to blow out the lantern. She then lay back down, still facing away.

Spence was drunk and fearless at this point. He moved his body forward slightly so it touched Morgan's from head to toe. He worked his right arm beneath the pillow and wrapped his left arm around her.

"What are you doing?" Morgan asked, her voice tinged with sleep.

"You know the dangers of drunk people rolling out of bed. Safety first."

"Oh, yeah. Good point. Then hold on tight."

Spence's heart raced, even despite his drunkenness. He felt Morgan's warm body pressed against him. Despite the swim in the swamp water and lack of good hygiene, he was a teenage boy, and she was a sexy teenage girl. He wished he could stay awake longer and savor the moment, but he was too sleepy and inebriated. But he fell asleep the happiest and most content he had been in...forever.

***

"That makes things more...interesting," Ra said.

"Ah, yes," Artemis replied. "Two young lovers forced to lead their armies against each other."

"What if they form an alliance?" Odin asked.

"Oh, I am sure they will. At least initially," Enki said. "But no matter. We are finally getting our war. There will only be one victor."

"What have your dwarves and their new leader decided?" Artemis asked.

"They are marching north, toward your elves, as we speak. They will attack hard and try to force a quick surrender. If not, they will use fire and axes to fell Sabekha. Then they can combine forces with the survivors and march toward Argos. If the girl does not reach the elves soon, she will not have an army to lead," Odin replied.

***

A knock on the door woke Spence. He sat up and took a few seconds to recall where he slept and what had happened the night before. Light shone through the window. Morgan stirred in the bed beside him and sat up too.

"Morgan?" Caleb's voice called from outside the door.

"Oh, crap!" Morgan whispered to Spence. "Yes?" she said for Caleb to hear.

"It's time to eat breakfast and go. I'm going to try to find Spence. Meet you downstairs."

"Should I feel awkward?" Spence asked.

Morgan gazed at him, her face unreadable. "Do you?"

"No...not really. Other than feeling hungover, I feel surprisingly good."

"Well then, there's your answer. Now, get the hell out of my room so I can freshen up. Meet you downstairs." She flashed a slight grin, so Spence knew she wasn't angry.

"Yes, my queen."

They arrived downstairs in the dining room at the same time. Qishti and Caleb sat eating at a table in the center. Only a few Draconians sat around the room; Spence figured they were a little late for breakfast.

"Where have you been?" Caleb asked Spence.

"Huh? Oh. I just woke up a little early and went exploring." Spence didn't dare make eye contact with Morgan or Qishti.

They ate a quick meal of smoked fish, coarse bread, and the eggs of some type of animal. They drank a hot, bitter, coffee-like drink.

"What's the plan?" Caleb asked Qishti.

"Well, my people will follow the instructions of our new leader, Spence. You and Morgan must decide whether to stay with us or depart to lead your peoples."

"Oh, yeah," Caleb said.

"But first, I think we should gather some of the swamp rose. We will need as much as we can harvest, and you may take some to your peoples when you leave."

"What's the swamp rose?" Spence asked.

"It's a rare flower found in some of the thickest parts of the Forsaken Swamp. You can make a poultice that will stop bleeding and greatly speed healing. We will take a boat to harvest it. I know of some growing directly to the south."

"Sounds prudent," Spence said, glancing at Morgan and Caleb. Their plan would sound convincing to the gods or anyone else watching and listening. "We'll take our breathing masks too, just in case we need to do any swimming."

CHAPTER 54

The boat resembled a canoe, except longer and broader. Qishti had asked two Draconians to accompany them and man the two sets of oars. The four sat in the middle, with a rower in the front and back of the boat. The water was calm, and the sleek vessel glided swiftly past the islands. They saw various lizard men on the landmasses and entering and exiting the water. It appeared as if most were fishing or gathering plants from the water and water edges.

"Can I ask you something?" Spence asked Qishti.

"Of course. You are our leader now."

Spence glanced at Morgan, raised his eyebrows, and grinned. "Can you and your people live away from the water? In case we have to march across Nibiru to battle the dwarves?"

Qishti made a clucking noise that might have been a laugh. "Yes. We live on and in the water because this is where Enki chose to place us. We enjoy the water and have developed a great ability to swim and hold our breath. But we do not need it for survival. We would only need some training on acquiring food since fish is the main source of our diet, as well as the plants growing in and around the water."

"I assume the other races will face similar challenges," Spence said thoughtfully. He hoped their plan would work, but he had to start figuring out how to lead an army of lizard people if it didn't. That caused him to reflect on a more painful thought. Morgan would have to leave him to join the elves. Since last night, his outlook on everything had changed. They were both drunk, but he knew spending the night together might have meant something. Morgan could have simply asked him to leave. Was it just the loneliness and isolation from other humans their age? Or did she actually have feelings for him, as improbable as it seemed? But now, would they even have a chance to find out?

"Do you think we can swim with everything on?" Caleb asked quietly.

Spence hadn't considered that. He could slide his staff beneath the straps on his pack. It would slow him, but he could manage. His boots would make it more challenging, though. Caleb and Morgan had more serious issues. "I think I'll be OK."

Morgan frowned. "I guess I can keep my bow over my shoulder. But I'll need some way to secure my arrows."

"Scoot back. Let me see if I can tie up your bow and arrows." Morgan did as he asked, and Caleb went searching through his pack. He withdrew the rope and cut several small pieces. He then deftly secured the arrows to the quiver and the quiver to the bow. "There. Nothing is going anywhere. Hopefully, you won't need to use it in a hurry, though."

They entered a large stretch of open water after they passed the last of the small islands. Not long after, they began seeing trees and thick patches of reeds. Spence couldn't gauge whether the water was shallower or supported islands covered with growth. The rowers guided the boat between the ever-increasing thickets. Soon, it seemed like they were picking their way through a mangrove swamp.

Their progress continued to slow as it became harder to navigate the growth. Eventually, they reached a solid wall of tangled vegetation that they could not find a way through or around. "We are here," Qishti spoke. He pointed to the land in front of them. Several red flowers grew from one particular type of bush. "Those are the swamp roses."

The growth was too thick to get out of the boat and walk on the land. The rowers turned the boat parallel to the bank, and Qishti picked the roses as they floated slowly past. He placed them into a canvas sack he had brought with him. Spence and the others studied the surrounding swamp. The water was pitch black, and it didn't seem it could be too deep with so much growth reaching out of it. But he remembered the giant worm also living among the islands and trees.

After a few minutes of harvesting, Qishti turned to his guests. "This might be a good spot to explore the waters. The thick, white plant roots are edible. You might want to harvest some of them." Qishti reached inside a pouch on his waist and pulled out a clear, tear-shaped gem. He squeezed it, and it glowed a soft white. "Take this with you; the waters are dark. Also, remember, you only have an hour of air."

A thought occurred to Spence. He rifled through his pack and brought out the carefully wrapped yellow bread they had eaten during

280

their first night in the forest. He unwrapped it and handed a piece to Morgan and Caleb. "A little snack for our swim." They all ate it, and once again, Spence experienced the rush of energy and adrenaline. The effect wasn't as powerful as the potions he and Caleb had drunk, but it would definitely help them with the task they faced. He returned his pack to his back.

"I thought you only had one piece left?" Morgan asked.

"Oh…oops. Or three," Spence said, grinning sheepishly.

"Although the time is wrong, I suppose my watch still works." Caleb grabbed the gem, and the three placed the breathing devices into their mouths. Spence secured his staff beneath the pack straps. Caleb also checked the shield on his back. His sword was secure in its sheath. "It's three o'clock. Qishti, if we're not back in an hour, we're not coming back. Squad, let's go diving."

Caleb rolled backward off the boat like a scuba diver and disappeared under the surface. Morgan turned and dove off headfirst, also instantly disappearing. Spence tried to dive, but he did more of a belly buster. He flopped and kicked until he, too, submerged into the black depths. He found it easier to sink with his pack and boots on, but his staff dragged a little in the water. However, it would be challenging to swim back up if their plan didn't work. He soon spotted the glowing gem and the others not too far ahead.

A tangled wall of roots and vegetation stretched in front of them. The thicket appeared to grow out of a floating island, which allowed the roots to grow through to the water. He saw some of the long, thick white roots Qishti had mentioned. Of course, they weren't concerned with harvesting food.

Spence caught Morgan as they followed Caleb deeper into the water. He felt powerful from the bread and swam much easier than he had the day before. As they descended deeper and deeper, his ears began popping and hurting from the pressure. They were at least thirty feet deep when they finally arrived at the end of the growth. Caleb swam beneath the thicket, forming a dark, tangled ceiling above them. The bottom of the swamp was only four or five feet below. The surface was dark and thick with some type of vegetation.

Spence suddenly began feeling claustrophobic. If the floor elevated much or the roots extended further down, they would be trapped or at least blocked. He wondered how long they had been down. He guessed around fifteen minutes. Then the time-fear hit him. If it took longer than thirty minutes to reach the dome's wall, and they couldn't break free, they would all drown. His heart raced, and he gulped bigger breaths of air.

Then he realized he would have even less time now. He forced himself to calm down. *God, please keep us safe and show us the way.* He began holding each breath for thirty seconds before breathing again. He had to conserve air.

Spence knew Caleb was having similar thoughts because he now swam faster. And Caleb had the watch, so he knew the exact time. Spence swam as hard as he could, but despite the energy gained from the bread, swimming was difficult with boots, dagger, pack, and staff. The harder he swam, the more breaths he had to take too. The bottom did elevate some, reducing their swimming space to three feet. He wondered if the gods had thought of this possibility, and the area would totally close off, preventing them from reaching the wall.

Caleb slowed and turned ahead of him. Morgan also pulled up, allowing Spence to join them. Caleb tapped at his watch and then pointed to his mouth. Spence's stomach tightened. They had traveled thirty minutes. Caleb shrugged his shoulders and then pointed straight ahead.

CHAPTER 55

Should we continue? Part of Spence wanted to turn around and go back. Then he considered what that would mean—losing Morgan and leading the Draconians into the gods' war. And eventually, he would be forced to fight against Caleb and Morgan. Drowning in the swamp would be a quicker and easier path than what waited for them if they returned. Spence pointed forward and nodded. Morgan also nodded. She added a wink to Spence that Caleb couldn't see.

Caleb continued swimming forward. They passed a few large fish swimming in the depths. Spence hoped there wouldn't be anything to fight. There wasn't room to maneuver, and they didn't have enough air for the exertion. Plus, Morgan's arrows would be useless down here, and Caleb's sword wouldn't be much better. Would his staff work underwater? That's something they hadn't discussed in much detail. Then he wondered how he would even activate it. Was the floor hard enough? Since the staff was technological and not magic, could water even short it out?

He forced those thoughts out of his mind and focused on Morgan in front of him. She had learned swimming quickly and now made it look easy—her long arms and legs were suited for it. Caleb was a natural. Spence had improved but still had trouble keeping up with the others. His body definitely wasn't designed for swimming—floating or sinking, possibly—not swimming.

Spence looked down and realized the bottom was even closer. He saw no sign above of the roots and vegetation receding. If they didn't reach the dome soon, it would be over. They barely had enough room to swim as it was. They continued for another few minutes when Caleb suddenly stopped swimming. Morgan nearly ran into him and then Spence into her.

Caleb curled around in the tight space and motioned for Spence to swim to him. Spence reached him, and Caleb grabbed Spence's hand and extended it in front of him. It suddenly stopped and struck something that wasn't water. The surface wasn't hard, though. His hand pushed into it several inches and then gradually stopped. He visualized the dome as being like a silicone breast implant. He still couldn't see the wall; it just appeared as if the water continued.

Spence knew it was now or never. He reached behind him and, after a few tugs and pulls, slid the staff out from under his pack straps. Maneuvering was tricky in the tight space. He then pushed the butt back onto the bottom. Nothing happened. The ground was spongy, and the staff only sank several inches into it. He looked up at Caleb, his eyes wide. Caleb's eyes were also big, but he just shrugged. Spence tried again, but it still didn't work. He didn't know if his internal clock worked well, but there couldn't be much time left with the breathing devices.

Spence wished he had one of the *Limitless* potions. Negative thoughts flooded his mind. They couldn't make it back now. The only way they could survive was if he could blast a hole in the dome. But he couldn't even activate his staff. He inhaled a costly deep breath and tried to settle his nerves. Then something grabbed his right hand. He turned and saw Morgan's hand on top of his. She squeezed it. He could tell she was smiling even with the disk in front of her mouth. He returned the smile and instantly felt calm. The clutter in his mind melted away. *I can do this. I have to do this.*

He tapped Caleb and then swirled his hand, motioning for Caleb to turn around. Caleb stared at him for a moment and then nodded. Caleb turned his body around and allowed himself to sink until he lay on the bottom. Morgan removed her hand, and Spence extended his staff as far from his body as possible. Then he slammed it through the water with all his might. It struck hard in the middle of the shield on Caleb's back, pressing him firmly against the floor.

The tip of the staff illuminated. The glow was bright in the confined space, much more luminous than the stone Caleb held. Caleb swam up beside Spence, and Morgan floated by his other side. He glanced at Caleb and then Morgan. Caleb tapped on his watch again. Spence nodded and placed his finger over the exposed buttons in the staff. He brushed over the first one; the lightning bolt would probably electrocute them. The fireball would likely only fizzle out or bounce off the invisible barrier.

His finger stopped on the third one. The shock wave would send out a tremendous force of energy. At point-blank range, he wasn't sure what would happen. The barrier wasn't solid, as they had seen from Tom's arrow striking it. The shock wave would undoubtedly have an impact on it. The question was if it would open a hole or whether the surface would merely absorb it. There would also be a danger to them if the wall did deflect it. The shockwave might knock them unconscious or worse. Although with just a minute or two of air left, that might be the easiest way to drown.

Caleb tapped frantically on his wrist. Spence placed the staff's tip up to the barrier and inserted it as far as possible. He began to push the button but then removed his finger. Maybe the wall could interfere with the blast or absorb it easier if the orb were stuck into it. He pulled the tip out until it was a foot away. He motioned for Morgan and Caleb to move back.

Spence was going to hold his breath but realized he was no longer getting oxygen from his breathing device. He was breathing, but it felt like breathing into a paper bag. He closed his eyes and pressed the third button. The staff surged with power. Then the force sent him rushing back through the water, something Spence hadn't accounted for. He opened his eyes and could only see bubbles and churning water. He finally dug his feet into the bottom of the swamp and halted his momentum. He panted into the breathing device.

Caleb and Morgan had been blown back some, but they were able to stop sooner. The water slowly cleared, and Spence saw the massive ripples in the now visible wall. It looked like a piece of ice in the water. The surface was cupped deeply, several feet deep, as if a chunk had been scooped out of it. But it hadn't broken.

Spence watched Caleb pull his sword out of its scabbard and swim forward, both hands on the hilt. Spence began swimming frantically toward the wall too. He stared ahead and watched as Caleb paddled his feet hard, and then his sword entered the depression and disappeared through it as his body crashed into the wall.

Spence briefly saw a small hole of light appear around Caleb's blade. Then the hole expanded, but the light faded to a dull glow as the water rushed through it. The opening sucked his body toward it, along with the surging water around him. Caleb withdrew his sword, grabbed Morgan with his free hand, and pushed her toward the opening. She extended both arms and disappeared through the wall. The hole reached its maximum size of three feet and then slowly began closing back together. The depression was filling, pulling the tear closed. Caleb motioned for

Spence to hurry. Spence kicked his feet as hard as he could and held his staff pointed in front of him as Caleb had done with his sword. He was getting lightheaded and began seeing spots of light in the water.

The staff punched through the wall, and Spence suddenly felt cold air on his hands and arms and then on his face. Then something squeezed his chest and stomach. He realized in a panic that the wall was closing shut—on him! He struggled hard, but he was stuck. His body would be crushed and then cut in two. *No!*

Then something began pushing on the bottoms of his feet. At the same time, hands grabbed his arms and pulled on him. The opening in the wall slowly slid down his body. Then suddenly, he was through the wall and free of the water. He opened his eyes. He was no longer in the dome.

***

"Most unexpected," Ra said.

"What now?" Odin asked.

"We are running out of time. We must quickly persuade them to return to the dome. Those two could prove most useful to us," Enki replied.

"And if we cannot persuade them?" Artemis asked.

"Then we must eliminate them," Enki said.

CHAPTER 56

Spence lay on hard-packed dirt, wet from the swamp water that had rushed out from the hole they had opened. Morgan jerked him to his feet. He turned around and realized Caleb hadn't made it through. "Caleb!"

He frantically searched for the hole in the dome but only saw crumbling buildings, ruin, and dirt. It was as if the dome had vanished, and they stood in the middle of a destroyed, modern city. He extended his staff in front of him. It stopped with a clack. He stepped forward and extended his hand. The dome wall was still there but was hard and felt like glass. He couldn't see it or the world from which they had escaped. He struck it with his hand but didn't create a ripple or feel any give. Morgan joined him, and they both began pounding on the invisible barrier. Nothing.

"Oh my God. Caleb!" Spence shouted. He struck his staff on the ground, but it didn't activate. "I'll blast another hole! We'll get Caleb out."

Then he slowly turned around and slid down the dome until he landed hard on the ground. The energy from the bread was gone, and exhaustion filled its place. Tears rolled down his cheeks. Morgan sat beside him, laying her head on his shoulder. He heard her sniffle too. Spence barely noticed when she reached over and placed her left hand in his right. He squeezed it absently.

Spence stared at their new surroundings. The landscape was flat, with gray dirt stretching out in all directions. On top of the earth stood the crumbling remains of a city, the buildings ranging from total piles of stone to massive chunks and half-standing structures. None had glass in their gaping windows. Sections of paved streets peeked out here and there from beneath the rubble and layers of dirt and dust. A strong, chill wind whipped through their clothing and hair.

The sky was gray, with streaks of brown swirled throughout. The clouds swirled and moved swiftly across the sky, with occasional streaks of lightning flashing within. The water around their feet rapidly disappeared, the dry ground hissing.

"Well, we escaped," Morgan said.

"Yeah, but to where? And what now?"

They heard a scuffling sound to their right—rocks skidding across stone—and rotated their heads to locate the source of the noise. Spence detected movement coming out of a dark opening in the ruined base of a building. Half a dozen shapes detached from the darkness, their bodies and heads covered in dark, hooded robes. The group moved toward them in an unsteady gait.

"Fuck!" Spence wasn't even startled at the word that just issued from his mouth. He was numb. He had never given up hope of returning to Earth or succeeding in Nibiru throughout the quest. But now, it was obvious that they weren't going to survive. There would always be another monster to fight or another twist to the game. Eventually, they would lose.

"OMG! That's the first time I've heard you curse! And the F-bomb at that. Good job."

"Sorry. First time in my life I've felt the need. I think the wait was worth it, though." He tried to muster a weak grin.

Spence wiped his eyes and regained his feet; Morgan rose beside him. He drew a dagger and slashed the ropes binding her bow and quiver. She grabbed her bow and quickly nocked an arrow, and Spence struck the butt of his staff on the ground. Enough time had elapsed since the tip glowed again, and the compartment slid open. He wanted to use the staff to attempt to save Caleb, but then it wouldn't have time to recharge to face their new adversaries. Without Caleb's sword and muscle, his staff would be critical to his and Morgan's survival.

"Out of the frying pan, into the fire." He would at least go down fighting whenever he lost that final battle.

"Yep. Just the way we like it," Morgan replied.

For More Information & Updates:

Follow on Facebook
https://www.facebook.com/crsturgillauthor/

Visit Website
http://www.crsturgill.com/

Other Books by C. R. Sturgill

Sea of Hearts

Blood Tides

Dreams from the Heart: Tales of Hope & Love

www.ingramcontent.com/pod-product-compliance
Lightning Source LLC
Chambersburg PA
CBHW071308170626

46809CB00001B/374